PENGUIN BOOKS

# THE JOURNEY HOME

1613

Dermot Bolger was born in Finglas, North Dublin, in 1959. His first two novels of Dublin life, *Night Shift* and *The Woman's Daughter*, have received the AE Memorial Award, the Macaulay Fellowship and the *Sunday Tribune* Arts Award. He is the author of five collections of poetry, and his first play, *The Lament for Arthur Cleary*, was one of the major hits of the 1989 Dublin Theatre Festival and received the Stewart Parker BBC Award. His second play, *Blinded by the Light*, was staged by the Abbey Theatre in Dublin on their Peacock stage in 1990. Dermot Bolger is editor of Raven Arts Press, one of Ireland's most radical publishers, and a member of The Arts Council of Ireland.

*The Journey Home* was shortlisted for the Irish Literature Prize in the *Irish Times*/Aer Lingus awards.

# THE
# JOURNEY
# HOME

---

## DERMOT
## BOLGER

PENGUIN BOOKS

PENGUIN BOOKS

Published by the Penguin Group
Penguin Books Ltd, 27 Wrights Lane, London W8 5TZ, England
Viking Penguin, a division of Penguin Books USA Inc.
375 Hudson Street, New York, New York 10014, USA
Penguin Books Australia Ltd, Ringwood, Victoria, Australia
Penguin Books Canada Ltd, 2801 John Street, Markham, Ontario, Canada L3R 1B4
Penguin Books (NZ) Ltd, 182–190 Wairau Road, Auckland 10, New Zealand

Penguin Books Ltd, Registered Offices: Harmondsworth, Middlesex, England

First published by Viking 1990
Published in Penguin Books 1991
1 3 5 7 9 10 8 6 4 2

*For Bernadette,*
*Without whose love and support*
*this novel would never have been completed*

# GLOSSARY

*Ard-Fheis:* A political party conference

*Baby Power:* A bottle of Power's whiskey containing one (Irish) measure

*Ban Garda:* A policewoman

*Boreen:* (*From the Irish*) A very small country road

*Bounce, the:* Playing truant from school

*Crack:* Enjoyment generated in other people's company. Cheaper than the American version and a great deal more fun

*FCA:* Ireland's reserve army – mainly joined by boys in their late teens

*Fainne:* Rings of varying precious metals (depending on the wearer's proficiency with the language) worn on the lapel by Irish-language speakers.

*Hard Chaws:* Tough men (or women), street arabs

*Jockeybacks:* Piggybacks

*LDF:* Ireland's local defence force during the war. A forerunner of the FCA

*Leb:* Lebanese dope

*Mitch:* The same as going on the bounce

*Mot:* A Dublin term for a girl or a girlfriend

*Nixers:* An unofficial piece of work done outside (or sometimes inside) working hours

*Spots:* Pounds

*Three Cross Doubles:* Three doubles and a treble in the one bet

*Turlough:* (*From the Irish*) A lake without obvious sources, which vanishes in summer and suddenly fills up during a wet winter

# CHAPTER ONE

## *Sunday*

The branches were strewn above them like distorted mosaics of crucifixions, the hawthorn bushes blocking out the few isolated stars to ensnare them within a crooked universe of twigs and briars. Nettles raised their leaves in the wind like the ears of startled dogs to sway a few inches from where his hand lay. Hano could feel their sting on his wrist and longed to rub it in the soothing grass. But he lay motionless, his other arm around her shoulder in the position they had landed when they slid into the overgrown ditch, and listened to the heavy boot-steps ring out on the tarmacadam above his head.

The feet halted with a squeak of polished leather inches from his skull. Hano, gazing at the figure who stretched skyward, could see the man's thick moustache when he shone the torch up before his features were lost as the arc of light picked its way along the hedge and fields by the road. Hano moved his hand down to cover Katie's lips though he felt himself more likely to cry out than her. She lay crushed against him, her body relaxed despite their awkward position. It seemed as if danger was a more powerful drug than any peddled on the street and she was adrift, eyes closed, lips slightly open, within its depths. The slow, regular inhaling of her breath came so faintly that she might have been a small night creature in its natural habitat. His own breathing sounded explosive to him. The man was bound to hear, to shine the light down and call out to the others, to finish it before it had begun. This was her world, not his, and he was lost within it. His numb fury had evaporated and all he felt now was fear.

He swallowed hard, trying to block the recurring images from his mind. But flames lit the space behind his closed eyelids, smoke still seeming to fill his nostrils. The boots moved, spraying gravel down on to his face, beating so harshly on the tar that they might have been pounding his skull and as they retreated he had to restrain himself from moving. He realized how desperately he wanted to be caught, that whatever terrors lay in the cell under the station could be no worse than the unknown journey ahead through the dark. The fallen gravel covered his hand. To shift even a finger would send it trickling noisily down. All his life he had obeyed; the instinct ingrained within him. An image came back from childhood, his father climbing the stairs as he hid after a quarrel, wanting to be found, knowing that his father would gruffly forgive him. A radio crackled from inside the car. There was the click of an automatic weapon being uncocked. The boots paused on the roadway like a parent on the stairs. How warm it had been under that bed, his father's voice coaxing, the scent of cooking from downstairs. The boots drew closer again.

His arm ached to move yet still he held back. If he were alone he would be in the squad car now, the first blows raining against his skull. But she would be there as well, a witness again to his cowardice. Without warning, Katie's teeth bit softly into his fingers, reassuring him with her own fear. The need to protect her gave him strength, a role in which he could imagine himself strong. With a click the boots stopped and a car door opened. Only when the noise of the engine faded did her teeth ease their grip. Gradually the unfamiliar night sounds reasserted themselves: the beat of wings in the blackness above; tiny paws scuttling through the coarse grass; the sight of a dreaming beast in a field nearby, where high branches creaked like dried bones. They waited for the noise of the motor to return. Overhead a pylon hummed as it stretched back towards the city they had come from. To move was to make a decision, to break the isolated spell of the ditch. He lay against her till he heard the words, 'They're gone', spoken so softly he was uncertain whether they came from her lips or his mind, and felt the dampness of the grass penetrating his side as she untangled her body from his. She scrambled cautiously up on to the roadway and gazed back the way they had come. There was still a glow in the distance and though it was a mile away he could not shake off the tang of smoke. His clothes seemed to reek of it, his hair, the very pores of his skin. Any part of him that wasn't frozen tasted of fire.

'Listen to me, Katie,' he said climbing up beside her, his voice low as if the trees could be informers. 'It's time you started back, do you hear? Otherwise they nail us both when they catch me. They've nothing to connect you with it. Just go home. Follow the road back to the city.'

Although he barely discerned the outline of her head against the black mass of trees, he knew she was staring at him with the same cold, unblinking look. How he had grown to hate that cold face behind which she observed him, the eyes where he read only contempt, and the jealousy of his intimacy with Shay which she had never broken. Her voice from that afternoon returned, fists clawing at him as she screamed, 'You just stood up here and let them! You were his friend and you let them. You let them! Let them!'

'Are you deaf or what, Katie?' he said again. 'Can you not hear me? Take the road back and just watch out for the cops. Listen, I've done all I can for Shay. Now will you bleeding go, I've to find somewhere to hide.'

He knew the eyes were still staring, the mouth expressionless. He waited and, when she didn't reply, turned and began to walk deeper into the countryside. After a few yards he heard footsteps echoing his own and when he stopped heard them cease as well. He walked on and they commenced, beating behind him. He stopped. They stopped. He began again, then stopped in despair as she followed. He shouted behind him.

'Leave me alone for fuck's sake! What more do you want? Go home Katie, please, go home. Listen, I've nowhere to take you. I don't know where I'm going, I don't know what happens next.'

The moon broke from behind a deep whorl of cloud and Hano caught sight of her face beneath the cropped black hair. She looked tough beyond her sixteen years, the jacket pulled up around her neck, the blue pullover, the dirty jeans, the mud-stained sneakers. Her body was poised, unsmilingly observing

3

him. Two days it had taken to lose everything. Now there was no Shay to turn to, no one left to differentiate right and wrong. He grabbed a stone from the road, raised his fist in frustration and shouted at her. Her expression never changed. He let the stone fall and stared at the ground.

'He's dead Katie, and I can't bring him back for you. You know I'm a poor substitute. Now for Christ's sake leave me in peace. What more do you want of me? What more?'

The clouds reined back the moonlight and he turned to walk forward, listening as the other footsteps gradually caught up with his. They plodded on, neither looking at the other until he heard her voice, again almost inaudible.

'Don't want fucking nothing,' she said. 'Just be your fucking self.'

Suddenly her warm hand hesitantly touched his and found its way in between his numb fingers. He closed them over her knuckles and, when he dared to glance down, saw her face was screwed up, scanning the darkness in front. He didn't want the squad car to return. Though nothing could lie ahead but capture, it didn't seem important now that she was ready, for a time at least, to share whatever would come.

Katie or Cait – whoever you are. Can it be just three nights since we lay in that ditch, since you followed me mutely out the black roads? I've grown so used to darkness, have learnt to see things better here. That hole in the corner where the ceiling has collapsed and creepers, like the limbs of a giant spider, descend to wrap themselves around the smashed wooden rafters, or the daddy-long-legs which stumbles drunkenly towards the beam of the torch shaded by my hand. The fire has crumbled into a nest of ash. What light escapes my fingers filters across the downy weeds left after we cleared the stone floor and catches a few loose strands of your hair.

I never knew you could be at peace until I saw you asleep. Not the Katie I knew back on those streets. I'm half jealous Cait of whatever world you dream of where you belong so well. Last night a sound woke me in alarm. You had laughed in your sleep. You did it again. I looked down and in the half-light could see the faintest of smiles. I've never asked you

4

where you dream of – the city, the country – which world at night becomes your home. I feared ghosts here when I was younger, before I learnt to fear the living. Now I love this darkness, the kiss of winged insects blundering against my skin; the faint drip of water from a broken gutter; the sighing of branches.

There's so much I want to tell you, the parts you know and those you don't. If you were awake I'd never have the chance, even if I could be this honest. You'd interrupt me, dispute facts, want your version to be told. So now even if you can't hear I'll tell you anyway Cait, tell those few strands of hair lit by a torch. Just this last time I'll bring Shay back to life before we move on.

I know it was him you loved, who you came to see each evening when we stared each other out at the doorway, but I don't think you ever knew him, not the Shay I met first, the figure who vanished into that continent. You loved the man you met when he came home, but I mourned the part of him that was left behind among those autobahns and bahnhofs. Because I loved him too Katie, loved as a brother, loved him selfishly for daring to be what I was afraid to be myself.

Where does our story begin? The first morning I crossed the park to work? No, even before then our paths would have crossed. How often did our parents pass on the main street of the village while the labourers' cottages were being bulldozed and the estates, like a besieging army, began to ring the green post office, the pub with the skittle alley, the old graveyard with its shambling vaults? But my parents and Shay's would not have mixed, being from different worlds, with different sets of experiences. I think of my parents, younger than I can really imagine them, taking the single-decker bus out beyond the cemetery, returning, as they thought, to the familiar hawthorn bushes and streams, to the sanctuary of the countryside. Shay used to laugh about how his father cursed the Corporation for casting them out into exile, complaining about bus fares to work in the brewery he had always walked to, bewildered by the dark lanes behind his house without the shouts of neighbours or the reassuring bustle of traffic.

Years later my father told me that the Church of Ireland

built my estate, some half-arsed scheme for a Protestant colony among the fields. They couldn't fill it from their own flock so the likes of my parents were allowed to pay their deposit and transport their country habits from bedsits along the canal back to the laneways again. A place of streams I'm told it was, each in turn piped underground as more people came. Once a row of gardens collapsed to reveal the water running underneath.

They planted trees in the image of their lost homeland, put down potato beds, built timber hen-houses. I woke to the sound of chicks escaping through the wire mesh to scamper among rows of vegetables. A dozen streets away Shay must have woken to the noise of pigeon lofts, that city man's sport, backyards ringing with displaced Dublin accents. Briefly we played in the same school yard before he was expelled, though neither of us remembered the other. We spoke of it in awe as from another century; the monstrous thug of a vice-principal wasting with cancer among his array of canes; the tricolour flown from the mast beside the concrete steps; the screeching of seagulls which hovered, waiting for boys to be drilled into lines and marched to class, before swooping to fight over the littered bread. I wish I could remember Shay there, those all-important two years older than me, among the swarm of lads stomping after a plastic ball. But I can recall little beyond a hubbub of noise; the stink of fish from a ten-year-old who helped his mother in the processing plant each evening; the twins who shared one pair of plastic sandals for a week, each one barefoot on alternate days. And the ease with which, among such crowds, I could remain invisible. I can still repeat the roll-call of nine-year-old future factory hands and civil servants, but it's myself that I cannot properly recall. I was like some indistinct embryonic creature, a negative through which nobody had ever shone light. Was I happy or sad? I have no memories of being anything more than a sleepwalker feigning the motions of life, living through the black-and-white rays of the television screen.

Each evening my father came in from Plunkett Motors, took his spade from the shed, and joined the chorus of rural accents across the ruck of hedgerows. I'd hide among the alder bushes bordering the hen run to watch the men dig and weed with the expertise of country hands, while my mother washed clothes by hand in the sink, light from the open kitchen door filtering through the lilac. I felt that square of earth was home, a green expanse formed by the row of long gardens. I'd pull the branches close to me while across the suburb Shay played among the red-brick terraces built by the Corporation. The gardens there were tiny with hardly space for a shed. Shay's gang would scatter with their football if a squad car showed, then resume their games on the next concrete street, voices still calling when only the vaguest shapes could be seen dodging between the street lamps.

We grew up divided by only a few streets so you'd think we would share a background. Yet somehow we didn't. At least not then, not till later when we found we were equally dispossessed. *The children of limbo* was how Shay called us once. We came from nowhere and found we belonged nowhere else. Those gardens I called home were a retreat from the unknown world. When the radio announcer gave the results of the provincial Gaelic matches the backs would straighten, neighbours reverting to county allegiances as they slagged each other. *And remember, if you feel like singing, do sing an Irish song*, the presenter of the Walton's programme urged and, as the strains of 'Kelly, the Boy from Kilane' and 'The Star of the County Down' crackled from the radio, all the stooping figures who knew the words by heart hummed them in their minds, reassured of who they were no matter what incomprehensible things were occurring outside.

As long as I remained among the hens and barking dogs I too could belong, but each walk home from school by the new shopping arcades, each programme on the television religiously switched on at half five in every terraced house, was thrusting me out into my own time. I began bringing home phrases that couldn't fit in that house when we still knelt for the family rosary. I hid photographs of rock stars beneath my mattress like pornographic pictures, wrote English soccer players' names on my copy book feeling I was committing an act of betrayal.

When I was twelve my father brought me back to the farm bordering the Kerry coast where he had been born. I stood awkwardly in my city clothes, kicking a football back and forth to my cousins across the yard. None of us spoke as we eyed each other suspiciously and waited for our parents to finish reminiscing. Next morning before dawn he took me out to the milking shed lit by a bare bulb. I never saw him so relaxed as when he bent with ease to squeeze the teats, glancing back proudly, urging me to grasp the teats of a huge lurching cow I was frightened of. For the first time I felt the division between us.

I didn't understand it then, but I grew up in perpetual exile: from my parents when on the streets, from my own world when at home. Once Shay told me about visiting his uncles and great aunts left behind in the Liberties. They welcomed him like a returned *émigré* to the courtyards of squalid Victorian flats and led him around the ramshackled streets choked with traffic, pitying him the open spaces of the distant roads he played on.

How can you learn self-respect if you're taught that where you live is not your real home? At fourteen I tried to bridge the gap by journeying out into my father's uncharted countryside. I'd rise before dawn to cook myself breakfast and when I ate at the kitchen table he would come down to place money on the oilcloth beside me and watch from the doorway as I set off to find Ireland. I arrived home with reports he couldn't comprehend: long-haired Germans in battered vans picking up hikers; skinheads battling outside chip shops in Athlone. Then came the final betrayal of something even he couldn't define when, at fifteen, I chose the first friend of my own. 'That old Protestant woman' my father always called her, though she had not been inside any church for half a century.

Looking back, my life was like a candle, briefly sparked into flame in that old woman's caravan among the fields, and extinguished again until I met Shay. The years between speed up – the new intimacy of class-mates in the months before exams; nights studying in each other's houses; weekends stumbling home drunk on two pints from town. I had been a loner before, so used to solitude I didn't understand what loneliness was. But that last year in school I felt enclosed in the company of friends, finally seeming to belong somewhere.

8

On the night of the final exam we walked out to Mother Plunkett's Cabin at Kilshane Cross, were barred before closing time and staggered home through country lanes off the North Road in hysterical laughter. After that I rarely saw them again, the release from school shattering our intimacy, leaving us half-embarrassed when we met, reliving the same stale memories. That autumn passed into winter. Sometimes I cadged the money for dances; mostly I just walked the streets putting off my return home. Some mornings polite rejections of my application forms for work lay like poisoned fish washed up on the hall floor, but normally I stared down at an empty, mocking square of lino, and began the same futile rounds of the industrial estates.

I thought my father would never let the garden run to seed even as he grew older, but that year after school I watched it happen without comprehending. The world of the gardens had changed. Where neighbours once kept the city out with hedgerows and chickens, now they used broken glass cemented into concrete walls. A decade had worked its influence. The alder bushes were gone, the last of the hens butchered. Patios had appeared with crazy paving, mock Grecian fonts made of plastic, and everywhere, like a frozen river, concrete reigned. Porches had sprung up bearing ludicrous names, Ashbrook, Riverglade, The Dell, each neighbour jockeying to be the first to discard their past. Only our garden had remained untouched, the potato beds becoming overgrown and the roof caving in on the felt-covered hut where my hands had once searched for eggs in straw.

Every evening that winter my father's face was like ash, gathered from a burnt-out half-century and spread in a fine crust over his bones. His eyes were more jaded than any I had ever known. He'd come home from work with stories of Pascal Plunkett's moods, collapse into an armchair by the television and stare at his idle eldest son. He said little and I learnt to match his words. We sat in a silence broken only by my mother's fussing, while outside the weeds and nettles choked his dreams. Sometimes he'd cough and, looking up, ask me to chop everything down. 'Tomorrow,' I'd say. 'I'm tired now.' I would mean to put on his rubber boots, take the tools hanging between nails in the shed and walk out as I used to watch him do, but those photocopied rejections seemed to have sapped my strength. I sulked instead, brooding on the few words that passed between us, although it wasn't what he said that hurt but the disbelief in his eyes when I'd mention all the places I had tried for work. In the end I just said nothing. The present made no sense in his world. He stared blankly at the evening news while they carried the victims of the bombings and hijackings away in black plastic sacks.

Christmas froze into January. Blue nights alone in the overgrown garden, making tea in the kitchen at three in the morning. That year had become a posthumous existence. At night I'd smoke joints in the bathroom, leaning on my toes to blow the smoke out the window, constantly alert for an opening door. I seemed to have lost the power to sleep, gradually losing track of the everyday world. February came and then March, fresh weeds squeezing through the dead grass.

At two o'clock one morning I walked down the garden, wading through weeds like a field of barley. Lines of new extensions stretched on both sides, a lone light burning in a garage twelve doors down. I thought of Jews hiding in cellars, snatching only a few seconds of air before dawn. Now I slept while others worked, rose in the afternoons, seemed to come to life only when darkness came. I had fallen from the cycle of life, with no longer the will-power to struggle. The queues each Tuesday afternoon, men pushing like a human battering ram against the door of the employment exchange. The letters posted out sending one hundred people for interview for a single job that I had to attend in case they checked up and cut my assistance. The fear of daring to hope in case it turned to bitterness when I was turned down; the hatred of leaving the bed and having to face the empty letter rack in the hall.

I turned to go back inside and saw my father standing at the gate beneath the arc of bare lilac bushes. At first I thought it was an apparition from the past. He had pulled on a white shirt and a pair of trousers held up by ancient braces. I walked towards him in the blue moonlight, both of us embarrassed, neither knowing how to talk.

'What's going to happen to you, son?'

His voice was low, humble with bewilderment. I would have liked to touch his shoulder, to somehow reassure him. Looking at him I knew that I would leave home soon, that only poverty was keeping me there. Ever since our fight about the old woman in the fields we had both lost the simple ease which had once existed between us. I knew that he was thinking about days further back, times I'd waited beside the lilac bushes wanting to feel important, hoping he'd ask me to fetch some tool from the shed. I longed to say, *Tomorrow dad, we'll take those tools down, fix up the garden the way it used to be*. But I couldn't. I had to turn away.

'I don't know. You go back to bed now. I'm just getting some air.'

He shook his head and I watched him turn and walk up the path. There was a nettle swaying near my hand. I pressed my fingers over it. It stung badly, but at least the pain felt real.

Then one morning, grey and ordinary, a letter from the Voters' Register's office came. The offer was a temporary position starting on the first of the month. I felt there should be bands marching from the kitchen, majorettes turning somersaults on the lino. Instead my mother was scrubbing floors in Plunkett Undertakers, my brothers and sisters were at school. Happiness seemed to underline my isolation. I went out into the street hoping to meet somebody I could share the news with. Behind the supermarket I saw my father in the forecourt of Plunkett Motors. Younger men asked him questions as they stripped an engine. He pulled on his cigarette, coughed and spat on the tarmacadam. I couldn't find the courage to go across and tell him.

On the way home I remembered a television programme I'd seen about flowers buried in the desert which hibernate for years waiting to burst through their whole life cycle during a single day of rain. I felt strong again, like a young bird about to take flight. And I realized why I'd never touched the quarter-acre of garden where all my childhood memories were buried under bamboo stalks of nettles and clumps of weeds. I had been trying to hold up time, to live on in the past having no future to put in its place.

But now the anticipation of change raced in my bloodstream and I wanted to be rid of that shadow. I returned to the silent house where the stained oilcloth on the table, the flaking paint on the wood, the faded wallpaper in the bedroom which light never entered till evening all seemed to be mocking me, reducing me to the child I'd always been. I took the bailing hook from the shed, donned my father's old boots, and as I worked every blow was like an act of finality, a foretaste of the separations to come.

At five thirty my father walked down to the hedge. I still had the letter in my pocket. *Your tea son*, he said, and I shook my head. He watched me work on for a few moments then turned. I swung fiercely at the last bushes until I stopped, my blood calmed in the afterglow of labour. As darkness fell I lit a cigarette among the ghosts of hen-runs and alder bushes and watched the lit windows of the house occluded by the overgrown lilac I hadn't the heart to touch. I felt severed finally from the life of that terrace where I had been delivered, red and sickly, by a country midwife. The bonfire of branches and old timber that I had dosed with paraffin and lit was smouldering. I remember a flatness about the evening as if the whole street had been becalmed in time and then, with a swift flapping of wings, a formation of returning swallows swooped over the rooftops and wheeled upwards in a V across the gardens and out into the distance. And when I looked down, the rotten timbers of the hen house had caught and the carnage began. The shorn surface of the garden looked like a nightmare landscape, fragments lit up and snatched away by the flickering light. Straight black smoke rose to be dissipated into a swirling pall. I watched my childhood burn, the debris of those years borne off into the sky, my final links with what had been home disintegrating into bright quivers of ash.

I'd no idea what lay ahead, all I knew was that as soon as I got my first pay packet I would start the search for a new home, for my own life to begin. I took the letter from my pocket and walked in.

*Katie, I smell of clay, I dream of earth, remembering until there is nothing more to forget. Where is this place? One square of fading light high up, one night sailor riding the sky. Old bits of glass and stones, leaves that have blown in. Somebody was here before me, I'm waiting for someone to come. Still can't make sense of it, this dreaming waking coma. Why here, seeing your life run like a film through my skull? Things I could not have known, images I couldn't have remembered.*

*They start with the click of footsteps that mark out your days. Shifting between one set and the next. Afternoons when weak sunlight catches the long windows of the upstairs classroom. The murmur of schoolgirl voices, a rustle of papers, heads perpetually bent down but you have gone so far Katie, so distant from that room. A nun, white and obsolete, in robes, leans across your desk to examine the smudged paper before you. She smiles, mutters inaudible words and when she lifts her hand she leaves behind five chalky fingerprints like the mark of a skeleton implanted in the wood. You stare in fascination at the dead hand as the footsteps dully click their way back to her desk. A bell rings and you move in a shower of coats and blouses down the waxed corridor by the plaster statue and out into the air. Voices call, bicycles manoeuvre through the crush of bodies, birds take off from the single tree inside the gate. You pass the pub, the bookies beneath my flat, cross the metal bridge indistinct in a babbling group and stand outside the shopping centre by the glass front of Plunkett Auctioneers to place the first cigarette to your lips. You have learnt how to return woodenly the glances of youths, a hard woman of fifteen idling in the click of boots that mount the concrete steps by the bank, watching the swollen queue encircling the bus with trolleys and prams, the taxis loitering by the monument. You put it off, you light up again, joke with the girls positioned around you. But soon you will have to stub that cigarette butt against the rough surface of the wall, lift your bag and walk back across that span of metal, down the twilit laneway by the ruined cottages. You will cross the darkening green where the horses are tethered, the piebald and the white, the young foal anxious beside its mother, and* move, *through the glare of headlights, across the main road into the embrace of the estate. The creak of a pram two children push, the gang of lads at the corner who shout. They will not find you out. You have hidden yourself well in parallel jeans and a tight sweeater. Your accent cold as a robin stretched dead in winter, your stance blending into the roadways. The depleted trunks of two trees stand as forlorn sentinels of another time. You hunch your shoulders in the cold. You do not allow yourself to remember.*

*The scent of frying from the kitchen. A television shrieking through a wall. Hanging up your coat you hear them, the steps of your uncle overhead crossing the landing to the stairs. He marches down briskly like a man with some purpose, impeccably dressed in his working clothes. His polished shoes go before you towards the table which is set. And each crippled, helpless step is like a hammer beating away at your skull, reminding you of an uncle you once loved. He sits at the head of the table as you sit among his children and sense his eyes scanning the oilcloth, anxious that all of you are fed.*

*You long to scream your rage for him as he stalks the house like a caged animal. Instead you lower your eyes to avoid the pain concealed in his. His donkey coat hangs by the door. Soon he will rise and take it, walk out through the dark streets to join his ex-workmates. Cigarettes will be lit, the day's news examined. All that will not be mentioned is the sense of shame each carries on his shoulders since the plant closed down. Tradesmen who were proud of their skill, the blue overalls perpetually clean, the brown wage packet carried home with calm assurance. It was to be like that for ever: a thousand Sunday mornings when children crowded into a car; a tray of pints carried in an evening; a child's eyes wide with half crowns. New words have entered their vocabulary since then. They will not spend long with each other, each inventing some task to take them back to a sofa and a television, the library book unopened with its ageing stamp, the white dot that will summon them finally to bed.*

*But you will be gone before he returns, back to the street's anonymity. The window ledge of a chip shop, the smell of watered vinegar. A radio on a wall, a squad car slowing as it passes, a boy's hand on your shoulder which you shrug off. It's late now and you know he will be waiting to hear the door. You know that he will search for words in his bulky frame. And you will stand, wanting to run and kiss like once before. But the same stiffness will be inside both of you now. Your feet click out your final moments alone along the deserted streets.*

What did I expect that morning as I walked down the park steps at Islandbridge to work? It had rained overnight and the stones were streaked with rusty rivulets of water and oil. I was exhausted at the unfamiliar hour. The letter said the office was located on the top storey of the court-house beside the hulk of the abandoned jail. I crossed the river and walked up past the barracks, going over the litany of names in my mind. It was where Emmet and Ann Devlin had been held and tortured; where Ernie O'Malley had escaped with the help of Welsh guards; where James Connolly had been strapped to a chair and carried in by the British to be shot; where the poet Joseph Mary Plunkett had become bridegroom and corpse within one hour of dawn. When Patrick Plunkett first stood for election in the sixties he used to fake a connection by quoting verses from his namesake in the election leaflets that Pascal made my father and other workers deliver door to door.

Now the jail was empty, an echoing presence beside the court-house where a small crowd had already gathered. My stomach was twisted with anxiety as I entered and paused for directions. The barren hallway made me want to run – the bare flagstones where two children played sailors in cardboard boxes, the single bench along the wall with paint flaking overhead from a once ornate ceiling. An elderly couple rose, the man beckoning with his stick as the women tried to hide behind him.

'Excuse me sir,' he whispered, 'my wife was mugged in Ballybough last year and she's due to give evidence. Her nerves are bad since and we're terrified to meet those young men again. Is there nowhere we can hide?'

15

It was the first time I had ever been addressed as sir. I mumbled guiltily and pushed on, leaving them looking more nervous and ashamed than the offenders casually standing around. I followed the staircase to a high, cold room partitioned by a warren of stacked shelving and three long benches besieged by chairs. No one looked up from their newspapers when I entered, each clerk sunk in those final moments before Carol arrived jangling the three keys from the different locks of her old bicycle like a bell, before Mooney's brooding presence mooched wordlessly into his inner office and the morning's work began.

How often in the following months did I enter that room to find a new person standing as I had stood, left to wait awkwardly till someone condescended to look up? I hated them that morning, hated the bowed heads, the odd murmur of voices; hated the same phrases I'd hear over and over: *Are you doing the interview? Did you hear there's a transfer list soon?* Yet later, when Shay left, I often did the same, sinking down beneath Mooney's presence which lit the office like a black bulb draining each breath of life from the room until no one bothered doing one action more than necessary, knowing how he would snap at them for the least step out of line.

Mooney appeared behind me, paused to insert his name on the attendance book and was gone into his office across the room. Though no one moved, I could sense the stiffness entering their shoulders and the relief, like a silent exhaling of breath, when he had passed. His tall, country frame was like a prison warder's, his lined face lacking sufficient bones to hang the red folds of flesh upon. I watched him slam his door, a black-suited Buddha turned bad, the pioneer pin stuck on his lapel, and from deep within I felt an involuntary shudder.

And then Carol was at my elbow like a diminutive burst of light, gripping it and joking as she led me into the centre of the room and jangled the keys of her bicycle locks for attention. She called my name out to everybody before she had bothered to check it, and suddenly had the clerks scurrying, one showing me where to put my coat, another finding space at a table for

16

me and a third poised to teach me the elemental filing with which I was to pass my days. She was tiny and plump with fading red hair, in her late fifties, as active as Mooney was static, nervous energy bubbling as she shouted commands in her precise south Dublin accent over the dying rustle of newspapers, covering up for her superior with her own work-load. She drew the red line in the attendance book as carefully as a heart surgeon with a scalpel, and had clapped her hands for attention when the door behind her opened. She stopped and pursed her lips as a young man strolled in with a leather jacket over his shoulder, then drew a long breath up through her nose, arched her nostrils like a nervous foal, as he approached.

'Hello, mum!' He grinned and bent to peck her on the lips before slipping past to take the vacant seat beside me. Shoulders stiffened at the tables like trees bending in a forest. Carol stood frozen in the position she had been kissed. Then she turned and ran towards the inner office. Almost before the door had slammed the white intercom on the wall was buzzing hysterically and continued to do so while it was being answered. The young man grinned again, held his hand out and asked me my name.

'Francis,' I said. 'Francis Hanrahan.'

'What do they call you at home, Francis or Frank?'

'Francy.'

'Good Jesus! Where did you leave the spade?'

He looked at me closely.

'You're no more from the bog than I am. Would you settle for Hano?'

The buzzing had stopped. The girl replaced the receiver and called over.

'Shay. Mooney wants to see you!'

He grinned and rose to stroll towards the door. When he went in people began whispering about the incident in little huddles. What they said I wasn't sure, I wasn't listening. I think I felt a mixture of admiration and resentment. His words had made me feel relaxed for the first time since entering the room. I was elated and yet suddenly scared, for if the others seemed content to ignore me, now I felt threatened by his very openness. Suddenly I resented him because he

17

seemed all the things I was afraid to be, because I was certain he'd see through me and ridicule the defences I'd built between myself and the world. I wished he was sitting elsewhere, that I was among some anonymous clutter of silent clerks. Charles, a clerk with a face like a slapped arse, a perpetual white shirt and tie and a nose to judge precisely which arse to lick, leaned over disdainfully and whispered, 'Dangerous to know.' I nodded and began filing the cards in front of me, copying the hand motions of the girl on my left side. The door opened and Shay returned to sit beside me. I sneaked a glance at him. He was only twenty-one but looked older. His jet black hair fell slightly down his shoulder, his skin was dark, as if he were descended from an Armada survivor, his hands were fingering a neat moustache. From somewhere I found courage.

'Well,' I said tentatively. 'Was she a panter or a screamer?'

He threw his head back to laugh in that room of whispering clerks and replied, 'I just said *take your false teeth out, Carol, and wrap your gums around that!*'

I grinned back at him. We bent companionably down and started to work.

They had walked in silence for two hours through the narrow roads that skirted the back of the airport. Like a discarded prop from a B-movie, a radar dish revolved its head slowly at a crossroads by the perimeter fence. A car rocked in the lay-by, one bare leg swaying against the rear window when they crept past. Beyond the fence, snakes of landing lights slithered through the grass, seeming to merge in the distance where the dark hulks of planes were parked. A security van sped across the concrete between floodlit hangars. Then Hano lost all sense of direction. Katie led as they threaded their way through tiny lanes, bypassing the huge expanse of light where he remembered the village of Swords. Three times a vehicle's lights sent them tumbling into a ditch. First it was a tinker's speeding Hiace returning to the camp site they later passed, an island of three caravans in a field of wrecked chassis and upturned wheels stacked like the upturned ghosts of the city's dreams. The second was a squad car cruising past, and the third time the light stopped and started like a will-o'-the-wisp behind them. He sweated as they climbed in and out of ditches, certain it was the police mocking, herding them like sheep towards a check-point. They watched the headlights beginning to draw level with them as they knelt among the weeds and refuse sacks, his hand squeezing Katie's, waiting for the doors to open. It was an old farmer so drunk that he fell asleep every few seconds and woke with a start. The car appeared to be driving him home. Shot with whiskey, his glazed eyes looked through them as the car creaked past.

Neither had spoken since she'd taken his hand. He clung to its outpost of warmth, his fingers the only part of him that felt alive. Like a scratched record, the screams from that room echoed in his mind. Could it have really been him? He remembered her fingers dressing him like a child, her hands pushing him from the burning house, his numbness as if cast from stone. Once again part of him longed to be rid of her, to be allowed to sink without trace or responsibility. It wasn't the shame of what he had done afterwards but the shame of what she had witnessed at the start which haunted him, making him afraid to look at her as they plodded through the countryside. It was better not to think at all, to sink into this numb cocoon where he just had to concentrate on keeping his footsteps steady.

Hano had no idea where they were heading. Each time they reached a crossing he followed her blindly. Two miles beyond Swords they crossed the main Belfast road, quiet at that time, rows of cat's-eyes dead for want of light, awaiting the noise of trucks in the distance.

She brought him down a side road where a solitary street light lit a row of old labourers' cottages. A dog padded out from a garden, wagging its tail as it jumped up against him. It was lonely and desperate for attention, following them to the edge of the light and whining mournfully as they were swallowed back by the dark. Without warning, Katie began to whisper like a drowsy person drifting towards sleep.

'You know,' she said, 'this is what I remember best. Did I ever tell you . . . about being lost out in it, hidden from the world. You know, in Dublin . . . sometimes I'd lock the bedroom door at night and curl against the wall, but no, it wasn't the same, you know what I mean, not like I remember it. Too artificial, like, who the fuck were you fooling. There'd be voices on the road, street lights. You knew you weren't cut off.'

Katie paused. She might have been addressing herself more than him. Hano listened, uncertain what she was talking about. Her voice was harsher, more like her own, when she continued.

'I killed this feeling, made myself forget. Murdered each fucking memory one by one. Wasn't going to be like my uncle, like his friends. Jesus, the same accents, same phrases they used forty years ago when they worked the land. They sound so stupid, so fucking pathetic. When you leave something Hano you leave it, you go on, you know what I mean. God, I hated those bastards for always reminding me.'

Hano remembered the evening her uncle came looking for her, the same huge hands his own father had, the same outdoors stance, his awkwardness in the tiny hallway. He said nothing, afraid to break the spell and cast them back into the bickering they had always known. Katie's voice mellowed again.

'Funny thing is, you can't kill it fully. Keeps coming back to haunt me . . . nights like this. Waiting for dada to put out the gas lamp in his room before I'd get out on to the shed roof. You know, twice he caught me and leathered me black and blue, but I still did it, even when he threatened to tie me to the bed. I was eight but I was in love with danger. Not what you'd think now, spacers or being raped by cider heads, but, you know, werewolves and ghosts waiting for you, trees with malicious spirits you have to pass – all that sort of shite Tomas filled my head with.

'Two miles it was from the road to our house, the tar-macadam gave out quarter way there. Except from Tomas's gaff, there wasn't a light for miles. And every few yards you'd shiver, daring yourself on, because you knew the further you went the longer the journey home would be. And that was the real thrill, Hano, that was fucking it. You know, you'd creep forward, shivering at every bush and shift of moonlight, till finally something – I don't know, the creak of a branch, a plastic bag in a ditch – set you off racing back through the dark, knowing that whatever the heck was behind you was gaining at every step, was about to touch your shoulder. You'd long to scream but your throat would be too dry, your legs covered in scratches, your clothes caught by briars, but you wouldn't care. Your lungs were bursting, legs pounding, but Hano, Jesus, Hano, the thrill of it, you know what I mean, the thrill of the journey home. Like being shot through with electricity. All the pills, all the booze, they were nothing to that.'

He remembered her uncle speaking, with his hands awkwardly gripping the leather belt of his trousers. 'If Katie's here tell her to come home tonight. The aunt gets worried. She can't help herself, keeps wandering off.' Katie stopped and shouted across the dark fields.

'Not bleeding scared of you now goblins or vampires. Come out if you dare!'

She relaxed her grip and began swaying along the road in front of him, teasing him to follow. And despite what had happened his mood lifted and he laughed, running with outstretched hands to chase her. They could have been any young couple on a midnight escapade as she screamed and dodged his grip, twisting and turning on the road, stumbling against the ditch and blundering on. He ran towards her, forgetting everything. Two dogs outside a nearby cottage began to bark and the chorus was taken up in all the other farmyards along the road as they raced past, occasionally catching hold of each other, more often careering freely along. The moon slipped its moorings of cloud again and threw shadows of leaves like crazy paving on the road before them. She turned to look at him and slipped into a deep ditch, barely missing a clump of nettles. He looked down in panic at her crumpled body lying awkwardly where it had fallen. The countryside was alive with outraged dogs. He climbed quickly in, cupping her neck gently in his palms as he bent to study her face. There seemed no sign of life. He pressed his face closer and suddenly her mouth was open, her tongue burrowing like a saturated animal between his lips. As suddenly as their first kiss had begun it

21

was over, her shoulder pushing him to one side as he lay confused, watching her climb up to the roadway, her face closed, staring ahead as she started to walk onwards into the dark.


It's strange how a city grows into your senses, how you become attuned to its nuances like living with a lover. Even when you sleep it's still there in your mind. Out here Cait, it's a different kind of isolation, a living one. Later on, when I'd walk home at dawn from work in the petrol station, I'd feel a sense of the suburb as being like a creature who'd switched itself off, leaving street lights and advertising signs as sentinels. But out here, even in the dark I can hear the noise of branches shifting, of hunting and hunted creatures. Here nothing really sleeps except with one eye open, alert for danger.

I keep trying to describe that office in my mind. I should know its every mood. Yet there is only a blank when I try to recall it, a dull collage of afternoons staring at an antiquated clock; of childish games played to relieve the monotony, rolls of sellotape hurled across tables, infinite rounds of twenty questions, fencing with the long poles required to open and close windows. In winter two Supersers heated the room. Those nearest the heater were scalded; those further away wrapped their coats around their shoulders and bent their heads under the long electric lights. That first morning it felt like a crypt, but it took time to realize that underneath the silence people were living a subterranean existence with a private language and private jokes, each clerk equipped with his or her own technique of surviving the tedium. I had always thought of work as involving some personal skill. As a child I'd bring my father down his lunch in Plunkett Motors and watch the men hammering out panels or respraying cars. There seemed a purpose to it all, a definite end-product. The figures worked in their oil-stained overalls with a curious dignity, self-assured in their skill.

That's how I had imagined the adult world. But here there was just the endless procession of blue files and green files to be sorted and stamped. I was earning as much money as my father but was ashamed to tell him what my work involved. After a fortnight I began to imagine some higher official was playing a joke on me, unsorting files at night and putting them back. The names seemed the very ones I had sorted the day before, the details of offspring over eighteen familar before I wrote them down. Shay and Mick had invented a game where they would call out people's names and addresses and make us guess by their ages what the children were christened. Shay said you could learn to date the fashions in children's names like the vintages of fine wines.

Each morning the crocodile of clerks looped its way through the crowded hallway down to the narrow canteen. We drank tea and talked the gossip and rumours of the office while through the window above the door a garda sergeant called out the names of those charged. It seemed an invisible world to the clerks: they pushed their way past junkies trembling on the steps, past clusters of hard chaws supporting the walls or mothers burdened with children and infinite, helpless patience. Only Shay would nod, pausing to joke with some old lad drinking a bottle of milk on the stairs. Once when we came out they were bringing in a tinker girl. She was no more than fifteen, in the first bud of womanhood. It took four officers to carry her into the courtroom, her body twisting in a grotesque, sensual dance. The clerks paused and then turned to mount the stairs to the dusty shelves while her screams echoed through the building.

What else can I tell you about? The gnawing, all-consuming hatred of Mooney who rarely spoke, confident of his power as he placed his hand on some girl's shoulder to enjoy the tremor of unease that rippled forth. I'd imagine his tongue lightly wetting his lips each time an increment form came on to his desk, or a temporary position came up for renewal. His days were spent making neat reports to personnel on every mistake, drawing black marks with a sensual pleasure. A black-and-white photograph of his wife and two children stood on his desk. Occasionally he would mention them in his Monaghan accent to some new girl, his brow knitting with anxiety about their progress through college, his tongue lolling over their achievements like a lullaby. Then an hour later he would stand behind her, screeching about her overuse of sellotape.

Six months before I joined a girl was tested for cancer. The hospital decided to keep her in but she insisted on taking a taxi back to the office first. Everyone was at lunch so she left a note for Mooney on the back of a blank voter's form before returning to the surgeon's knife. She woke up without her breast, but slowly recovered, painfully learnt to face the world, to venture out and then return to work. On her first morning back she was sent to personnel. On the desk lay the offending voter's form in a blue folder with a report on the abuse of official stationery.

And finally there was Shay, like a light switched on in a projector. When he came in the office seemed to burst into life. He'd steal some girl's cigarettes and make a show of passing them round, give mock radio commentaries of the Blessed Virgin landing at Knock, secrete sticks of incense in the filing cabinets. Above all he drew people out, spending days, if a new girl came, just getting her to talk. He had worked there for three years before I began and knew every nook where one could hide, every trick to waste a half-hour. The curious thing was that he was the one person Mooney kept his distance from, cautious because he could not put him into any slot. They measured each other like chess players: Mooney, a grand master baffled by the seemingly ridiculous moves his young opponent made; Shay, knowing that the more outrageous his actions were the more Mooney would stall, terrified of being tricked into making any decision.

Most of the girls queued for lunch in the small coffee shop across the road where Carol held court with tales of neighbours in Deansgrange and former clerks who had gone to the bad. As I hovered outside on my first morning Shay took pity on me, whistled softly and nodded across the street towards the Irish Martyrs Bar & Lounge. There an inner circle met. Mary, the longest serving clerk, scapegoat for Carol's tantrums and humours, and Mick, quiet and small, grinning to himself as he wolfed his way through pints of Guinness. The bar was jammed in an uneasy truce between policemen and criminals, nodding familiarly as they waited to be served by the old barmen. When I complained that it was my first day and I was afraid to drink, Mary reluctantly bought me an orange juice and then spiked it with vodka when my back was turned. That lunch-time I began to see the humour behind their serious faces.

Mick was the occupant of a Rathgar bedsit, expelled from college after three years of playing pool, degreeless and a disgrace to his strong farmer father, but with a highest snooker break of seventy-six, a love of German films and a poker fixation. He rarely spoke till the afternoon, as he nursed each morning's hangover in. Mary had just passed the wrong side of thirty. She had joined after school, intending to stay for a year and never managed to leave. Even that first day I knew she never would go now. She told the bluest jokes in her Liberties accent as she spent every penny she had on you, but rarely mentioned her three-year-old child at home, never spoke of the daily struggle to cope alone. Between them Shay sat, egging them on as they mocked the size of each other's sexual parts while surreptitiously pouring drink into me.

At two o'clock they helped me cautiously back up the stairs, Mary shovelling mints into me to disguise the smell. After every few steps they'd pause to agree how awful they were, then burst out into laughter again. That first afternoon passed in a hazy blur, wedged in between Shay and Mick hiding me at the bottom table. The room swayed in a welter of flying sellotape and blue jokes, the elbows of the lads prodding me whenever I teetered towards laughter.

It seemed unreal when I got home again to face my mother's eager questions. I stood in the shorn garden trying to sober up, suddenly resentful of Shay with his permanent position. He was safe in a job for life. All they needed to give me was three days' notice. He knew the rules while I was being led blindly down. But soon I realized I was not. Shay kept beside me as the first week rolled on, his intuition so refined he could warn me the instant before a door opened or a buzzer rang. And the work was so tedious that despite my apprehension I was drawn in, fascinated by his cool good nature, his audacity. Some mornings Mary gave him a conspiratorial wink and he'd disappear until break time when he discreetly emptied the baby Power in their cups at the top of the table, slipping the empty whiskey bottle back into his pocket before Carol arrived. In the afternoons the voices of solicitors and policemen wafted through the air vent as we blew smoke from the joint out the downstairs toilet window; his eyes amused at my terror whenever their footsteps came near. And gradually I learnt to surrender my trust to him. He kept me always just the right side of the line, teaching me how to look busy by perpetually carrying a pile of files as I wandered through the room or by stacking work up in front of me to create the appearance of speed.

By the Friday I knew everything about the job that needed to be known. My hands could file the forms away in my sleep. Indeed, when I closed my eyes on the first nights I automatically saw piles of registration forms being ticked and passed from tray to tray. The forms came in cardboard boxes that were carefully stored and returned. Those boxes that had burst open were burnt. That afternoon Shay beckoned me out to the landing. Below, the guard was calling out the last few cases before the weekend. Without looking down I could sense the crush of bodies piling against the court door. Shay selected four of the sturdiest cardboard boxes and reefed them apart with an expert left foot. He handed me two and we were gone. The incinerator was two concrete slabs placed against the wall of the old prison. We burnt each box individually, dutifully standing over them until the last one turned to ash. That was when he told me about the girl with one breast.

'Mooney made Carol do his dirty work, of course. She had visited young Eileen in hospital twice a week. I found Carol up there that lunch-time, her cardigan over her shoulder, eyes raw with crying.'

I was drifting slowly into friendship with him, the very casualness of it disguising its grip. I had stuck close to him at first simply to learn the rules of work but even after five days it had become more than that in my mind. There was a sense of excitement being in Shay's presence. His friendship made no demands; it was simply given, asking nothing in return, making no attempt to conscript you to any viewpoint or take sides in the petty office wars. The discovery that we were from the same suburb was made not in terms of common links but of differences.

I remember once as a child missing the bus stop at the village and being carried up the long straight road into the Corporation estates in the West. I was terrified by the stories I had heard. I could have been a West Berliner who'd strayed across the Iron Curtain. When I was eight the new dual carriageway made the division complete, took away the woodlands we might have shared, made the only meeting point between the two halves of the village a huge arched pedestrian bridge. He listened incredulously when I confessed to not having been in the Bath Wars, then described how each summer's day the boys in the West would gather on the hill overlooking the river valley that had miraculously survived between them and the next suburb. Below lay the only amenity for miles: a filthy, concrete open-air pool. On the far hill the enemy was massed with strict military ranks observed. Daily pitched battles were fought for possession of the muddy square of water. That Friday by the prison wall Shay lifted his shirt to show me the scar left on his back from the evening he was captured on a reconnaissance mission and beaten with a bicycle chain. I think now of Ernie O'Malley escaping through the gate that stood behind us that day, both wars a struggle to reach adulthood. To Shay the scar was as much a part of growing up there as Black-and-Tans smashing doors was to his grandfather. I told him instead of my world of hen-runs and potato beds, of opening the back door one night to find a hedgehog trapped in the light, pulling its head in and squatting for hours till it could escape into the dark.

Shay had left home when he started work at eighteen, and perpetually moved from bedsit to bedsit since. I envied him for having made the break. The world he spoke of was magical – late-night snooker halls and twenty-four-hour kebab shops where the eyes of a waitress at four in the morning were lit by Seconal, walking home from a poker session to a flat at dawn with thirty pounds in change. That Friday afternoon I desperately wanted his friendship, wanted his respect, wanted to become a part of his world. I tried to lie and invent experiences but found I hadn't the confidence.

Instead I tried to prove my manhood by cursing Mooney and speaking of the hatred already building in me. It was contagious in that cramped office where no one knew who would be reported next. Only once had I been inside Mooney's inner office where the blinds were kept drawn, giving the room an air of perpetual twilight. An old-fashioned lamp with a metal shade burned on his desk, highlighting his joined fingers, and a white circle of disordered papers stretched away into the dusk at the table's edge. Leather-bound volumes coated with dust lined the walls except for the space behind the desk where the largest map of the city I had ever seen was hung. The political boundaries had been drawn and redrawn on it as successive governments reshaped the constituencies to their advantage. Once a year when Mooney went reluctantly on holiday with his wife and children, Carol worked in a frenzy to make sense of the papers before his return. I had been sent in to deliver two completed folders and Mooney had ignored my knock and my query about where to leave them. Only when I was leaving did he speak. *I see everything in this office*, he intoned. I turned. In the lamplight it was impossible to see his eyes, only the joined hands motionless on the desk. They picked up the nearest paper, dismissing me. But as I cursed him by the wall of the jail I realized Shay was the only person who didn't share in the collective orgy of hate. For him it would have given Mooney a stature he didn't deserve.

He kicked at the ashes, enjoying the last few breaths of air.

'Listen Hano, that's his world up there. Do you not think he knows how they hate him? I tell you, the man gloats on it. Not only has he got them for eight hours a day, but before work, after work; every waking hour they spend discussing how they hate him makes him the axis of their lives. He lives off it for fuck sake, it gives him importance. Just ignore the cunt. That's what really kills him.'

Shay grinned and began to walk back towards the office, teaching me the golden rules of survival and promotion. Do nothing unless you absolutely have to. Make no decisions whatsoever. Perpetually pass on responsibility. Remember that no extra work you do, even if you stay till midnight, will ever find its way on to your record. Only your mistakes will be marked down, black marks on your file for ever. Any innovation will be seen as a threat by those above you. Therefore those who do least, who shirk all decisions, will always progress. It was why Mooney, who spent his day brooding behind an *Irish Times* at his filthy desk, now commanded his own section, while Carol, who ran and fetched, who kept the office running single-handed, blundering her way through the work he refused to touch, would never progress beyond being his useful assistant. She had committed the fatal mistake of making herself indispensable and would remain there till Mooney finally retired and some white-shirted graduate came in to modernize the office over her head. I had been wrong to imagine work as an adult world. The same old roles of childhood were played out there. As we walked up the steps I wondered suddenly would I be there till sixty-five, learning to rise the ladder and lick higher arses? The thought frightened me more than the unemployment I had known a week before.

Back in the office Shay and Mary played games to spin out the afternoon. If Mooney was safe from them, Carol rose to their bait every time. At half-four, Shay cocked his head like an Indian tracker, then clicked his fingers. Mary had reached the Ladies before Carol even opened Mooney's door. I watched Carol discreetly check the locked door as Shay and Mick bent their heads dutifully down. She pretended to examine the stacked shelves beside the toilet, shifting uneasily from foot to foot as the minutes passed. Beside me Shay and Mick took bets and softly hummed 'Singing in the Rain', until after a quarter of an hour Shay raised his head, touched my shoulder lightly and switched his humming to 'Here We Go, Here We Go'.

'Is the post ready, Paula?'

'No, Carol. I'll have it finished in five minutes.'

'What have you been doing all afternoon? Must I do every little thing in this office myself?'

She clenched her fists against her scarlet face and skipped up and down like a child with a rope as she screamed 'There's none of yous good!' Shay watched her flee the room and race across to the toilet in the pub, then picked his watch up.

'Fifteen and a half minutes,' he told Mick. 'You jammy bollox.' He passed a pound across the table and rose to tap three times on the door. Mary emerged with the paper, glanced around surreptitiously and used it to put the clock on five minutes.

At five to five we stampeded down the steps. The weekend, which had been the worst time of the week when I was unemployed, suddenly stretched joyously before me. I stood enjoying the late spring sunshine. Shay had left just in front of me.

'Good luck mate,' I shouted. 'See you Monday.'

He waved back and then paused.

'What's your hurry?' he said. 'Fancy a pint? Celebrate your first week of survival.'

He stood a few feet from me, happily indifferent to whether I came or not. I thought of my mother at home, my father due in from Plunkett Motors at half-past five, washing his hands in the deep enamel sink, my little sisters running in and out the kitchen door behind him. I didn't want to admit to being expected home.

'Ah, I'm a bit skint. Had to work a back week, you know yourself.'

'Jasus, there'll be enough times when I'll be broke. Get into the car for fuck's sake if that's all that's wrong with you.'

They would wait till the Angelus came on the television, neither praying nor speaking till the chimes stopped, then they'd cover my plate and leave it in the oven. There would be no questions asked when I got home, just silent hurt filling the room of plywood furniture.

A battered Triumph Herald was parked by the prison wall like a relic from Black-and-Tan days. 'My only love,' Shay said, patting the canvas roof, and with great difficulty managing to lower it. The rusty bodywork had received more blows than a punch-drunk boxer. After four attempts the engine reluctantly spluttered to life and we moved off towards town. I felt both guilty and elated, filled with a sense of liberation. And perhaps because we had spoken earlier of our home place, all the way to town we talked of travel, each charting more mythical journeys across the European continent. Paris, Berlin, Lisbon; places that to me were just names from subtitled films glimpsed when my parents went to bed, but for Shay they were real. He spoke of them like women he would one day sleep with.

30

That evening was my first glimpse of Shay's Dublin. It was like an invisible world existing parallel to the official one I had known, a grey underworld of nixers and dole where people slagged Shay for actually having a job. One summer he'd worked as a messenger boy on a motor bike and knew every twisted lane and small turning. I kept intending to go home after each place we visited but then he'd suggest another and we'd be gone. There was no premeditation, the evening just drifted on its own course. I'd imagine my mother's plain cooking gradually stuck to the plate, the meat drying up, the shrivelled vegetables. Then Shay would park another pint in front of me and that would put an end to that. I began to see how Shay survived the office without bitterness or hatred. To him it was just a temporary apparition, eight hours of rest before he entered his real world.

At nine o'clock Shay insisted on buying me a Chinese meal, joking that the seagull's leg refused to stop twitching. By then I was talking as I had never talked since I sat in the old woman's caravan, living off every word he spoke, making him laugh with stories about my father's boss. But I shied away from any reference to my home, ashamed of it suddenly as I envied his freedom, his experience, his accepted adultness. Two girls sat at a nearby table. Occasionally one glanced across at him.

'What do you think?' he asked. 'Will we give it a lash? It's up to yourself.'

I got frightened of being caught out. I was not a virgin but was terrified of the direct approach. My few successes had been scored hurriedly after dances, brought to a messy climax, before bolting as though from the scene of a crime. If we approached I knew I would be tongue-tied. I hesitated and, trying to feign an experienced air, suggested they might not be the type. He grinned at them and gave a mock wave of his hand.

'I don't know,' he said. 'Cute country girls in their bedsits. They may have lost their virginity but they'll probably still have the box it came in.'

But it was obvious I was nervous and when they rose to leave he blew a kiss after them and suggested we play snooker instead.

The hall was a converted warehouse with no sign outside. The old man behind the counter was watching a black-and-white television. He greeted Shay like a son and asked him to mind the gaff while he slipped out to the pub. The walls had been whitewashed once but only vaguely remembered the event. We chose the least ragged of the vacant tables. Shay broke, then leaned on his cue to look around the semi-derelict room.

'I used to live here after I was expelled from school. Old Joe had great hopes for me but I knew I hadn't got it. The place is in tatters now but no wankers come in. I tried a few of the new ones. Deposits, video cameras, and toss-artists who think a deep screw is a mot with a BA. Fuck this, I said, I must be getting old.'

It was ten o'clock when we left. The old man still hadn't returned but occasionally men left a few quid behind the counter as they wandered out. 'Is it cool?' Shay asked. 'You sure you don't have to head home?' I lied again and followed him through the feverish weekend crowds beneath the neon lights, then down towards a warren of cobbled laneways off Thomas Street. The pub we came to looked shut, the only hint of life being a fine grain of light beneath the closed shutters. A tramp passed, stumbling towards the night shelter. He mumbled a few incomprehensible words, one hand held out as though his fingers were cupping a tiny bird. Two children sleeping rough watched us from the doorway of a boarded-up bakery. Shay tapped three times on the steel shutter and I had the sensation of being watched before it swung open. A middle-aged Monaghan man with an old-fashioned bar apron beckoned and welcomed Shay by name. The downstairs bar was thick with smoke, countrymen nursing pints, a figure with a black beard gesturing drunkenly in the centre of the floor. Two old women sang in a corner, one lifting her hand with perfect timing at regular intervals to straighten the man beside her who was tilting on his bar stool. Nobody there was under fifty, no one born in the city that was kept out by the steel door.

'Gas, isn't it?' Shay said. 'Knocknagow on a Friday evening.' He gazed in amusement, then headed downstairs to the cellar.

Here the owner's son reigned, the father never coming closer than shouting down from the top step at closing time. Four women with sharp, hardened faces sat in one corner drinking shorts. The dozen people at the long table shouted assorted abuse and greetings at Shay as he grinned and waved two fingers back to them. He called for drink and introduced me to his friends. I began to suss how the locked door kept more than the industrial revolution out. The girl across from me was rolling a joint; the bloke beside Shay passing one in his hands. He took three drags and handed it on to me. The pints arrived. I dipped into the white froth, my head afloat. Two of the women in the corner rose and ascended the stairs, bored looking, stubbing their cigarettes out.

'The massaging hand never stops,' Shay said. 'Pauline there left her bag behind one night so I brought it over to her across the road in the Clean World Health Studio. She was clad in a leather outfit after skelping the arse off some businessman who was looking decidedly green in the face as if he'd got more for his forty quid than he bargained for.'

'Forty quid?' I joked as the next joint reached me. 'Well fuck Father Riley and his bar of chocolate.'

It was to be the first of numerous nights with Shay in haunts like that, always tucked away down crooked lanes. I think he had a phobia about streets that were straight. But that night in Murtagh's stands out because everything was so new and spinning faster and faster. It had all reached a blur when the young man in the check suit appeared, with features so familiar I drove myself crazy trying to place them. As he spoke he clapped his hands like an American basketball player, his body perpetually jiving as if linked to an inaudible disco rhythm. Shay frowned slightly when he saw him approach. He was the first person there Shay seemed to tolerate more than like. The young man slapped Shay's shoulder and shook hands with me with a polished over-firm grip.

'My main man Seamus. A drink for you and your friend.'

He returned with three tequilas. I copied Shay in licking the salt, drained the glass in one gulp and sank my teeth into the lemon. It was like electricity shooting through my body. I slammed my fist on the table and shook my head. The young man laughed so much he insisted on buying another round. Shay grinned sardonically as he watched me trying to place him.

'Add thirty years,' he said, 'four stone of fat and a bog accent. You've already mentioned him twice tonight.'

I studied the figure arguing animatedly with the two women left in the corner. My brain slowly reconciled the two opposites.

'Plunkett,' I said. 'My da's boss. He's something like him, but Pascal's a bachelor.'

'Fuck your da's boss. He's chicken shit. Who's his famous brother?'

His face had stared at me from lamp-posts at every election time, his eyes gazing from cards dropped into the hallway with fake handwriting underneath. I tried to match the features in front of me now with the image of Patrick Plunkett I had last seen, repeating rhetorical phrases on a current affairs show as he refused to answer the interviewer's questions.

'Your future, smiling local TD,' Shay said. 'A genuine chip off the old bollox. Justin. So christened because of his one-inch penis. I see he's dispatching the last of his troupe. Would make a great newspaper headline for any editor wanting to go out of business fast.'

The two women in the corner were about to leave.

'Surely the cops know,' I said.

'What fucking country do you live in Hano? You know any guard wants to get transferred to Inisbofin? It may be an embarrassment to the government to have it open; it would be an even greater embarrassment for the fuckers to have to close it down. Youth must have its fling. The party knows he'll drop it when the old bastard expires and he's called upon to inherit the seat. He's being groomed already, two or three funerals a week.'

For the first time I detected bitterness in Shay's voice. But to be angry would be to admit he was a part of their world. Shay shrugged his shoulders and suggested we go upstairs. When I closed my eyes I felt like a boat being rocked from side to side. At the doorway Justin Plunkett pushed a glass into my hand. I heard Shay slagging him about the suit, his good humour returned. Shay's hand was on my shoulder, steering me up-stairs, past the country men in their bar, up two more flights and into a tiny room in darkness except for a blazing fire and a single blue spotlight. It shone down on a long-haired figure on a pallet strumming a guitar. A man crouched beside him, keeping up a rhythm on a hand drum. I found a seat among the stoned crowd and tried to follow the singer's drug-ridden fantasies. Each song lasted quarter of an hour, filled with tortoises making love and nuns in rubber boots.

I felt sick and yet had never felt better as I gazed from the window at the tumbledown lane outside. The sleeping children had gone. A man with a cardboard box and a blanket jealously guarded their spot. Far below, Dublin was moving towards the violent crescendo of its Friday night, taking to the twentieth century like an aborigine to whiskey. Studded punks pissed openly on corners. Glue sniffers stumbled into each other, coats over their arms as they tried to pick pockets. Addicts stalked rich-looking tourists. Stolen cars zigzagged through the distant grey estates where pensioners prayed anxiously behind bolted doors, listening for the smash of glass. In the new disco bars children were queuing, girls of fourteen shoving their way up for last drinks at the bar.

And here I was lost in the city, cut off in some time warp, high and warm above the crumbling streets. I think I slept and when I woke the owner was shouting time from the foot of the stairs. The singer had stopped and accepted a joint from the nearest table. The lad beside me who had been eyeing the guitar stumbled up to grab it, closed his eyes and began to sing:

> Like a full force gale
> I was lifted up again,
> I was lifted up again,
> By the Lord . . .

He wore a broad black hat with a long coat and sang with his eyes closed, living out the dream of Jessie James, the outlaw riding into the Mexican pueblo, the bandit forever condemned to run. He opened his eyes again when he had sung the last refrain, handed the guitar back apologetically and moved down the stairs towards his dingy Rathmines bedsit. I thought of home suddenly, the cremated dinner, my parents waiting for the dot on the television, exchanging glances but never asking each other where I was. I felt guilty once more and yet they suddenly seemed so distant, like an old photograph I'd been carrying around for too long.

'You alive at all Hano?' Shay's voice asked. 'You don't look a well man. A tad under the weather I'd say. Listen, there's a mattress back in my flat if you want to crash there. And I'm after scoring some lovely Leb.'

'What about your wheels?'

'Leave them. Not even Dublin car thieves are that poor.'

Home, like an old ocean liner, broke loose from its moorings and sailed in my mind across the hacked-down garden, further and further through the streets with my parents revolving in their armchairs. I could see it in my mind retreating into the distance and I stood to wave unsteadily after it, grinning as I took each euphoric step down after Shay towards the takeaway drink hustled in the bar below and the adventures of crossing the city through its reeling night-time streets.

*Hope. A four-letter word. Hope. Mornings are the worst Katie. You wake when your cousin rises, tumbling into the warm hollow she has vacated on her side of the bed. Two years older than you, she dresses quietly for her work in the fast-food restaurant in town. She arrives home each Thursday with sore arms, tired feet from dodging the assistant manager and ten pounds more than on the dole. When she is gone you lie on, luxuriating in those private moments alone in that room. Then you hear his footsteps start through the wall beside your head. Rising at the same time he did when he walked down for the early shift. You hear the smudging sound of the brush over his boots before they descend the stairs. The routine, that is what is vital for him, the pretence that there is still something to be done. The front door closes and you know he will walk to the mobile shop with the same dilemma, ten cigarettes or a newspaper. You rise quickly before he returns, the situations vacant column always the winner. You will try to have finished your breakfast when the footsteps restart in the hall and hurry to the door before he spreads the page of close type over the Formica to stoop like a man holding a mirror to the lips of a corpse.*

*Hope, Katie. That is what he pretends to have. You cannot bear to watch the bowed head, the finger moving steadily to the bottom of each column. You reach the school long before the lessons start. Remember, you ran here so eagerly once. Now it is no more than a sanctuary from the despair of that house. There is a wall to smoke behind. A girl says, 'Are you game? The Bounce?' And you slip quickly back out that gate, skirting the road he will take at half-past nine to the Manpower office, not going in if the same girl is on the desk as the day before, afraid he will lose face by appearing too eager. You run down by the side of the Spanish Nun's, past the green and gold of the Gaelic Club, by the mud-splattered row of caravans, till you find the gap in the hedge and are running fast across the overgrown car-park to reach the vast cavern of the abandoned factory.*

*Here is education, here you belong. A dozen girls are gathered in the dripping shell where their sisters once bent over rows of machines. Here at last there is no pretence, no talk of imaginary futures. Sometimes they sit in near silence or play ragged impromptu games; sometimes boys come. Somebody lights a cigarette, somebody has pills. A small bottle passes down a corridor of hands till it reaches you. You hold the capsule in your hand, a speckled egg to break apart. You pause, then swallow. Hope. Four-letter words punctuate the jokes you laugh at. A girl leans on your back in tears as laughter almost chokes her. There are colours to watch. The concrete refuses to stay still. There is warmth. A circle of faces to belong to. The sound of a chain being pulled from a gate, the engine stops in the van. The girls by your side pull you on as the uniformed security guard unleashes the dog. You race exhilarated across the grass, the sky twisting and buckling. You can hear barking behind you and the girls begin to scream. The wall rushes at you, automatically you jump. The*

*sharp surface grazes your knees before hands pull you clear
and down on to the path beside the carriageway. The footsteps
are racing now; you join them — a flock of pigeons circling
back towards the estate.*

Hano and Katie had followed the weak scraggle of street
lights which petered out beyond the green with its pub next to
the closed-down swings beside a battered caravan in the tiny
amusement park. To their left a new estate of white council
houses slept with an unfinished look, out of place among the
fields. On their right through the blackness they could breathe
in the sharp tang of sea air blowing across the expanse of
sucking mud exposed by the low tide. The road wound
upwards through moonlit golf courses and the flaking paint of
holiday chalets, until it levelled out into a car park on the very
brink of the cliff. Hano stood with his arm around Katie when
they reached the edge, mesmerized by the scene below. The
whole of Dublin was glowing like a living thing sprawled out
before his eyes, like the splintered bones of a corpse lit up in
an X-ray. Hours before he had still been a part of it, one cell
in a vibrant organism. Now up on this headland where Katie
had led him he was cut off and isolated from the lives below.
She stood almost indulgently beside him while he gazed, then
took his hand again to pull him on through the dark. He
panicked for a moment when her form vanished before him,
thinking she was intent on some suicide pact, before realizing
that she had begun to climb carefully down the black and
seemingly impossible rock face towards the foam flashing
below them. She gripped his hand, never speaking or looking
back, but instinctively choosing the correct path along the
slope. Once she slipped and as his arm was jerked forward he
heard the noise of pebbles tumbling down to vanish into the
sea below, but she didn't cry out though her leg must have
been grazed. She was up a second later, nimbly finding footholds in the rock face again. The sea wind blew into their faces,
stinging his exhausted eyes, but keeping his limbs awake. He
focused his mind solely on reaching the strand alive, no longer
wishing to think of the events which had led him here, or the

promise of what might happen when he reached solid earth again. His life, as he had lived it, was finished, but there would be time for decisions later; now it was enough to be led. Her warm hand brought him through the teeth of the night, where swaying lights winked across the water, neither judging nor demanding, but human and alive, a tiny embryo of hope.

She stopped and his momentum sent him careering against her back. They had reached the bottom. Without speaking, they walked across the sand which parted beneath their feet, slowing them so they seemed to move in a dream. A dark outline against the V of the cliffs took the shape of a concrete bunker as they approached. On both sides steel shutters glinted in the dark from the closed toilets. There was a narrow exposed entrance at the side of the shelter and a large open space at the front overlooking the sea. Most of the bench against the wall inside had been hacked away, but occasionally a strip of wood still ran between the concrete supports. When Hano struck a match he saw the walls covered in graffiti before the wind choked the flame. Sand and litter had been blown in across the floor and from one corner the smell of urine lingered. Yet when he squatted below the open window at the front there was shelter from the breeze. Katie was standing beside him, leaning on the concrete sill to gaze out at the waves.

'How do you know this place?' he asked.

'What does it matter?' She replied and huddled down beside him in silence. But after a moment he heard her voice.

'Seems like a lifetime,' she whispered. 'I don't know, so fucking long ago. Often lads would steal a car at night, arse around the streets in it, looking for a chase. But sometimes, you know, they'd just drive out into the country. You'd be with them in the back, killing time, seeing what the stroke was. I loved it and hated it . . . brought back things I didn't want. We were so spaced you wouldn't think I'd remember any of it. But I know every laneway here like the veins on my wrist. They're the only shagging things that do seem real.'

Katie laughed and leaned against him.

'Last day I went to that kip of a school some teacher starts looking over my shoulder. We'd taken tablets the night before and things seemed to be shooting across the room. My eyes kept jerking round to follow them and I couldn't hear a word the old biddy was saying. She screamed at me and when I looked up she was like some bleeding ghost you know, all the features indistinct, out of focus, like. But they were all that way by then ... figures from another world, days rolling together in a blur, nothing real about it.

'But I remember every second driving out here – it was vivid, Hano, you known what I mean. One time we almost drove as far as Leitrim. I was shouting directions from the back, like a lost animal finding its way home. I got frightened when we got close, screaming for them to turn the car round. They thought I was fucking cracked. "Faster," I kept shouting as we sped back. "Faster! Faster!" Just like that little girl running through the night again, only this time I was racing away from her.'

She was silent and, just when he thought she wasn't going to continue, her voice came out of the darkness again.

'No matter where we went we always wound up here on the coast. I don't know why. Walking down the pier in Rush in the dark or outside the closed-down amusements in Skerries. The cove at Loughshinny or out along the arches of the railway bridge. Out here was my favourite, around Portrane and Donabate. Watching dawn break, you know, all sea-birds and grey light over the water.'

Her voice softened as though the litany of names were soothing her. The edge of hysteria was gone that had always been present in the flat, except for the nights when she just sat sullenly for hours wrapped up in her duffle coat.

'What happened when you reached the coast?' he asked, taking his jacket off and spreading it over both their shoulders. They leaned close together as she searched in her jeans for cigarettes, lit two and handed him one. He watched the red tip burning upwards towards her lips as she inhaled.

'Fuck all,' she said. 'That's the funny bit. All the screaming and slagging stopped when we hit the shoreline, like we were at the end of a journey. When the wheels touched the sand there'd be silence, all of us just staring out at the sea. It belonged to nobody, no little bollox in a peaked cap could come along at midnight and turn it off. We'd get out then and throw sand, skim stones, that sort of shite. Git and Eileen could swim so we'd smoke a few numbers waiting for them. And you know, blokes who were half-animal in Dublin would talk to you about things they'd normally be ashamed of, mots they had fancied or nightmares or the future stretching away before them. They were too thick to know how bleeding short it was.'

Like a cancer gnawing inside, the stab of jealousy shocked him and he hated the words even as he spoke.

'Have you spent a night with someone here before?'

'What if I did?'

'Who was he?'

Her shoulders hunched defensively and she became that huddled figure in the flat again. Her voice was hard, almost contemptuous.

'For fuck sake Hano, what does it matter to you? You're not a child any more. Aren't we screwed up enough without raising old ghosts? The past is as dead as Shay, you can't own it or change it. So don't explain yourself to me, Hano. I don't want to know what the fuck you were at in that room back there. And don't ask me questions, right. You're still alive, I'm still alive. That's all that bleeding matters for now.'

She was right, but after what she had seen he still needed to prove himself. But the gesture of placing his arm around her shoulder which would have been so natural a moment before now felt awkward and contrived and her shoulders stiffened beneath his touch. He moved his lips down and while he encountered no resistance, there was no life in her mouth. He knew he should stop, yet like an overwound spring, in his exhaustion and self-disgust, seemed unable to prevent himself – though he knew she would twist away, hurt and withdrawn, with her back turned to him. He laid his head against the wall, his eyes closed, and sighed. The only sound in the hut was of the waves carried in on the damp air. Then, to his surprise, he felt fingers in the dark searching for his hand again.

'What are you trying to prove Hano?' she whispered. 'That you're better than them, or the same or different? You don't need to. Listen, this place is full of ghosts for me. Git and Mono, they're both doing time now. A vicious attack – no reason for it, no excuse. They shared a needle with some junkie inside. They're locked in the Aids unit, wasting away, waiting to die. Beano's up in St Brendan's after burning every brain cell out. Six months ago the world looked up to them in terror. Now the kids on their street wouldn't want to recognize them. Burned out so fast, Hano, like violent, brutal stars, you know what I mean. Never heard them laugh those last days, just sitting there, no brains, no words, slumped on the canal. "Hey Beano," I said last time I saw him, "remember the night we crashed the car up in Howth?" He looked through me like that drunk back along the road. They're gone now Hano, like dada walking across fields to work, Tomas with no light in his cabin. This place was theirs Hano, let them rest here. We'll find our own maybe, somewhere.'

Then she leaned back until her head lay snugly against his chest and, rolling on to her side, drew her legs up against his and was still. Hano could feel the frustration draining from his body and knew that he was tumbling downwards into a warm drowsiness where sleep would come, as unstoppable as the waves below, crushing on to the wet strand, fainter, and fainter, and faint . . .

# CHAPTER TWO

## Monday

Hano dreamt of whiteness. Winter time. He was walking from a grey estate of houses down an embankment towards a new road. It had been snowing in the night. Now a single set of footprints curved downwards towards the noise of water. A new steel bridge bypassed the old hunch-backed stone one which was cut off by a row of tar barrels. A circle of Gypsy caravans squatted on the waste ground around it.

Hano knew the place now, the Silver Spoon, the bathing place Shay had often spoken of. The summer evenings when mothers from the West had sat on the grass, watching children in short trousers splashing in the water, their hands holding slices of bread and jam. The footsteps were Shay's, yet there was no sign of movement in the camp site they led to. Scrap iron, parts of cars, a washing machine with one side dented lay on the river bed. To move was like walking through a wall of ice, cutting into his flesh, amputating the movement from his hands. The Gypsies had left clothes out to dry along the tattered bushes near the bridge which had grown solid with frost, rigid to the touch. How long had he been walking like this, searching for Shay? He passed the clothes and then looked back. A pair of old jeans were stretched between branches. Just above them was a ripped check shirt and then, three inches further up, Shay's face grinned at him, also made of cloth, completely flat and stiffened. There were no hands, no feet and just a necklace of leaves where his neck should have been. Shay seemed to be trying to speak but his features were too frozen to allow him. Hano reached out slowly to touch the face and as his fingers encountered the icy brittleness of the cloth he shuddered and woke.

Hano tried to focus his eyes in the harsh sunlight reflecting

43

off the bare stone of the bunker and, failing, closed them again, leaning his head back and banging it on the wall. The pain shocked him to his senses and he realized that he was freezing and alone. The memory of the dream disturbed him though the details were already obscure. All that remained was the sensation of eternally searching for Shay. Then the memories of the previous night returned and with them came paralysis. He grew rigid with fear, unable even to turn his head towards the doorway. Somehow he had expected that morning would bring normality, a return of his old world. Katie had placed his jacket neatly over him before departing. He told himself he was relieved that she was gone. There would be no responsibilities left in the hours before they caught him. He could wait here shivering in this filthy bunker or walk outside. It made little difference to the outcome. Yet he huddled to whatever small warmth the jacket and his cramped position gave him. What if they already knew he was there? The squad car parked on the beach; two guards calmly smoking on the bonnet as they waited for him to appear? What if Katie hadn't abandoned him, but was crammed into the back seat, a burly hand over her mouth? What if the guards weren't there? He grinned to himself. What if he had to go on, alone and hungry? There was no fight left in him. He stood cautiously up and turned around. The strand was deserted. An autumn sun was trying to thaw out above the cold waves where, in the distance, a local fishing boat bobbed like a toy Russian trawler. He put his jacket on and walked stiffly out, slapping his legs to restore the circulation.

Then he caught a glimpse of Katie bent between the boulders and limpet-covered rocks where sunlight glinted among the green rock pools. He almost shouted in relief but turned instead and waited by the water's edge till he heard her approach. Relief had given way to defensiveness, like an embarrassed stranger trying to claw some dignity back the morning after a party. He remembered those few mornings when he woke with some girl from work, both toying with life, automatically talking when there was nothing really to say. Now when everything was urgent neither Katie nor he could speak. He realized that he had never really spoken to

44

her until last night, that they had shared the same room dozens of times, muttered the same few words to each other without ever knowing who the other was. He knew she could sense the tension within him.

'I thought you'd gone,' he said at last.

She didn't reply.

'You don't have to stay you know. There's no reason.'

'I'll go if you want,' she said. 'Piss off and leave you here.'

'You should have last night. It's him you always wanted. Why come with me?'

'Maybe I didn't come with you,' she said. 'Maybe I just came along, you know what I mean.'

Driftwood was strewn on the beach. She moved away to hurl a piece of rotten timber back into the foam. He had always thought of her as retarded for some reason. He remembered the distaste he felt once when drinking by mistake from her cup. She was indistinct to him from dozens of girls he'd seen lining street corners around his home, jeering at passers-by, listlessly watching each day pass, smelling of boredom and adolescence gone stale. It had always puzzled him when Shay called her the country girl.

'Maybe I just hadn't anywhere to go back to,' she muttered after a moment. 'Maybe I couldn't take another morning of it, another night. What the fuck do you know of my life anyway? Your friend killed it for me back there, made me so I could never fit in again. Would have been better if he'd knifed me.'

Hano watched a woman in a grey overcoat with a dog approach from the far side of the beach. She was the first person he had seen since the previous night. He shivered, realizing that every stranger was a threat, to be watched and avoided if possible. It was too late to move back to the bunker. Katie had hunched down watching the wood drift back towards her. The waves crashed in, splashing his feet with spray.

'You scared Hano?' she asked suddenly.

'Yeah.'

'Then I'll go with you. Because I'm scared shitless too.'

'Don't know where I'm going Katie. I've nowhere to go.'

She was silent. He imagined Mooney's desk, the red line being drawn, the unreality of it all.

'Hano?'

He looked up. Her face was drawn, the hair ragged, eyes tired. She mumbled something and, when he looked blankly back, repeated it again in a whisper.

'Will you come home with me Hano? Will you?'

'You know I can't. They'll be looking for me.' He felt a sickness in his stomach as he spoke.

'Not there Hano – *home*. They took me from it one night, half-asleep in the back of a car. Miles of darkness and then I remember waking to street lights flashing on and off like a lighthouse beacon when we'd pass under them. Thinking if I screamed loud enough I'd wake and my parents would come. And all the time my uncle's face staring down at me, his hands stroking my hair and saying in that gruff voice of his, *You've a new daddy now. A new daddy.*

'You know, I told myself I didn't miss it. Drinking with the girls I'd make them laugh with stories. The soldier Ryan who slept in a concrete pipe in his field and moved his cattle into the new house the County Council gave him. Old Tomas's tales, even the way my da . . . dada used to speak.'

'But how long has it been . . .?'

'Eight years.'

'Were you ever back?'

'No. That night with the girls in the car . . . but I told you, I got scared. You know, at first my uncle tried to talk to me about it but I'd put my hands over my ears and scream. One time he even decided to bring his family down to the grave and I bit his hand when he tried to get me into the car. Can't explain it Hano, I waited for months in Dublin for them to come for me, then I blamed them, I cursed them. I was eight, Hano. I didn't want to understand, I just wanted them back.'

Without a glance in their direction, the woman had begun to climb the steps leading from the beach. He became aware of how hungry he was. Katie was looking at him, waiting for him to speak.

'Why not just go Katie? Why do you need me?'

'Listen Hano, don't you think I've tried? All those nights

I've slept out, thinking at dawn I'll go. Walking down to the carriageway and watching the trucks, waiting till one stopped and then always just standing there, unable to move. There's an old man there Hano, he could help us.'

'Your man Tomas? Who is he anyway?'

'He's just an old man, a farm labourer. He worked with dada. Two miles into the hills Hano. You'd be safe. He'd take us in.'

England was the place to go. It always had been. The enemy which gave refuge, the dull anonymity of Leeds or Bradford, the digs and building sites his father had flitted between, dreaming always of returning home. If he got away now it might be possible to gain a new identity, start again. Here it was only a matter of time, there would be nowhere to hide. Yet instinctively he knew that he wouldn't run as he'd done all his life. He had never been bright like Shay but he could be stubborn. He remembered the farewells in Murtagh's, no longer cardboard suitcases and cattle boats, but green cards and holiday visas. Illegal emigrants melting into the streets of American towns. As the airport posters proclaimed, they were the young Europeans, fodder now not just for factory floors but for engineering and computer posts. But once you left you were gone for ever. Shay had tried to return and failed. Hano knew it would be his last way of keeping faith, as senseless and futile as the night he'd sat beside the tramp in the hospital after the fight.

'What if this old lad's not there? He could be dead.'

'Have you a better idea?'

Hano stood up and, pulling his jacket tighter, shrugged his shoulders. Anywhere was as good as nowhere and it was dangerous to stay here. She touched his shoulder.

'Do you still hate me?' she asked.

He shook his head.

'I don't even know you,' he replied.

'I never knew what hate was till I met you,' she said. 'You know, every night walking to the flat I'd pray you'd be out. I'd put my ear to the door to guess whose footsteps were coming down. Shay's were loud and quick in his old boots; yours were a dreary tread. Every time I heard them I'd pray to

47

God you'd fall and break your neck. You should have seen yourself, opening the door like a nightclub bouncer and mumbling, "Are you coming in or what?" Without you, I thought Shay could be mine. So don't make me ask you for anything, Hano. But I'll go alone this time if you won't come.'

He put his hand hesitantly on her shoulder. She didn't look up or pull away.

'I can't fill his boots, Katie. And I've lived in his shadow so long I don't know what to do without him.'

She touched his hand for a moment and let it fall.

'He's dead, Hano, and I don't want some sort of substitute. You stand or fall by yourself. So don't lead or don't follow me, but if you're going let's just get the fuck away from here together.'

'You know if you're caught with me they'll probably charge you as well.'

She stared back at him without replying.

'Another thing,' he said.

'What?'

'Where the fuck is Leitrim?'

She smiled for the first time, then turned, and without waiting for him, began to walk towards the edge of the rocks. He looked back once at the bunker and followed her. He took her hand as they fought for footholds among the crevice pools and boulders confettied with seaweed and damp moss, but when they had climbed up to the unpaved cliff walk that mimicked the twists of the rock face he let go of it again, uncertainly.

A seal's head bobbed below them like a lost football. A lone sea-bird stood its ground on a rock, head constantly brushing the underside of its wing. There were tentative drops of rain. In the silence the horror of the previous night returned and he felt giddy with terror. He kept trying to justify it in his mind but knew it made no sense to anyone except perhaps to her. The images came back with the clarity and detachment of a horror film that seemed to have no connection with him. His past might have happened to somebody he'd vaguely known and lost contact with. When he'd hang back as Shay plunged them into another bout of lunacy, the older lad would say, 'One day Hano you'll go wild and leave us all only trotting behind you in a cloud of dust.' There was no Shay to see it, but Hano knew he had been thrust from his cocoon and could never manage to climb back. He followed the small figure with the cropped black hair along the cliff path knowing that this time was a bonus, with every second worth fighting for.

A single rusted strand of wire ran between them and a sheer drop. A stone wall with tiny flowers clinging to the crevices divided them from the fields on the far side. Before them a tall water tower rose like an upturned pint glass dwarfing the imitation round tower beside it. It had been built as a folly by a landlord in famine times but a century of weathering made it indistinguishable from the real thing. Behind it the cluster of red-bricked Victorian buildings which formed the Portrane asylum began to appear, flourished with turrets and Gothic trappings like the mansion of some cursed inbred clan. Silent as ghosts a stooped line of its patients appeared slowly around the corner ahead of them, a nurse's white uniform blazing among the shabby greys and browns of their clothing.

When Hano and Katie reached the first couple they drew back towards the safety of their minder. The line stopped and shied away towards the wall until they had passed. The old men's faces twitched under caps as they watched. The final old woman had a radiant girlish smile and waved back at them from a drugged stupor. Her eyes were the brightest Hano had ever seen. Beside her a bald man in his forties was turning in a constant circle with a slow and perfected step, like a child trying to be dizzy. The others simply looked old, bemused and abandoned. The nurse smiled and motioned her charges into life again. A middle-aged man was doing press-ups on the lawn in front of the hospital. It was impossible to know if he was keeping count or aware that he was being watched. He stretched face down on the grass, gravely raising and lowering his body as though determined to prove his strength or keep the flame of sanity alive in his mind. Katie shuddered and turned away from the wall.

'Christ, I hate asylums,' she said. 'Always remind me of the one at home. A former workhouse it was, a rambling, run-down ruin. It wasn't just for the sick, you know. It was a

49

dumping ground for anyone they didn't want, stuck out on the edge of the town. Whenever we had to pass it, I'd beg mammy to cross the road before we reached the gate. I was always scared she'd leave me there. That was her biggest threat, not dada's strap or the bogeyman but we'll send you off to the home.'

In Dublin Hano rarely remembered her mumbling more than a few words, and then they had always been of the streets outside. Now that she had begun to talk of Leitrim it was like she'd never stop.

'The time the nuns in the school asked my uncle to take me to the psychologist was when I ran away first. Three nights kipping out in an old car by the Tolka. All I could think of was the spinsters locked up in that place because they couldn't be married off and the backward kids shut away so as not to shame their families before the neighbours. I mean, I knew it wouldn't be like that, it would be all shagging ink blobs and when d'you start using dirty words, but it was the same fear inside me.

'There was this woman, our next neighbour after Tomas, called Mary Roche. She was twenty-five years in that home before her mother died and some relative back from England found out and signed her release papers. Mammy often brought her in because she could hardly feed herself by then. She lived on crackers, single-wrapped slices of cheese. Anything that came in plastic was good because it was what visitors had brought in for the other patients. If mammy left the kitchen she'd sit with her arms in front of her on the table for hours on end.'

'What happened to her?' Hano asked.

Katie shuddered, looking back down the path as if she could still see the line of patients.

'She was only twenty when it happened. Some carpenter down from Dublin fitting out the family shop. One night her father found her bed empty and caught them in a shed at the back. The carpenter was in hospital a week before he managed to slip out. She was kept locked up. You know I think it wasn't just what she was doing but who she was with. If it had been the doctor's son they would have all been indignant and yet delighted. But it wasn't, so they beat the skin off her back. Once she escaped to Dublin. Her father caught up with her after five days, famished, still in the same clothes, looking for the carpenter's digs. Doctor O'Donnell signed the committal papers. He'd have signed over his granny's corpse for a brandy.'

Katie leaned against the stone wall, staring at the hospital as she spoke. Hano put his hand on her shoulder. She shrugged it off.

'The year I was born, Hano, there was a scandal in the town. No papers carried it, nobody spoke to strangers, but people knew. One evening Mary Roche told my mother. They didn't know I was there, against the side of the dresser, hardly daring to breathe as I tried to make sense of her words. I didn't understand them all but I understood the terror in her voice.

'On weekend nights The Railway Hotel stayed open after hours for select customers. When the owner finally got sick of their drunken talk, Doctor O'Donnell would bring a few cronies across to the asylum – the chemist, the draper, a few big farmers with sons at college, the local councillor with his fainne. I could see them all in my mind as she listed them. They'd drag the retarded girls out of the wards to use them as whores. Can you imagine it? The stink of whiskey off their breaths and their laughter billowing down the corridor. Do you want the really funny part, Hano? The punch line? They'd bring in little boxes of Smarties for the girls. The two night nurses stayed quiet, they had jobs and families. It could have gone on for ever only some guard, fresh out of training school, reported the whole thing to his superiors and got transferred to the arse of Donegal for his trouble. The only charges were against the publican for after-hours serving. The doctor got the hint or maybe the inspector got in on the act.'

Hano stood back, afraid to touch her hunched-up shoulders. The man on the lawn had finally stopped. He lay face down, motionless.

'When I was eight, Hano, they unveiled a statue to some poor wanker who'd been shot at eighteen by the black-and-tans. They'd a pipe band, a priest and altar boys, the usual old shite, the FCA strutting round with empty rifles. The organizing committee had a row of seats on a raised platform. As each of their names were called out I could hear my mother trying to hush Mary Roche as she intoned like the response to a psalm, *He had me! He had me!*'

Katie turned to look at him. Her voice had grown shrill and he saw tears in her eyes.

'So why the fuck do I want to go back? To that fucking pain? Dada waiting in the square for those bastards to give him a day's work. You know I worked beside him every evening when I finished school. I can see them still arriving in their cars to survey the lines of workers, their eyes watching me stoop in a child's frock and a man's rubber boots to pick potatoes from the muck. I was only eight but I remember the look in their eyes, I knew what it meant. I can still see the leers on the faces of every last bastarding one of them!'

She turned and walked quickly ahead of him, her back hunched as if part of it were broken and all the toughness gone, so that momentarily she looked like the sixteen-year-old child she was.

That first weekend with Shay it was Sunday afternoon before I got home. One event had simply folded into another. I remember lying on the mattress in Shay's flat after Murtagh's in the early hours of Saturday morning, the glowing tips of joints passing back and forth. He had the stereo on and the curtains undrawn so that each number was rolled in the street light filtering through the high windows. I remember the outline of his face in the bed above me, the teeth white as he laughed at some joke, the hands folded behind his head on the pillow as he waited for the joint to return. People arrived and departed from the house all night – the strains of music upstairs, the creak of a bed, a girl's voice on the landing. I don't recall going to sleep. I just woke next morning, my throat raw, my chest on fire from alcohol. Shay was standing beside the two-ringed cooker near the window wearing only his jeans. He lifted the first pancake on to a plate, smeared it with butter and honey and placed it on the floor beside me.

'We need food badly,' he said. 'Or we'll be rightly destroyed.'

The house was on the corner of a road in Ranelagh. Across the street a greengrocer piled his goods on to the pavement, the fruit gleaming in the sunlight as he stood in his apron to chat with passers-by. The road curved away in a mass of old trees. The pub on the corner was dark, a Lourdes for quiet men seeking the cure. Shay spread the racing pages of the paper on the table in front of us and accepted whispered advice from the two men on stools at the bar. I drank the first pint slowly, savouring its bitterness on my tongue and I thought of home, my mother in a phone box probably phoning the hospitals.

I knew that what I was doing to them was cruel but somehow it seemed necessary. Every hour away gave me a small thrill of power at making them aware of the difference within me. Maybe I was just afraid to go back and face them, but I think I was so mesmerized by Shay as to be incapable of leaving before he told me to go. I wanted to be a part of the world he moved in, feeling more alive in his presence than ever before in my life.

I'd promised myself I'd go home after the last race when we stood on the steps at Leopardstown that afternoon. Then Shay met a friend who had won a share of the tote. Out of obstinacy he'd refused to take a cheque and we waited to escort him back to town by taxi with a plastic bag full of small notes and coins. Again I swore to leave after we had a drink with him, then after we'd eaten and then on the last bus.

The party was on the far side of Rathfarnham, a girl from the office's twenty-first. In the hallway of the house she rented with four others Shay found a bottle of whiskey and one of gin. He emptied them secretly into the basin of punch and went round with a spoon ladling it out. A bonfire blazed in the backgarden. Mick sat on a swing, a six-pack between his legs as he rocked back and forth, the glow of a roll-up sweeping in an arc through the air. Figures fluttered in the semi-darkness. I collapsed into a hedge and fell asleep. Shay and Mick must have carried me inside to the living-room floor. I woke next morning stiff as a cloth left out on a line in winter, the blanket placed by Shay still over my shoulders. I found him asleep upstairs, his arm around some girl. He woke and winked, untangling himself discreetly.

Scowling, we wandered through street after street of new homes, completely lost in that new suburb at the foothills of the mountains as remote to us as our own had been to our fathers. The brickwork on each house looked too new, too consciously trying to be old, not to seem like Noddy houses. We grumbled in the clean air, among the brightly painted doors and privet hedges, speaking of the poetry of rusting steel, our favourite old factories, crooked laneways decked with glass and graffiti. Families were climbing into cars for Mass, a dog came proprietorially out to investigate and fled to the sanctuary of his porch when Shay knelt to bark at him. After an hour a bus came. An old tramp sat across from us in the back seat playing a mouth organ and banging his feet in time to the tunes. I knew I finally had to go home. I left Shay in the city centre looking for his car abandoned on Friday night and nervously got a bus. I tried to rehearse words to myself, remembering the speeches I made to my father in my mind about the old woman. Now the same phrases come back again five years on. This time I swore I'd say them.

But in the end I said little and they said less, though I could see the hurt in their eyes. My young brother told me they had gone to the police earlier that morning. I kept wanting to explain but as soon as I stepped back inside their house I knew that, like trying to talk about the old woman, it was impossible to bridge our worlds.

But this time I think my father wanted to tell me he understood. I had sensed his attitude to me change the first day I returned from work, but to my mother I was still a child. I could hear her scolding him in the kitchen for not being firmer as I lay in my room. I wanted to go down and apologize but by now it had become more than just a weekend. I was punishing them with my silence just for being what they could not help being. A mother and father I loved but no longer belonged to. It was time to enter my own world yet it seemed I couldn't make the break without causing them pain and deliberately denigrating the memories that bound us. What had once united me with my parents now seemed ridiculous – those memories of gardens and jockeybacks. From that Sunday I was like a wound inside their house, festering without air, living only for the evenings when I could take the bus to town.

Because now it was Shay that I lived for. In the weeks that followed I didn't just want to be with him, I wanted to become him. Sometimes it seemed I had almost succeeded. Towards closing time in a pub, if I lowered my head for a moment with his voice still in my ears, I felt physically locked inside his body, seeing through his eyes, sharing his thoughts. At work the girls slagged me for unconsciously imitating his gestures as his key words found their way into my speech. Even Mooney treated me with caution as an appendix of Shay.

Each night spent wandering through bars and parties with him made my home seem more distant. I was split in two, my personality changing each time I opened the front door, the afterglow of being with him reinforcing my isolation in that room where my parents sat trapped before a television. In their company I was sullen, closed in on myself, but once I left I could feel myself change. I would shout and embrace him when he entered the pub and he'd laugh, calming me down like a young puppy. Drink gave me courage to become all my imaginings. I hid behind it, stumbling down alleyways after him, falling, singing, hopping up to ride on his back to shout like a Horse Protestant. I became a jester unleashed, knowing only exhilaration, yet capable of being stilled and made to feel childish by one look of irritation from him.

I longed merely to be allowed to take a blanket and curl up on his floor below the huge bay window. As each evening progressed I'd grow nervy, ordering that last drink for us just a fraction too late for me to reach the bus stop on time, glancing at the pub clock, dying for him to suggest that I stop over. Sometimes he'd be chatting up a girl or just tired and wouldn't bother and finally I'd have to face the long walk back to my parents' house, with the night oppressive on my shoulders. But more often he would offer me a mattress and I'd casually accept, trying not to sound too excited.

The night would wind leisurely back to his flat, via kebab shops and snooker halls. Shay kept a small axe under the seat of the Triumph Herald and auctioneers' signs and advertising hoardings on quiet corners we passed often vanished in the darkness. Back in the flat he'd chop them up, hold a match to the fire-lighters thrown beneath them, and we'd sit across from each other at the Victorian fireplace, talking over dope and tea about our pasts and our plans. Often the front door banged at two in the morning and Mick would arrive with a group of mates. I'd clear the table while Shay searched for the cards. Dealer's choice for any poker variation; Klondikie, Southern Cross, Ace High, Blind Baseball, Seven- and Five-Card Stud, under a barrage of wisecracks while Ian Dury and Wreckless Eric revolved in the cramped space beneath the sink. If the game flagged he'd throw in a few rounds of In-Betweenies, and we'd dare each other to go for the pot, laughing when somebody lost and had to stoke it.

If dope was plentiful Shay would produce an ornate water pipe from beneath his bed. Slowly it passed along the lips of the gamblers. I'd close my eyes and lean backwards to feel the room lurch and buckle in my mind, white colours merging into brilliant shades that blazed against my eyelids. I'd open them to arguments about who should go for skins to the twenty-four-hour shop. I'd offer to go and stand blinking in the bright shop, feeling like a criminal as I asked for washing powder and sliced ham as well in an effort not to buy the cigarette papers too conspicuously. The boys would crack up when I returned, clutching the bag of shopping guiltily under my jacket. They'd break for coffee and, still slagging me, hold putting competitions on the carpet with those who were knocked out, betting on those who were left.

Some nights people brought bags of magic mushrooms which Shay fried on a pan with oil and salt despite protests from all. They took time to take effect. On the first night I had forgotten them when the colours began to explode. Shay was sleeping in bed. I lay on the mattress beside the embers of the fire like a man strapped to a galloping horse, feeling the drug like a Martian from a B-movie coming alive in my body. For two days at home I still felt them as I sat before the television with my father, frightened to speak or make a sudden move, paranoid that he would notice the twitching I imagined I had developed.

One night Mick fell asleep lying on the side of the bed. Shay took every poster and cartoon off the wall to collect the Bluetack on the back. He rolled it into a long sausage stretching from Mick's hands which we joined at his groin up to his mouth. We smeared the tip with mayonnaise and, carrying him gently outside, left him to wake on the front steps. That was the night Justin Plunkett came by with a slab of black from Morocco smuggled in through the diplomatic bag. He was out of place, deliberately slumming it in his expensive leather jacket among the cluster of jeans and grubby sweatshirts. He left soon after, blown out by the lads' indifference. On the steps outside he woke Mick.

'Hey, my man, it's not cool, you'll catch cold.'

'Go and fuck yourself!' Mick said and, after thinking about it, added to the retreating back, 'And fuck your politician daddy too', before stumbling back inside. Then, as always, it was back to the cards, money still passing across that table when dawn greyed the window. Finally Shay would kick them out, curl up on his bed, and I'd lie again beside the fire, knowing that in a few hours I would screw up my eyes in the light and walk with him to work, the smell of drink on our breaths, our stomachs empty, our heads sore, our feet stinking and no love for Jesus in our hearts. And that evening I would turn the corner with a shiver of dread, returning to worried looks – my father's sunken smile, my mother's silence, her eyes close to tears – and I'd hate myself for the stab of triumph, as though I could only measure my independence by their growing bewilderment and pain.

The tenant in the room next to Shay's drifted in and out of institutions. Once he had returned home to his native Galway and after two weeks in an asylum there one morning, instead of medication, they gave him thirty pounds and a one-way air ticket to Manchester. Now meals on wheels came once a day to feed him, harassed social workers calling most evenings. At night we could hear him pacing his flat, perpetually walking in circles. At two o'clock each morning he'd take his dishes out to the front lawn in a basin and wash them kneeling on the grass. He had a key attached with string to some part of his body but rarely managed to find it beneath all his clothes which he wore at once. Most nights when we'd reach the house he'd be standing on the steps, his hands scrambling through his three coats, kicking at the door in desperation.

'Shay!' he'd beseech in his Galway accent. 'Let me in Shay. I'm praying for you Shay, you and your young friend.'

He'd corner us on the step for quarter of an hour, droning on excitedly about how many Masses he'd attended that day and how many miles he had travelled on his free bus pass. Shay claimed that one day there would be plaster-cast statues of him in the glass panels over every Catholic doorway in Dublin, that we should keep the tin-foil containers they left his meals in to sell as future relics. Yet Shay was the only person in that house to rise, at no matter what hour of the morning and with how many curses, to let the shambling figure in. I'd lie on the floor listening to Shay calming him down enough to get him into his room. The other tenants were noises I could rarely put faces to. Their lives were shadows on the landing, the noise of footsteps in the hallway, a locked toilet door, the clink of six packs, a raised television, whispered evacuations on the night before rent day.

In the backyard the landlord had stacked old rotten timbers of doors and window frames from the four other properties he owned along the street. In times of shortages Shay hacked away at them steadily with his axe. I'd hold a torch, shivering in the night air, and listen to the rhythmical chopping while the lights of a hundred bedsits flickered out across the black, abandoned gardens. That's what I remember most about his small flat, the glowing embers like a bird's nest as I drifted to sleep, and waking, stiff-limbed and hung-over, to the scent of wooden ash.

One night stands out from those first months when everything was so shockingly new. High up in a warren of bedsits, while far below Rathmines was awash with litter and tacky lights. At two in the morning there were still queues in the fast-food shops, music from pirate stations blaring through speakers where girls knifed open pitta bread, flickering shifts of colour carried through windows on to the street from the video screens above the counters. Traffic jammed the narrow roads where the last old ladies lived in crumbling family homes, taxis outside the flats unloading party goers who shrieked and embraced and then quarrelled about splitting the fare. A tramp was slumped on his bench where he slept each night beside the swimming baths, oblivious to the noise around him.

Earlier in the pub beside the canal I had found myself talking all evening to a girl. It had happened spontaneously, we were both drunk and at ease together, laughing in the ruck of bodies against the bar, teasing each other with the anticipation of what might come. Across from us Mick and Shay were joking with some girls from work. He caught my eye and winked in congratulation.

I cannot remember whose party it was, it was merely a succession of stairs till we reached an attic. Thirty bodies danced in the crowded room where the only light came from candles stuck in bottles. Whoever rented the flat only owned three records which were played over and over. The girl had come with us, she was half-slumped against me as we waltzed until I was almost carrying her. Yet still I raised the bottle we were sharing to her lips, watched the gin dribble down like tears on to her dress. What did she want from me? Would I know what to say to her when I was sober?

But it wasn't really her I was thinking of as we danced. Above all else I wanted Shay to see, I wanted to prove myself. Steps led up to a tiny bedroom with a low, sloping roof. I kicked the door open where a young boy lay unconscious from drink on the bed. I called back to Shay and Mick who took him between them, carrying him down those long flights of stairs to the back garden where they walked him in circles, his bare feet trailing through puddles, till he woke without a clue where he was. The girl had swayed against me so I had to catch her as we watched them carry him past. I led her in and as I turned to lock the door she collapsed without a sound on to the carpeted floor. Light came from a low window divided by a wooden lattice which threw a shadow across the floor in the shape of a crucifix. In a flat across the street I heard a child crying and imagined a young unmarried mother pacing up and down her few feet of space trying to pacify it before the other tenants complained.

I had to crawl on my knees to find the girl, help her up,

59

manoeuvre her on to the bed. I doubt if either of us got any pleasure. I struggled to stay erect, fumbling in the dark for condoms, trying to undo buttons as people banged on the door; she slept through it, waking occasionally to mumble another man's name. All I kept thinking of was Shay outside, walking with the drunken figure, knowing that for once it was me up here. I came half-heartedly and lay spent in the dark, holding her clumsily in my arms and listening to the commotion on the stairs. I realized I'd forgotten her name, where she worked. I had sobered up but I was scared now, not knowing how to approach her when she woke. I wanted to ask Shay but knew that would make me feel small again in my mind.

When she began to stir I helped her up, got her dressed, hurried her down to the street outside. She wanted to be held a little longer, wanted some words to make sense of what had happened. I wanted to talk to her, ask her to meet me properly again some evening. We walked to the main road, sat on the pavement saying nothing until a taxi approached and I hailed it, helped her into the back and gave the driver a bundle of pound notes and her address.

The police were leaving when I returned, a siren's blue light rinsing the pavement as heads watched from windows along the street. Shay had thought the party had everything except a police raid so he'd phoned them. The host was in the hall, screaming at Mick and him to get out. Behind them an old black bicycle was unlocked. Shay mounted it and wobbled down the steps on to the footpath. He shouted at me to jump on to the crossbar. The bike swerved as it took my weight, then nearly unbalanced when Mick climbed on to the carrier at the back. The owner ran behind us screaming, as we weaved along the grass verge till we collided with a tree trunk, got up, left the bike there and walked home. Like a puppy with a stick, I waited for some acknowledgement, but neither of them mentioned the girl and I realized that nothing I could have done in that attic would have made Shay think less or more of me. They would have been as cheerfully indifferent if the girl was walking now along the shadowy roads back to find space beside me on the floor of Shay's flat. I thought of the silent taxi driver speeding towards the outer suburbs, of what might have been if I hadn't been afraid it would come between myself and Shay.


*What time is it Katie? It stops when you pass into the twilit hangar of the old factory. Intimate afternoons of pills and laughter. Choices are discussed. One girl talks of pregnancy, the independence of a flat and an allowance. Another speaks of England, a bedsit shared with an older sister. Someone repeats stories of council bed-and-breakfasts in Bayswater: Asian children crammed into one room; breakfast a fried egg and a slice of bread in a plastic bag. None speak of the land outside, concrete melting into greenery that stretches away decked in alien foliage. Now all that is real for you begins here. The cold sitting-room light is forgotten; your uncle's fist clenched around the nun's neat handwriting; a television with the sound turned off; the steel rivets of accusations, his shame at your expulsion. What is his name, can you even remember? Good. What is your own? Even better. One girl disappears with a youth into the gloom where cobwebs hang from girders and torturous water drips at the far end of the cavern. 'Are they?' you ask. 'No,' somebody laughs. 'She has a vampire's teabag in.'*

*Outside light is glaring. You lurch across the carriageway, past the old cobbler's bypassed by the builders, by the gothic bare-stoned mansion ensnared by Corporation terraces, up the hill of the main street, shivering in the afternoon light. The schoolgirls have been released in trails of bright colours. From outside the clothes shop you watch them come. Who was the girl who laughed among them a few months ago? Another stranger inhabiting your body in limbo. The security guard's uniformed back turns as you slip past into the shop. A voice of metal crackles inside his walkie-talkie as the skirt fits neatly underneath your own. Like arrayed ghosts the clothes hang on racks. An assistant laughs as he chases after her down through the tunnel of clothes and you are gone through the unguarded shop door. Back to twilight, back to warmth, a dozen items laid out on a floor. The young fence lifts them up, hands one back as worthless. He leaves in their place a variegated row of*

*pills, a thin, dung-coloured slab in a tiny plastic bag, a trace
of white powder. He retreats from you with patent leather
footsteps.*

*When you speak now it is in a private slang, birthdays
and older girls' dole days your only reference points. Your
landmarks bordered by a bus to town, a view of sky through
corrugated iron, a black road leading inexorably home. One
night you sit with two friends by the low carriageway wall
where the woodland once stood. A child behind you with
his father's axe is chipping away at a young sapling surrounded by mesh. Two youths stop in a stolen Ford, they
coax and the three of you climb in, voices singing from the
back seat. The last remaining red light is broken. The car
shoots on like a released prisoner, but to you, half-stoned, it
could be in slow motion. By Mother Plunkett's Cabin it
flies, twisting down towards the ancient castle. Overgrown
branches whip against both sides of the windscreen, the girls
shrieking as the wheels cascade through the flooded hollow.
Chained dogs grow frantic inside each farmyard as the car
skids against the side gravel and veers sharply right. They
slow near the snakes of landing lights laid out around the
airport, the flickering reds, the rows of coloured bulbs rising
up to meet the belly of the dropping plane. But you have
grown quiet now, watching the moon keeping track through
the hedgerows. The songs and voices do not penetrate. What
nightmare journey are you remembering? What night when
he cradled your head in his arms as you cried in the seat;
what car that sped under a canopy of branches away from
that house; what names of dead parents whom you called
out for? If you spoke now how would your voice sound; if
you yearned for home which direction would you turn? The
car speeds through a tunnel of trees, the shuttered moonlight
between the trunks distorting your features so you look like
two different persons.*

Hano let her walk ahead of him, silent now like he remembered
her from the city. The cliff walk led to a small cove with the
ruins of a burnt-out store. Somebody had torn the election

posters pasted on the concrete blocks over the windows so that only strips of the candidates' faces were left. Katie paused, then chose a clay path across the deserted golf course towards a hollow crammed with caravans and shabby wooden chalets. Summer was past, the grass grown tall again after the trampling of sandalled feet. They huddled in the porch of a chalet with their backs against the flaking white wall in the morning sunlight. With his finger, Hano traced the name 'Sunnyside' in forlorn black letters on the door.

Katie pressed his hand and slipped around the side. He gazed anxiously back at the flags on the greens as the tinkle of breaking glass came. There were footsteps on wood, rusty bolts dragged back and then he was inside, searching with her for food and warmth, anxiously drawn every few moments to peer through a broken window.

It was musty in the chalet, the spartan furniture riddled with the pinholes of woodworm. They found two blankets, wrapped themselves up and waited for darkness. Both knew how vital it was to get away but were paralysed by fear, reluctant to make a decision as though the night could somehow protect them. Outside a wind was blowing up. Far off they heard a tractor and later the noise of music and slogans being broadcast from a speeding van. Towards noon a dog barked as a woman called its name. They rarely spoke until hunger drove them out in the afternoon to plunder the empty caravans. It made little difference what he did now but he still shivered at each smash of glass.

Back under the blankets they shared what little they had found: a crushed bar of chocolate, stale biscuits, a can of beans they opened and ate cold. Katie had discovered a small radio. He hesitated before turning it on, wanting to prolong the time when he could at least pretend he might return to his past. It ranked second in the news bulletin after the report of a low morning turn-out at the polls. The party spokesmen were trying to twist the turn-out to their advantage: the government claimed it proved the people had not wanted an election, while the opposition blamed the level of apathy on disillusionment with the current administration. Both predicted that their supporters would be out in the evening. The longer they waffled on the more Hano allowed himself to hope it had all been some bizarre nightmare.

Then the details of the fire were given, with rhetorical condolences by the same spokesmen. Since morning the government had been turning it into a late campaigning ploy, knowing the opposition wouldn't dare interrupt the saga of one family's grief after two tragedies in a single week. The Junior Minister spoke of being glad of the burden of office at the present time, that the responsibilites of state were shielding his mind from the awful grief in his heart. When the votes were counted and the country's future secure he would return to his native countryside and mourn among his own. Hano could see Patrick Plunkett in the studio, lips pursed over the microphone, eyes dry as he calculated the chances of bringing home the third seat with his surplus that would ensure they couldn't deny him a full cabinet position next time. The gardai were following a definite line of inquiry but Hano's name was not mentioned on the air. He switched the set off.

'Fuck them,' Katie whispered beside him. 'We'll get away. Tomas will hide you till you decide what to do. He has to be alive. I can feel it. He has to be.'

It could only be a matter of time. When his name was broadcast her uncle would realize. The police would check her old home even though she had never gone back before. But where else did he know outside Dublin? A blurred succession of roadways he had hitched on; the farm his father had come from; the small wood belonging to the old woman. Katie lay calmly beside him like a different person from the one he had known.

'Home?' he said uncertainly.

'That's all Shay ever spoke of,' she said. 'Trying to get home from Europe at the end; I never thought of going home till he began talking about it.'

Shay had simply arrived back saying nothing to him and Hano had never dared to ask. Automatically he made a note to ask Shay now and winced, cursing his memory for letting him forget. He felt sickened after the voices on the radio.

'Never spoke about it much to me,' he said.

'Coming home, trying to fit back, that sort of thing,' she said. 'If you asked him he'd clam up, stare into space. One night I said to him that when I was stoned I started thinking they'd sucked the air out of Dublin, you know what I mean, and people around me were opening and closing their mouths with nothing coming in, nothing going out.

'It sounded bleeding thick when I said it but he just rolled another cigarette and stared out the window. Then he started talking about nights up in the loading bay of a canning factory in Denmark when he'd look down from the hoist at four in the morning on the workers below, nobody speaking, the limbs just moving automatically. He said he'd start thinking the conveyor belt and the loading machines were alive, that at half-seven they'd stop and the arms of the men would keep on moving back and forth till some cunt remembered to press a switch.'

Those months Shay spent in Europe puzzled Hano like an oppressive weight. He didn't know why they were important, but if he could fathom what happened there he might understand why he was here now. He had the facts that Shay had finally told him on the last night, but they alone could not explain his unease. It hurt to have to ask Katie what he had said as if it somehow gave her possession of part of Shay. He leaned his head against the wall and listened to her.

'Often, you know, I wasn't really sure what the fuck he meant by things. Once he said you could never go home. It was some old Turk in a hostel filled his head with it.'

Hano listened to her describing Shay's bed with three others in the dormitory, the steel locker, the piece of wall for the pin-ups and photographs, the Yugoslav woman who served them meals on metal plates without a smile. He remembered the easy boredom of the Register's office, the cardboard boxes burning between the blocks as they leaned against the prison wall smoking.

'Anyway, the Turk said you carried home around inside you. It was more real there than when you went home. It didn't change and you weren't changed seeing it.

'It was some week when Shay was broke and spent each night sitting with him. Your man used to scorn the younger Turks for drinking and looking at whores at night. Time went too slow that way he claimed. He'd sleep instead and every hour slept was a victory. He said he was cheating time, making it work for him so he could go home sooner. I told Shay that Beano who did six months in the Joy once said that was what the old lags did as well.

'But no matter what you did this old Turk said, when you went back to your village you were a stranger inside and always would be. You know, Shay'd repeat that like he was bitter, then just look out the window and wait for you to come home, Hano. I don't know what the fuck he was remembering but it was like he'd forgot I was there. Jesus, he'd look so old then, sitting in the shadows, the cigarette burnt away to nothing at his elbow, just waiting for you. I'd curse you Hano, whatever you knew that kept him apart from me.'

Hano remembered the silence in the kitchen when he'd opened the door, Katie's bitter eyes turning to stare at him. How many lifetimes ago did it seem? Once you left home you could never go back. They lapsed into silence, waiting for darkness, to blunder forth, knowing that nothing lay ahead of them.

At dusk a golfer took them to the main road. He chuckled at Katie's dishevelled hair, taking them for teenage lovers returning to face the music after a night sleeping rough. A van brought them to Balbriggan half an hour before the booths closed. Cars sped down the main street with loudhailers, party workers desperate to get each last vote in.

Hano and Katie queued for chips in The Pop Inn, the crowd joking about the air of frenzy outside. It had been two days since he had eaten anything hot, and now the smell of the boiling grease made his stomach turn. An election agent poked his head in, scanning the faces for somebody. A policeman passed. Hano lowered his head, trying to keep the tremble from his legs. The few late voters were jostled by the canvassers as they made their way to the booths in the town hall. Nobody noticed them as they walked through the square except the punks who sat on the court-house steps with bottles of cider in plastic bags at their feet. They whistled after Katie.

Hano grabbed her hand when she seemed about to shout back and steered her off the main street through the terraces of houses by the closed-down hosiery factory. Ornate plaques high on the wall commemorated medals won at trade fairs in Vienna and Paris before the turn of the century. The names of rock groups were sprayed on the brickwork below. A few boats were tied up at the small harbour, coloured lights reflected on the water from the disco bar on the pier. On the hill the lights of the new estates glowed over empty concrete streets. They passed again into darkness and began walking along the Drogheda road.

A farmer picked them up not far from Gormanstown. He was returning from voting in the city.

'Could you have not voted closer to home?' Hano asked.

'I did, I did,' he chuckled. 'This afternoon. But the brother always gave his number one to Patrick Plunkett and sure there's no reason Plunkett shouldn't have it now just because me brother's dead. Especially this day, the poor man. A fierce fire that was. Ah, but you can be sure the Brits were behind it. And you know why? The Plunketts were the men to stand up to them, like their grandfather did, that's why.'

The booths had closed when they reached Drogheda, the town looking like a dancehall car-park after a holiday weekend. The pubs were jammed. The only faces left on the streets stared from election posters on lamp-posts and leaflets piled like autumn leaves along the ground. There was little traffic. Unloaded trailers of lorries were parked on the quayside beside the crumbling Victorian warehouses. They climbed on to the back of one, stretched on the bare boards and stared at the railway viaduct spanning the mouth of the Boyne. Katie's head rested tiredly against his shoulder. He stroked her hair, closed his eyes and leaned back against the tail-board. The flashlight came from nowhere. Both knew it was a garda before he spoke.

'Hey! What are you at up there? Come here to me!'

He was running around the side of the trailer before they had jumped to the ground. They heard him call as they dodged through the narrow cobbled streets by the storehouses. The lights of a car turned the corner and bumped down towards them. Hano froze, waiting for the siren to come. Katie pulled him on as the headlights sped past, catching the figure of the garda puffing and slowing down as he cursed their backs.

They didn't stop till they reached the darkness of the Slane road. They rested in the gateway of a field watching the lights of occasional cars heading for the town. When lights came the other way they pressed back against the bushes, afraid to hitch now. To their left the Boyne ran sluggishly towards the sea, silvered occasionally by rocks. They walked on, listening anxiously for the noise of an engine behind them. Twice they pressed themselves flat against the ditch as cars passed, cursing their fear when they were plunged back into darkness in their wake.

They had travelled over a mile before Katie stopped and listened carefully.

'It's a lorry Hano. Fuck it, we'll take a chance.'

The lights were higher off the road, the noise of the engine deeper. Katie placed one foot on the tarmacadam and thumbed it. It roared past and they had cursed the driver before it skidded to a halt twenty yards in front of them. The driver was in his early thirties. He grinned down at them as they climbed into the warmth of the cab. He was returning to Sligo, having driven since seven the previous evening from Belgium through France and then up from Rosslare. He didn't ask questions, didn't want conversation. He just drove, grey eyes ringed from lack of sleep, smoking cigarette after cigarette as he manoeuvred through the narrow streets of each small town – Slane, Kells, Virginia, Stradone, Ballyhaise, skirting the border beyond Belturbet, before moving down through Ballyconnell. He offered them cigarettes and large bars of continental chocolate, talked about the traffic police on the continent, the rigs of the other drivers waiting in the ferry port. Tomorrow his brother would take the truck to Galway to collect a load for Ostend. He would rest for two days till the truck returned. His wife would still be at home, the two children put to bed. Four years more was all he'd drive. The regulations were stricter now, spies in the cab regulating the hours you were supposed to drive, strikes among dockers, the same hassles always with the customs in England. Where was the profit for a haulier now? Missing the children growing up, feeling a stranger at times in your own home. But the bungalow he'd built from it, that was the best in the district. Last year he'd taken home a fireplace from a shop in Brussels. This time it was a chandelier, the only thing left in the back after unloading in Drogheda. Hano thought of it swaying absurdly from the ceiling of the container behind them, the young woman waiting at home with the firelight flickering and all the lights turned down. The driver wore a stained blue jumper with no shirt underneath.

'You can't beat it,' he said. 'Going home.'

Katie's eyes stared ahead, her lips moving each time they passed a road sign. The driver pressed a switch on the dashboard and country music began to play. In Dublin with Shay, Hano remembered mocking the corny three-four playing of the Irish country bands. But now, as the headlights swept along the low bushes and stone walls bordering the road far below him and Katie curled warm against his side, the awkward lyrics were magical. Stories of wedding rings and lost love letters, of crossroad meetings, of blankets laid beside rivers. He closed his eyes, never wishing the journey to end. The driver sang along to himself. They passed Bawnboy and Glengevlin in silence and were only miles from Dowra when Katie tugged his hand urgently.

He looked down but she seemed afraid to speak. Her fingers were pulling at his jacket as if trying to tear it off.

'Here,' Hano said uncertainly. The driver stared across at him.

'You sure? It's the arse end of nowhere.'

Katie nodded slowly and the man shrugged his shoulders. He braked and bumped the wheel up against the loose gravel. The air rushed in, freezing when Hano opened the door. Katie jumped and he followed her down. The driver reached under his seat and threw another large bar of dark chocolate after them.

'Don't know what the fuck you're at,' he said, 'but good luck.'

*

For me those evenings with Shay were reality at last, a tangible sensation that I sensed coursing through my body. But even then I think Shay was merely playing at living his life. Like that moronic office where decades stood still, the poker sessions and crowds swamping his tiny flat were somehow an elaborate joke, a marking of time before he chose to enter whatever real world he was destined for. He was growing sick of his address being famous, people calling at every hour of night. I would wake on his floor to hear heavy thumping on the door and listen to Shay curse as he waited to see if they'd go away. The knocking would continue, startling the Galway man who'd begin his anxious pacing next door, until Shay pulled on his jeans and went down. I'd hear loud voices, then the light would tear at my eyes. One couple on the dole never called before two o'clock. They were both nineteen with short, spiked hair. He would make them tea and they'd sit staring around the room, mumbling about obscure rock bands until they had filled up the time before they decided to sleep.

Shay kept the place neat as if fighting to impose some order on his life, but people kept arriving, bringing friends, leaving the flat in chaos. I began to feel self-conscious calling on him but felt, or wanted to feel, that he rarely resented my presence. I could never understand why, but we seemed to share something I could not define.

One night we returned to find his record player stolen. The door had not been broken down and nothing else was touched. We both knew that some visitor had pocketed a spare key. So many feet had passed through and so much drink had been spilt since Shay moved in that the square of carpet where the record player had been was a different shade to the rest of the room. He sat on the bed, staring at the space like a map of two years of his life, then walked to the twenty-four-hour shop in Rathmines with his hands sunk in his pockers. He bought an evening paper and began to draw circles down the accommodation columns. At two o'clock the knocking began on the door. He never raised his eyes from the columns of print and I said nothing, placed the cup of tea at his elbow, took my place beside the empty grate and listened to the silence return after the final arrogant flurry of knocks.

Over the next fortnight I accompanied him most times he looked for a new flat. Off-duty policemen grinned in doorways, their official trousers and boots still on. They showed us up damp staircases covered in peeling wallpaper into spartan rooms with cheap furniture. Often some reminder of the last tenant remained – a crooked poster on a wall, a chipped mug on a shelf. There was a sense of desolation about each room, airless, dusty, catching only a few moments of light in the evening. The landlords eyed him up to see if he would be a good payer with the same experienced glance as a poultry farmer selecting a laying hen. I shook my head whenever Shay looked at me and we'd tramp out towards the next address past the youngsters queuing down the stairs. The landlords grunted at the next in line, knowing they would always find someone desperate enough not to complain about the damp patches, the hissing tap or the rigged electricity meter.

But it was more than just the squalor of each flat we tried that was wrong, it was their size as well. There was room for only one and, without a conscious decision, we had begun to think of the place as being ours to share. It had grown naturally into an unspoken understanding which I never dared mention. Already the girls in work regarded us as a pair, always leaving the seat beside me free if Shay had not yet come in. Whenever he phoned in sick Mary would tease me in the Irish Martyrs lounge about pining for my boyfriend.

'What do you think Mick?' she'd asked. 'Are the pair of them bent or what?'

Mick would raise his pint and pause, shaking his head in earnest thought.

'Don't know about Hano, but I have my suspicions about Shay,' he'd say. 'There's always a fierce taste of shite off his penis.'

I'd laugh with them, but when I would try to define our relationship in my mind, though I shied away from the word, for me it was as close to love as I had ever known. Not in any physical sense, not implying possessiveness. But, for me, Shay was freedom and life; he was everything I never had the courage to be. I have no idea what he saw in me. Maybe some younger version of himself, kicking a football between cars on

71

those streets where horses were raced along the pavement, dreaming of leaving, still tied to the parents he never mentioned.

Was I his past, what he was escaping from? There were parts of his mind I never knew what went on in. I remember one night in a pub shortly after I met him. Two blokes from Coolock were acting tough, trying to wind up Mick because of his Donegal accent. Shay said nothing, smiled up from his pint and let them believe he was from the bog too. Finally their girlfriends arrived and the two lads went to leave. Shay waited till they had reached the door before calling. They stopped and looked back. Shay spoke slowly as though instructing a child: 'You roll it down over your dick!' They were about to go for him when the entire bar broke into spontaneous applause. Then one of their girlfriends giggled. They turned and vanished meekly through the door. Shay took a sip of his pint.

'That's what gives me a pain about this city,' he said. 'Everybody who comes from it is so cocksure of themselves, they think they're all so street-wise. That's your charm Hano, you're the most uncool guy in the world.'

It was the only time I heard him make any comment about me and I couldn't figure out if it was a compliment or an insult.

By the end of that fortnight we had looked at twenty-seven bedsits. The last one we saw overlooked the canal between Rathmines and Ranelagh. It was a narrow room divided in two by a plywood partition that split the window in half. Even after Shay told him he was not interested, the landlord insisted on showing off his prize feature, a new shower unit with a meter in a tiny cubicle to be used by all twelve flats in the house. He spoke of the money it had cost him, like a father after giving away his daughter at a wedding. At any moment I expected him to produce an umbrella and invite us to stand under it. We finally got away from him and crossed the street to where plastic bags floated as gracefully as swans on the dark water.

'It's about time you began paying rent, you bollox,' Shay said. 'We could get a good gaff with a bit of space. I'm sick of looking at these single rooms. Are you into it?'

72

'All right,' I said, trying to keep my voice as casual as I could. On the far bank youths were drinking from plastic cider bottles outside the timber encampment of old people's chalets. We followed the tow-path down towards Baggot Street. I remember an early cluster of prostitutes chatting under a bridge and passing a tramp with a cardboard box who was digging himself in under the roots of a tree for the night. And I can still see the half-moon of Shay's face when he paused beneath the branches to light two cigarettes and pass one down to the unshaven figure who grunted his thanks before we resumed our discussion about the plywood mansions we could now afford to look at.

But if anything the double flats were worse. The best of them was a single room with a kitchen bar in one corner, two cheap chairs, a sofa and what had once been a small corridor down to the bathroom converted into a narrow bedroom with two bunk beds. One could smell the toilet at the end without opening the door. A young couple with a child arrived when we were leaving. The rent the landlord quoted them was twenty pounds a month dearer than he had asked from us. The girl's eyes had a glazed look, like a refugee shunted between transit camps. I knew that no matter what he asked they would take it.

Despairing of flats, we tried for a small house off the South Circular Road. Behind the run-down terrace the grey blocks of Fatima Mansions rose. Only weeks before the families there had forced the heroin pushers out with marches on their flats at nights. I remembered a photograph of one banner in the march carried by The Concerned Criminals Against Drugs.

Paint had been spilt on the roadway outside the house to let and green and blue tyre tracks careered off in all directions. Across the road three boys looted a rubbish skip, a toddler nonchalantly smashing the bottles they threw down against the kerb. Every second house had a weathered For Sale sign; one was handwritten with just the words 'Five thousand pounds and it's yours'. We both recognized the estate agent who arrived in his red Saab. We'd seen him in Murtagh's once or twice with Justin Plunkett. He kept nervously glancing back at his car as he led us in. Sooty black footprints led down the stairs to the front door. We followed them up to the bedroom where we discovered somebody had just ripped out the fireplace. The estate agent sighed.

'Well, it's cheap,' he said, 'and we never had any trouble before. It could make a really cool bachelor pad for you guys.'

'Isn't that kid fierce young all the same to be driving a Saab?' Shay remarked at the window. We followed the estate agent out at our leisure. The kids had stopped emptying the skip and were watching him wide-eyed as he held possessively on to the door handle of the untouched car and tried to get his breath back.

'You just can't trust a word some *guys* say,' Shay reminded him as we walked off.

After that Shay seemed to lose his enthusiasm for house hunting. He was sick of landlords, sick of agents. In his flat he sat beside the twin bars of an electric fire when it was cold, no longer bothering to chop wood in the yard. The atmosphere in his room had changed. I called less, sensing that not even I was welcome. I couldn't bear to spend time at home and began to walk each evening around the streets of that suburb where we were both reared.

That was how I noticed the sign above the bookies in the old village. I told Shay about it at work. It was where he had placed his first bet. He laughed at the thought of living back there. Katie, were you one of the girls sitting on the carriageway wall that evening, watching vacantly as the car turned under the metal bridge? It was my first time there with Shay. I began to see the same streets through his eyes. We were early and cruised through the estate he had grown up in. Ponies were tethered on the green, the telephone box so smeared with graffiti it was impossible to see into. He paused outside the house where his parents still lived. I don't know how long it was since he had been back, but that night I knew he liked the idea of returning home. We drove back up the main street where coach horses had once halted. The shopping centres ringed the crest of the hill – before us Plunkett Auctioneers; behind us Plunkett Stores; down a lane to the left Plunkett Motors; and, beside the Protestant church across the bridge, Plunkett Undertakers on the right to complete the crucifixion.

The atmosphere of that old street was different from the other places we had seen. It was just before dusk when it's quiet and the air is clear high above the city. The row of shops dated from when the village only had two streets. There were three rooms to the flat up a long staircase. From the window we could see over the roofs of the abandoned cottages across the road into the old graveyard behind them. I remembered that road vaguely before the dual carriageway split it in two. A small stone bridge over a stream where lorries now thundered by. The sweet shop next door hadn't changed since then, the same rows of comics arranged on twine in the window, the antiquated cash register that had held my six-penny bits after Mass on Sundays. We stood together gazing out past the cottages at the graveyard. Through the Gothic arch of the ruined church wall the shopping centre rose like a space-age monster. People were starting to stroll towards the pub across the road.

'Sanctuary at last,' Shay said. 'We'll open a massage parlour for the punters downstairs, install Mary as a madam, and call it "The Winner's Enclosure".'

The bookie stood behind us, amused at Shay's talk. He was no professional landlord, merely a man with a space to spare. We took it there and then and arranged to move in on the Friday. We paid a deposit and he gave us the keys at once. After all my plans I was leaving home to go only a quarter of a mile and Shay somehow was coming home. When the bookie left we sat on in the twilight, congratulating ourselves, remembering things that had occurred on that road when we were children.

Shay offered to drive me home but I wanted to walk back across the bridge. My father sat in the dining-room like a grey puppet someone had draped on a chair. It was near bedtime, my mother stood at the back door calling my young brothers and sisters who were playing in the gloom. I walked past her into the garden that had grown up again in the last three months, choked with weeds and nettles, and wondered how I would find the words. It was late at night when I broke the news. I no longer wanted to hurt them but the words seemed harsh and awkward. As soon as they were spoken I felt occluded from their home. My mother cried like I was going to Australia. My father sat quietly, trying to calm her.

'Hush Lily, he's growing into a man now. It's natural. We can't hold him back.'

Yet his eyes betrayed his bewilderment and now it was I who was the stronger. I felt no satisfaction in that realization. I climbed the stairs to my room, my actions already seeming to belong to another life. My brothers were sleeping in their bunk beds. I lay awake for a long time memorizing the sounds of the house. The jangle of milk bottles, him drawing the chain on the front door, her voice calling from the kitchen, their footsteps together on the stairs. That bedroom where I had been born enclosed me with its warm familiarity. I wished I could have been gone at that moment without the hurt farewells always brought.

On the Friday night Shay called with his car. We carried my clothes out in plastic sacks, a cardboard box full of records, a handful of photographs and some books. As a child on summer holidays when my father went to work I would stand on the doorstep till he reached the corner, waiting for him to turn and give a final wave before vanishing from sight. That evening it was him who was left awkwardly there watching the car move slowly towards the bend. I twisted in the seat to wave to him and suddenly noticed how much weight he had lost. He stood stooped beside my mother, his hand raised like a geriatric child.

Next morning I woke to the noise from the bookies below, the girl's voice on Extel reciting the non-runners and form. The odds were repeated like litanies at Mass as the punters shuffled in or gathered on the pavement outside. I pushed open the window to experience the sounds of the street, women pushing their washing up to the launderette, the barking dogs, a car nosing into a parking space. I sat taking it all in while Shay cooked breakfast. He emerged with a tray and a racing page. Sunlight filled the street. Below the window a girl laughed. We ate quietly, listening to the punters chatting. The weekend stretched before us, a kaleidoscope of possibilities.

'Here we are again,' Shay said, 'back to nowhere. The fuckers will never find us here.'

*

*I dream of clay, I smell of earth. Katie, where is this place where I'm watching you take three pills from your pocket. Now you place them in your palm, lift your eyes to the screen and stare. Swallow, sit back and soon you will begin to scream. The double horror bill flickers before you, a hand breaking forth from a grave to grab the leg of the single mourner. You scream and scream until the usher picks up the four of you with his torch. The daylight startles you in the lobby as you are pushed out. Across the road the cabs wait, coloured beetles with round legs. The driver puts the paper down as you all cram in. 'Where to, girls?' The wall of laughter begins again. Before he throws you out you manage to say, 'Just out into the middle of the road and do wheelies!'*

*You go along now, the time for thought has gone. Some nights you do not get home. Once your uncle came searching for you, you heard footsteps at night entering the empty factory. He paused when he found the group, cider bottles spilt, a scent like herbs. When you heard his voice you turned cold, like a joint of meat in a butcher's fridge. He waited for you to come, embarrassed, gruffly calling. If the two boys had not appeared he might have turned away defeated. One sniggered, releasing him back into his own masculine world, a fist catching the side of the youth's skull before he pulled you by the hood of your duffle coat like that child again screaming, being torn by him away from your home. You did not come home for three nights after that, sleeping in back sheds and cars, fighting off attacks with your nails, while he stalked deserted factories and closed parks. When you heard he had stopped and gone home you returned, ravenous and jaded, by yourself.*

What do I remember most about the three months spent living with Shay? Sunday mornings with the trees in Phoenix Park still drenched with dew, light glistening in the hollow as we drove towards the cluster of lads togging out for a match at the Fifteen Acres. The golf course in the foothills of the mountains where the old man who took our money listened all day to opera on a ghetto-blaster or leaned placidly on the wall to watch golfers curse as they waded through the treacherous marsh that served as a fairway on the shorter holes. At the ninth a figure in wellingtons always emerged from the swamp, a token club in one hand, the other offering a selection of balls for sale. He was there even when we played at seven in the morning and, leaving the money under the door, were finished our round in time to drive down for work. Evenings devising a miniature putting course that wound through all the rooms of the flat, teeing off from beds and behind chairs. The week he spent teaching me to drive at dawn each morning on Dollymount Strand. The evening, a week later, when I caught him trying to tear a piece off my provisional licence when he was stuck for roach paper. And nights just doing nothing, drinking coffee and smoking tipped cigars, letting the darkness envelope the room as we lazed in armchairs.

It was an oasis of curious tranquillity. Faces remained from our childhood: the old headmaster who lived on the corner, the red-faced doctor long past retirement age. Any excuse in those days would cause Shay to go sick from work – once he stayed at home to watch Playschool. As I sat among the clerks I'd see him in my mind leaning out the flat window at four o'clock to wave the flex of the electric kettle and call *Coffee girls? Coffee?* as the convent emptied and the men milling outside the bookies grinned up at him. I don't know how he did it, but twice I arrived home to find a school bag embroidered with rock stars' names in the hall and opened the kitchen door to catch a flash of light brown thighs before the green uniform was quickly pulled down. We were far enough from town not to be disturbed by unwelcome guests, but still only twelve minutes drive from the city centre. The distinctive drone of the Triumph's engine became famous on that street in the early morning hours.

One night we met a Spanish girl holidaying in Ireland. We had been at the races that afternoon, winning for once, drinking shorts between races to celebrate. Food kept being postponed as we left the Phoenix Park and began to drink around town. By ten o'clock we were in Murtagh's, giddy on our empty stomachs, rolling numbers on the Formica tables. The girl was drinking by herself at the bar. She might have been twenty-two or three. Only a cool and seasoned traveller could have nosed out that bar and found her way past the shutters on the door. After a time I realized that Shay wasn't listening to me anymore. He finished the number he was rolling, walked over and offered it to her. She laughed and shook her head. I saw him bend down to catch what she was saying. They talked on in gestures and then she came over. We communicated in sign language and broken English.

At closing time Shay pointed first to the door, then placed his palms together and laid his head sleepily on them, leaving the choice to her. She kept laughing as she imitated him with the palms and the cupped head in the Triumph Herald on the way home. There was a bottle of whiskey in the flat. It died a brief death. I could hear his bed shaking through the wall as I undressed alone, and then without warning the noise of Shay being sick.

'I'm sorry,' he kept repeating. 'No food today. Jesus it's all over your skin and all. Wait, I'll get a cloth. Never happened before. Really sorry. Really.'

It was the only time I ever heard Shay embarrassed. The girl kept trying to play it down. 'It okay, it okay,' she was saying, 'you lie down now, lie down.'

The last thing I heard was the bed jangling. I woke with a filthy hangover the next morning and noticed the front door open from the top of the stairs. There was a curious scent from Shay's room and flies were buzzing near the bed. Shay was naked, deep in sleep, with one hand limply hanging down towards the floor. The girl was gone, having pulled the sheet neatly down to his waist. On the centre of his white chest lay a slender, curved, light-brown turd.

I slagged him about it for days, no longer just an observer but finally part of his world. I joked across the office with Mary and Mick, dodged Carol, ignored Mooney, made friends with the girls in the room, falling in love with each briefly and individually. Some nights I sat beside Shay in Murtagh's listening to the guitarist bop. Each week someone else there would be leaving for London, Berlin, New York. The postcards began to line the mirror behind the bar while those left compared places and contacts.

As I watched I sometimes imagined my father sitting in some Kerry bar in his youth while his friends debated which boat to take. It was different now, the scent of hash, the music in the background, the certificates and degrees. Yet their eyes must have looked the same, the jokes to hide bitterness, the feeling of being already gone once you had made the decision. My father had clung to some vision in his heart, managing always to return from each English factory, digging in, clinging to his vision of home. I doubted if many of those drinking in Murtagh's would return. The gap was smaller now between home and elsewhere. They would lose the accents quicker, be easily assimilated. They would not meet signs proclaiming *No Blacks, Dogs or Irish*. Now they were literate, white, equal Europeans. Those equipped with new passports showed them off, the smaller EEC version replacing the green Irish one. And it wasn't just unemployment that drove them away, rather they were going home to the world they had grown up with in their minds: the American films, the British programmes, the French clothes, the Dutch football they watched on satellite channels. For most, the fields their father's worked would have been exile; now they were catching planes to their own promised land.

Justin Plunkett moved among them, shaking hands, buying final rounds. He told them the best bars in Berlin, explained how to buy a tageskarte on the U-bahn, dispersed knowledge from across the continent where he vanished for three days of every month. One night when I was drunk I saw him as the angel of death, moving in gaudy colours through the bar, slapping the shoulders of those who would have disappeared by the following Friday. Perhaps he was just carrying on his father's work: clearing the country of debris, propelling it towards its destiny as a pleasure ground for the rich, a necklace of golf courses encircling the city, a modest number of natives left for service industries.

That same evening his father's face had been on the news making a speech to visiting EEC ministers. Justin had asked the television to be put on and had stood gazing at it, oblivious to the dozen hands raised in mock Nazi salutes behind his back. I cannot remember the speech word for word. There's no need to, it was just the standard phrases that could be joined together like Lego to suit any occasion:

*We are just a small nation in this great community. But our heritage abounds with saints, with poets, with dreamers. We in government are realists, first and foremost. We know we cannot all live in this one island. But we are not ashamed of that. Because young people are to Ireland what champagne is to France! Our finest crop, the cream of our youth, nurtured from birth, raised with tender love by our young state, brought to ripeness and then plucked! For export to your factories and offices. My fellow European ministers, we are but a small land with a small role to play in this great union of nations. But a land with a great history. Long before Columbus set sail in 1492, long before Amerigo Vespucci gave his name to that great continent, our missionaries in their boats of animal hide had already discovered the new world. Through all of the dark ages we have gone forth to spread the word of God among you, to petition you for arms to repel our invader, to fight your wars. Once more we entrust to you the flower of our youth: not black or yellow but white; not illiterate or backward but qualified; not as migrants or illegals but as equal Europeans. We know they are ready to take their place; we know you will not turn your back on this greatest of assets.*

Okay, okay, maybe I've embellished it slightly, I'm exaggerating, but it was some such shite.

Living with him, I began to see the conflict that was always present within Shay. I still don't fully understand those two sides of his nature, the fear of being trapped perpetually clashing with the sense of belonging somewhere. At first the move home to the new flat seemed to still his restlessness. But if he had run away from home at eighteen, in some ways now home had begun to run away from him. Our suburb had been planned without shape, so each time you seemed to hold it in your grasp when you looked away and looked back there was something else new, something else changed, not only buildings but moods, levels of despair. As long as Shay had kept his flat by the canal he could forget his past, but once he moved back it seemed to hound him. People who could not find it on a map spoke of the place like a suburb of Beirut when he told them where he had moved to. Without wanting to, he began spending his time defending the streets and the people he had grown up among. And then, late at night, we'd return to those streets, a thousand miles removed from the columns of news-print about them, those sleeping rows of houses where people thrown into nowhere were building their own lives, their own homes. And we knew nothing we could ever say would explain the hold of that place for us.

I could see a new tension develop in him. In work he was like a child growing bored of a game, spending most of the day on auto-pilot. He began to clash more with Mooney as the old man found that he could needle him indirectly by abusing the new clerks coming in. I knew Shay hated himself for being drawn into the politics of the office. At weekends when there was a party with somebody leaving I would have to force him to go, reluctantly driving back into the flatland he had left.

I remember one night how he kept the whole company laughing by acting out sketches – like Mooney's wife wrapping a new fur coat over her shoulders after his cremation and lifting the lid of the urn to blow his ashes out of the window with the words: 'Well dear, here's the new fur coat I've been asking you for these past twenty years and here's the blow-job you've been asking me for.' The clerks clustered on the floor at his feet, drinking from bottles, laughing at every song he invented, every impersonation. Shay fed them for over an hour with a comedian's perfect timing, then suddenly shut up, growing sullen as if disgusted with the whole spectacle. As we walked back to the car he said curtly:

'I'm nobody's fucking court jester, Hano. Listen, they'd live their lives off you if they could. But we're just the light enter-tainment on their way up the ladder. They're sitting back there now, feeding the pair of us into a mangle with their talk.'

Now his talk grew filled with images of Europe. He started sitting with Justin Plunkett at weekends, asking questions, filling out his knowledge of the continent. I ignored those conversations. My new world was too perfect to contemplate it ever changing. But one morning at twelve o'clock he put on his jacket without a word and walked out of the office. Mooney and Carol were at a meeting and Mary managed to cover up his absence. I found him at home, sitting beside a row of coffee cups. The ash tray at his elbow was choked with butts.

'I'm wasting away Hano,' he said. 'I can feel my mind drying up with every day spent in there. It's no longer a joke, mate. It's not funny anymore.'

I tried to reason with him. I wasn't scared for his sake but for my own.

'Forty years you could spend there doing the same fucking thing,' he said. 'What's at the end of it all? Just enough money to survive every fortnight. Three and a half years of it Hano and I'm no richer, no more qualified to do anything than the day I walked in there.'

'But you've good crack. You enjoy yourself outside.'

'I'm sick of it, the job, this town, they're just too small and they're making me too small. Can you not imagine it Hano, anonymity, losing yourself in some foreign city where nobody knows who you are and nobody cares? What do you say? Are you game? We could just go, now, in a few weeks time, the pair of us, together.'

Shay looked up at me, cigarette in his hand, his eye with that old gleam as if suggesting a party somewhere. But this time I was frightened, he had gone out beyond my depth. I wanted to go and yet I knew I hadn't the courage. He was waiting for an answer. What was keeping me here? It wasn't ties or commitments, it was the simple fear of being swallowed up by the unknown. Yet I was even more terrified of being left behind by him. He was smiling just like that first night with the girls in the Chinese restaurant, only this time there could be no excuses, no games of snooker to put it off. This time my bluff was being called.

'But this is my home,' I said lamely.

'Home! Good Jesus, Hano, what's that? Do you think it wants you? That it has any use for you? Phone up Patrick Plunkett now and he'll pay for the taxi to the airport. Home is where you make it, not just where you're born. A chicken doesn't spend its life squatting on the fragments of its shell does it? Hano, I can't breathe in this kip anymore. And you've fuck all to look forward to. Don't you realize you're temporary. In two months when you come up for renewal Mooney will be able to give you the chop. What have you got in front of you then? The dole? Some scabby Manpower scheme? It's a sinking ship. Come on, let's get off while we're ahead.'

Every word he said was true. I had no answer for it beyond the simple paralysis of fear.

'What would we do over there Shay? How do you know it would be any better?'

'Take the risk, just once in your life. *We are the young Europeans* they keep telling us. Screw them Hano, we'll get out. Just think about it, at half-eleven tonight when the pubs here will be closed and the last bus gone, people will be just going out to drink in Amsterdam, strolling down the Ramblas in Barcelona, gawking up at the whores starting work in the Reeperbahn. Hano, you're just turned nineteen, I mean you're a big boy. We'll find work easily enough. Give it a lash for a while anyway then we can come back. Come on, what do you say?'

Shay spent the evening trying to convince me, but I was like a man trapped on a ledge, scared to go back in, terrified to jump. I kept thinking, it's just a passing whim, tomorrow he'll wander back to work. But he didn't. He neither resigned nor phoned in sick. Mooney smiled as he dictated the first letter to Mary. It was returned with the scrawled message over it, *Go fuck yourself!* When Mick heard of Shay's intention he laughed quietly to himself, but it was Mary who took it badly. I never knew how close she and Shay had been, their heads always bent together, hatching tricks, covering up for each other. Somehow she saw his action as a sort of betrayal. She made bitter jokes about him in the office. He had started work when she was still in her late twenties. As long as he was there she could remain joking in that perpetual state of youth. Now his departure seemed to bring her age home to her, reminding her of all her own failed chances to escape before her child had arrived. Suddenly the figure of Carol fussing in the office, of cycling home to a lonely home in Deansgrange and existing only in those hours of work, began to scare her.

Yet what was interesting was how quickly Shay was forgotten. For a week clerks speculated at the tables, the conversation gushing in a thrill of excitement. Then one morning something else happened, more current, belonging to that cloistered world he was now excluded from. People still asked me how he was but he was spoken of in the past tense like a man who had passed away. A new girl started. To her he was just another name among a hundred who had worked there once.

Personnel sent him two letters before the resignation form. He ignored them all. The final letter of dismissal contained a cheque for his superannuation. He was back to his best form, excited and joking. Even then I kept thinking he wouldn't leave.

'What will you do?' he asked one evening.

I shrugged my shoulders. I hadn't allowed myself to think beyond his departure and after the first night he never pressured me to go.

'Talk to the bookie. He's an honest bloke. All he really wants is the space filled. He'd probably knock a bit off the rent for you. I'll leave you some bread. It's not fair of me to run out on you like this.'

'No,' I said, 'you'll need it more than me.'

I could no longer put the question off.

'When are you going Shay?'

It was the first time I had brought myself to mention the subject. He looked relieved that I had asked him.

'Saturday morning. No long farewells, eh.'

That left four days. On the Friday I phoned in sick. He cooked a huge breakfast. I opened the windows and we sat down to eat. Twelve weeks had passed since the Saturday morning when I had sat listening to the punters talking on the road outside. The street was deserted except for one old woman with a shopping trolley. Shay made some joke but neither of us laughed.

85

After breakfast we drove out into the countryside and parked at the bridge in Knocksedan. He led me down through the overgrown river valley, across wire fences and hidden tracks to the reservoir. An old man was hunched by the water's edge, black hat down over his face, watching three youngsters fish. He grunted at Shay, an animal sound as we pushed on through the wilderness. I had always seen Shay on city streets. It surprised me how well he knew his way in this jungle of bushes and trees. He led the way upwards towards an overgrown mound. We stood on its dome and looked around.

'Man-made,' he said. 'See how circular it is. Before the time of Christ they built it with stones and clay. I used to mitch from school out here, bring some girl out who'd go sick from class to swim in the river with me. Two hours getting them to take their dresses off for five minutes in the water.' He grinned. 'But it was worth it. You know, some evenings I'd climb this mound by myself in the dusk and it was as though you could almost hear it saying to you: "I know you. I know everything you will ever feel. I have felt it all before. Whatever you will do I have seen men do. Wherever you go I will have seen them go.' I brought this Argentinian girl out here once who claimed she was psychic. She shivered up here and ran down, said she felt blood, that it had been used for sacrifices.'

He was standing, gazing back down the river valley. The sun had gone behind a cloud and it was suddenly cold. It felt eerie listening to him come here to say goodbye to something that I couldn't understand.

Justin Plunkett had agreed to buy the Triumph. We drove out to his apartment in Clontarf at five o'clock. The ministerial Mercedes was parked in the courtyard. Justin came out to the door of the block in a mourning suit. The white collar of his shirt was standing up where he had been fixing the black tie. He looked tense.

'Jesus mate,' Shay said. 'Have we called at a bad time? Is it somebody in the family?'

'You're okay Seamus,' he said. 'Listen, I can't ask you in just now. The old man's in a bad way inside.'

'Is he sick?'

'Ah no, nothing like that. Hassle in the constituency. The chairman of the East's Residents' Association and the mother of Tommy O'Rourke who has that pub in the village are after both kicking the bucket yesterday. One's being brought to the church in the East at six, and the other to the church in the West. We can't work out who's going to get the bigger crowd. We're trying to figure out which one he should go to and which I should attend in his place. Eh, either way you're going to insult somebody. Two fucking stiffs in the one day. God I hate fucking stiffs.'

He paid us in cash, crouching down as he peeled notes from a wad without taking it from his pocket. We caught a bus back into town. We were both in drinking form. Having accumulated enough money for his trip, Shay seemed intent on leaving most of it behind. The pubs were empty in that lull between tea-time and evening when we began. They filled up as we wandered from bar to bar, meeting more of his friends, becoming a larger and larger procession.

He was like a whirlwind all night, sweeping people up in his wake, sending them reeling off again. I sat on the stool next to him at every counter, drinking like never before, wanting the night to last for ever. We met Mick near closing time. They embraced and sang 'Bandiera Rosa' till we were thrown out. Five of us wound up somewhere off Capel Street, bar men roaring at us to leave long after closing time. We exited with half-finished pints in our hands, finished them in one gulp and hurled the glasses into a doorway. The buildings kept swerving before my eyes, the pavement was unsteady. A pound note was blowing along the ground. I stamped on it.

'Here, Shay,' I said. 'For when you're skint some night in Germany.'

'A good-luck charm,' he said, accepting it. 'Not to be spent on women or drink. I'll keep it, Hano. I mean it.'

There were road-works being carried out on the quays. Shay stole a flashing lantern and shoved it up his jumper. We lost the last two of his friends and wandered up by Christchurch with only Mick at our side. A guard stepped from the porch of the cathedral.

'What are you at, boys?' he asked.

'Nothing, guard,' Shay replied innocently, his jacket illuminated every three seconds. The policeman took it from him for safe keeping, laughing as he told us to wander on home. We headed back down Dame Street. One moment Mick was there, the next he was gone.

'I'm hungry,' I said, and Shay led the way into the first Chinese restaurant. They refused us service and we wound up in an old German place we used to visit whenever we felt rich. The waiter was dark-skinned, like Heathcliff gone wrong. One could never quite understand what he was saying. I ordered Chicken Maryland with roast potatoes, chipped potatoes, sautéd potatoes, fried potatoes and baked potatoes. They brought it out on a huge plate with one sprig of parsley. I said it was perfect, then fell asleep with my head in it. They helped Shay to clean me up, called a taxi to the door.

I don't remember the journey home, only paying the man off at The Bottom of the Hill pub. There was an old cobbler's there, the last remaining cottage in a block surrounded by the carriageway. It looked incongruous, with one pony tied outside and a single tree bereft of leaves. I lay on the low wall and got slowly sick before rolling over to look at the stars. I could still go, apply for a passport and follow him. I knew that Shay was thinking the same. Neither of us spoke.

Past The Bottom of the Hill there was a litter bin, crammed with newspapers and tin cans. I pulled a can out and threw it at him. He ducked, snatched up a coke can and flung it back. We began a mock fight up and down the main street. There was nobody about, as if the world was deserted except for us. We used the lamp-posts for protection, aiming punches and kicks at each other as we ducked and bobbed. I wanted to hurt him; I wanted to just touch him. What I wanted I'm not really sure. If he had stopped and opened his arms I would have walked towards him; I would have laid my head on his shoulder and embraced him; I would have sat on that kerb all night with him.

We stopped at last, and lowered our heads, exhausted. He came towards me, making the sign for a truce. We touched hands briefly, then we turned and walked up that wrecked main street where no car or person had appeared, across the metal bridge and, with a final nod, into our own bedrooms. When I woke the next morning he was gone. My head hurt just to rise from the pillow. The bedroom door was open. There was a scrawled note on the table.

*You were sleeping so sound I didn't want to wake you. You must have been a lovely baby. Look after yourself kid.*
   *Shay*

He didn't like long farewells.

*Black skyline of earth breaking up, like clouds the pink flowers forming. They grow between the worn bricks of the laneway by the backs of the houses. They treasured you Katie for your slim hips that could squeeze through any window. A lean-to kitchen had been added; the two youths lifted you up on to it. Don't look down, just keep on – the window latch comes undone. You are terrified you will get stuck but they whisper urgently. You squeeze, the wood grazes your hips, then you are through. Once inside you feel scared. The quiet dusty room with its sparse, woodwormed furniture. You descend the stairs hurriedly, undo the bolts on the back door. When they enter no one speaks, you know that they can sense it too. You keep together as you sneak through each deserted room. Musty pictures of St Teresa, a schoolboy with a prayer book and crooked fingers in a photographer's studio. Lining a drawer you find a paper dated forty-five years before. There is nothing to steal, nothing has been purchased in the last quarter-century. The presence of sorrow fills each room with a heavy enveloping vapour. In the bedroom you have left you hear footsteps on the lino; you rush back into the stillness to hear them now on the stairs. The atmosphere has grown oppressive as though the walls were imperceptibly closing in Is it the pills, the speed? You feel them coursing through your bloodstream, suddenly you want your own body back. Pushing your way down the stairs you see through the hammered glass of the front door the shadow of a figure reaching up with a key. You crest the back wall of the garden, career down the laneway. 'Who was he coming in? What did he look like on the path?' you scream at the look-out on the corner. She looks back puzzled and shrugs her shoulders, 'Who was who? What are you talking about?'*

The driver slammed the door, leaving them in darkness as the lorry moved off. Hano watched it till the tail lights vanished at the bend. He hunched down, raised his arms to his shoulders and hugged himself. The stars were extraordinarily clear. A car passed. He closed his eyes, held back tears till it was gone. There was a low wall beyond the ditch. Katie was leaning against it, staring at a row of tree stumps on the bank beyond.

'Poplars they were. A lovely rustle off them in summer coming home from school. You know, even the fields look different. Seems to be all grass Hano or can you see? They grew crops there once, there wasn't a rood of it my father didn't plough and all for other men. And not a field where I didn't help him lift spuds. Dozens of us in a line filling sacks in the muck.'

He wiped his eyes with a sleeve, glad she couldn't see, and stood up. The fields stretched uphill to the state forest. To their right a bog lay sullen in the darkness. A line of bungalows were set back from the road. A dog barked in one, sensing strangers.

'They grow cars instead now,' he said, pointing to one upturned on the bog, stripped of everything that could be removed.

Katie laughed. 'There were always cars. Blackie McDonnell on the far road lived in one. Said it was the best thing yet. The laneway is just down here. Two miles, no problem to a hard man like you.'

The largest bungalow had a split roof in a Spanish style with white walls raised off the ground by a base of local stone. The driveway was lit by lamps which ran down to a wooden gateway inlaid with two huge wagon wheels. A high pole had been erected on either side to support a crossbar which bore a sheep's skull and the words 'The High Chaparral' in floodlit letters. The lawn stretched to the bushes by the lane, a cool line of shrubs marking the border. On the slope behind the bungalows they could barely discern the shape of a roofless cabin crumbling in on itself.

'Mary Roche's,' Katie whispered. 'The only light there ever was a mile either side of this place.'

The sides of the laneway were so overgrown it was like entering a tunnel. The reflection of branches threw crazy shapes on the pot-holed tar and a strip of grass which grew like a horse's mane down the centre.

'I suppose you walked it in your bare feet,' Hano joked, trying to keep the tremor from his voice.

'Aye, with stones in me pocket to keep me from blowing off the path.'

After a hundred yards the branches grew so thick that all light was blocked out. It was like a laneway forgotten by time. Hano could not believe anyone still lived up it. They slowed down, unsure of their footing in the dark.

'I'm scared Hano, scared shitless,' she whispered to him. He took her hand, it was cold. She shivered. 'I walked it a thousand times without it ever seeming lonely, but it feels lonely as hell tonight.'

'Don't know what's up there,' he said, trying to reassure her, 'but it can't be worse than what's behind us.'

They walked on, hands raised to protect their faces from the low branches, feet stumbling on the uneven tar.

'What if he's dead Katie?' Hano finally asked.

'He's not.'

Hano could barely hear her voice.

'He's . . . not the kind. It sounds thick, but like, he was just one of those unkillable old lads, you know what I mean? You couldn't imagine that they'd ever been young. The same grey clothes, the same worn faces looking the same age – sixty or ninety or as old as the hills. Never sick, never stopping work, never going beyond the nearest town. Tomas was like a tree or a rock, you know, like a part of the place. Birth or death had fuck all to do with him.'

She spoke as if trying to convince herself.

'Only outing was Saturday night when he'd walk to the pub in Dowra. I'd see his light come on through the trees when he'd get home around two in the morning. He'd fry bacon, no pan or anything, just throw it up with a lump of lard on top of the stove and eat it with white bread and tea from the shop at the front of the pub. Always said it was the best part of his week. No work on the Sunday except a few hours in the morning. You know, I'd watch for his light each Saturday like a guardian angel, pinching myself to keep awake, sitting up at my window to guide his journey home.'

The hedgerows gave way to trees, the tarmacadam to clay and stones. They were passing through the state forest, tall lines of cheap wood on both sides, the noise of creatures scurrying through the undergrowth.

'Eight years Katie. It's a long time. He could go to the police when he finds out.'

Even in the darkness he could sense her smile.

'Listen, Tomas was the only man to court me. I don't mean anything dirty, he'd never put a finger near me though I teased him often enough. No, like I've known blokes in the city but that's not what I meant. My father was my father and my uncle, whenever he came back down, was my uncle, but Tomas was a man and I was the only woman he'd ever known. If he's still alive then I tell you Hano, we've come home.'

Hano remembered when he'd last walked through a wood like this, the old woman beside him, clusters of rhododendrons grey in the moonlight. Five years, a lifetime ago, but the same illicit sensation as now. Katie was tugging his hand, pressing forward, half in expectation and half in fear. The forest ended and the track narrowed, rising to where a new locked gate blocked their way. Katie touched the iron bars, unable to believe they were real. Hano had to coax her to climb over.

'He could have put it there Katie,' he said, his voice losing conviction. She ran towards the next bend without replying, raising her arms to her head as she rounded the corner. When he reached her she was standing still, gazing into the darkness in front.

'The lights Hano. You should be able to see his lights.'

'Maybe there's a new ballroom in Dowra. He could be dating a widow with a tractor.'

He shut up and took her hand. If he hadn't taken it she would not have gone on. She held back as they approached, whispering, 'Good Christ, Hano, no, no.' They made out the exposed rafters first, standing like bones against the sky. The bushes beside the cottage had begun to grow through the windows, still blackened in the aftermath of a fire. The front door lay like a headstone in the long grass, scattered knick-knacks of a life littering the overgrown path. They stepped carefully through the nettles to the low doorway. Glass crunched beneath their feet, their fingers feeling black when they touched the walls. The panes were smashed in both tiny windows. Hano was amazed at the depth of the walls. They crumbled under his fingers, made of loose stones and clay. He lit a match and surveyed the debris before the light flickered out. A wooden chair with one leg missing lay on its side. Katie was on her knees, stroking something cupped in her hand. She spoke without looking up.

'I filled it for him Hano, whenever he'd let me.'

He felt the shape of the smashed pipe she pressed into his hand and wanted to hurl it against the wall. A rat brushed his leg as it bolted for the door. Startled, Hano dropped the pipe, almost screaming at her as she scrambled to find it.

'Let's get the fuck out of here,' he said

She was still kneeling, sifting fragments of wood and glass through her hands. Her head was bowed as though she had forgotten him.

'He was an old man before you left for Christ's sake, not a rock or a bleeding tree. Life doesn't stand still. He's dead. Dead, Katie.'

The slivers of wood hurt his face when she flung them at him. She grabbed a second handful and held it up.

'Shut up! Don't say it. I want him back. I want to talk to him, want to ask him things.'

She stopped and he heard the debris slipping through her fingers. Her voice went quiet.

'No I don't Hano. I hope he's dead, not stuck in a home

somewhere. That would be worse for him. It's only here he belonged, not in some ward full of old men coughing.'

Hano helped her up and steered her towards the door. She put her arms around him, pressing her face against his jacket.

'Maybe he was dead for weeks,' she whispered, 'before anyone found him. Here alone with the rats. Can you imagine it Hano, dying here alone?'

'There's nothing we can do for him, Katie. If he's dead maybe in some way he knows you came back.'

'Does Shay know, Hano? Can he see us? Do you believe it?'

When she mentioned Shay's name he began to cry. He no longer tried to fight it, just let it blubber out of him.

'Jesus Katie, I miss him, how I fucking miss him. I want him back Katie. I don't want to be alone.'

She was crying too, soothing him as he tried to soothe her.

'I know Hano, I know. All my life I've known. Christ, I miss him too. People keep leaving. If I could only say goodbye to him or to them I could let them go. Told a lie to you Hano. I would have gone down here once, for the funeral. But my uncle wouldn't let me. Never forgave him . . . felt if I could just see them to tell them how I missed them they'd come alive again.'

Shay would be in Glasnevin now, his first night underground, the fresh flowers that were strewn down over the coffin crushed under the weight of soil. What would he look like? Hano tried to stop his imagination but the face came, withering up as he buried his head in her hair. Masonry was crumbling against his back. He lifted his face into the sharp night air.

'Come on Katie, we've got to get somewhere warm.'

She stared through the caved-in doorway as he pulled her away, shaking her head when he tried to coax her up the track.

'It will just be another ruin Hano, like visiting a graveyard. I don't want to see it. Please.'

He sensed the fear inside her but pushed on. His teeth chattered. There could be frost by morning. She pulled at his hand, trying to drag him back as they approached her old home. Water trickled over rocks to their right, forming small pools as it soaked across the earthen track to disappear into bracken. A few stumped trees grew, twisted grotesquely by the wind. Their feet touched wood as they crossed planks laid across the banks of a black stream and to their right the walls of the house appeared. Katie cried out in shock and dropped his hand.

'No Hano. Jesus, it couldn't be.'

'What's wrong Katie? What do you see?'

The girl turned back. Her breath was loud in the darkness.

'Like time stood still. Same as the night I left. God, maybe they're in there Hano, still waiting for me.'

'Jesus Katie, you've me as scared as you are. It's deserted, can't you see. It doesn't even look lived in.'

They approached cautiously. The house was uncanny. It was a traditional labourer's cottage, but too perfect, too untouched by time. He thought of the bungalows back on the road, the tumbled-down walls where Mary Roche had lived. What light came from the stars, caught the freshly white-washed walls. Hano expected to see a Ford Anglia parked at the back, girls in sixties dresses coming to the door. A story from childhood troubled him, the witches home in the wood made of bright candy.

'That was my bedroom window,' she whispered. 'Look in for me, Hano. See if there's a small bed and a wooden dresser with a mirror and a cracked basin for water. There should be red roses on the far wall and chinamen and bridges on the left one where dada ran out of paper. See if it's the same, Hano, see.'

Katie backed away as he peered in. The floorboards had been polished and two sheepskin rugs put down. The walls were painted to match the cubist prints hung on them. Speakers from a hi-fi were mounted in each corner. The deck rested in a glass cabinet with a video on top. The chairs were of tubular steel with leather seats. He called back to her and she cupped her hands to peer through the glass.

'We had the loan of a black-and-white television once,' she said, 'and dada and Tomas wouldn't watch it without covering the screen with the yellow cellophane from a bottle of Luco-zade to protect them from the rays.'

95

The fitted kitchen had a microwave, a dishwasher and a tumble-drier. Above the electric cooker two posters hung in German. There was a concrete bunker behind the house. The locked iron doors led down into the earth.

'The first sign of trouble and they'll fly in here from Munich or Bonn,' Hano said, trying the handle. 'Close the doors, let the big boys get on with it and the locals burn. I never saw one before Katie, except in pictures. Must be somebody's bolt-hole, holiday cottage in the sticks. It's nobody's home.'

'It was mine once.'

'It could be again,' he said, looking out over the black mountainside. 'There's probably enough food here to last a war. I'm staying for as long as it's safe.'

He paused, trying to keep his voice steady.

'Stay with me Katie, for a while at least.'

They were silent, suddenly awkward like strangers at a dance. Then she reached down and found a rock.

'What the fuck are you waiting for?' she asked gruffly.

He took the stone, smashed the glass in the small window, opened it and reached his hand down. There was a lock on the latch of the main window. He fumbled till his fingers were sore.

'Lift me up,' she said.

'You'll never fit.'

'Just do it.'

He held her legs and watched as she smashed the rest of the glass, then manoeuvred her body through the narrow frame. Her hands reached down to the sink and she tumbled backwards out of his sight. He called her name and, when she didn't reply, started banging on the glass anxiously until she called him from the door at the side.

'Hano! We're in. We're home.'

He walked towards her, blinded for a moment by the light flooding the doorway, highlighting her body as she flicked the switch.

The bedroom had two long shelves of German books. The few in English were computer manuals. Hano laid the soup bowl on the floor and searched in the drawers for socks and a shirt. Wooden blinds covered the window. Katie stared through them across the darkness of the hillside. He leaned back on the bed, knowing if he closed his eyes for a moment sleep would come.

'Do you think they're still here, Hano? Still trapped?'

'Your parents?' He thought for a moment. 'If they are they must be very lost by now.'

'This was my favourite spot,' she said, 'Their window . . . Felt important to be allowed here. If they were both out I'd stand here, watching for their return. This is where I stood that night, Hano. Eoghan Davitt from across the hill had loaned them his car. I doubt if my father drove more than twice a year.'

She paused, her fingers a few inches from the window pane as if fingering an invisible lace curtain.

'Cancer. It's strange, couldn't say the word for years. She was wasting before my eyes and, you know, I'd no idea why. "Mammy, why are your arms so thin? Mammy, why are you lying down in the afternoon?" Maybe they knew, Hano. Maybe the doctor in the hospital had told them how long she had. You know, my father never spoke much, just worked all his life. Met Tomas before dawn, walked to whatever farmer would have them. We had gas lamps, Hano, one tap, a covered bucket for a toilet. I'd see him briefly at nine or ten at night.'

He watched Katie run her fingers along the blinds. They swayed, knocking against the sill with a wooden thud. Light came from a red lamp in the hallway. Pale slats of moonlight criss-crossed her face. One moment he could see her eyes, the next they had slipped into darkness.

'I ran home from school and waited here as they'd told me. At the window, holding the lace curtain back. What was dada thinking Hano? That's what haunts me. Him and me alone in this house, winter nights walking home to a cold bed. There were women's things we could never have spoken of, you know what I mean? Was she crying, Hano, as they drove? Was she thinking of me standing at the window? Some nights in dreams I see his face, staring at the road ahead, at the bend with the ramp and the bog far below. All he had to do was keep his hands steady, keep staring.

'I stood here till it got dark, till I saw the lights of the police car bumping down the track and Tomas crossing the hill, running down, caught in the revolving blue light.

'I've never told a sinner Hano, but when I turned she was there in the doorway. Like I remembered her once. Smiling. She'd her arms outstretched. You know, her flesh, it was luminous, like the statue of the Virgin somebody brought her from Lourdes. She opened her mouth, gazing straight at me. "Look little Cait," she said, her voice full of wonder. "My arms are no longer thin."'

Katie was walking towards him with her arms stretched out. He was too terrified to look towards the door.

'I used to pray Hano. Out here in the woods, waiting for Our Lady to appear like in the film they took me to. And when I prayed long enough it was like everything was white, behind my eyes, all whiteness.

'When my uncle stole me I prayed, Hano. I knelt on the lino and prayed and prayed. The whiteness never came. They said I was mad, you know, my cousin's friends up in Dublin, laughing at me, jeering my accent. Couldn't pray anymore, couldn't get white by being good. Like God had left me on those buckled streets, the grey houses, the grey shagging gardens. They said I was backward, teachers in the school, couldn't figure my accent whenever I tried to talk, so I shut up. But I got back to whiteness, Hano. Took glue, took cider, took every fucking pill I could lay my hands on, but I closed my eyes and I got there.'

She had stopped a few feet from the edge of the bed, her voice like the hissed intonation of a prayer. Her face was in shadow. He felt scared; sensing her pent-up energy about to explode.

'I cursed this place Hano, tried to rid myself of it. Tomas's eyes, my mother's hands. One time, there was this old man in Dublin. We tricked him, led him on so we could rob his house. You know, I looked at his jowls, big awkward hands trembling and Tomas's eyes came back. But I didn't feel any shame. No, I wished he was Tomas, I wanted to desecrate every fucking memory still haunting me. I wanted to say, "You see me Tomas? Where's your world now; where did it fucking bring me?"'

In the half-light she had slowly begun to undress. She turned her face towards the doorway, moisture glistening on her cheek like a snail's trail. Hano tried to stop her but she pushed him away.

'So what do you say now Tomas, eh? I don't believe in ghosts, not yours, not theirs. Don't want yous. Do you fucking see? You deserted me, left me alone. Oh Jesus, Hano, hold me, I'm cold, so cold.'

He put his arms around her. Her back was cool like ivory, warm like fever. He buried his head in her hair, brought her down beside him on the mattress edge.

'You got anything Hano, a rubber?'

'We don't have to do it.'

'I know. I want to.'

She pulled the quilt over her and watched as he searched in his wallet for the small packet. He undressed in silence with his back to her and swung the door half-shut so only a thin strip of light came through. He walked towards the bed and she pulled the cover back.

'Hano?'

She paused, wanting him to understand.

'Hano?'

When their tongues met he thought of Shay, saw him standing some evening grinning from a doorway. Her kiss tasted green and glistening like sap in a bud, his head shifting as their tongues twisted. Her small breasts were beneath him, her slender limbs turning. He felt himself stiffen as tentative fingers brushed against him. He reached his hand over to the bedside table, tore at the packet and drew the condom out. He twisted to his side to pull it on, turned back to her, closed his eyes and stopped. The face was no longer Shay's. He jerked away.

'Can't do it, Katie. Jesus I can't. His face, Jesus, breath stinking of whiskey. Oh Jesus, Katie, oh God.'

She pulled him down, kissed him urgently, ran her fingers along his back. He had slackened, felt the rubber hang loosely against his leg.

'Fuck them, Hano, we'll fuck them to hell together.'

Her tongue burrowed deep within him, suffocating every

memory, leaving him choking for air, swamped with heat. When he entered her she bit his hand to stop from screaming. It was only afterwards, when he lay curled against her, that he noticed her blood on the sheet along with his.

# CHAPTER THREE

## *Tuesday*

Against the window a small branch was tapping irregularly in the light breeze. Sleep should have come, Hano's limbs were straining in tiredness as though strapped to the bed. Even to turn on his side seemed an impossible task. Yet his eyes remained open and he knew Katie's were open too, close to his head, staring up at her parents' ceiling split into thin slats of light and shade by the long drift of moonlight through the blinds.

'I wanted Shay to be the first,' she whispered. 'Every lad I met tried it on with me at some stage. Mono, Git, even two of Justin Plunkett's men. You'd know it would always come down to that at some stage in the factory or a stolen car. But I wouldn't do it, though I'd let them pretend I had if they wanted. Anything else, but not that. I was keeping it for somebody I thought would never come along. Used to wonder what it felt like. It wasn't pain I was afraid of, or God, none of that shite. It was just mine, the only thing really mine since I left here. I'd stripped away all the nonsense they'd taught me, I was a hardened woman but, Hano, I couldn't shake the notion there was somebody among those streets who could change things.

'Then, after that old man in his kitchen, I felt so dirty inside, I didn't want to find him. It didn't feel like me, I just woke up with an empty pain and found the pill to fill it. You know, I'd stopped feeling Hano; it was better that way.

'And then, one afternoon by the carriageway, there he was. I'd seen him a year before when I was one of those girls babbling in a uniform as he waved a kettle from the window over the bookies. You know, in class we'd giggle about what happened up those wooden stairs. He vanished then and when

101

I saw him again we were both like different people, survivors of something, I don't know fucking what.'

Hano wanted to reach beneath the covers to take her hand but he knew he was not a part of this story. He listened to her describing the afternoons sitting alone by the carriageway, feeling the lorries' slip-streams blow against her face. She always saw Shay crossing the metal bridge after lunch in that stillness when the women had finished their shopping, the kids were not yet out of school and only a few old men shuffled down to the bookies. Shay would stop sometimes to nod down at her, both staring at each other between the passing trucks.

'He appeared behind me one afternoon,' Katie said, 'and asked who I was waiting for. I looked up and said I was waiting for a juggernaut to take me out of that kip. I saw him grinning and he started telling me that the Juggernauts were idols of Krishna carried around in big cars that disciples flung themselves under. Then he told me there were fuck-all Hindus in Meath and I'd have more chance of a coffee. I thought he was taking the piss till he showed it to me in a dictionary.'

That first afternoon Katie went with him without thinking. She kept trying to stay cool but he was like a slow flame drawing her reluctantly out of her dead world. Hano listened, remembering a year and a half before, how alive he had felt the first night in Murtagh's.

'I knew at once Shay was the man I wanted. Figured nothing more would come of it, be just one afternoon like dozens for him. But I wanted that one moment of life to happen. But after an hour in your flat I didn't know if Shay was bent or something was wrong with me or what. We smoked, played music, talked. I knew why he'd asked me and he knew I knew . . . the same reason any man ever asked me anywhere. There was no bullshit, you know what I mean? And I kept waiting for him to move but, like, each time he seemed about to, he'd check himself. Then at six o'clock you arrived and I thought, *Fuck this, a pair of queers; what am I doing here?*

'I wanted to forget him, Hano, but next afternoon I went back, hating myself for knocking. And, you know, Shay didn't turn me away. He made me tell him things, about the girls and the factory or my uncle's house, just listening till I found myself talking like I'd never done before, things I'd made myself forget – my parents, this house we're lying in. I couldn't believe it.'

Those afternoons became her life. She went there to remember. The grey world stopped outside his flat, kept out by coffee and music, the smell of dope and by Shay. She realized there was nothing but a strange bond of friendship between Shay and him, and guessed from their talk how many women had passed through Shay's room.

'I was frightened he'd grow bored with me,' Katie whispered. 'Felt like a child plaguing him. I mean, if he'd only touch me, take me, I'd feel I was giving him something. I couldn't figure it, Hano; I waited, letting him know I was available. The girls began jeering me for spending so long in your flat. They used to give odds on what position he'd last screwed me in. Once I tried to claw Carmel's eyes out when she asked what his sperm tasted like. But you know, the longer I spent in your flat, the less I saw of them. I just couldn't fit back there. They were strung out more: now it was gear, smack, stuff I didn't want to get into. I didn't want to kill each day, Hano; suddenly I wanted to live it. I didn't need speed or pills, I just needed him.'

Hano listened, closing his eyes, feeling sleep about to swamp him. One morning Katie had called after he'd left for work. Shay was still in bed. He came down to the door in his jeans and, with that same amused smile, let her in. She had lain awake till four that morning listening to her cousin sleeping beside her. Then she had dressed in the dark and gone walking the deserted streets. Hano could see the carriageway in his mind as she described the lights coming on in the dairy and the crates being stacked on the vans. She kept walking in the blue light through miles of streets and all she could think of was him.

'I was in love, Hano, you know that; suddenly I was able to feel again. I wanted him to make me clean. When I made him laugh he'd call me his little sister but I wasn't. I was a woman of sixteen, Hano, I wanted to know love. I kept thinking something must be wrong with me that he didn't want to touch me; I needed to know why.'

When Shay had gone to wash in the bathroom she entered his room, felt the sheets still warm from his body. She had planned nothing, just found herself like a little girl stripping away her clothes, removing the T-shirt and the jeans, then the socks and the bra and panties. It was cold there, she told Hano. She remembered trembling with goose pimples lining her flesh as she waited by his bed. Finally the door opened and he came in, wiping his face with a towel. He stopped when he saw her. She meant to stare him out but found herself lowering her eyes, feeling foolish, wanting to cover herself but even more wanting him to take her, to do what any man she'd known before would have done without thinking. Her teeth began to chatter and, though she didn't want to cry, huge sobs rose up in her throat. She made to run past him but he caught her, placed the towel over her shoulders and eased her down on the bed beside him. He held her against his chest, stroking her hair as she clutched him and cried on and on till there was nothing left inside.

'"What's wrong with me, Shay? What the fuck's wrong? Why don't you want me?" I kept asking.'

He had said nothing for a time, then very gently laid her back on to the mattress with her legs hanging over the edge. He knelt between them and slowly began to circle with his tongue, pausing every few moments to change direction, the tip of his tongue revolving back, causing ripples of heat through her till she was unable to keep her legs from trembling. How long he continued she didn't know. She could hear the loudspeaker in the bookies but it could have come from another planet. There was only a slow, drowsy journey towards pleasure. She tried to fight it when it came, feeling exposed by its intensity, but his arms pinned her down though she tore at his hair. Then she was there and cried out and he stopped and, exhausted, rested his head on her thighs as she lay back, drifting into a dreamless sleep.

'When I woke, Hano, the curtains were pulled so it seemed like night though the battered travelling clock beside the bed told me it was half-four. It felt funny, me lying between the sheets and him sitting, fully dressed, on a chair in the room, watching over me with that same half-smile. He left the room and came back with a cup that he placed beside the clock. I smiled and drank from it. I didn't know what the fuck to say to him. My clothes were folded at the bottom of the bed. He went out and came back with toast, smiled again, left and didn't return.

'After a while I dressed and went out. It was weird emerging into daylight after his room. And, you know, he never mentioned it, Hano. Like it had never happened. I wanted to get out of there before you came home. It was only at the door that he put his hand on my shoulder and said, "There's nothing wrong with you, Katie, and never was." Just that. Then he closed the door, and when I stood on the street it seemed so unreal, I could have dreamt it, and yet all the tension was gone from my body. You know, I slept so well that night, Hano. Jesus, I'd love to sleep as well again.'

Katie was silent and at that moment it seemed to Hano there were three people in the room. Ever since his death he had been trying to say goodbye to Shay, and yet Shay seemed more alive to him now than in the months when he had wandered through Europe. She must have known he was thinking of him because her hand reached out and she said:

'You know, I never understood that man, Hano, but he didn't expect you to. He had his ghosts he never spoke of. I think he was being true to them.'

They must have both slept then, face up in that awkward position because Hano was still lying that way when the click of the switch woke him. He opened his eyes and shut them quickly again in the glare of the electric light. Eventually he managed to focus on the well-dressed, middle-aged woman watching from the doorway. He thought of Katie's mother, waiting for her to stretch her arms towards them. Then he woke fully and knew before she spoke, from her carriage, her clothes and the contempt on her face, that she was foreign. He still had Katie's hand in his. He tugged at it, trying to wake her. She mumbled sleepily and shrugged his hand away, curling over on to her side. The woman stared as he shook her again.

'Sleep . . . Hano . . . tired now,' Katie muttered, but when the pressure on her shoulder continued she woke and with a start pulled the blanket up to her neck as she saw the intruder. In the silence Hano tried out a tentative smile. The woman's eyes narrowed as she began to scream.

'*Dreckige Irische!* Gypsies! You filthy Irish worse than pigs. First you murder the old man now you want to murder me. *Los aus meinem bett!* Out of my bed! Get out of my bed!'

She grabbed an ornament from the coffee table in the hall and flung it at them. They both ducked beneath the covers as it smashed on the wall above. Then he heard Katie's voice.

'It's not your home, you stupid bitch.'

'My home you robbers, thieves!'

There was another explosion of pottery against the wall. Hano regretted the abandon with which he had undressed. He held a sheet around his waist as he climbed from the bed to search the floor for his clothing, avoiding the woman who kicked out at him when he came too close. He called to Katie to get dressed but the two women ignored him as they traded abuse.

'You murdered him,' the woman screamed. 'One of your own. You burnt the roof over his head.'

'I was going to marry him. I filled his pipe for him when he let me. You never did that, you shagging old hag. Fuck off back to Germany with your bleeding microwave!'

He gathered up parts of her clothes and, pulling her from the bed, bundled them against her bare flesh.

'Get dressed Katie and let's get out of here,' he hissed, but she ignored him and stood shouting at the German. He pushed her towards the door, picking up the clothes as they fell from her arms. The woman struck out with her fist as he pushed Katie past her in the doorway.

'Back to the side of the road, you pigs!' she shouted.

Katie turned and kicked with her bare feet, screaming:

'Back into a field, you shrivelled old cow!'

Suddenly they were locked together, tugging at each other's hair. On the table Hano saw a bunch of car keys and, pulling Katie free in a headlock, he opened the door and ran towards the car. He had the passenger door open and Katie thrust into the seat before the woman realized what was happening. She raced down the path as he tried to open the driver's door.

'The button, Katie, lift up the button!' he shouted through the glass, but she had seen the woman approach and was climbing back out, shouting:

'This is my house! My house!'

Cursing her, he ran back to separate them, having to push the woman on to the ground to do so. He got Katie inside, locked the door and clambered over her into the driver's seat. But before he could start the engine the woman had climbed on to the bonnet and was banging on the windscreen. Hano gestured to her in despair and began to drive slowly in circles to dislodge her. She clung on, her face pressed against the glass inches from his head, her fists pounding, until finally he braked and, as the car jolted, watched her roll off into the darkness. He swerved to avoid her and accelerated down the track, the car bumping wildly over the uneven surface. He braced himself and called to Katie as they reached the gate but he was still thrown against the glass by the force of the collision. The gate was half-down. He reversed and this time was able to drive over the tangled remains of the bars. One of the headlights had been knocked out and they drove through the trees in semi-darkness. Katie was hunched down in the seat beside him, clothes strewn on the floor as she muttered angrily to herself. There was a fleck of blood on her cheek where the woman's nail had caught her. He put a hand out to stroke her hair and she shrugged it away.

'The old bat,' she muttered without looking at him. 'With her layers of make-up. My mother would never have allowed her inside the front door like that.'

With Shay gone the flat was too big, the rooms too empty, the evenings too long. It is hard to describe that loneliness. I was his sidekick, our old haunts had no magic without him. I found that I no longer belonged there. In Murtagh's they would ask if I had any word from him, then dry up having nothing more to say to me. Mostly I drank alone in the early evenings before the pubs got too crowded, a single man feeling conspicuous and awkward. Then I'd walk in and out of the bars, always pretending to be searching for someone. Often mates of Shay would hail me, but I'd panic and push on with a wave, unsure of myself alone with them.

There were so many nights of walking home alone, the strange melancholia of passing through back streets on a Saturday night away from the noise of laughter and glasses, prolonging the time before my lonely return. The steel shutters on the shops, the litter blown about, a steel moon reflected in a gutter filled with rain. And always keeping up the pretence of going somewhere, queuing outside phone boxes as though I had someone to ring. I hated the last bus full of couples and gangs of youths. I'd walk instead, taking the short cut home by the prison and canal, the scent of bread from the small bakery filling my nostrils as I passed.

That summer the workers had been sitting in at the closed flour mill. When their men were jailed for contempt of court, the wives and children slept in tents on the grass verge beside the offices on the canal. A lone garda car always kept watch as the women sat talking beside the bonfire. Cider drinkers had killed a young boy on the tow-path earlier in the year, stripped him and tied him to his bicycle before they pushed him into the water. It was dangerous to walk there but it was the way Shay had always come. It was my way of keeping faith with him, a gesture as futile as that of the women camping below the blind plate-glass eyes of the multinational.

All the way home I'd keep thinking a letter would have come. Surely he had written and it just hadn't arrived. I'd get in around one o'clock, convinced that there'd be something in the hall, some late post, some letter delivered by mistake to a neighbour. I knew it was crazy and hated myself for daring to believe such a thing, but every night I ran the last few yards home and cursed myself afterwards and cursed him. I rarely turned the lights on, walked in the darkness from room to room. I'd lie on his bed, trying to imagine where he was at that moment. His absence was like a phantom pain inside me. Once the phone rang at three o'clock in the morning. It's him, I thought: he knows that I'm sitting here thinking of him. It was a wrong number, a young girl looking for someone. I kept saying 'What? What?' as she tried to explain until she got frightened and hung up on me.

And then there was work, completely torturous now. I'd never bother cooking for myself. I lived from chip shops and Chinese take-aways, growing so haggard-looking that Carol began to worry about me. There was a huge kindness within her that you rarely saw when she was shouting commands and covering up for Mooney. Some lunch-times she'd grab me before I could go to the pub and serve me home-made soup from a flask with her own brown bread in the office.

Up to a decade ago, married women were not allowed to keep their jobs. I sometimes wondered what decisions she had had to make: did she lie awake some nights not wanting another dawn? But it wasn't just her work that tied her down. Carol's father had been a doctor in south Dublin, Mary once told me. He had died when Carol was eighteen, having just moved his family into a large house which had cost every penny he had. Carol was the eldest, the only one who could bring in a wage. She saw her four brothers and sisters through school, cried at their weddings, and nursed her mother through fifteen years of illness. She kept the house brightly painted the way her father would have wished, and would sit in the freezing kitchen at night, having only soup for her dinner, cycling discreetly on the old bicycle from Deansgrange in the rain. She had lived alone there for the past twelve years, nephews calling reluctantly on Saturday afternoons, her family rostering her between them at Christmas and Easter. I'd always seen her charging through the office like a flame of energy. But now she sat quiet and concerned, watching me eat with the same instinctive care she had shown for her brothers once, reassuring me over and over that she'd put a word in with Mooney to have my temporary contract renewed.

But with Shay gone Mooney could turn all his antagonism against me. From the time I signed on each morning he was watching. I'd sweat as I sensed him at my back, knowing I had to make the work in front of me stretch till five o'clock. And the girls in the office made my loneliness worse because it was like they were not addressing me but some after-image Shay had left in his place.

It was only a matter of time before the letter addressed to me was left in the attendance book. And yet, sitting among the clerks, it seemed that my life there would continue for ever: an infinite succession of dull afternoons lit by the brief joy of a cheque every second Thursday and the relief of the weekend. And when I found it there one Monday morning as the rain lashed down outside, I was still shocked. Mary came in behind me and 'touched my shoulder. We both knew what it was without opening it.

'The old bollox,' she said. 'He could have renewed that for another nine months. He's getting back at Shay through you.'

Mooney was a constant presence that morning, a smug grin on his face. I tried to remain impassive, knowing that Shay would have. I worked as slowly as possible, yawning and stretching my arms as I gazed at the clock. But they were petty gestures, he had me by the balls and we both knew it.

'He's nothing to pin on you,' Mary said, trying to console me in the pub. 'Personnel keep your name on the computer. If you're still out of work in six months, you'll probably get back in for another spell. But sure shag him anyway. Why don't you just take off? Find Shay if you can. There's fuck all for you here. I wish to God I had before I had a child. You'd get work in a factory easy enough in Germany. You couldn't be any worse off than you are here.'

I considered it during the two weeks I worked out my notice. But would I ever meet up with Shay? How many thousands of Irish men and women were moving like a retreating army across those frontiers? If Shay had written now I would have gone to join him at once. But I was frightened of making the journey alone, scared of losing the small hold I had on life here. I still clung to the hope that one day he'd return to the flat and it would all begin again.

But during that fortnight I changed my mind. I joined the huge queues in town at the passport office and sought out the house where Shay had been reared to sit drinking tea with his parents. They too had no address for him. One night they'd received a phone call from Munich and later a card with a postmark from Hamburg. Apart from that there had been silence. I promised myself nothing, just paid over my money and waited for the passport to arrive.

Most weeks somebody would be celebrating a birthday or being transferred to another office. After work on Thursday the clerks would gather in the local pub and the hard core would remain on until closing time. I seemed to be expected to fill his shoes and most Thursdays I played along, aping Shay's jokes and imitations, trying to keep the evening afloat and vibrant as he had once done. And towards closing time the talk always returned to him: the Christmas when he had kicked down the canteen door; the morning he'd pretended to Carol that anal intercourse was a clue in the crossword; the day he put the live chicken in the cramped space between the new tiles and the old ceiling. I'd drink on, warm and united in the comradeship of the group, till we spilt out on to the midnight streets, singing as we made our way back to some girl's cramped bedsit.

But always the fun was jolted out of the night by the interruption of the journey. We'd sit on the floor around an electric fire, opening six-packs and trying to get back into the happy ambience of the pub. But slowly the conversation froze back into the endless dissection of work and promotion, character assassination and grudges. Some nights a girl might happen into my arms, more often I would drain my last bottle and slip out, glad now to avoid a night spent with eight others on a square of carpet, and the collective straggle into work next morning.

The final Thursday night came when it was my turn to receive the card with the kisses and good wishes. At two in the morning I left the bedsit we had adjourned to and walked back through the Phoenix Park. It could be dangerous at that hour when furtive men sought each other. Often their footsteps would follow yours, you'd glance over your shoulder to see their eyes, both menacing and menaced.

I got a taxi at the North Circular Road gate, paid him off at the top of the carriageway and walked through what was left of the old village. Up the steps of the ancient graveyard the Neather Cross stood, indistinct in the shadows. I slipped through the laneway beside it and had reached the front door when a slight figure stepped from the shadows. For a moment I thought Shay had returned. I moved forward quickly and found Colm, my younger brother, with his anorak hood pulled up over his head. He was shivering. I think he'd been standing there for hours.

'It's da,' he said. 'You've got to come, Francy. They've taken him into hospital.'

I walked beside him, across the metal bridge, through the streets I had played in as a child. There was a sick feeling in my stomach as though life was starting to slip away from me. My mother sat at the table in the kitchen. She had been crying. Sean, who was twelve, sat awkwardly on one of the chairs, not knowing how to console her. I sent both boys to bed, took her hands in mine, and let her tell me in her own time.

'He used to complain now and then about a pain,' she said. 'But sure he hadn't mentioned it for months. Only that I walked into the bathroom while he was washing ... God knows if he'd have ever done anything. Like a little ball it was, all raw.'

She paused. I lit a cigarette and placed it between her fingers for her.

'He was afraid to go near a doctor, son, kept thinking it would go away if he ignored it. You know how Pascal Plunkett is about sick days. Took me hours to persuade him to go down to O'Rourke in the village. He sent him straight home for his clothes.'

She looked fiercely at me.

'He'll be okay son, won't he? He's an awful man, an awful man.'

I felt numb as I lied for her sake, eventually reassuring her enough to get her to go upstairs and lie down. I came back down and walked out into the garden. It was overgrown again after that summer. I should have known all along what was wrong, but I'd fooled myself just like he'd been trying to do. It would have had to be more than tiredness; my father was too much a country man to let that garden go wild. I would like to think I felt sorry for him and for her. Later on I did, but that night all I felt was the sense of being trapped. Then, when it was suddenly too late, my heart yearned for those autobahns that Shay had spoken of.

My mother had loaned my bed to a neighbour. I knew she would never ask her for it back. I closed the door and spent the night on the sitting-room sofa.

Next day at work I felt like a ghost. Already I seemed excluded from so many conversations. Soon I would be a memory, in time just a name. Mary called me out and asked me to escort her to the bank. All the way down past the prison wall the autumn leaves were piled up in multicoloured drifts, a low sun slanting into our eyes. On that walk we never mentioned leaving, we just shuffled along through the banks of leaves like schoolchildren on the mitch, and when she grabbed a pile and flung them at me I filled my arms with leaves and threw them back. We chased each other in and out of the trees, stems clinging to our hair and clothes.

I think I loved her that day as we lingered outside in the warm air. Mary with the docker's tongue; Mary who'd slipped vodka into my mineral on my first day; Mary generous on Thursday and broke by Monday. I realized that if I was sacked, she was sentenced to be left behind.

People were expecting me to join them across the road for a final drink at five o'clock but I knew this walk was my farewell. I kissed her timidly on the lips before we went back in. At ten to five I slipped on my coat and went while Carol was in Mooney's office. Most of all, for some reason, I didn't want to have to say farewell to her.

*The nights you could not sleep. Sheets damp beneath your face, a sleeping cousin's warmth against your back. Remembering. That is the first mistake: to remember, to think back. Go on, move out into the crush of bodies spilling from the car across from the petrol station. Factories sleep like well-fed adolescents, snug in the warmth of security lights. There is a hole in the wire, the gravel tearing at your fingers as you crawl through to where lines of rusting train tracks slumber in the siding. Steel scrapes against steel until a lock snaps, two cardboard boxes selected with vodka and whiskey. Then the long slide down to the canal bank and the shouts when you are out. Run, Katie, run; don't think, don't look back. Your uncle cannot catch you now no matter how you might wish him to. An estate of new houses nestles between the crossed arms of the cemetery. You break into the old part, the boxes planked down on a slab, and soon there is just the sensation of fire in your throat and that blessed numbness swirling inside your head again. One wants you to and you kiss him, then push his hands back when he starts. You slip past him and begin to run, dodging your way through the ramshackled tombstones. Your body tingles as he pounds behind you, his doc martins crunching over wreaths and stones and you look back over your shoulder, wishing this chase could just go on and on. You let him catch you by the curved railings, the shaved head bending down towards your own. And you are far away from the others now where only the dead can witness. White breasts in a graveyard lowered on to a moon-greyed tombstone '. . . who fell asleep in the year of our lord, 1831 . . .' So gentle now when he is alone but still you will not let him. Just touch him there with your fingers and soon it will be over. He will strut back to his mates, a huge, simple child of violence. Let him go, let him invent this conquest to put against each cold morning when he will wake and walk across the green, without work, without cigarettes, clenching the useless strength in his fists to prove to himself he is still alive.*

*You lie on the slab when he has gone, the shapes of yew trees swaying above you. If you could melt down into the soil without pain or thought would you ever rise? Better not to think. You lift yourself, adjust your jeans and blouse. Someone has lit a fire; it helps to guide you back. A bottle explodes within its heart, the fragments smoke-brown. Two skinheads have begun to shout curses at the dead. A sole decked with steel studs sparks against a granite slab. A line of green-gold urine splashes on a mounted photograph. A stone smashes when it falls, a name splintered into two, and everyone is kicking out now against the sculpted inscriptions over bones that lie, even more futile than them, bereft of flesh or habit, mutely in the soil.*

\*

The hospital was due for closure. But being run-down made it seem more human. My father had never missed a day sick in his life. His illness was like a vice not to be spoken of. On the first evening I told him I'd move home till he was well again. He nodded apologetically, then leaned forward in confidence, his voice seeming to lose strength.

'They won't tell me how long I'll be here,' he said. 'It could be weeks before I'm back and you never know with Pascal Plunkett; you can never trust him.'

'Twenty-five years, da,' I replied. 'He can hardly quibble over a few weeks now.'

He leaned back against the pillow, fretting.

'You don't know him, son. You don't know his breed.'

'Don't worry, da,' I reassured him. 'I'll hold the fort.'

'Just till I'm up,' he said. 'It won't take long.'

When my mother came nervously into the ward, I left them to be by themselves, to say in private whatever words their fears allowed them.

The clocks went back the Sunday I brought my possessions home. When I explained the situation to him, the bookie gave me back the deposit and the week's rent in advance.

'I'll miss the pair of you,' he said. 'There were some queer scents emanating from up there but you were good lads.'

The queues had grown longer in the employment exchange, the heave of bodies more desperate when the doors opened. I was shunted from hatch to hatch till all the forms were sorted out. I had grown used to having money in my pocket but suddenly every purchase had to be carefully considered. Sometimes in town I met clerks from the office who invited me to parties, but now I felt excluded from that comfortable circle.

It was an old school mate who told me about the petrol station. I walked out along the carriageway to it one afternoon. The manager showed me over the pumps, the floor safe for the money, and gave me three night-time shifts starting at the end of the week. When he told me the wages I knew why it was black. Even if I was doing sixty hours there it would have been hard to survive. The next Wednesday morning I put the thin wad of notes in my back pocket and stayed up walking around town till it was time to draw the labour.

My father came home after four weeks, having finished the course of treatment. All he said was that it was like his insides were burnt out. He felt the cold more now that it was harder to walk, and cursed the fact it might be another month before he returned to work.

Christmas came, and he spent the morning in bed. My mother fussed, getting a fire going in the sitting-room for him. She rearranged one of the cards more predominantly on the mantelpiece.

'Every year the same,' she said. 'Patrick Plunkett never forgets us.'

I told her the handwriting was done by a machine. Patrick Plunkett probably never even saw them.

'Don't you be always running that family down,' she whispered sharply. 'How could he do everything by hand and he a minister in the government?'

'Junior minister,' I said.

'Hasn't he the car?' she pointed out, as if to a child. 'He never forgets us.'

She stopped speaking as we heard my father's footsteps slowly descend the stairs. After dinner he fell asleep before the television like an old man. I had bought my two sisters skateboards and could hear them practising on the pavement outside. My mother came in with a blanket and placed it over his legs, and we sat on either side of him, neither of us speaking as his breath became laboured. Whenever I looked at her, she lowered her eyes. I sat there till he woke, pretending to be absorbed in the television programme.

Did he know all along? That's the question which haunted me every morning I went in to see him shrunken more into himself in the bed. Was he pretending he might get better for our sake or had he somehow anaesthetized himself from reality?

I still don't know. There was an unreality about his plans for when he had recovered. Not only did he intend to continue things he had been doing prior to getting sick, but now he spoke of taking on larger projects that he had never mentioned before. The whole back garden was to be redug and potato beds laid again; a back kitchen was to be added to the house;

116

a holiday home beside the old farm in Kerry was to be purchased — even though every penny the family had was slowly wasting away, like his diseased liver. Yet no matter how farcical his plans, his eyes always blazed into mine as he spoke, with complete conviction.

I had always disliked that bedroom which the sun never entered until late in the evening, filled with the noise of children and dogs from the neighbouring gardens, but now I dreaded entering it as though stepping into a crypt. If the day was warm my mother would light a fire in the dining-room and I would help him slowly down the stairs, one step at a time, his body smelling of the room where he had lain. He would sit by the fire and answer the same three or four questions she always asked him. Near the end his answers grew blurred and frequently out of sequence. But if either noticed, neither of them said so.

And what of my mother? Did she know she was soon to be a widow? To see the father I had loved and grown apart from waste away was a torture, but never to be able to speak of it was worse. Sometimes when the children were at school and she went into the kitchen after turning the television on loudly, so that he and I were both forced to watch the idiotic movements of cartoon figures on the screen, I would wonder — as the eldest son, as the heir — was it my duty to speak, to break the torpor the house seemed to languish in? Yet even I was terrified to say the words that would finally take away the possibility of hope.

I felt the need to question him about all sorts of half-understood memories, pieces of my own childhood; and further back to his own school-days which ended at fourteen, the names of great uncles and grandparents, the history of fields and rocks that I remembered from my one visit to the farm. I no longer wanted to see him just as a parent, but to imagine him at my own age out on a hillside some dark night, or taking the boat to Liverpool during the war, the ammunitions factories; the money orders sent to his new wife serving as a maid in a house in Rathgar, the weekends home when they had taken the single-decker bus out to that place I called home — a warren of green fields then with its tiny village — and walked

117

through the whitethorn blossoms along laneways to the field where white crosses marked the outline of the first houses to be built.

We had not spoken like this since the quarrel over the old woman had driven us apart like the breaking of some invisible taboo. Our lives since then had been like two dialects of a lost tongue growing ever more incomprehensible to each other.

It was during his third stay in hospital for radiation treatment that my mother asked me to go with her to Pascal Plunkett for the first loan. I had just returned from working in the petrol station.

'Who else have I to turn to?' she asked.

I sat facing her at the kitchen table.

'That bollox,' I said. It was the first time I ever cursed in her presence. I could see how upset she was by it.

'He's your daddy's employer,' she told me. 'The money for the food you ate as a child came from him. Don't think you can start calling him names just because you're bringing a few shillings in. Pascal's a hard man, but he gave your daddy work when nobody else in this country could. Before him it was money-orders coming home from England. He kept this family together; we'd have had to sell this house in the early days and move over there if it wasn't for him.'

I apologized awkwardly.

'Then you'll come down with me so?' she said, hopefully. 'For Sean's sake. For Lisa's.'

In the garage below Plunkett's office each of the mechanics came over to ask about him. They had already had two whip-rounds and sent the money up. Plunkett appeared on the stairs and beckoned her. He eyed me for a moment before I turned away and walked out among the new cars in the forecourt. Eddie the foreman came over. He knew, like everybody else, why she was there. It was a relief to be able to talk openly to another person.

'How's the da, son?'

'Fucked.'

'Does he know it?'

I shrugged my shoulders. He shook his head and smiled as though I had made a grim joke.

118

'Tell him I'll be over soon.'

My mother called me and I went back in. Plunkett was standing beside her at the foot of the stairs. Eddie walked beside me towards them.

'That bastard takes a pound of flesh every time,' he said. 'You know that?'

I nodded as he slipped away into the garage.

'Shake hands with your daddy's boss, Francy,' my mother said, as though addressing a child.

I nodded to Plunkett. His palm was sweaty as he gripped my fingers hard and seemed reluctant to let them go. Perhaps he was too used to keeping everything that came into it.

'He was very understanding,' my mother said as we crossed over the carriageway. 'Two hundred pounds just like that.'

'At what per cent?' I asked.

She looked hurt as though I had insulted a close relative.

'He's a generous man, Mr Plunkett,' she said. 'I'm sure many people take advantage of him. And he's given me more hours cleaning in the undertaker's. From six to eight each evening. You'll keep an eye on the little ones won't you? Anyway, when your daddy's back at work we'll pay this off without blinking.'

The newspaper man outside the supermarket was packing up the unsold copies, while the tea in the plastic top of his flask cooled on the pavement. I had turned to enter the glass doors when she stopped me.

'You couldn't expect him to have that much cash on him on a Friday morning? No, he gave me a note for Plunkett Stores. I can buy what I like there and use the rest as credit whenever I come down again.'

Plunkett Stores was a quarter the size of the supermarket, the prices a good 15 per cent dearer. I wheeled the trolley for her while she chose each item carefully to sustain a family of five children for the week ahead. The cashier rang a small buzzer when she handed her the note, and after a moment a man my own age in a suit came down from the office, looked over the note and initialled it. We put the groceries into plastic bags and he held the door open for us. My mother thanked him repeatedly as she left. He smirked condescendingly at me above her stooped back, then let the glass door swing shut.

After ten more days my father was sent home from hospital. I arrived in from work and my mother came rushing down the hallway. She looked almost youthful, her face radiant.

'He's home again,' she whispered. 'Last night in an ambulance after you left for work. Daddy's home.'

'But the next course of treatment,' I said. 'Why . . .?'

'The doctors say he's got a touch of pneumonia. It's too dangerous to continue the treatment till he's better. So he's home.'

She paused while the joy left her voice and doubt replaced it.

'Is that good news or bad news?' she asked.

'That's good, ma,' I lied. 'The best.'

His lungs were burning after the first half of the treatment but he was so delighted to be home that he rarely complained of the pain. Even in those ten days he had grown more sluggish. The old man who relieved me at half-six in the morning in the petrol station shook his head when I told him.

'That's it son,' he said. 'It's reached the stage where there's nothing more they can do for him now. Any excuse to get him home for a while with the demand for beds. It will be faster now. I saw it all with the missis.'

'What do I do now?' I asked him.

'You wait,' he replied.

'Do they know?' I asked.

He looked at me as he took the keys from my hands.

'What do you think?'

Whatever the doctors had told him in the hospital he had twisted round into a message of hope. His story had changed now. There would be no full recovery. He would just have to live with the fact he had this and maybe once a year for the rest of his life he would have to go back for treatment. And yet he must have known the truth because early on that first week I arrived home to find paint and brushes in the hall. I painted the front door and the windows as I was asked, while my mother knelt inside, shampooing the carpet in the sitting-room that was still used only for visitors.

They were preparing themselves for the invasion which soon began: the uncles and aunts arriving from Kerry and

Donegal; the bottles of Guinness and the ham sandwiches; the talk of events forty and fifty years past. Sometimes he would begin to nod in the chair, the untouched glass of Guinness he could not drink, but which was still poured for him, going flat on the arm of the chair. The room would go uncomfortably silent, the relations awkward, before he jerked back awake to ask the same question he had asked five minutes earlier. The room would breathe again as the same answer was eagerly delivered.

'You will be down for the Christmas, won't you? We'll have a few glasses in Farrell's,' they'd say as they shook his hand, and his eyes would turn bright at the thought.

'Will we? Do you think?' he'd ask with a sense of wonder in his voice, and they'd laugh.

'Sure we'll order them on the way back,' his brother would say, 'and what with the good weather coming in, you won't feel the time flying.'

They were good people. I wished that they were mine but they were not. Whatever world they and my father came from had died among the rows of new streets built here, and I was cut off from that past as surely as if ten generations stood between us. I know they cried silently, driving out through the long darkness of the Irish countryside, leaving behind their brother to die in this alien world.

The petrol station was owned by one of the largest firms in Europe. Those of us who worked nights paid no tax, no insurance. Those who demanded such things were easily got rid of. There was no shortage of workers. From half-eleven to half-two was the busy time. Often the four pumps would be engaged at the same time while a queue of local people who had climbed the hill for milk and biscuits were pressing their money into the two-way hatch. Drivers had to pay in advance, but there was always the danger that if you were distracted they would keep pumping after their limit if you didn't cut them off. Then, from half-two on the weekday nights there was almost no business. I would cradle my head in my arms, sitting on that stool among the humming cables, or watch the video screen switch between the six cameras positioned around the station. Sometimes, if business was very quiet a taxi driver would come in at three or four to have his car washed.

121

Always there was the danger of robbery. Some weeks before I joined, two youths had arrived with an empty can, paid two pounds to have it filled and then poured it into the hatch. They held a lighted match in the air above it and asked politely for cash. Often by five o'clock I would not have seen a person for over an hour. Dawn would begin to break over the tombstones in the cemetery across the carriageway and I'd think of him, lying awake in pain in that bedroom, while she slept or lay awake holding his hand, praying to her litany of saints, believing like a child that their names alone could shield him from harm. Then the old man would come. I'd unlock the door to let him in and stand out in the yellow light of the courtyard, breathing in the fresh air before climbing the carriageway, up by the stream and the dairy, to the village.

'It's like time standing still back there,' I said to the old man one morning. 'Nobody willing to talk about it, nobody wanting to face the truth.'

'Death isn't something you believe in,' he told me. 'Up to the very last, deep down you think it won't get you. I could see it with the missis. We both knew and yet . . . it was like we were each waiting for something, the cavalry on the hill I suppose. It made no sense, we hated ourselves for it, but we clung to that . . . right up to the last few hours.'

He gave a short laugh like an exhaling of breath.

'Then there was nowhere to hide,' he said. 'I don't think we said anything; I don't suppose there was anything to say. All the words – we'd said them too often, elsewhere. We're all scared of it, son, and we're right to be.'

I looked at the cigarette I was smoking and stubbed it out beneath my heel. The old man was gazing across at the cemetery.

'It's like a train,' he said, 'and sometimes when I wake at night I can hear it coming.'

My mother would have risen, despite my protests, to have a breakfast ready for me and, when the children had left for school, I'd climb into the lower bunk of the bed in my old room with the sheets still warm from the body of my younger brother, having arranged a blanket clumsily over the curtained window.

I gave all my wages and dole to her except ten pounds, but twice more during his final illness I made the journey with her to Plunkett Motors, shook that sweaty hand and endured the stare which seemed to say: *Soon I will own you too.* Once the Junior Minister himself was there. He stood sympathizing with my mother in the forecourt for five minutes. Eddie came over and put his hand on my shoulder.

'There's a man on the horns of a dilemma,' he joked grimly. 'Your da gave him number one in every election. He's wondering now whether to hang on or bring the government down before he snuffs it.'

'Just because my old man dies it doesn't mean his vote can't live on,' I said, watching my mother fawning over him. 'I'm sure they'll see to that.'

'There's this story,' Eddie said. 'Before the last election, Plunkett and two of his election workers are up in the cemetery at midnight registering people for the vote. Patrick's writing down this yellow fellow's name he's after coming across who used to own the Chinese take-away up there in the village. "Ah Jasus Patrick," says one of the workers, "he's not even Irish." Plunkett looks up indignant and says, 'We'll have no racism here. He's as much right to vote as anyone else in this cemetery."'

I grinned bitterly. My mother had finally let go of the minister's hand and was walking towards me.

The doctor came each morning when his surgery was over. He had been born in the village long before the estates were built. My father had been going to him for forty years. He was a gruff man, racked by illness himself. He never lied about my father's condition, neither mentioning recovery nor bringing any note of finality into the talk. Early on, when I was showing him to the door and for some reason my mother had stayed behind in the room he simply said, 'You know, of course.' I nodded and he drove off, a list of calls neatly written on the slip of cardboard in his breast pocket.

I began to stay later in the petrol station each morning. The old man was the one person I felt I could talk to. Once, I asked him what it had been like.

'The daughters came home from England,' he said. 'The son

was all set to come from America, but sure what was the point. He works in some nuclear processing plant over there. I said to him on the phone your mother's bad enough without her seeing you glow in the dark if the lights go out.

'I'd have sooner not had them around at all in the end. There was something morbid about it, sitting in a circle not knowing what to say, just waiting for it to happen. They made the missis nervous. I knew she was worrying about all the trouble she was causing: the plane tickets, people to mind the grandchildren, the expense. In the end she felt like a nuisance for still being alive. I would have preferred just the pair of us.'

He paused, remembering.

'So would she.'

A car pulled in and the old man leaned over the small microphone. His voice was distorted by a loudspeaker outside as he asked the driver to pay in advance.

'When did you move out here?' I asked him suddenly.

'Forty-eight,' he replied, taking the money in. 'The first estates. Around three years before your houses were built.'

'What was it like?'

'We were just poor,' he said, 'and wanted to be left alone to lead our own lives. We still are and still do. That's the only history I know. The rest isn't worth a wank.'

It was a time my father rarely talked of. He was always trying to get me to be part of another world, another history. Only once had he told me about borrowing a lorry off a friend, loading up everything they owned, all their hopes, heading off into the fields, into nowhere.

I remembered an Italian film I'd once seen. It was set in a town after the war where everyone was a refugee, everyone dispossessed, pushing their belongings in handcarts with their children plodding behind. In my mind that's what it was like: leaving a ruined landscape behind, leaving that country from the history books, starting afresh with nothing; building a world not out of some half-imagined ideal but from people's real lives and longings.

The old man was staring after the departing car.

'The bastard went five pence over,' he said.

When the time came the hospital could not send an ambulance for him because of the shortages. The doctor himself paid for the taxi. I helped him down the stairs. He grumbled about the bother of going in when he would probably be sent back home that evening or the next morning. His pneumonia was no better. It was too soon to resume the treatment. I was unable to speak. I helped him negotiate each step until we were out on the concrete path. A few neighbours called across gardens to him. He raised his hand weakly to them. On the street outside I paused in case he wished to look back for a final time at the house he had spent forty years working to pay for. A green expanse of fields turning slowly under concrete. He pulled at me to get him into the taxi.

'The meter's running,' he said.

Perhaps to look back would have been to admit that he was leaving for ever. She sat beside him in the back while I sat beside the driver. He kept his head turned deliberately towards the driver's neck. None of us spoke. The pretence had gone too far for us to keep the terror out of our voices.

I had begun to think of the cancer as a human thing. Like some torturer in a prison camp saying: I will not break him yet, I will give him some relief today; or else, I will turn up the pain and see how long he will last. In my mind I started to address it on those daily visits to the hospital where my father lay drugged with pain-killers. *Don't do this*, I would say, *have you no mercy? Can you not wait a while?* Or else *Now please, take him while he's sleeping. Spare him any more pain.* Sometimes he woke convinced he was back at home and only gradually realized, with intense disappointment, where he was. I questioned him now more and more about the past. Often he would stare back blankly at me as though already parts of his mind were dead. There was something I desperately needed to know now while he might still answer me, and yet I couldn't get clear what it was in my mind.

The Tuesday before he died I had been sitting there for ten minutes before he twisted suddenly in the bed. He called out, half a shout, half a mumble.

'Son!'

I leaned over him.

'Huh. What ... oh good Jesus.' His voice grew more indistinct. 'Is that you Francy?'

125

I gripped his hand.

'It's me, da,' I said.

He was silent for a moment and I thought he had drifted back to sleep.

'Is that you, Francy?' he asked suddenly again.

'I'm here, da,' I said. 'Feel my hand.'

'Yeah, I know,' he mumbled. 'I was dreaming I was home.'

'Soon, da.'

'This place, Francy?' his voice was scared. 'Will I ever get out?'

'You will, da,' I said, with sudden intense conviction. 'We've the garden to do, together, eh. When you're a bit stronger. We'll dig it again, put down potato beds, have it like it first was, eh, da. Right.'

He twisted his head away from me to stare at the ceiling. His breath came with difficulty.

'I . . . all sorts of things. Dreamt I was home. You know . . . the feel of a room. Never liked that house, son, all the years I never told your mother that. Only liked the garden cause it was long. Felt free out there. Felt . . .'

He went silent and then whispered.

'Francy?'

I had to lean over him to listen. It felt strange hearing him speak for so long after all the years of silence I had known. His voice was muffled, drugged. Even though he looked at me I still wasn't sure if he knew I was there.

'They all went,' he whispered. 'Killed me to see them go. Boston, Leeds, London. Nine in my family, one left on the farm . . . the others scattered. That's why I kept coming back, to try to keep a hold of something. Before you were born. Every year put potatoes down in the garden, got the boat, sent the money-order on Fridays, hoped to get holidays in time to harvest them. Your cousin Ned from Kerry, he went when he was eighteen. I loved that lad, used to spend hours with him out in the fields. Meself and your ma brought him to Dublin once, showed him all around. I met him when he came over to London but I could see he didn't want to know me there. When you've looked up to someone you don't want to see him in digs like your digs, doing work like your work. I kept

126

thinking what if it was my son . . . over in this place . . . nothing Irish about him. That's when I came home for good, went to work for that bastard Plunkett. Then we had you . . . Early sixties, seemed so different then, like the lives of you and Sean and Colm and the girls would be able to stay . . . in your own place. Seemed like I was building something . . . for you. I don't feel good son . . . like I want to sleep for ever, but can't with the pain.'

'That's just the treatment, da,' I said. 'You'll see. We've the garden to do. Like we promised. You and me . . . together, da. I swear.'

He turned his eyes towards me with difficulty.

'You wouldn't lie to me, son.'

'I've started it,' I said desperately. 'Sean is helping me in the evenings. We'll have it dug and all, ready for you to start the sowing when the treatment's over. Used your old spade and the new rake you bought the year before last.'

He stared up at me. His voice was flat, emotionless.

'That spade broke, son. Lisa was playing with it, when you were away living in your flat.'

His eyes turned back to stare blindly up.

When I arrived on the last evening I knew by his breathing and his face, stretched as though the bones were straining to break through, that this was the end. My mother was due in an hour after she had finished cleaning in Plunkett Undertakers. I phoned there and asked for her. There was no phone in our house and I had never spoken to her on one before. Her voice sounded so different, so scared at being called to it, that I could hardly speak. I just told her to come at once and bring the children. Then I went back. He was still asleep but woke after a time. He called my name when he saw me and began to mutter something but found it too much effort to continue. He was very weak but relaxed, obviously the drugs had done their work and he was in no pain.

Once we had been so close. I remembered the long garden being dug, him working between the rucks of potato beds while I sat on the ridge, proud to be allowed up so late to watch him. I would gather the weeds he pulled and bring them over to the unlit bonfire in the corner. And then when it was almost completely dark he would send me up for the can of paraffin. I would hold the handle while he unscrewed the lid and poured the liquid over the weeds and shreds of clipped hedge, and I'd hold his hand thrilled as we watched it burn together. I think he always wanted it dark for that moment, to banish the city with its terraces of houses, and just have himself and his son standing among the grass and trees in the hypnotic light which seemed to close us in and cut us off from everything.

Then in adolescence the world beyond the garden and that terrace had begun to claim me and I was lost to him. Once it was his stories that had fascinated me, now it was music, clothes, films he could not comprehend. He would stand in my bedroom examining a record sleeve, his face troubled and then angry. For years we had hardly spoken and now I wanted all those stories back, wanted all the years that were lost to me.

We were both strangely at peace for that half hour we spent alone while he drifted in and out of consciousness. Once he woke and looked not at me but beyond my shoulder. His eyes grew blue and for an instant vivid with recognition. I cannot swear what I heard but it seemed that he whispered the names of his parents. Then his eyes faded again but his face relaxed into a smile. I did not question him and he did not speak.

It was only when my family arrived that the horror began. While I had been there alone it was possible for us both to pretend that it was just one more visit. Now as the curtains were pulled and chairs arranged around the bed there was nowhere left for that unmentionable fear to hide. My mother tried to say a few words to him but was unable to continue. She sat stiffly, her fingers clasping the handles of her bag as though they were rosary beads. My two younger sisters fidgeted, both bewildered and frightened by the silence, still with no real idea of what was happening. One clutched an exercise book in her hands.

He began to pluck at the sheets, desperate now to rise from the bed. His eyes were pleading with me and when I lowered my face I could hear his hoarse whisper: *I know I'm dying son and I don't want to*. At that moment he was a man of the country; he knew that hospital beds were for death. All he wanted was to be up, to be out in the air for one last time. I could see him visibly fighting to hold on. He stopped trying to speak after a time and just stared back at us as though defying death to take him. My sisters had stopped twisting. The word death had become flesh in their nine- and ten-year-old vocabularies. They held each other's hands, both crying silently. His brother arrived from the far side of the city and I let him in to take my chair. My father recognized him. When he tried to say his name it was more like a gasp for breath. I could see him trying to tell his brother something, trying to pronounce their parent's names. I knew by my uncle's face that he could not understand him.

Then I had to leave. I couldn't bear to be a part of that vigil any more. I walked out into the corridor and down the steps to the courtyard. I found a cigarette and lit it. How often had I walked out into the night air? Felt it blow about me after the heat of some room? I had never realized how precious such a simple thing was before. If I had been stronger I could have pulled him from that bed, carried him down the corridor and out on to the damp grass to die beneath the clouds. Instead he was caged behind those curtains, chained to drips and meters that could not save him, and all I could do was stand and experience the cold nocturnal breeze, the lights filtering out over the loose gravel, and inhale the rough taste of tobacco. I smoked it for him, knowing by some instinct that when its light had burnt out his life would have gone. When it had burnt down I cradled the tip between my palms till the wind had blown each loose red worm of ash away. My uncle's hand was on my shoulder. It felt for a moment like my father's. Then I realized I had no recollection of him ever touching me except on those nights years before, walking up from the garden. I patted it to thank him for telling me, then walked out into the darkness of the grounds and cried.


They drove through the night without speaking. Beyond Dowra he pulled in and they dressed in silence. Katie had lost a runner and his shirt was so badly torn that he bundled it up and stuck it into a ditch. It was vital to put as many miles as possible between them and the woman by morning, yet no matter how far they drove the car it would still leave a trail to wherever it stopped. He asked Katie to lie in the back and try to sleep and, to his surprise, she did so without arguing. Hano found it hard to keep his own eyes open. He was terrified the car's other headlight would go and they would have to abandon it on a main road. Before dawn he wanted to find a bog track and if possible leave it where it might go undiscovered for days. Although there was little light yet, a white mist covered the fields they passed. He felt his tiredness lift as the light began to sketch out his surroundings. The speedometer had jammed, there were no cars on the road and he kept his foot down.

As he took a steep bend he saw the milk container parked in the centre of the road. He was about to swerve past when the light of an oncoming car blinded him. He applied the brakes and eased himself against the seat as the car skidded, very slowly it seemed in his mind, into the back of the container. He remembered thinking how remarkably calm he felt, how detached from the scene, as the container grew and grew until with a shuddering halt he was thrown against the windscreen. Falling back, he saw how the top of the bonnet had caught the rim of the lorry and prevented it from bursting through the windscreen to decapitate him.

'Katie?'

He closed his eyes, afraid to whisper her name. In reply her hand pressed against his shoulder. Neither moved until the door beside him was pulled open. A rough pair of hands lifted him from the seat and was slapping him on the back.

'A grand piece of driving, young fellow! Mighty entirely! Eased it into the back of the van like you were patting a woman's arse. Oh sorry miss, didn't see you there.'

Katie had climbed out over the seat to stand beside him. He looked at the three men who had run from the house that the truck was parked outside. Electric light came through the trees from a milking shed. One of them stood back to obscure the number plates of the vehicle. They were watching him to see if he would cause trouble. For now their own fear about the truck being illegally parked outweighed their suspicions about him being in such a car, with a torn shirt and a girl wearing one shoe.

'That's a fierce amount of damage for one wee collision,' the man blocking the number plates said. 'The oul speeding is a terrible habit.'

'Will it still go?' Hano asked.

'Ah sure why wouldn't it?' the driver of the lorry replied. ''twas hardly a touch at all. Not if you'd seen the mighty crashes we've had on this corner. Do you see that ditch over there? Three lads killed last year after a disco in Boyle. Straight over, never a chance, cut out stiff by the firemen. And a head-on collision the year before. They had to cut the woman out – were still wiping the blood off the road a week later. Yours is hardly a crash at all. Sure this is the best spot in the whole of Roscommon for the crashes. Queen Maeve's country you know?'

The man listed the accidents with pride in his voice. His two companions nodded and added case histories of their own. Hano still felt strangely calm but a delayed shaking was starting in his legs. The men pushed the car back to survey the damage. A young child with an overcoat over his pyjamas came out of the house and was sent back for water.

'The old tank is leaking,' the lorry driver said, squatting down. 'But we'll give you enough water to get to the nearest town anyway. Do you know where you are at all?'

When Hano said he didn't nobody offered him the information. The bonnet had been twisted so much that it refused to stay down and the men had to tie it with twine. They stood back now, taking in his appearance, confident there would be no trouble. He could hear them making jokes about Katie's one shoe.

'A good trick that. Stop the heifer running away,' the youngest mumbled and they laughed.

To his surprise, the engine, after coughing a few times, started. The steering pulled badly to the left but he could drive it. Katie sat in the back as he pulled away, her face pale in the light. Dawn had come and the flat, poor fields stretched out for miles around them, broken by stone walls and whin bushes. The bonnet tugged against the twine until he was frightened it would come through the glass. After a mile he stopped and threw it into a ditch that was already strewn with rubbish. His major problem now was the oil shooting up on to the windscreen. He tried to clear it with the wipers but only succeeded in blurring the whole surface. His body shook so much that it became almost impossible to drive. Everything seemed heightened, as though occurring in borrowed time. He saw a small boreen leading off into the bog and chanced turning down it. A narrow ridge of grass grew between the two brown grooves worn down by tyre tracks. The boreen wound upwards for over a mile, narrowing until it petered out near a small lake. He stopped and turned the engine off. Behind him he heard Katie crying softly. In his efforts to keep the car on the track he had blacked her from his mind. He turned to console her.

'I never liked those runners anyway. We'll buy you a pair of shoes next time.'

She sat up and tried to laugh, wiping her eyes with the sleeve of her jumper like a child. There was a half-stripped turf bank by the water's edge and when he scaled it the whole of the desolate mountainside stretched out before him, ascending gradually to a barren peak. The morning light seemed solid as crystal. He heard Katie climb out of the car from which steam was hissing angrily. There was only him and this infinite world of brown water and scraggly bushes twisted by the wind. Far off, white dots of sheep stood out like dandruff. The ridge behind hid the blue ribbon of main road. Sentinel stacks of turf were parked like motionless robots about the landscape. He had left behind the suburbs and torn headlong back into a world as alien to him as to any creature from space, all green flesh and gadgets, exploring this nightmare terrain. He felt Katie's hand against his jacket and looked down at her holding her single shoe in one hand.

'I'm sorry Hano,' she said. 'I brought you nowhere.'

'That was Shay's favourite word,' he said. 'Where he said we came from in the first place. That woman saw you with me Katie. They'll be looking out for you now as well.'

At least Katie had some right to imagine she could go back. She had known a house, parents, a neighbour who might have offered shelter. He knew it wasn't just stubbornness that had made him choose this desolation to hide in, instead of trying to reach the anonymity of England. He'd been like that boy again, hitching down roads in search of a place that didn't exist. Ever since his father's death the old myth had gnawed at him, the idea of some sort of lost homeland he could belong to. He'd stored up the handful of stories from the hospital. The day Master Brady closed the polling station at five to nine when the two big farmers, too mean to let their men off earlier, brought them down in wagons to vote for their cousin. The calf his father had dug out of a snow-drift and carried home at dawn across the fields, proud of his strength. Children stealing a saucepan to try to make toffee in the wood behind the farmhouse.

Now he remembered his cousins again, the rutted farmyard where he had felt as lost as if he had landed on the set of a film in the Russian outback. The only time he'd seemed at home was with that old woman in the caravan, but it hadn't been the forest or the village that had claimed him, but the woman herself, who was more an outsider than he was even now. Would he ever feel that warm again? He closed his eyes and saw metal bars, a concrete corridor, steel stairs rising to a set of doors.

Two birds were circling high over the bog, even their names unknown to Hano. He was no prodigal returning home. A fugitive with a few pounds left and a girl with one shoe, an intruder in a landscape he could never call his own. How could he be sure that the police were not closing in even now? How long before a helicopter circled this shelterless hillside? Katie was silent beside him. He wondered whether she was thinking the same thoughts as him.

How deep was that small lake – more a turlough really, filled with water in autumn and winter, a dry hollow in summer – and would the car restart for him? If he asked her to climb back in and wind the windows down, would she do so without questioning? As water poured through the window and he tugged frantically at his belt, wanting that last chance now it was too late, would she sit serenely beside him, her eyes closed, the water rippling over her face, the twin trail of

133

bubbles up to the surface until both of them lay slumped together? He remembered the look on her face when he turned with the knife, half terror, half expectation. Katie shivered suddenly beside him as though guessing his thoughts and tugged at his arm.

'I don't want to die Hano. I don't want to fucking die.'

He put his arm around her and turned his back on the desolate mountain. He helped her down the bank and tried to restart the car. The water had drained out and three times he went to the lake to fill his shoes before, after choking several times, the engine caught with an unhealthy rattle. He released the brake and edged the car forward. Katie was watching him, hunched down against the turf bank as far from the car as possible. She looked ready to run in her bare feet up the incline into that wilderness. He had the driver's door open. The car was gaining speed down the slope to the lake. The water sparkled in the low sun which had begun to glitter in the east. He thought suddenly of her father, the bend before him, the child at home waiting by the window. As the front wheels splashed into the water he jumped clear and was drenched in the spray as he rolled away.

The car was floating with the bonnet down and its back wheels raised like a duck scavenging for food. It bobbed its way round to face him and, as it took in more water, began slowly to sink until, gradually, the turmoil on the lake surface subsided and the last ripples spread out to touch the shore. He watched it sink with a sick feeling, imagining himself strapped into that seat. When no trace was left he rose and walked back towards Katie. She was hunched in the same position and crouched even lower when he approached as though suddenly afraid of him. He knelt and she backed away. He held his hand out, and very tentatively she stretched hers out to take it.

'Don't know what to do Hano. Will they catch us? Will they?'

He found he couldn't lie. He nodded slowly.

'Sooner or later. If the police don't, Justin Plunkett will. Rest a few minutes here before we move on.'

He put his arm around her and they huddled together against the damp brown clay. The overhang gave them some shelter from the wind and they could see the end of the boreen clearly while being concealed themselves. Katie shivered.

'Talk Hano, just talk.'

There was a slight bulge in his jacket pocket. He felt it and found one cigarette in a crumpled packet. He struck a match, inhaled and handed it to her. She cupped her hands around the red tip as though it could give warmth. Then he told her the story of the woman with the house in the forest.

*To be without it is to be excluded from warmth. She convinces you in the subterranean light of the factory, describing the house as the two youths laugh. That evening the men will come, two to keep guard outside, one walking between the puddles on the concrete floor, his face indecipherable in the gloom. You must have money then. The snap of the locks on the briefcase is amplified by the walls. To be empty-handed when they click is to remain in the cold.*

*Once when the man was sick his boss himself came, the neat suit, the youthful face of a politician's son. You arrived late that night, pushing your way in with the notes held in your fist. He was leaving. He laughed at your haste, said the chemist's was closed for the night. Remember his hand over your shoulder as you pleaded in the dark passageway, how it lingered on your breast when he deliberately paused to see if you would pull away. And you stood there, not moving as it made its way slowly across your jumper to pluck the notes. The package placed into your hand like sweets given to a baby. And then he was gone and you walked unsteadily on to where the group huddled, sharing needles and jokes.*

*Be numb, say nothing and you will survive. You follow the youths out and through the lane to the stolen car. At your side she hums and stumbles slightly. You turn by the canal and railway tracks, cruise through red-bricked terraces till you find the house. 'The brother was laying a new carpet here last week,' the driver's voice drones on. 'He'd the drawer open and the notes almost in his hand. The old git just came up too quick, too quick.'*

*Leave your jacket in the back, creak open the gate. Above*

135

the door a plaster Infant of Prague. You knock. The old man comes slowly from the kitchen, a blurred figure in the glass. You step forward when he opens the door. Surprised, he steps back. A long dead pope is marooned in a sea of Latin on the wall; beside him a madonna hovers over a holy water font. A smell of damp penetrates your nostrils. Beside you she begins to move and you make yourself follow suit, two T-shirts peeled off to reveal the upraised teenage breasts. He startles back as though struck, his eyes seeming to magnify. You smile now and move forward till you are almost touching. His breath comes loud and unsteady, his hands tremble as they rise. They fold like a corpse's across his chest as if it were he who was exposed. You are gaining yard by yard, never speaking, staring him out. He tries but cannot lift his eyes from the. pert white breasts. You have never seen such terror before, such bewilderment, such unwanted desire. You have reached the kitchen now and still he stumbles back against a wall bedecked with icons and sepia photographs, still unable to find the will-power to lift his eyes. You stare at the veins on his hands like a living coloured flex strapped to his flesh, the jowls on his neck drooping down, the peeling texture of his forehead.

And then the first crash comes, hard against the floor-boards overhead. His eyes lift up for the first time, enveloped with horror and self-disgust. He pushes you back but as he moves the thunder of footsteps descend the stairs. You both turn to run as a youth calls in, 'You dirty old man you! You dirty old man!' They are already in the car, with the rear door flung open. They know he will never report the robbery. You dive into the seat, scrambling for your clothes. A youth snaps the elastic band on the roll of discoloured notes, throws the jewellery back over his shoulder. She picks it up beside you on the seat and says 'That locket is worthless'. The car is already speeding as it is thrown from the window. The glass breaks when it hits on concrete, cracking into a hundred pieces over the face of the dead country girl with the curling hair staring out from the cheap frame.

*

They came from Donegal, from Leeds and Liverpool, Bradford and Stoke, his brothers and sisters who only gathered together now for funerals. I was eight when I last saw them all together, and to see his brothers now, like so many distorted reincarnations of him, was a shock. We packed into Plunkett Undertakers for the rosary before the lid was placed down, but I could not bring myself to join the procession up to kiss that mouth tasting of powder and lipstick. I already had enough memories both painful and sweet, I didn't want the last one to be of a painted figure who had once been my father.

In the church the neighbours filed slowly past us. I sat in the front pew beside my mother, the man of the family now at nineteen. I kept thinking for some reason that Shay would appear, the final person up, having known somehow on his travels what had happened, understanding my pain yet piss-taking the whole ceremony in a low voice, keeping sanity alive. *Only one destination in the final taxi.* The lyrics came back from those poker sessions in his flat, not defiant now but mocking. And it was only the neighbours and the men from Plunkett Motors who trailed up, awkwardly shaking hands along the line.

Both Plunkett brothers appeared at the graveside. It was the talk of the house afterwards when the mourners came back. Very few funerals saw them together. Their presence conferred a posthumous importance on my father in people's eyes. I watched Patrick Plunkett scan the crowd with a sure professional eye, tending his flock carefully – a chosen word, a sympathetic smile. Pascal stayed at the back of the crowd, ignoring everyone as he stared transfixed through the mass of bodies towards the crater of earth. I kept praying that Justin wouldn't appear as well, that my father would not be another dummy run for the future minister. The hole had been dug by a JCB which was moving away along a mucky track between the headstones, its bucket nodding sagely.

When they had lowered the body down and covered the hole with the green awning the crowd filtered slowly away. I found myself walking beside Pascal Plunkett.

'You're just idling up in that filling station I believe,' he said.

I nodded.

'Black money, I suppose?'

'As the ace of spades.'

'You have the exams and all I'm told. Not like me and your daddy, we'd no need of them things. He was a good worker your daddy. Never missed a day, never caused trouble. No talk of unions or labour courts. No shite if you get my drift. Do you think you could be as good?'

We had reached the two hired cars that were parked near the railing of the cemetery. The chauffeur was holding the door open as my mother arranged her children inside. He stiffened respectfully as his employer approached. I hadn't replied to him.

'I've told your mother to send you down to me on Monday. I promised her nothing now, but we'll see what we can do.'

The state car was about to leave. Patrick lowered the window.

'I'll give you a lift, Pascal,' he called.

I remembered from the newspapers that Pascal had had his licence endorsed and been suspended from driving for a year. One rumour had it that he had been sacrificed, willingly or unwillingly, by his brother as a public relations stroke to show his impartiality as the Junior Minister for Justice.

He grunted at his brother, walked toward the car and climbed in beside him. My mother climbed out of the car and almost ran to catch Pascal and begin her thanks again. He disentangled his arm gently and closed over the door of the Mercedes, leaving her standing on the gravel alone before neighbours circled around her. I got her into the car and the cortège moved off for the house.

When the final visitors had gone that evening and the bottles and stale sandwiches were taken away, I took my two small sisters in turn on my knee and told them that I was their daddy now and I would look after them. They slithered away still excited after all the visitors and the pound notes passed into their palms, and went to play, jumping from the bottom of the stairs. I knew they were not willing to let each other believe what had happened yet. With my two brothers I was more awkward suddenly.

When we had got them to bed I sat my mother down and made her take out all the bills, the bank statements, the I O Us to Plunkett. She went over each item eagerly, anxious to try and forget the silence that awaited her when she closed the door of her room. It took a long time to add up everything we owed.

'Mr Plunkett gave us credit on the funeral bill,' she said. 'But sure, the only way I could have paid him would be to borrow the money off himself.'

My father had never offerred me advice about work. I have only one memory of him ever mentioning the subject. On Saturdays as a child when I used to bring him down his lunch I briefly became fascinated by the garage. One day I told Eddie it was where I wanted to work when I was grown up. I still remember my father lowering his mug of tea on to the scarred work-bench and bending down to say quietly: 'You can be anything you want, but no son of mine will ever work for a Plunkett.'

After my mother had climbed the stairs and I was alone I put my jacket on and went walking in the streets. The pubs had closed an hour before and there were few people to be seen. Occasionally I'd pass a young couple pressing themselves into the shadows of a doorway, an old man walking slowly nowhere or a young girl in bright clothes half-running in fear. Beneath the amber lights I walked for hours, past Plunkett Motors where a light shone in the watchman's office, by the church where he had lain, criss-crossing the village until finally I gave in and stood below the flat I had shared with Shay.

The bookie had still not let it. I had a key and let myself in, climbing up the stairs like a burglar afraid to put on a light. I wanted Shay back. I wanted to ask him what to do. Just months before we had drunk in that room where the moonlight now crept in over the dusty floor and it had seemed that I was free, about to enter a life of my own. Now here I was trapped, suddenly a father to four, alone.

I walked into Shay's bedroom and lay down on his bare mattress, wondering in what bed Shay was lying that night. In what corner of Europe was he – ready to move on to the next town, the next girl, the next experience? It felt as if I had imagined him. I knew that no matter how long I waited in those rooms, how many stories I remembered, it would make no difference. I had no choice but to walk back into the garage where my father had worked out the last twenty years of his life, to climb those wooden stairs and knock respectfully on Pascal Plunkett's door.

On my final morning in the petrol station, I unlocked the glass door and stood beside the old man in the bluish light. When I told him who I was going to work for, he spat on the concrete steps.

'I remember him well, thirty years ago, traipsing round from door to door selling sets of saucepans on the tick. Sure half the housewives thought he was giving them away for free. The missis came in to me with three of them gleaming under her arm to ask me what I thought. "Take them if you want," I told her, "but if you do you can take yourself with them out of this house and trail around the streets after that knacker."'

On Sunday mornings Shay had always loved to clear his head by following the course of the Tolka as it wound through the Botanic Gardens. On the far bank was the convent, a green expanse where occasionally cattle wandered past a small stone grotto where an old bath-tub had been left out as a trough.

The Sunday morning before I started in Plunkett's I returned to the gardens for the first time since Shay had left. The keepers were just unlocking the gate and the avenues of flowers and tree-lined walks were deserted. I turned right at the glasshouse for the giant water lily and went down the steps towards the water. There had been heavy rain over the weekend and the river was swollen and murky brown. For my father's sake I had wanted the church service to mean something to me but it had just been cold words still familiar from my childhood. When people die you need to say farewell to them before they pass on to wherever they go. That is what I believe anyway, but it is as hard finding the words to say goodbye in death as it is saying you love them in life.

When the river had risen it had carried off whatever junk was left on its banks. A battered fridge was stuck among the rocks by the large weir near the bridge where the river split into two. The relatives had gone home; the fuss of the burial was over. I stood alone on the bridge with a dozen unsolvable memories and watched an old car seat floating down the river towards me. At first I thought it would be swept off in the rush of white water tumbling down the weir. But it was too close to the bank and instead was borne slowly onwards beneath my feet and down the meandering canal that snaked through the gardens for a hundred yards before rejoining the river.

I found myself following the seat's slow passage, and remembering those stories about the funeral biers of old chieftains cast out on to the ocean, until in my mind I was following my father's bier as it slowly spun and bobbed its way down to join the rush of water that would carry it out into the sea. I walked in step with it, promising him to look after those he had left behind, and when the car seat bounced against the wooden gates of the tiny lock and was trapped on the surface of the water, I found a stick to push it down until it slipped beneath the planks and was free to career off in the white torrent of water away from me.

I had imagined that Plunkett himself would interview me. Instead when I arrived on the Monday, Eddie handed me a brush and told me to sweep up and generally pretend I was busy. It felt eerie being where my father had worked. In his final months he had wasted away so much that he bore only a slight resemblance to the man I had carried lunch down to. Now whenever I saw a figure in overalls bending over a bonnet or a pair of heels underneath a car, for an instant I imagined it was my father or his ghost.

Sentiment was not a quality associated with Plunkett and the men were surprised but pleased to see me. I knew how few new hands he took on. As the recession grew so did the workload of the men in the garage. Those who left were frequently not replaced. The men grumbled among themselves but few were foolish enough to argue. I knew their faces well enough to feel relaxed among them. Most found a quiet opportunity to mention my father and then it was open season for slagging. I went home that first evening with a dozen new nicknames relating to laziness, enough dirty jokes to turn Stalin's shirt blue, and still no real idea of what my job was supposed to be.

141

It was two days before I saw Plunkett. I was helping George, one of my father's closest friends, to clean the inside of a Ford Fiesta when he appeared from nowhere and began to abuse the man loudly about a car which had gone out the previous day. I worked on with a cloth in my hand, embarrassed at having to overhear their conversation. Later I was called to the office where two of the younger mechanics were being grilled. I turned to wait outside but Plunkett beckoned me back, forcing me to stand there while he called them incompetent and threatened to sack them. They replied defensively, but I knew from their tone how my presence unnerved them, making them feel awkward and exposed. When they were gone he looked down at the papers on his desk until after a few moments it was I who spoke.

'Did you want something Mr Plunkett?'

'Oh yes, Francis. Or Francy is it they call you?'

'My name is Francis.'

'How are you settling in . . . Francy?'

'Fine.'

'Well, aren't you the great man, so. Now close the door on your way out.'

At lunch-time the younger men played football against the side of the garage where somebody had painted the crude outline of a goal. I could sense a difference in the attitude of the two mechanics towards me. As I walked back into work beside them they ceased speaking.

Over the next week Plunkett continued calling me up to his office, enjoying my discomfort as I stood before him and dismissing me again after asking some meaningless question. I'd walk down the wooden steps in dread, knowing that immediately afterwards he would call up any person from the garage floor against whom he had a complaint.

You could not fart in one corner of that garage without the echo shaking the light fittings at the other end. Daily I noticed the men cooling towards me: the momentary silence in the canteen when I walked in; the way people pushed against me when I tried to balance a scalding cup of tea; the looks of suspicion whenever I offered to help anyone. At first the men had been glad of the extra pair of hands. I had only to lift my head from one job to have somebody else call me over to hold or fetch something. But now they kept their heads down when I passed and I spent most of each day sweeping up. My lack of purpose increased their suspicions. I had been there three weeks when Eddie came into the canteen one lunch-time and nodded towards the door.

'Hano, he wants you upstairs.'

Somebody laughed from the crowded table at the end of the room. A laugh of contempt. I stayed seated, alone at the table in the corner. Eddie nodded again.

'I'm having my lunch Eddie,' I said. 'Tell him to go and fuck himself.'

Conversation stopped in the room. Though nobody turned I knew they were listening. Eddie waited a moment, then shrugged his shoulders. He had always liked me. He was the only one there who didn't believe I was a grass.

'I'll tell him so kid,' he said. 'Another funeral in the family so soon.'

Even as I'd spoken I was terrified, knowing that my mother was at that moment probably wheeling her battered shopping trolley down the aisles of the supermarket, neighbours still consoling her as she chose each item, luxuriating in being able to pay cash again to the bored girl at the check-out. It would not have been so bad if she had simply taken the money when I gave it to her each Thursday evening, but she insisted on telling me how every penny would be spent, like a schoolgirl reporting to her teacher, and thanking me and praising Plunkett over and over. Both the men and myself knew that as we waited Eddie would probably be putting my cards in order, calculating up to the hour what I was owed, placing the notes and silver Plunkett gave him in the narrow brown envelope.

Half-one came but we still waited. Nobody wanted to miss the end. At twenty to two the canteen door opened and Plunkett entered, looking at his watch.

'A national holiday is it? Feast day of St Clitoris, patron saint of bollox-lazy mechanics?'

The men shuffled out past him until there was only him and me left in the room. He kicked the door shut behind him.

'I called you.'

'You're always calling me Mr Plunkett. But you never want anything.'

'Do you think you're smart Francy? Insulting me in front of my men. You're not. You're scared. Scared shitless. Or you should be.'

He took a small book from his jacket pocket, threw it down on the nearest table and waited till I rose to pick it up. It was my mother's children's allowance book.

'Tuesday mornings she comes here and I give it to her. I'm not a hard man wee Francy, I let her keep some for herself when she brings it back. Collateral it's called. You need security off people as poor as you.'

I wanted to say it again to his face, like I'd wanted to say it to countless others: teachers, Mooney, the manager in the petrol station, but I hadn't the courage and he knew I hadn't. He leaned back against the door, taunting me with his power. I couldn't stop trembling.

'You've had a sheltered life, Francy, too sheltered for your own good. If you knew the work I had to do when I was your age . . .'

'Selling saucepans on the tick door to door.'

'I'm ashamed of nothing, so don't try any of your smart-arsed educated sneers. I left school at twelve, shovelled shit on the sites of England, did anything to get that brother of mine through college, to get myself out of the slime. And then when I had cash I came home. Oh yes, I sold saucepans, but that was only the start. A shilling a week, then something bigger, a bed or a table, then a loan. And was I that awful? I gave loans to people no bank would have looked at and if I hadn't been here most of them would have been sitting on orange boxes. Be smart for once Francy, I saw this place grow from nothing. Oh, not your part, the safe little world, except you've fallen from it now. No, but the estates that came later, the people just dumped to fend for themselves. At least I was here; nobody else gave enough of a damn to even exploit them.'

I wanted to get out. I knew Shay would have. I remembered all the bogus phone calls we had made to Patrick Plunkett, the ridicule in Shay's voice when the family were mentioned. But Shay was gone and all I had left was fear. I sat and listened.

'Did you ever see men beg Francy? No, of course you haven't. I see them come in here with their degrees and honours and they'd sweep that floor for nothing if I let them just to feel they were working. And do you know why? Because this is my country, in my image, that's why. We made it what it is – poor uneducated men like me. We did the hard graft, and now young pups come along with their degrees and their sophistication as though we owed them a living. Well they can do their bit, they can knuckle down to it as it is or they can bugger off elsewhere.

'You had it easy for a while by all accounts, Francy, a nice little temporary state job. Moving around bits of paper and inventing fancy terms for it. But there's none of those jobs left Francy, there's just me and my kind now. Now, I'm doing you a favour because your father was from the same neck of the woods as I am. We're the same stock Francy, we're both Kerrymen beneath all that Jackeen shite of yours.

'You've turned all my da's old mates against me,' I said.

'Them?' he said. 'Fodder. That's where your father began. Where he deserved to end up too. You're different Francy, better. Or is it that you fancy spending your life under a car till someone decides they don't need you, eh, throws you away like an old sack in a gutter. Eh? Think about it. Oh, they might take you back on in that petrol station a few nights of the week, or maybe you'd fancy working with the kiddies in the silly hats in some hamburger restaurant? But if you don't work for me you're not going to get a real job with anyone else in this town if I say the word. Now, can you drive?'

I nodded, slowly.

'I didn't hear you boy. I must be going deaf.'

'Not really, not very well,' I said. 'A provisional licence.'

'Well, I called you Francy to drive me somewhere. Now I wouldn't force you to do anything you don't want. This door behind me is open, you're a free man to walk out. But if you want to stay you pick up these keys and when I call you you come.'

He flung the car keys on to the floor. They jangled as they slid across the tiles and under a table. I stared at him. He held my gaze until I had to lower my eyes. I bent down, pushed aside the chairs and found the keys. When I stood up he had left the room. I walked out quietly through the garage, the men turning their heads to stare as I passed. Eddie looked quizzically at me. I moved past him, out into the sunlight where Pascal Plunkett sat in the back of his car, the driver's door left open for me. I climbed in and started the car with difficulty.

'Where to?' I asked.

'Just drive, son,' he said, with a surprising gentleness in his voice.

They left the shelter of the turf bank and began to cross the brown landscape, skirting the pools of black water, manoeuvring their way across the flooded stretches by stepping from tuft to tuft of coarse grass. After a mile the ground improved and they could walk more freely. Their feet were sodden. Katie found it so awkward without her left shoe that she flung the right one away and stepped carefully in her stockinged feet. When they came to rocks or prickly heather he carried her on his back.

Because it was the only feature in the landscape they made for the dolmen on the edge of the mountain. The ground softened again as they approached and Hano lost his footing and stumbled as he lifted her on to his back to wade through the marsh. He righted himself and drew his foot out of the mud with a popping sound, anxious that the shoe might be left behind. The dolmen itself was built on a small island of solid land. They sat resting with their backs against it. The only sign of man was the high-frequency wires strung out between humming pylons that bisected the sky. Otherwise the landscape looked the same as had greeted druids who tramped here to lay down their dead thousands of years ago. The eye of the dolmen was narrow, one slit of light piercing three stones. Hano walked around to the far side. Somebody had lit a fire between the stones and a mound of black ashes remained like a cremated ancestor. Four crushed lager cans littered the ground and the words 'Liverpool Football Club' had been sprayed in white letters on the burial stones. He returned to sit beside her.

146

'Tell me more about the old woman,' she said.

Hano shrugged his shoulders.

'Little to tell. It's from another time, like your Tomas. She'd be long dead by now.'

'Finish the story anyway. You never talk of anything except the times since you met Shay.'

He paused and looked around him. That fifteen-year-old hitch-hiker sleeping in school yards and telephone boxes and living on slices of corn beef placed between unbuttered bread seemed so distant he found him hard to make real again.

'Well, it was all drummed into me subtly,' he said. 'Places like this were meant to be more Irish than the streets I was born in. It was weird, all twisted up in our heads, wanting to blow up the Brits and following their football clubs. All the teachers with bog accents talking about Iosagan and Peig like this glorious shagging kingdom you were excluded from. It was gas, neighbours would call across the hedge to my father, *Have you been down home, John?* After thirty years they still asked.

'It became like a phantom pain building up, so much so that when I went back with him I thought I'd get this sense of homecoming at seeing the farm. But it was just awkward, it was another world, shag all to do with me.'

He leaned against the dolmen and kicked one of the Harp cans away.

'So I set out to find it for myself; in places like this, looking for ... I don't know, some sort of identity or something. My father never liked it but didn't stop me. It's strange, in Dublin I was tongue-tied but hitching I was like a different person, inventing other names, other lives. I remember sleeping in a shop doorway in Sligo and being kicked awake by a policeman's boots. The next night in Donegal another policeman was feeding me pints in a jammed pub at two in the morning where some old fiddler was playing.'

'And the woman?'

'We'll walk on,' he said, though he had no idea where to go. 'I'm starving.'

He carried her back across the marsh. The ground grew firmer as it rose. Occasionally a sheep raised its white face and surveyed them before nervously lurching away on thin legs. He described how he had met the woman that summer hitching back from Donegal. He had told his father he was travelling with school friends, ashamed to admit he had none and knowing he would not be allowed to go alone. He'd followed the chain of hostels around Donegal, meeting the same people in each, enjoying the sensation of independence. Then he got lonely, self-conscious at being alone in the crowded common-rooms.

He was hitching back through Sligo when he found the wood, an unpaved track up through a state forest. A farmer had left him off on a by-road towards evening and he'd wandered in, expecting the usual long ranks of conifers and pines. But after a hundred yards he'd reached a small gate with a hand-painted sign saying *No shooting, no hunting*. He crossed the shaky wooden stile beside it and followed a curving avenue upwards. The trees were different here, much older and more varied. He left the path to climb among them. It was like a copper-plated undergrowth which later on she taught him the names for: rhododendron, day lilies, brambles and bluebells. In places the trees were cramped together, branches twisted towards the sun, galaxies of green stems shooting up at their feet. It was growing late and the sun in the west flickering through the tree trunks frightened him suddenly as he ran, waiting for ghosts to appear on all sides.

He stopped running when he reached the grassy avenue again. A storm had partially uprooted one tree that was bent low over the top of the avenue, its leaves obscuring most of the view. Through the gap beneath he made out the shape of a house and approached cautiously. Beyond the tree the avenue broadened out into a small plateau of an overgrown lawn swamped with clusters of wild flowers. It was a large, single-storey house with two wings converging into an ornate hall-way. The windows were boarded up with creepers growing over them. Through gaps in the boards he could see old wooden shutters and beams hanging from the high ceilings and names scrawled on the exposed brickwork. The same person had painted a notice above the hall door: *Please do not vandalize. This is my home.* The house frightened him. At any moment he expected some Victorian figure to emerge from within. And yet he couldn't turn back. A fascination made him edge through the bushes at the side and peer down the slope through the basement windows which were not boarded up. He climbed down and, suddenly scared, had turned to find the woman standing above him.

As they reached the curve of the hill Katie and Hano could see the boundaries of small fields leading to a handful of cottages and bungalows below. He looked back at the bare hillside, trying to decide which way to go when Katie took his hand and began to walk towards the road glistening in the morning light.

'She was a tiny, fragile woman,' Hano continued, 'dressed in a yellow oilskin and wellingtons with a small bag on her shoulder. What light was left was slanting by the side of the house so I was in shadow and she was caught fully in its rays. Her hair was short and silver, her features sharp like a bird. She must have been seventy-five or eighty, I'm not sure, but her smile was that of a girl. I knew I was trespassing and waited for her to order me out of the wood but instead she climbed down beside me.

'"People in the village would say you're either brave or foolish," she said. "None of them will go in there. When I came here first local girls wouldn't walk down the avenue at night. Isn't it strange how old stories cling on. Would you like to go in? Just be careful where you walk."'

Hano remembered how, without waiting for a reply, she lowered herself through the cellar window and beckoned him to join her. They walked through the narrow basement rooms and up a crumbling flight of stairs into the hallway that was lit by thin shafts of light through the boards. Despite the fallen timbers and vast cobwebs suspended from the carved wood over the doorways, Hano could imagine how the rooms had looked a half-century before. The fireplaces were still intact, standing with forlorn dignity among the jumble of wood and glass where green creepers curved down through the girders from outside.

He asked her if it didn't make her sad to come here and she shook her head.

149

'No,' she replied. 'It's a mistake to ever get sentimental. The past was both good and bad and anyway it's gone now. Isn't today exciting enough?'

As she led him back down towards the basement he paused on the stairs, unsure of what he felt, but with some instinct making him stare towards the smallest of three cubicles in the cellar. They were each the size of a narrow prison cell with space for a small pane of glass in the wall between them. The sensation disturbed him, a sort of melancholia, an echo of regret. The old woman saw him pause and said:

'You must be sensitive to these things if you can feel it too. It happened a hundred years ago. Some money went missing and my husband's grandfather accused a servant of stealing it. He'd been with the family all his life. The same morning that they discovered that the children had hidden it as a joke, they found him hanging in that wine cellar. The pane of glass in the wall was smashed. They put in pane after pane in the months that followed, but the next morning it would always be smashed. Then they tried to brick it up but the mortar would never dry.

'When I first came here in the 1920s I could still feel his presence in that cellar. My husband's family never spoke of him, they were sliding away into bankruptcy while the village waited. All sorts of legends had grown up about him but I never felt threatened. I don't think he wanted to harm anyone. He was just trapped in there and needed to be released. It took me months to overcome my fear but one evening I took their old family Bible and stood on the top step reading it aloud. Every evening for a week I read to him till I began to feel a kind of tranquillity, as if his burden was lifting in some way. But there is still something left, maybe just an echo of that pain growing fainter, or else he's still trapped, hanging down there, but, if he is, I think he knows I'm nearby and thinking of him. These days I feel his presence some evenings like a form of company. I don't believe in their God down in the village but I think maybe in another life I'll meet him and we'll know each other.'

It was five years since the woman had told Hano the story.

'Nobody had ever spoken to me like that before, Katie.

Nobody since either, except maybe Shay. I never mentioned her to him, I was always afraid he'd laugh. But I think he would have liked her.'

Hano and Katie had come close enough to the bungalows to hear children playing in the gardens that bordered the small brook. The news was on the radio coming through an open kitchen door. At the sight of people Hano grew tense again, paralysed with fear. Katie crouched behind a hedge and beckoned him down. He strained to hear the radio clearly, unsure if it was the start or finish of the bulletin. Votes were being counted all over the country, both parties claiming they would be able to form a government. The programme finished without mention of him and, though he knew he should have been relieved, he experienced a sense of anticlimax. He felt suspended, not knowing even if the police were looking for him yet.

Two young girls in the garden were running in circles around a baby who stared impassively ahead. Their mother was hanging washing on a circular line. A paperback lay open on a deck-chair on the concrete path. The eldest girl might have been thirteen. Katie surveyed her carefully and then, with a sudden pressure on his arm, beckoned him to keep still and slipped away into the ditch. He crouched down petrified, wanted to call her back and yet afraid to be heard. Katie vanished through the undergrowth and shortly afterwards he caught a glimpse of her jacket among the bushes at the rear of the house. The woman would soon be finished with the clothes. She was bound to go indoors, to find the intruder. The final peg closed over the sheets and she turned, picking up the plastic basket. Hano watched her walk into the kitchen.

On every part of their journey they'd left a cumbersome trail. Now this was the final indignity. A man appeared in the next garden with a basin of water. He placed it beside his car and rolled his sleeves up, calling to a youth who appeared at the window. Hano waited for the woman's screams to alert her neighbours, knowing that he wouldn't run, that he'd be caught too trying to rescue her. The woman re-emerged and beckoned quickly to the girls. They vanished into the kitchen. Hano tried to stop his hands from trembling. The kitchen

151

door burst open and the girls ran out holding slices of bread in their hands. He breathed out and was knocked over by a sudden thump on his back. He swung round, fists raised to protect his face, and found Katie laughing at him. She was wearing white sneakers that looked too small for her and carrying biscuits and cheese in her hands.

'She was that close,' Katie whispered. 'Only a door between us. Come on, let's go.'

She limped slightly in the shoes, sharing the food with him as they walked back towards the desolate mountainside.

From then on Pascal Plunkett rarely went anywhere in the daytime without me driving him in his BMW. In the fields beyond St Margaret's he had received planning permission to build two small terraces of houses. To reach them I had to turn off a narrow country lane and manoeuvre the car down a mud track with the tyre marks of earth movers deeply scored into its surface.

When Plunkett was in his office I spent my time out of the men's way in the garage forecourt cleaning the spattered mud from the car. Some days I still took lunch in the canteen there, a litany of licking noises trailing me as I left the room. But mostly I ate at the bar in Mother Plunkett's Cabin while he drank his ritual two neat Paddies from the fresh bottle placed at his elbow which he then topped with water before going over the previous night's takings with the manager. The pub was in two sections: the bar in front paved with flagstones like a scene from *The Quiet Man*, with old black-and-white photographs of Kerry lining the walls; the door of the cabaret lounge at the back was in the shape of a horseshoe and the green carpet had a design of gold stetsons and wagon wheels.

I was surely the worst driver he could have chosen. My only experience had been at dawn in Shay's Triumph Herald and frequently in those early weeks the BMW would cut out at traffic lights or I'd finally have to get out and let him park it in some narrow space. My inexperience with everything amused him: those inept sagas of reversing and stalling were the first occasions I had seen him in good humour. I'd watch him in the mirror letting me sweat until he decided to show me how to do it. Surprisingly he was a good teacher, better than Shay. I would think of the business clients he was keeping late as he sat beside me in the front until I had got the procedure perfect. A fortnight after I began driving him, in a sudden burst of confidence I came too quickly out of the driveway of Mother Plunkett's Cabin and had to swerve up on to the ditch to avoid an oncoming car. I slammed on the brakes and glanced nervously in the rear-view mirror. Pascal Plunkett was looking delightedly back at the furious motorist who had stopped behind us and was climbing out of his car. He hit me on the shoulder.

'Would you look at the sour face on that cunt. Drive on young Francy and stick to the road this time.'

All the way back into the garage he kept chuckling to himself and impersonating the motorist's indignant face until by the time we pulled into the forecourt I too was bent over the wheel with laughter. When he went inside I realized with a chill that for the first time since going to work for him I had enjoyed my morning.

I was spending less time in the garage and people elsewhere were getting used to me. In Plunkett Stores I glowered at the baby-faced manager who fidgeted nervously whenever I was there, terrified that I was discussing him with Plunkett. One evening my mother told me she had been there and he had insisted on pushing the trolley for her around the shelves. The men in the pub and on the building site were more casual and I began to make friends among them. I carried on a nervous but intense flirtation with the receptionist in the auctioneer's. The only place I hated was the undertaker's where some evenings when I walked in my mother would look up with pride from where she knelt with her bucket and scrubbing brush. My wages were better than in the Voters' Register but still not enough for her to give up work or stop making that weekly journey from his office to the post office and back. It was something she never mentioned though once I saw her across the street waiting for me to leave the forecourt before sneaking into his office.

Sometimes I gripped the wheel of his car with anger when I

remembered my mother's face that day; yet in a curious way I had begun to admire Pascal. It was like he was a river in torrent and I wasn't strong enough to resist being swept along by the current. Since the confrontation in the canteen I had done everything he had asked without question, and he in turn had never raised his voice to me. I was seeing a side of his character which few people knew. As I drove along he would mimic with a vicious accuracy those people who managed his businesses. I saw how much he played along in the role which others had cast him in. He would storm off the building site, shouting back angrily at the foreman, and slam the car door, shouting for me to drive on. When we reached the tarmacadam I'd glance in the mirror and find his eyes waiting to spot mine, alive with amusement as though looking for applause for his performance.

He was gaining my trust slowly, introducing me to his empire, ensuring that everyone treated me with respect. I was like a fish, cautiously moving out from under a rock, and he was an angler gaining my trust, luring me further and further out. I had been driving him for a month when he orchestrated my next compromise. It was a morning in March and I was sitting in the car waiting for him to finish a meeting with two of his men, O'Brien and Flynn. They drifted from premises to premises, occasionally bouncers in the Abbey, sometimes even standing in for chauffeurs at the undertaker's. But mostly they just came and went after a few words with Plunkett. They were tough men whom I rarely spoke to. Even to be in the same room as them made me feel nervous. They came out of the garage and had climbed in the back of the car before I realized what was happening. I turned around.

'You're driving us today, Francis,' O'Brien said. 'Take a left at the lights there and just keep going straight.'

I drove towards Ballymun, listening to them casually discussing football behind me and admiring the women on the footpath. At the roundabout by the shopping centre they told me to go left and then turn in, across a rubble-strewn car-park till we stopped outside one of the tower blocks.

'Will you be long?' I asked.

'You're coming with us kid,' O'Brien replied, and when I hesitated he half-pulled me from the car.

154

Neither man spoke as we waited for the lift in the hallway. Two women came out with prams and we got in. It smelt of urine, the walls covered with IRA slogans, a crude picture of a penis painted on the inside of the doors.

'Time to earn your keep kid,' O'Brien said. 'Just like the rest of us.' From inside his pocket he produced a small pistol and pushed it into my hand. I was shaking so much I couldn't hold it. Flynn bent down to pick it up.

'I don't like it,' he said to O'Brien. 'Fucking working with kids. There's no need for him or for a shooter here.'

'You take your money, you take your instructions,' O'Brien replied sourly, taking the gun from me. He opened it to show me that it was empty, gripped my right hand firmly and placed it between my fingers. The lift stopped. He put his body in front of mine in case anybody was looking and stepped out into the empty corridor.

'Listen to me,' he said, 'There's nobody going to get hurt unless you fuck up. You just hold it inside your jacket so they can see a bulge. All you have to do is stand at the door and pretend to look tough – if that's possible. If the boss says you're to come along it's nothing to do with us.'

The lift behind me was closing. If I had run I might have reached it. I didn't. I turned and walked between them.

When the young woman opened the door slightly at his knock, O'Brien put his weight against it so that she fell back on to the floor. She scrambled up in her dressing-gown. She looked maybe twenty-two or three, still pretty but her face had lost its glow like a cake gone stale in a shop window. Her husband sat in a string vest and jeans on the sofa, his moustache making him look older.

'Ah Jesus lads,' he said. 'Could you not pick somebody rich to rob?'

His wife backed away towards the sofa. He rose and put his hand protectively about her shoulder.

'If there's robbers here don't look in this corner,' Flynn said. 'I'm just collecting for what we're owed. Ask your missis.'

She kept her head down while her husband looked at her.

'Oh God,' she said. 'Oh God.'

'What money? Jesus Christ Maria, what money do you owe them?'

His hands were shaking her now. She shook him off and stared into his face.

'Open your eyes Mick will you. Where do you think the money came from when Sharon was sick? You kept saying you'd be back at work when you were better. It wasn't much, Mick – only three loans of a hundred when we were desperate. Remember the time I told you the welfare gave me for the ESB. The fuckers gave me nothing. Nothing. I'd nowhere else to go. It's been eight months since you worked Mick. She was sick, you were sick. I kept thinking I could pay it back from the housekeeping when you got your job back.'

The man seemed to have forgotten us. It looked as if he was about to strike her. Then he stared at Flynn.

'I didn't know mate. Honest I didn't. I had a fall, off a scaffold. Been on disability ever since. You'll get it back, every penny. Just as soon as I'm well.'

O'Brien walked over to the small play-pen in the corner, set back a few inches from the wall that was discoloured by damp. The tiny girl inside it looked up at him with curious brown eyes. He looked back at me as though waiting for a nod from his boss, then picked the child up by the leg. He walked towards the balcony door with the screaming child. Her mother tried to run towards them but Flynn pushed her back on to the sofa and produced a steel bar from inside his coat. O'Brien turned the key on the door and stepped out into the air. He held the frantic child by one leg over the balcony and said in a calm voice:

'I'm going to count to fifty. After that you won't need to worry about her being sick again. Move once from that sofa and it'll be so much daughter under the bridge.'

The woman kept screeching her child's name like a prayer. The father just sat there, hands crossed over his chest like a laid-out corpse. Inside my jacket I gripped the gun. I was leaning against the door. If I'd tried to stand by myself I think I would have fallen. At thirty the woman ceased screaming and took her eyes off the balcony to stare desperately at me. I didn't want to look at her but I couldn't lower my eyes. We stared at each other as the count continued, our eyes filled with terror and disbelief. She was pleading with me, knowing there was no mercy in the two men. At fifty we both closed our eyes. O'Brien walked quietly back in and replaced the child in the play-pen.

'Twelve o'clock tomorrow. Don't be late,' he said, making his way towards the door. Flynn followed him. The woman had begun to sob. The men left the room and I was left staring at her. She looked up.

'Go on!' she screamed. 'Go on you bastard!'

No one spoke in the lift on the way down. O'Brien reached in and took the pistol from my jacket. The doors opened.

'A messy business,' Flynn said, almost to himself. 'No need for shooters or half of that carry on, whatever the fuck Plunkett's at.'

I had the car door open when it came over me. I raced down towards the tower block wall and vomited violently at the side of the steps. The men waited inside the car. My hands were so unsteady it took me several minutes to start the engine. We were almost at the garage when O'Brien spoke.

'I've two little ones myself,' he said. 'She was never safer than in my arms. Even if he told me to I wouldn't have dropped her.'

When I got home that night I climbed into bed. My sisters had moved in with my mother, my brothers into their room and I had the box-room to myself. I could hear children playing on the street outside. All I wanted to do was sleep, to stop trembling and forget that young woman's face. I felt dirty, as if my body was consumed by leprosy. If I reached beneath the bedclothes I'd feel my skin peeling and rotten. I wanted to be back there, still with that gun in my hand, only loaded this time; wanted to aim it at O'Brien and Flynn; wanted to return to the garage, climb those wooden steps and aim it again at the wrinkled skin on Plunkett's face. In the darkness I could feel my finger squeezing the trigger and see his head explode in slow motion, splattering blood over the white wall behind him. I pulled that trigger again and again and still I couldn't feel clean.

I heard my mother listening out on the landing, anxious

that I had eaten no dinner. I pulled the blankets over my face in case she came in. I told myself that I had a choice: I could flee the country, I could go to the police and tell them everything. But I knew I couldn't, knew that even the couple in the flat wouldn't back me up. And if I left I knew my mother's eyes, my sisters' voices would follow me anywhere I went. I tried to recall the figure who'd wandered through the night-time streets with Shay, but it was someone so different from the person who lay sweating in bed that it was too painful to think about. I woke next morning with sore eyes and a twisted feeling in my stomach. My sister Lisa was in the room holding a breakfast tray.

'Mummy says I'm to give you this and thank you for the lovely new dress and the shoes you bought for me. Well, she bought them, but you paid for them.'

She paused and peered more closely at me.

'Your eyes look real cranky, like an old fellow's.'

I got dressed, avoided my mother, closed the front door quietly and walked to Plunkett Motors.

I drove him in silence to the building site and the pub. At three o'clock that afternoon Eddie came out and told me to go to the office. Pascal Plunkett had a brown envelope on his desk. He counted out twenty ten-pound notes and ten fives and laid one of each in front of me.

'Don't be fooled by sob stories,' he said. 'That's the first lesson. People can always get it when they need to. That's yours, take it.'

'I don't want it.'

'You were there. You were a part of it. Whether you like it or not Francy you've earned it.'

We stared at each other, like those old games of statues in the Voters' Register, only this time it was deadly serious. In the end it was I who lowered my eyes and picked the money up. At the door I turned and asked bitterly why, if he was such a tough man, hadn't he got the full three hundred back. Pascal's laugh was different from the one I knew in the car.

'I did Francy, but sure I loaned her back fifty. We don't want to lose a good customer, do we?'

He was still laughing when I closed the door. Later that

evening I put the fifteen pounds in a collection box for old people in my local newsagents. The girls behind the counter were stunned into silence but it didn't make me feel any less cheap as I walked on through the darkness towards the place I once called home.

At home I had grown more sullen. My sisters began to avoid me whereas once they had tumbled into my lap when I returned. At times I ventured back out to the pubs and snooker halls where Shay had reigned but I always felt uncomfortable, knowing that to people there I had been Shay's friend and nothing else. Sometimes I just walked the streets; sometimes I drank. Occasionally I hid in doorways to avoid meeting people from the Voters' Register and having to talk about the past.

Plunkett could sense the change in me. He knew how isolated I had become. I had grown to hate the hours lingering in the garage forecourt away from the men, and was happy when he suggested a more flexible arrangement. I began to come in at noon to drive him to Mother Plunkett's Cabin. Often, after the rounds of premises and the visits to offices in the city, I would find myself back in the Abbey for the last hour of opening time, drinking at the bar while the awful strains of a local talent contest came through the wall of the lounge. By now I too had acquired a briefcase and kept receipt books and invoices in it to remind him of them. But basically my job was still to drive. I'd finish each night by unsteadily driving those last two miles into the countryside, and having deposited him in his hallway I would return through dark half-built lanes to my mother's house and wake next morning, hung-over and sullen.

In working hours Plunkett was often silent in the car but he mellowed with drink each evening. Once as I drove him home we came to a garda check-point. I had rolled the window down nervously, knowing that I'd been sitting with Plunkett over a bottle of whiskey since eight that evening, when he leaned forward from the back seat and spoke in a more cultured accent:

'You are halting the Junior Minister for Justice on state business. Take down that guard's number, driver.'

Afterwards he invited me in for a last drink and giggled like a schoolboy as he imitated the guard's embarrassed and frightened apologies. He had made himself sound exactly like the minister and, as I discovered, the minister, when he lost his temper, sounded exactly like him. Although Patrick Plunkett rarely came to the garage itself, often in the evenings he would appear at the house. The two brothers would go into the drawing-room, leaving me to sit in the kitchen with the government driver and listen to the low murmur of voices.

Although the minister's name never appeared on any business documents it became obvious to me that he was a silent partner in all of Pascal's ventures. Sitting in that kitchen waiting for them to emerge, I began to piece together a thumb-nail sketch of their lives from what I had heard there and from what my mother had told me.

Patrick had been two years a national schoolteacher in the suburb when his elder brother returned from England in the early sixties with capital and ambition. Soon he had Patrick selling encyclopaedias to the parents of his pupils, checking up on their home backgrounds to give Pascal leads for his new business of selling door to door. In those days the two brothers were inseparable. Although Pascal was a year older, my mother said they looked like twins. At dances girls had problems telling them apart. But soon they were rarely to be seen at dances. They moved into lodgings with an old bachelor on the North Road where the light in the living-room was still burning no matter how late you passed the house.

By 1966 Pascal had opened the garage and found others to go from door to door for him. The fiftieth anniversary of the Easter Rising that year was the making of them. From his native Mayo they dragged up their grandfather, Eoin, who had been thirty-eight during the rising and was eighty-eight then. They brought him around the estates to meet the people. One night when we were drinking heavily, Pascal described him to me. Eoin had come to Dublin in 1916 looking for work and joined with Connolly's men only on the morning of the rising. He had stuck to his new leader's side and even helped to carry Connolly down when he was shot on the roof of the GPO. Before arriving in Dublin he had known nothing, but he came out of the internment camp in Wales a confirmed socialist. Wounded six times in the War of Independence, he had not died. Pascal used to repeat this bitterly. If only his grandfather had been killed I think he felt they could have both won seats.

After the dust had settled in 1923 he was still a socialist and still spoke out as one. They gave him medals reluctantly and eventually a pension, but he was not there in the carve up of jobs and power. At the time of the Graltan affair in Leitrim, he too had been denounced from the pulpits as a Bolshevik. Graltan on the run had often hidden in his house, and when he was deported to America the newspapers cried out for Eoin Plunkett to be dispatched as well. He survived, the aura of holiness around his Easter medal protecting him, until one night the locals set fire to his house. The brothers' mother had died giving birth to Patrick and their father had brought them to live with Eoin. After the fire, their father cursed Eoin, took the only suitcase and went to England. The sons never heard from him again. Eoin took them to his sister's house in Kerry near where my own father was born, left them there and was arrested and sent home when trying to board a boat to join the International Brigade in Spain. In 1939, when his grandsons were in their late teens, the police came for him again. He came out of the Curragh Internment Camp, a grey-haired man of sixty-seven, when peace was declared.

The brothers always resented the poverty they grew up in when they knew how easy it would have been for Eoin to secure a well-paid niche. He could barely walk when they got him reluctantly back up to the city but they quickly learnt how much he despised their new activities. Eventually, in desperation, each evening before they took him on their rounds of the estates they would remove his false teeth so that the people mistook his tirades against the snugness of the new state for the standard pieties they expected.

They shipped him home when the bunting came down, and in the next election Patrick Plunkett slipped into the last seat on the twelfth count. Eoin died as the first bombs exploded on Derry's streets. They forgot to remove the tricolour from his coffin when they lowered it down, and shovelled the clay on top of it. The local priest claimed a bedside conversion. I always wondered if he had prised the teeth out first.

161

In April the party had an emergency Ard-Fheis, giving rise to speculation of a snap election. At the last minute Patrick Plunkett was dropped from the list of speakers. That night, after the leader's speech he arrived at Pascal's house. I could see he had been drinking heavily. The brothers withdrew into the drawing-room, muttering angrily to themselves. After an hour Patrick emerged from the drawing-room and told his driver to go. Through the open door I could hear Pascal on the phone placing a bet with someone. I had been idling in the kitchen for hours, waiting to be told to go home. When I heard the receiver being replaced I reached for my coat and was zipping it up when Pascal came in.

'You're working late tonight Hanrahan,' he said, his manner abrupt as always in his brother's presence. 'Drive us back into the city.'

I could smell whiskey like a fever in the back of the car as I drove. It was after one o'clock when we got there, the streets almost deserted with the burger huts closed and the night-clubs still churning out music. We drove by Liberty Hall, crossed the river and cruised along Burgh Quay. Near the public toilets they beckoned for me to stop. Three youths leaned on the quayside wall, watching for men, obviously for sale. The eldest might have been sixteen. I could sense the brothers staring at them before they motioned me to move on.

Maybe twenty-five years ago it had been impossible to tell them apart, but the grooming of political power had lent Patrick a veneer of cosmopolitanism at odds with his brother's instinctive raw aggression. That night though, as they sat impassively behind me, it was like the polish had slipped away and they were one again. I drove slowly, with a sickness in my stomach, along the quays and down alleyways where dirty children huddled in groups with bags of glue and plastic cider bottles. Some spat at the slow car, others watched with mute indifference. Neither man spoke beyond instructing me to slow down or drive on. At times we moved at a funeral pace and those badly lit alleyways could have been some ghostly apparition of a dead city which we were driving through. Murky lanes with broken street lights, the ragged edges of tumbledown buildings, a carpet of glass and condoms, of chip

162

papers and plastic cartons and, picked out in the headlights, the hunched figures of children and tramps wrapped in blankets or lying under cardboard, their hands raised to block the glare of headlights.

Twice we paused where a figure lay, down a laneway between the ancient cathedral and the ugly squatting bunkers of the civic offices, before I was ordered to stop. Patrick Plunkett was bundled up in an old overcoat and hat. In the semi-dark of the car he could have been anyone or no one. This is what death looks like when it calls, I thought, watching him in the mirror, a black figure with no face. Pascal got out and approached the youth on the ground who tried to shuffle away when he bent to talk to him. He was perhaps eighteen. I saw him shake his head repeatedly before Plunkett produced two twenties and a ten pound note from his wallet which he held up and then placed carefully back among the wad of notes. Both were still for a moment before the youth picked himself up and folded the blanket under his arm. Plunkett caught his shoulder and, after arguing briefly, the youth turned and carefully hid the filthy covering behind some rubble in the lane.

He sat between the two brothers in the back. I could tell from his face in the mirror how scared he was. He wanted to ask them questions but was intimidated by the brothers' silence. Occasionally Pascal murmured to him, reassuring the youth as you would a frightened animal, or called out directions to me. Otherwise we made the journey in silence.

I thought I knew North County Dublin until that night. I know we passed near Rolestown and much later I glimpsed a signpost for The Naul, but generally the lanes we travelled were too small to be signposted. Two cars could not have passed on them and I had to negotiate by following the ridge of grass which grew down the centre. Just when they seemed to peter out they would switch direction. At one crossroads another set of headlights emerged and began to tail us, and this was repeated again and again until we too caught up with a procession of tail lights streaking out into the darkness ahead of us.

The cars slowed almost to a halt and we turned off the

tarmacadam and were bumping our way across gravel and then grass. In the field ahead of us a semi-circle of light was formed by the headlights of parked cars. We took our place and those behind followed until a rough circle of blazing light was completed. Men stood about in the grass. Patrick Plunkett addressed me for the first time since leaving the city.

'Get out!'

He climbed into the driver's seat and donned the chauffeur's hat from the glove compartment which I had never been asked to wear. He slammed the door and fixed his eyes through the windscreen on the trampled floodlit grass. Pascal had got out and was standing beside the open boot with the youth who was now stripped to the waist and shivering. Pascal was rubbing liquid from a bottle on to the youth's chest. He handed it to me with a sponge and plastic container of water, then placed his hand on the youth's shoulder to steer him out into the circle. From the far side of the ring of lights I saw a second youth being led out, as scared looking as the first. I knew the man at his side, a wholesale fish merchant named Collins from Swords who occasionally did business with Plunkett. He called out jeeringly:

'Is that the best you can do Plunkett? You must have fierce weak men up in the city.'

'Are you sure a grand won't bust your business Collins?' Plunkett called back. 'I know it's a lot of money for a small man like yourself to lose.'

The two youths eyed each other, desperate to make a deal between themselves. But even if they had tried to run they would have been pushed back into the ring by the circle of well-fed men who were closing in around them. A referee, stripped to his waistcoat, was rolling up his sleeves.

'Where did you get him?' he asked Plunkett.

'Back of Christchurch.'

'And yours?' He turned to Collins.

'Knackers. Camped out near The Ward.'

'Fifty pounds to the winning boxer. I want twenty-five each off you now.'

He turned to the youths.

'Nothing to the loser. Do you understand? No using your

164

feet, you break when I tell you and the first to surrender is out. Now you've got five minutes.'

We returned to the boot of the car. Plunkett put a jacket over the youth's shoulders and fed him instructions on how to weave and hit. Two men approached us and he walked off to cover their bets. The youth kept glancing at me as though I were his jailer. I wanted to tell him to run but I was too terrified, afraid that if he did escape I would be thrust into the ring in his place. The winning purse was less than the smallest bet being placed around me. The laughter and shouting, as if by an unconscious signal, died down into a hush of anticipation. Plunkett returned and pushed the youth forward.

'Fifty pounds son. Fifty smackers into your hand. Don't let me down now.'

I walked behind, noticing that Patrick had left the car and was standing unobserved a small way off from the crowd. A man staggered over to offer me a slug of Southern Comfort and thump me on the back.

'Good man yourself,' he shouted in my ear. 'I've a hundred riding on your man, but watch it, them knackers fight fierce filthy.'

There was a roar as both youths entered the ring. They circled cagily while the referee encouraged them forward. For over a minute they shadowed each other, fists clenched and raised, tongues nervously exposed. The crowd grew angry at the lack of action. They cursed and called the fighters cowards. Then the Gypsy ducked low to get in close and swung his fist up. He caught the youth above the eye as he moved back and flailed at the Gypsy who danced away. It had begun.

There were no gloves, no rounds, both fighters punching and clinging to each other as the men around them screamed, until after five or six minutes the Gypsy was caught by a succession of blows and fell over on to the ground. I expected the referee to begin a count but Collins just pulled him up and wiped the sponge quickly over his face. Plunkett grabbed the water from me and raised it to his fighter's lips.

'Don't swallow, just spit,' he said. 'It's going to be a long night.'

Then they were thrust back into action, a graceless, headlong

165

collision of blows and head butts. Both bled badly from the face. More frequently now they fell and the fight was stopped for a few seconds. After half an hour, the Gypsy got in under his opponent's defence and rained blows against his rib cage. He stepped back and the youth fell, doubled up on the ground. He kept trying to stay down as Plunkett pulled him up.

'Me ribs mister, they're broken, broken.'

'Get back in there. I've money riding on you. Finish the cunt off or you'll leave this field in a box.'

The youth stumbled forward with one hand clutching his side. Money was flowing on to the Gypsy. He approached, grinning now through the blood, sensing that his ordeal was nearly over, but as he swung his fist the youth caught him with his boot right in the balls and, as he fell to his knees, again in the face. There was a near riot of indignation among the crowd around me, their sense of fair play abused. Both youths knelt on the ground while the referee shouted at Plunkett:

'Once more Plunkett and I'm giving it to Collins. Do you hear me?'

The youth rose reluctantly and looked back to where I stood. I lowered my eyes and walked towards the gate of the field. I could bear to watch no more. To the south the lights of the city were an orange glow in the sky. The wind blew against my face. A tree was growing by itself in the ditch. I pressed my face against its cold bark, remembering suddenly the old woman's story of the oak trees in her wood that she would embrace to find strength in times of crisis. I closed my eyes and I could see her, not as that ancient figure I had abandoned, but a young mother in the early light running between trees. I saw her so clearly, as if her image had always been locked away inside me, part of the other me I never allowed myself to think of. I wanted him back, the person I kept nearly becoming – in her caravan, with Shay in the flat. From the shouts behind me I knew that the Gypsy was finishing it. Every eye would be watching the final grisly moments before clustering round the bookmakers. I wrapped my whole body against the base of the tree. I had nobody left to pray to so I prayed to it and to her and to me: to the living wood itself, to the old woman of the fields, to the memory of someone I had almost once been.

When the noise died down, I turned and walked back. The youth was lying against the side of the car. He was crying. I found his clothes, helped him to dress. I wanted to ask him his name but it seemed too late to do so. I helped him up and opened the back door where the brothers sat.

'Put him in the front,' Pascal shouted.

I eased him gently into the passenger's seat and started the engine.

'Leave us home,' Pascal said, 'then dump that tramp back where you found him. Bring the car into work at lunch-time. One word about this and your family will be living on sawdust.'

I let them out at his house. Both slammed their doors, disgruntled and, now they were alone, bowed their heads together to discuss the fight. I drove into the city. The Mater Hospital was on casualty. It was almost dawn but still the benches were jammed with drunks, with lonely people hoping to fool their way into a bed, with girls in party dresses who cried waiting for word of their friends behind the curtains. He hadn't wanted to go in and, if I hadn't sat there, would have stumbled his way back to his blanket hidden in the laneway.

Even the nurses were shocked at his appeareance. They called him in ahead of those waiting. When he rose I pushed whatever money was in my pockets into his hand. I knew that Plunkett had given him nothing. He looked at me but we did not shake hands. I watched the nurses help him on to the bunk and, staring back at me with mistrust, pull the curtain shut.

It was daylight outside. I thought of my brothers and sisters. At twelve o'clock I would be waiting at the garage to drive him, but now I left his car there and walked the two miles home in some futile gesture of penance, even though I knew that nothing would be changed.

*This is where I first find you. Child in a duffle coat, girl with cropped hair. Where you have lost all sense of yourself. 'Be like them,' you keep repeating in your mind. 'It's dangerous to think; don't listen to that voice. They were different men in different times.' So why then do his eyes bring the memories back. Mournful eyes staring from the window of a cabin, as dark always as that kitchen had been, the same musty smell of regret. The trembling hands, the rasping breath, so unlike the silent figure ingrained in your past, but it's the eyes that are haunting you. How they turned when you lifted the latch after racing in your one dress across the field to pause for a moment, shyly at his door. The same red mesh of burst blood vessels, the same shrunken resignation. Stop thinking Katie or you are lost; go back inside or they will talk. Trucks pass on the carriageway, their slipstreams blowing through your hair. Can you not hear the girls calling, whispering about you at the entrance?*

*The stink of urine from one corner, figures huddling in that dark. Slats of light run down their faces where the corrugated sheets have slipped. The time for pills has gone. A candle is lit, a teaspoon warmed. The next girl straps up her arm. She pinches for a vein, a tapestry of bruises from the wrist up. Her lips enter the circle's light, her eyes still left in the dark. You watch the shared syringe exhale into reddened flesh. Her head lifts back, the neck now caught, white skin bound up in the knot. Your turn will be soon, the next girl strips off her jumper, divining fingers seeking the vein like a blue river underground. Stay and you will still belong. Don't close your eyes, don't see his face again.*

*No one calls when your feet splash through the puddles of water and oil. So bright outside you blink, the wind against your face. A woman passes with a shopping trolley, her eyes never leaving the concrete. You wonder will they still come, the speckled capsules your friends have outgrown. Feel the old ten-pound notes in your jeans, smelling still of his mattress under which they have lain. Why are his eyes holding you back, feverish and terrified, gazing at your breasts? You had the needle in your hand. Guardian angels have many shapes.*

*They cease talking when you rejoin them, already sensing you have ceased to belong. You wander towards the carriageway wall, wait for nothing in the still afternoon. This is*

*where I will find you soon, your eyes a mesh of burst blood
vessels, ladened with shrunken resignation.*

I should have known where it was leading. Perhaps I did but
kept running away from it. We were climbing slowly from
debt. Not too fast, I knew Plunkett would ensure that, but
enough to keep hope alive. Every morning at home I woke to
the smell of frying, my mother keeping the breakfast hot till I
came down, a clean white shirt folded over the chair. I could
say nothing as she sang that man's praises. If I had told her
the truth she would have refused to believe.

But my mornings at home were more infrequent. Often, it
was so late when we left Mother Plunkett's Cabin, and I was
so drunk, that having barely managed to steer the car safely to
his house, I wound up sleeping on the living-room sofa. Those
nocturnal drives seemed unreal when I looked back on them,
the BMW shifting from side to side on the road, while behind
me Pascal mumbled on about nationalist politics and business
scandals, eulogizing the qualities of his mother who died when
he was one and mispronouncing the names of classical com-
posers he'd heard on drunken visits to the National Concert
Hall with his brother. Sometimes he'd attempt to whistle out
of tune highlights of their work, then lose interest.

'Tschaikfuckoffwsky my bollox,' he'd roar, and break instead into *The Kerry Recruit*:

> '*About four years ago I was digging the land,*
> *With my brogues on my feet and my spade in my hand,*
> *Says I myself what a pity to see*
> *Such a fine strapping lad footing turf in Tralee . . .*'

'Sing up there young Francy, ye Kerry Recruit,' he'd shout,
laughing at his own joke. But always at the back of the songs
and shouts was the veiled but unmistakable dropping of in-
nuendoes.

How can I describe how I felt then, or was I so numb as to
feel nothing? I have an image of myself as an embryo with
unformed eyes driving that figure through the blackness of a

womb. I was completely alone, with no one left I could speak to, hurtling deeper and deeper into the darkness that was Plunkett's world.

It came at three o'clock one morning. The only drink in his house was whiskey. I cannot taste it since without sensing evil. We were sitting in the kitchen at opposite sides of the table. Plunkett rose unsteadily and approached. He had been droning on about his kindness, how people always took from him but never wanted to give anything back. He swayed in front of me. I felt sick with drink, all evening I had been answering him back, smart-assed. He called me a wee Kerry pup, then put his hand out, saying *friends*, and held it there until I shook it. Then, so quickly that it took me a moment to realize what was happening, he was kissing me. I remember the sensation of shock and yet the total absence of surprise. More than anything else I felt my own stupidity at not realizing it was going to happen. It seemed to take for ever to pull my head back, stare at his sixty-year-old wrinkled face and, pushing my chair over, run.

The lights had been extinguished throughout the house. I was so drunk my legs could hardly hold me. I ran from room to room with Plunkett lunging drunkenly behind. I could hear him call.

'Come back, Francy, come back. I can be good to you, I'll be good. Let's just talk.'

There was a short flight of stairs leading into the hallway. I stumbled on them and he almost caught me. I drew my elbow back, felt it smash against his face and ran on. I was almost at the door. I had only to turn the lock and I was gone. And yet even as I reached for the handle I knew instinctively that he had locked the Chubb. I was still twisting it when his hands caught me around the neck and pulled me down in a headlock on to the floor. I lashed out with my feet and he punched me repeatedly in the face until I stopped and lay still. We were both breathing heavily. Neither of us spoke. Blood was trickling from my nose, he ran his finger lightly over the flow, trying to soothe me as he would a frightened calf. I shivered when I felt his touch. Then very slowly he brought his lips down to mine. When they touched I twisted my face around

170

and flailed out desperately with my legs. Again he drove his fist hard against my face until I was able to see nothing from one eye. Above my own screams I could hear his voice, insistent, animal-like, repeating:

'I want! I want! I want!'

Then we were both silent. He relaxed his grip and I slumped back against the door. My eyes were closed. I heard a rustling before he grabbed my hair with both hands and pulled my face downwards. I was crying. I opened my mouth to scream and felt his prick being shoved deep into my throat. It was stiff and hot with the taste of salt. I gagged. For a moment I thought I would choke. I tried to pull back and he tightened his grip on my hair. I felt strands of it come loose with a tearing pain but still I couldn't free my head. He was rocking it back and forth. I could feel vomit about to rise and kept thinking I was going to choke, I was going to die. Then he manoeuvred his fingers down to squeeze my nostrils shut and I was forced to open and close my mouth purely to try to breathe.

Pascal said nothing, even after he had come. He withdrew and I spat out whatever I could. He released my head, leaned forward against me with one hand clumsily draped on my shoulder, and after a time I realized he had lapsed into a deep sleep. I knew I had to get up now, not to search the kitchen for a knife and stab him like I longed to, but just to rise quietly and leave his house. To walk home across the fields, pack whatever few clothes I had and leave this country. But I could not. Even while he slept he exercised that same inexplicable hold on me. I felt guilty, as though I had been an accomplice all along, leading him on deliberately, knowing how it was bound to end. I worried that there was a part of me I had never known which he, with those animal instincts, had seen. I felt dirty. My face was puffed and caked with blood and there was a ringing pain in my head. But all I could think of was that somehow I was at fault. I sat watching dawn flesh out the hallway, my body trembling in shock as I wept, and listened to the loud peaceful breathing of Pascal Plunkett asleep with his head nestling against my shoulder blade.

I must have finally slept because when I woke I was alone in the hall. It would have been half-seven or eight in the morning. I tried to rise to see if the door behind me had been unlocked and as I did Pascal came down the stairs with a basin of water and towel. He was impeccably dressed in a clean suit, his hair groomed, leather shoes gleaming. I slumped back. He knelt beside me and began to gently sponge my face, repeating *you poor boy, you poor boy*, as though somebody else had inflicted the damage. I kept waiting for him to try to kiss me but now he was a different person, concerned, courteous, fatherly. He bathed the cut above my eye and placed a plaster over it, then helped me up and made coffee in the kitchen. He set the cup down in front of me.

'Are you all right?' he asked.

I nodded without looking up. I still hadn't spoken.

'You'll have to tell your mother there was a fight in the pub at closing time. Don't come in for a few days; rest up until you're feeling better. One of the men will bring your wages round. I'll drive you home now Francy.'

'I'd sooner walk,' I said.

'Are you sure?'

I rose from the table.

'Francy . . .?' he said, with a question in his voice.

'I've told you before, my name is Francis. Like you say, I'll rest up now.'

I found my jacket and left.

On the following Tuesday evening, when my mother came home from the undertaker's, she very deliberately placed the children's allowance book on the bedspread beside her when she came up to see me. She wasn't sure if I had known and I gave no sign that I had. Pascal Plunkett came the next night. I heard the knock and, from the bustle in the hall, knew who it was. He was dressed at his best, and just calling in, he told my mother, on his way to meet his brother at a reception in the Dutch embassy. She stood between us in the box-room for a moment, waiting to be dismissed in her own house. He smiled professionally and waited till her footsteps descended the stairs before turning towards me. The suit and Crombie coat lent him a curious air of dignity. He placed a

172

bottle of cognac on the bedside table. We stared at each other for a time, then he smiled again, a sadder smile, an honest one.

'I've one of the mechanics driving me, but it's not the same, he's able to drive straight.' He paused. A lesser man would have looked down but he stared me in the face. 'Francis I miss you, I want you to come back to work. Not now but when you're ready.'

I could see he wanted to sit on the bed but was afraid to. I said nothing and watched him stand awkwardly in the centre of the room.

'I'll tell you a story,' he said. 'It won't excuse anything but it might explain.'

He stared at me as if waiting for permission to speak. I looked away from his eyes.

'When I was your age there's nobody ever gave me nothing but a kick in the arse and a curse and told me to get the hell to England. What was there for me here? What could I be? You feel things as a child . . . feel different. Nobody ever let me be who I am. How could I . . .'

He paused.

'I saw them when I went Francis, those rented rooms in Cricklewood, old men with nothing of their own. That's what I was fodder for. Oh my grandfather would be proud of me, one of the workers at last, a pick in my hand and a union card in the other. And there's no one would thank me for climbing out of that pit. But I did, Francis, I worked hours no man would work, sent money home to get that brother of mine the hell out of Kerry and into training college, and saved money when the others were drinking to get myself the fuck out of there.

'Just once I allowed myself to be myself. He was a Galway lad, soft hands covered in blisters from the shovel. *Here's The Vaseline Kid* the men on the site jeered every time he passed. He was in tears one lunch-time, I just put my hand on his shoulder. I thought we were alone. I'd three ribs broken; the doctor thought I'd never have the use of the fingers on my right hand again.

'That taught me Francis, taught me gentleness was a luxury

173

for the likes of me. I switched cities, another site, worked my back off, rose to foreman, never let anyone see me weak again. Then I undercut, got contracts myself. Oh, I made the rules now and no one else. What they said I could never have I took by force. The English, thick as shite on a blanket. All straight mind, no curves. You play the thick Irishman and they smile their big empire smiles while you're running rings round them. Education my arse, any gobshite from the back of the bog would have more cop on than a hundred of them lined up with their degrees flapping out their arseholes. And I've got used to getting my own way. And to taking what I couldn't have by force. It's always been that way for me and always will.

'Because even now they'd pack me back to the arse of the bog if they could. I'll see it tonight at this Dutch bash, like a thousand other nights. They'll tolerate me with their cocktails and speeches because I'm my brother's brother but I can see it in their eyes. I'm just a savage even though I could buy and sell them all. You know me, Francis, you know how hard it is for me to come here, so don't make me have to ask for anything. Just come back to work Francis, for a while even. Nothing else, I promise. You owe me that at least.'

When I still didn't reply he smiled again and left. I imagined him all evening moving through the pin-stripe suits and clink of glasses, a tribesman from a vanished place, collecting snubs he would never forgive. For the rest of the week I lay in bed or went out only after dark to walk the streets alone. Most nights I'd stand outside the flat, looking up at those dark windows. One morning, before the punters came in, I went to see the bookie. The same female voice on the Extel machine was calling out runners. He was sticking up the cards for the English courses. He hesitated at first when I asked him, studying the bruises still on my face.

'It would be the same rent you know.'

'I know.'

'I wasn't going to re-let it. I was hoping to move the office back up there whenever I got time. Still I liked yourself and young Seamus.'

I carried my stuff down in cardboard boxes. My mother watched nervously as I packed the last one. She sent my sisters to play outside.

'You're different, son, it's like I don't know you any more. Yesterday you snapped at the girls when they ran up to you. You were never like that before. And now you're moving out again.'

She put her hand on my arm and I flinched involuntarily at her touch. She started back as though I had struck her. I could see she was close to tears.

'I'm just down the road ma,' I said. 'You'll see me most days and I'll still give you the same money each week. Sure you'll be better off without me to feed as well.'

I knew she was aware there was more to it than that. She didn't believe the story of the fight in the pub. But now I couldn't bear to be near anybody I had felt close to. I wanted to lose myself, just to be alone. That evening I wandered around the bars in town and met a girl who had worked temporarily like me in the Voters' Register. We swapped stories about Mooney and I laughed for the first time in weeks. We switched to shorts as closing time came. It was the most natural thing in the world to go with her to the nightclub she suggested, to let the night take its course and wake up once again cramped in a single bed in some Rathmines flat. But when the time came to leave the pub I lost all confidence. I was terrified that when I'd lie naked beside her in the dark it would be Plunkett's face I'd see, his eyes rendering me impotent and ashamed in her arms. When she was in the Ladies I slipped quietly out and walked home, cursing myself and cursing him.

The following Monday I returned to work. Plunkett handed me the keys and we drove from site to site. We spoke little. I sorted out what papers he needed and handed them to him. I drove him to the pub that evening and joked with the barmen about the last traces of bruising on my face. He had told them I'd been caught by a jealous husband and my prestige behind the bar had suitably increased. He came out from the back room at ten o'clock, told me I could go on if I wished to in the car and he would walk home. I told him I would wait. He was pleased. At half-eleven I drove him back.

'You know you're welcome to a nightcap,' he said, outside his door.

'I know,' I said.

He got out and walked with surprising dignity up the steps without looking back. For four nights it continued like that. I would leave the car parked in the garage forecourt and walk across the metal bridge to the empty flat. It was late on the Thursday night, when the wind was blowing up with gale force warnings on the car radio, that Shay came home.


Late that afternoon they saw the helicopter. The noise of propellers alerted them first. They looked uncertainly at each other, trying to reconcile the sound with the wild landscape, then simultaneously began running towards a small outcrop of rock nearby. They squeezed beneath it as best they could, Hano lying on top of her as the machine suddenly scaled the crest of the mountain and moved slowly past them, the whirling shadow of a crucifix transfixed on the gorse and rock as Hano peered out through the crook of his arm. After the noise died away they were still too afraid to move.

Finally Hano raised his head. Dusk was hours away and the bare mountainside offered no shelter for miles. He was hungry again though his body had passed beyond tiredness into a numb state where it moved automatically. Neither had mentioned their destination, though at some stage of his story about the woman, both had instinctively known. It might be no less futile than Leitrim but it would serve as a destination to lend some purpose to their journey. Now when he mentioned the woman it was like an unspoken code between them. Hano eased his weight off Katie. They lay face up, soaking in the autumn sunlight, afraid to speak of going there yet, trying to keep that tiny flame of hope alive.

'She had a caravan in a field beyond the village,' Hano said. 'My first night there I woke to this faint crying. At first I thought it came from inside the caravan but then I realized it was from underneath. She came out of her room in an old jacket and jeans. "Do you hear it too?" she whispered, and climbed outside. I pulled on a pair of jeans and followed her.'

176

Hano closed his eyes as he spoke and saw again the lone white light of the last street lamp at the corner of the road. The only other light had come from the stars. The woman had crouched down, shining a torch between the concrete blocks that held up the caravan. The crying had been replaced by a low whine. And when he bent down he could see it: the cat trying to crawl towards the torch. The woman reached in to cradle it in her arms, carried it inside and laid it on a woollen jumper on the floor. She had never seen the cat before. Its back was broken, as if a car had run over it, and somehow in its pain it had known where to crawl for attention. The woman stroked it, murmuring softly, giving it every piece of love inside her. The cat rested its head on her fingers and looked up pleadingly, silent except for the irregular rasp of its breathing. The woman sighed and fetched a bottle of chloroform and a swab of cotton wool from her room, sat with the cat on her lap on the floor and gradually, still stroking and murmuring to it, put it out of its pain. They had not spoken but Hano had been aware of the extraordinary sensation of peace in the caravan, her own three cats quietly watching in one corner, her dog lying at her feet as she gently rubbed the fur till she looked up, dry eyed, to tell him it was over.

'Next morning,' he said, 'I dug a hole in the field and we laid the cat there, still wrapped in her jumper. It's always haunted me Katie, the cat knowing where to go. I never knew death before that night, but it seemed so natural there, so simple just to pass on.'

Hano went quiet, wondering why then was he still unable to say goodbye to Shay, to think of him as dead and not somehow waiting for some final rendezvous?

He was unsure of their location. By road they might be forty miles from the woman's wood. Cross country he'd little idea of direction or distance. Katie had eased her runners and socks off. Her toes were reddened and looked bruised. He wondered who she was thinking of as she lay there: Tomas, Shay, her parents? The litany of the dead seemed endless. He remembered his father dying, the cool breeze in the hospital yard as the shrunken man in the bed longed for one last taste of real air. Jail would be something like that. You might get used to other things, but never to being unable to step out beneath the stars, to feel the air on your tongue like champagne. Oblivion or jail? Justin Plunkett or the police? Whoever found him first.

Hours before he'd stared at the lake, comforting in its finality. Now he knew he'd cling to each extra moment given to him on this journey. He remembered his first meeting with Shay, the anxiety he had felt, the fear of being exposed. With Katie it was like that again, only his apprehension had taken so much longer to overcome. Even now part of him held back, sensing the barriers still within her. At any moment he expected them to snap back into the frozen silence they had always known. So many emotions were clashing within him: an aching grief for Shay, a terror of what was bound to happen when he was caught, exhaustion, hunger. Yet overriding them all was an excitement in her presence like the thrill of those early days with Shay or the heightened elation he'd felt after his first stay with the old woman.

He remembered again the first three nights he had remained sleeping on the woman's window seat, often waking to find a cat sitting on his chest watching him with curious green eyes. They'd creep in the skylight before dawn after hunting missions through the fields, brush against him and pad to the bowl of water on the floor. Each morning stray cats, too shy or brutalized by other people to enter, would accept food or a slow pat from her at the door but dart away at his appearance.

One wall of the caravan held rows of pictures from her past: the house before the war; her family who were all dead; friends from around the world; everyone from street traders in Morocco to political prisoners in Turkey. She fought a hundred causes from the caravan. The postman brought mail from The Kremlin, Chile, South Africa, and places Hano had never even heard of. The only government she had no correspondence with was her own. Looking back, it was as if she had withdrawn from her own land, knowing it was impossible to change the Plunketts who carved it up, and had concentrated on creating her own country within her caravan instead.

At night she lit candles and they sat talking till late. Her words fascinated him though they rarely moved in a rational line, skipping through decades and countries till he could follow only the outline of what she said. But each conversation was another door opening in his fifteen-year-old mind to let in light and doubt, so that when he'd step into the dark field afterwards to breathe the night air, everything that he'd been taught to believe as permanent seemed transient and obscure.

In the afternoons he'd take her dog into the woods and report back on any overnight damage to her fences. On the last evening of his stay he climbed with her up to the top of the wood, carrying sticks to mend gaps knocked in the ditches so that cattle could get in to graze. Near the crest a line of five oaks raised their heads above the younger trees. Their trunks were coarse and indented, like ancient hardened skin. The woman began to talk of the 1930s, a time of great unhappiness when she was left alone there with two small children. A friend had written to her about a line of oak trees in a dream that had radiated strength and solace. The woman knew from the description that they were her trees. From then on, whenever she touched the fringe of despair, she would run at dawn, after a sleepless night, up through the woods to wrap her hands around a gnarled oak trunk, feeling imperceptibly an echo of its strength soak into her flesh, calming and soothing her until she was able to walk down again to face the bills and problems of a new day.

Hano reached for Katie's hand. It was smooth, alive to touch. He remembered the field in North Dublin, the noise of the men circling the boxers, the touch of the bark beneath his skin.

'What are you thinking of?' she asked and suddenly, for the first time, he was able to tell somebody about Pascal Plunkett, stroking her skin for comfort, no longer embarrassed but relieved at being able to say the words.

'You were always trying to be Shay,' she said when he'd finished; 'you never gave yourself any time to be you.'

He began to understand what she meant. He remembered the child hiding in the tree in the back garden; the figure lost among the screaming children in the school yard; the fifteen-year-old hiker inventing new names; the youth trying to bury himself in the shadow of his friend. To stand firmly against something you must first know who you are. He could feel no self-pity, he had allowed himself to drift where others could use him, willing always to fit into any role they gave him. The only time he'd openly been himself was in that caravan where nobody in his permanent world could have ever seen or known.

That same evening years before, when they'd repaired the fence, the old woman led him to a small clearing at the very top of the wood. Across the fields of cattle and obscured by a hedgerow that bordered the narrow road was an old quarry. A lorry was leaving, having dumped its load of white plastic sacks on to the mound already there. Some sacks had burst open, white grains like salt glinting in the evening sunlight. The two farmers with the cattle also owned the lorries. They drove them in rotation from the chemical factory near Sligo to dump the waste in their disused quarry. The company was banned from America and was not allowed in any other European country. The woman had heard that they operated two sister plants, in Africa and South America. Most of the government front bench had been at the opening. It was now the major local employer. Those who spoke against it were enemies of the community. There were mortgages to be paid, new bungalows to be built in place of the cottages Hano saw crumbling on the side-roads.

They watched the lorry cross the humpbacked bridge by the small crossroads and brake as a second lorry approached. The drivers stopped, their wheels slicing the grass verge on both sides of the road as they chatted together. The old woman began to walk back towards the ruined house, taking an overgrown path through the left side of the wood to show Hano leaves that were blackened and withered, a sward of decay cutting through the green foliage.

'A woman in the village asked me would I not prefer a house,' she said, crinkling one of the leaves in her hand. 'A permanent home, was how she described it. That's what they think they have Francis, like my husband's family trying to keep up the ugly old house down there for decades. There was a fire at that dump in March, although none of the papers reported it. If the wind had been from the west the whole wood might have been destroyed. Luckily only these trees were in the path of the smoke, plus all the farms and houses behind us. You could see the children coughing for weeks afterwards, their eyes bloodshot. Next spring we'll see if the leaves come back or the cattle are stillborn. Once I thought you could have a permanent home. Maybe it's just old age, but after watching those bags split open and death blowing around the quarry, I'm happier with my caravan out among the fields at the mercy of the wind.'

It was her strangeness that had fascinated him then; only now did her words begin to make sense. Permanency was what he'd longed for; life with Shay to continue for ever, neither ageing nor marrying, both locked into that flat for ever and ever like bodies trapped in a peat bog. He gazed at the mountainside around him and knew that what made Katie's presence with him more real and precious was the inevitability that they would be parted. Despite his terror, it felt good to lie there with the danger making each moment as intense as a child's first experiences. Once he would have kept trying to put a shape on their relationship. Now he said nothing.

She lay beside him like a shy hare crouched in the grass, whom only time and patience would coax out into the light. Her eyes betrayed nothing of her thoughts. He knew better than to mention Leitrim again. Katie turned, catching him observing her and smiled as she ran a blade of grass between her fingers.

'Go on Hano,' she said, 'I want to hear about her.'

If he had told his parents when he came home the first time, it might have been all right. He had meant to, but when he returned to Dublin there seemed no words that would bridge the gap between her book-lined caravan and the terrace house where his father shaved before the cracked mirror and walked in his overalls to Plunkett Motors. Twice a week a battered mobile library creaked on to the cracked concrete across from the post office, the bored assistants reading as the borrowers browsed through the same titles yellowing on the shelves. There had been no books in his world, only the blare of the television from half-five each evening, the inanities of quiz shows, neighbours gathering to watch the Eurovision Song Contest. Ghosts were meant for Friday night at eight, interrupted by ads, forgotten by nine in the mystery of *The Fugitive*. Young people and old people were like separate species in a zoo. The television serials said so. It would have seemed unnatural, even morbid to his mother, for him to have anything in common with the old woman. And he knew that to his father she would be 'an old Protestant woman', though it would not be her religion that he would find worrying. Half Hano's street were Protestants, they lived and mixed together as one. Differences were only mentioned when somebody died and people wondered what to send instead of a Mass card. It was her class that would be the problem, even though she was poorer now than anybody in her village. But she was still a part of that barbarous race who had once controlled the land.

So he said nothing, but sneaked back twice that year, inventing the most banal safe destinations. Each evening he'd wander up the wooded avenue at dusk but always stop when he reached the bend before her ruined house, daring himself on but unable to shake the notion that if he did a waiting figure would emerge from within it. He'd turn back, almost running, till the electric light at the village edge broke the fear within him.

A sheep appeared from behind the rock at Katie's head, stared unblinkingly at them and bounded away. Katie rolled over and closed her eyes.

'I could see how the men in the village thought of her as a half-mad nuisance,' Hano said. 'Walking miles in the rain to make them move their cows if they let them stray into the wood, or to complain when they beat a dog or allowed a sick calf starve to death. But they still had a curious respect for her, Katie. You know, because even though she had returned from wandering around the world to live in a caravan with only a few acres of woodland left, she remained the wife of the man who'd ruled the village, the last of the family name chiselled in stone over their church altar.

'Had she been an outsider, I think she'd have been found in a ditch with her head battered by a rock. But even though she was penniless and old, there was still an aura about her they couldn't shake off. Their wives went to her for advice, surreptitiously at first and then more openly. Some evenings I'd visit the local pub. They hated Dubliners there but her friendship protected me. One night a farmer filled me with pints. I wasn't used to drink and began to ramble on about the dump and the cattle while a sullen silence grew at the bar.

'"What the fuck would you know, ye fucking Jackeen," a young man muttered sourly. The older ones pulled their black overcoats tighter, their caps screwed down on their heads, and watched. I blathered about my father being from a farm in Kerry until the farmer asked his name and then, with a dismissive snort, started describing my grandparents to me. Your man had been in school with my father. I sobered up when his name was mentioned, feeling suddenly exposed. I could see the whole pub grinning, Katie, they knew they'd got the measure of me.'

Hano was back home a week before the farmer's letter came. He came in from school, it was the first time his father ever struck him. He looked down at his hand while Hano held his face, then began to shout about people wasting land, her refusing to sell her ten acres of wood so they could be levelled for cattle, denying her neighbours prosperity. Although it was thirty years since Hano's father had turned a sod of grass, whatever the letter had said, he took it as an insult to his masculinity that his son would visit such a person.

'They couldn't understand why I'd lied to them,' Hano told her. 'And I couldn't explain it, Katie. I could say fuck all – just stand there as the endless questions came. That night in bed I heard the murmur of their voices downstairs, the worry, the incomprehension. I don't know what they thought – that she'd corrupted me somehow, and she had, but in ways they could never have imagined. "We didn't shoot enough of them in '22," my father said the next day when I tried to talk to him. The words were so unlike him, Katie, it was like he was saying them to prove something to himself.'

'And that was it?' she asked.

Hano remembered how the younger children had loved her. He'd watch them arrive early to reach the caravan before their friends and bask in the importance of talking to her alone, gazing at the rows of old books on the cramped shelves and twisting up their noses at the unfamiliar scent of incense. The old woman would talk to them, knowing that in a few years they'd be embarrassed at having ever gone to her. On the bus that went twice a week to Sligo they'd sit away from her, deliberately boisterous with their friends, sniggering at the mad old woman. Hano knew that he could have gone back, could have written. But he had stopped, suddenly ashamed at the thought of her. He'd seemed to lose the sense of her, to see her only through his father's eyes. And it wasn't only her he'd forgotten, but all she had said, the sense of wonder in that caravan where the only clock was a broken one with the word *Now*! written on a piece of carboard stuck over its face. On the Saturday after the farmer's letter came he had gone down town and returned with a punk haircut. He remembered how happy his parents had been, his oddity now a recognized one, like the ones they saw young people condemned for on television.

'I wonder if she understood?' he asked Katie. 'She had a way of knowing what went on in people's heads.'

Katie opened her eyes and stared at him, the same unblinking look he'd known back in Dublin.

'Will she still be there Hano?'

'Her wood might be. The ruined house. Maybe.'

'What if it's not?'

He shrugged his shoulders. She looked away, prised her tight shoes back on and, without waiting for him, began to walk.

# CHAPTER FOUR

# Tuesday Evening

All evening as they crossed the mountain black clouds were lowering themselves slowly on to the hill like spacecraft coming to rest. Katie and Hano walked through the mist, their progress impeded by streams and patches of bog. They ignored the first soft drops that clung like vapour to their hair. Towards seven o'clock they reached a small road where an old man was digging in the tiny field behind his house, his felt cap pulled down, oblivious to the weather.

It was the first time that day they had seen land under tillage. The field had been laboriously reclaimed from the bog which lurked beyond the thick stone walls. There were rows of carrots and cabbage, a scraggy line of twigs separating them. They crouched behind a boulder, waiting for him to go in. Hano stared at the carrots, his dry mouth aching for their raw flesh. Finally the old man plodded towards the cottage, parking his spade against the white wall. They scrambled down, shoving against each other in their haste to reach the vegetables. When their hands were full they ran, afraid to look back, filled with shame and ravenous hunger. They cleaned the carrots in a small stream that trickled down rocks beside the boreen and ate them raw.

The rain was growing heavier. Hano found a plastic wrapper crumpled up in the ditch and gave it to Katie for her head. She slit the side of it and pressed it down over her hair as a makeshift hood. A car appeared far behind them, its headlights catching the drizzle as they crouched down till it passed. They were cold and exhausted. Nausea had displaced his hunger since he'd eaten. She cupped her hands to drink from the stream and climbed back up on to the road without speaking. He followed her hunched shoulders in silence.

They moved down the hillside in the drizzle. The wind had risen with an uncanny sound across the open expanse of bog, clearing the mist, bringing heavier rain. The road twisted past the ruins of cottages with plastic sacks strewn at the base of the County Council *No Dumping* signs. Terraces had been dug like mass graves in the bog, the turf piled to dry in stacks covered with plastic. The wind blew the rain into their faces. They reached a main road and swung left towards the gateway of a field hidden from the road, climbing on to the bars to rest. Occasionally cars passed at high speed, showering them with water from the road. Down the hill, near the lake, they saw the lights of a hotel, cars pulling in and out, distant figures chatting in the real world. Hano lowered his head, then raised it with a sick feeling when he heard an engine coming to a halt.

Katie's hand touched his as they gazed fearfully at the stationary white Volkswagon van. Two men in their twenties sat in the front, mocking grins beneath their neat moustaches. Hano stared in incomprehension till he noticed the blonde teenage girl in the back training a video camera on them. The men in front were pulling faces, waving their fists, trying to coax some reaction from them. Disappointed, the driver moved off, the camera still filming as the van was lost in the bushes.

'Fucking Germans,' Katie said. She thought for a moment before continuing. 'You know, when I was around eleven I started asking my uncle about the funeral. Before that I'd never mention it. But I began to think about it: what was it like; who was there? He was uneasy when I asked. Maybe it was so sudden, that he remembered shag all about it himself. All he ever mentioned was this car pulling up across the road from the graveyard as they were about to lower the coffins. The priest paused for a moment, thinking they were mourners who'd travelled all morning to reach there.

'It was a middle-aged couple, French or German, he didn't know which. They leaned against the wall to take pictures of the coffins being lowered on ropes and then, when everybody had walked away and the grave was covered by a green canvas, they came in. They were bent over the grave when my uncle looked back. He thought at first they were praying,

Hano, then realized they were reading the inscriptions on the wreaths. The man raised his camera again, there was a last click and they just drove on to the next spectacle.'

She shook her head, the saturated bag slipping off on to the grass. It was growing dark, time to move on. Just keep moving, that was all, imagining yourself one step ahead of the posse. A light shone through the trees before the bridge. As they approached they made out the plaster-cast statue of The Virgin. *Our Lady of Lourdes*, the inscription read, *Marian Year, 1954*. A spotlight had been placed at the feet of the crude image. Every village still had one, like an appendage of the past. All summer, crowds, abandoning faith in ordinary hope, had been gathering to watch such statues dance and sway and deliver cryptic messages. The eyes stared back at Hano, still and lifeless.

'It must be out of order,' he said.

It was an old joke, neither laughed. They crossed the bridge where a farmer was buying petrol at the one pump outside the hotel. An American in tweeds with a white bawneen on his head sat in the window over his dinner, the smell of steak wafting through the rain. Hano wanted to stand and breathe it in. He stopped outside the circle of light shining on the roadway. Katie tugged his hand, urging him onwards. There was nowhere to hide from the lights of cars now, they just climbed on to the mound of grass against the stone wall till each one passed.

Where the road levelled out again they found the dance-hall. The front door, below the *For Sale* sign, had been bricked up. The remains of a few posters hung there still. Somebody had painted FUCK O in large white letters and been too apathetic to finish the message. The car-park to the left had never been tarmaçadamed. The rutted surface led down towards a row of granite boulders and bushes bordering the water's edge. They walked around the side. There was no annex built on. The door moved inward under his shoulder and they were in the remains of a kitchen. Through the serving hatch he could see into the main dance floor. He broke the dividing door with his boot and led her in. What light remained filtered through the high windows along each wall where the glass had been smashed and iron bars jutted against the night sky. A ragged sign hung over the low stage, the barely distinguishable gold letters proclaiming *Welcome to the Crystal Ballroom*. A raised area had been railed off for tables, the wall behind it covered in scrawled names and curses. A few coloured tiles were still in place on the floor where an occasional chair lay, twisted and upturned among the black puddles. The light fittings had been stripped from the ceiling and leads of flex hung like worms burrowing through wood.

Hano thought suddenly of his father, forty years before, cycling to a place like this, the black bicycle left against the wall, the slice of sweet cake passed out through the serving hatch with the mineral. How many girls had waited along those walls like his mother had stood once? How many lads had looked for courage?

'Can you feel the ghosts?' he asked.

'Don't feel fucking nothing,' Katie muttered, pushing past him to pick up a chair and sit huddled on the dance floor. Their voices echoed in the emptiness.

'Do you know where we are?' she asked.

'I think so.'

'What if she isn't there? What if even the wood's gone?'

'Don't know Katie. Maybe . . . maybe it'll be as well if she's not. She'd be changed, different from what I'd told you. Maybe we're better off never to arrive anyway, just keep travelling till we're caught, quit pretending we can stop.'

'I'm cold, Hano.'

The lights of a passing car swept along the top of the wall and plunged them back into darkness.

'You could go home, Katie. Tell them I forced you to come with me.'

'Where the fuck is that?'

He wanted to put his arms around her but there was so much coldness and pain in those hunched shoulders that he was afraid to touch them. Her hands were folded tightly against her stomach and her head bent down almost touching the plastic rim of the chair. Her feet were placed apart among the jagged stars of glass on the floor, water dripping from them to form a fresh pool beneath the chair. In the indistinct

188

light she was like a figure in an old painting lost behind the grime of centuries of dust. He walked towards her and bowed slightly.

'I'm not very good at this, but would you like to dance?'

She looked up. Hano stared back solemnly at her.

'You asking?'

Her voice sounded as suspicious as any girl's had ever been in that cavernous hall. He nodded. Katie rose awkwardly, holding him at arms length as they began to shuffle through the debris. He hummed every tune that entered his head, ones he knew and those without words which came to him, murmuring anything to keep them revolving in slow circles, drawing closer to each other until her arms were draped over his shoulders and he half-carried her as they waltzed.

'Katie . . .' he whispered.

'No. Don't call me Katie, My real name . . . they gave me, the one I changed in the city. Call me Cait. I'm tired of Katie . . . tired.'

She laid her head down and they continued shuffling. Even his voice had stopped now. There was only the shuffle of their feet crunching the glass beneath them into the floor. Outside he heard the rain beat against the stone walls of the hall, the wind tearing at the loose sheets of metal still tacked to the windows. The noise made the darkness of the dance floor seem warm and trance-like. He stopped moving as though afraid of being hypnotized.

'Can I see you home?' he said.

'I don't know.' She looked up. 'Who are you?'

'My name's Francis. Can I see you home, Cait?'

'Please, Francis. Please.'

The wind had chopped up the surface of the lake. They could see white flashes through the bushes and rocks. There were fewer cars now. He tried to give her his jacket though it was soaked, but she refused and, wrapping her own around her, began to walk.


At five to twelve on the Thursday night I crossed the metal bridge. In the shelter below a young couple were standing

189

motionless with their arms around each other, waiting for my footsteps to pass inches from their heads. As I reached the flat old Mrs Finnegan who lived above the next shop opened her hall door and beckoned to me.

'There's somebody after breaking into your flat,' she said. 'Some dark fellow in a hat. I was just putting the bottles out when I saw him trying to force the door. I think he's inside now. Will I phone the guards for you?'

I searched hesitantly for my keys with her standing a few steps behind me. She had spent two hours keeping watch; now she was determined to miss nothing. The door seemed closed as usual, but when I opened it cautiously and peered up the stairs I could discern in the moonlight the outline of a figure sprawled at the top of the stairs outside the landing door. Maybe it was because he was the last person I had seen sleeping rough, but I was sure it was the young tramp I had left at the Mater Hospital, that he had traced me here and come seeking shelter or revenge. I felt exposed and guilty but also angry as if I was being forced to carry the sins of the Plunketts.

I motioned for Mrs Finnegan to remain where she was and, picking up a sweeping brush from the hall, ascended the creaking steps one at a time. The landing was in darkness except for a diminutive pair of luminous hands suspended a few inches from the intruder's head so I had to grope at the wall to press the light switch in with a soft, inhaling click.

'Listen, you can't sleep there mate,' I said.

The figure raised a battered hat from over his unshaven face and screwed up his eyes in the light.

'Nothing personal Hano, but you look an awful prick standing with a sweeping brush in the middle of the night.'

'Holy-for-fuck! Shay, is that you?'

He was dressed in a long overcoat of coarse black wool, with heavy boots that an LDF recruit in the forties must have abandoned, and a black rimmed hat which made him look like a preacher in some mid-west road show who knew there was no God. His eyes were circled and exhausted, his face darkened with the stubble of travel. A rolled-up sleeping bag served as a pillow and a travel clock kept time on the floor beside him.

On the newspaper beside him there was a half-eaten loaf of bread, a penknife, a packet of cheese, and, incongruously, an unopened bottle of champagne. He laughed as he rose to embrace me. It was only then that I remembered Mrs Finnegan. I looked down.

'It was only *him* was it?' she said in disgust and walked back, disappointed, to her book beside the window.

'I wasn't sure if you'd still be living here, Hano. Were you at a party or what?'

'No, I was at work.'

'Work? Has Mooney got you digging up the dead and registering them for the vote?'

I said nothing, I didn't even want to think about Plunkett. I wanted to suspend reality as long as possible, to pretend everything was the same as the night Shay had left. When I asked him why he'd come home he grinned.

'You've obviously never tasted Dutch beer Hano. Would you believe that I got homesick. I got this little thrill in my stomach tonight when I saw the lights of Ireland flickering in the distance. I imagined the last person on to the plane would have turned them all out.'

With a plop the wall timer plunged us back into darkness. Shay thumped it with his fist and jammed it with a broken match. He caught me staring at his haggard face and in turn stared curiously back at my own.

'Why did you really come home?' I asked.

'Is this a fucking inquest or what?'

For a moment Shay's face became guarded. In spite of my euphoria I could sense a change in him. His features had an older look and tiredness made his eyes seem watchful and serious. But there was something more than that, though it took me weeks to realize it, as if something inside him had broken and left him with a perpetual sense of unease which he was incapable of shaking off. I could see his eyes also taking me in, shocked by the traces of bruising.

'Kid, you look worse than I do,' he said. 'Have you another lodger or are you going to ask me in?'

I unlocked the door of the flat and Shay drop-kicked the sleeping bag into the corner of the living-room. I suddenly wanted to tell him how much I had missed him, how I had not been living here, how my father had died, about Plunkett. But the thought of that name chilled me, He produced a single battered key from his pocket.

'Couple of months back,' he said, 'I was after getting kicked out some factory and kipping up on the third bunk of a hostel dormitory. Don't ask me why, the bottom one was empty. The head wasn't functioning too well, I suppose. Middle of the night I rolled off. I'd have probably lain there till dawn if some good Samaritan hadn't picked me off the concrete floor and tucked me into the bottom bunk. Then he took my wallet as a tip. I went through my gear in the morning and the only things I still owned were my passport, an Irish pound note a certain person gave me on Capel Street Bridge and a key to this front door.

'Tell you a joke, Hano. Later on I went to the Irish embassy in The Hague and finally this ninth secretary agrees to see me – late thirties, ultimate career woman. *Oh no*, she says in a Foxrock voice, *I'm afraid it would be impossible to help you financially. We're here to help young Irish people in every possible way – except financially*. Well, I think about it for a minute, then I look at her and say, "Actually I haven't eaten for a day and a half so I don't suppose it would be possible to suck on your tit for a few moments?"'

'How did you get home then?'

'Listen, I got fucking home, that's enough,' he said sharply and closed his eyes. He opened them apologetically. 'Look, I'm sorry. I'm knackered. And I meant to write to you, every single day I meant to write to you. Right now I'd be heavy into a bed. I remember vaguely what one looks like so I should be able to find it.'

Pressing the champagne into my arms and leaving his coat, hat, boots and jeans in an untidy procession on the floor behind him, he fell in through the doorway of his old room. And before I had time to turn the lights off and set the clock I could hear snoring through the wall. I pulled the blankets over me and, for the first time in weeks, slept deeply myself, as though I too was an emigrant returning from a nightmare journey.

The storm which had been forecast swept across the city that night. I was aware of it in my sleep with the drowsy pleasure of being wrapped up listening to the torrential rain outside. The first phase blew itself out as I lapsed in and out of dreams, waiting for the alarm to finally ring. Time seemed suspended in a sleepy cocoon that went on indefinitely until finally the door was swung open, flooding the room in an arc of light, and I woke fully to the smell of fried bacon. For a moment I thought I was in my mother's house and then remembered that Shay was home as he stood silhouetted in the doorway with breakfast on a tray. It was twenty-five to one on the clock beside the bed. I would be late for work. I had one hand out to rise when he immobilized me by placing the tray down on my lap. The shock of seeing him in the morning light was almost as great as it had been on the darkened stairs. The stubble had been removed and the neatly clipped moustache occupied the centre of attention again. Only the hair that had grown long and shaggy seemed out of character with the stylish figure who had left seven months before. It was wet from the rain. He saw me looking at it and placed a wisp in his mouth.

'Doesn't taste half bad when you're starving in some railway station. You bollox, you never told me you'd changed jobs. I killed your alarm, you were sleeping too beautifully. I phoned Mooney to report in sick for you. Think I finally freaked him out. He said you'd left five months ago and he heard you were working for Pascal Plunkett. I told him Plunkett couldn't be a bigger bollox than he was.'

'What did you do then?' I asked, trying and failing to keep the fear from my voice. Shay looked at me curiously.

'I phoned your man Plunkett, told him you were sick and would probably be in tomorrow. He's one weird character. He boomed down the phone at me, *Who are you?* He sounded like Fu Manchu at the end of those films they made in Wicklow, *I shall return!* I said I was your flatmate and he slammed the phone down.'

He paused and stopped grinning.

'If you have any choice, Hano, stay away from that family.'

I could imagine Plunkett's rage as he stormed up and down

the office. I knew I would have to face it tomorrow. But suddenly, as I lay with breakfast in front of me and the old taste for misadventure returning, I didn't care. I laughed, realizing how long it had been since I had made that sound. I felt like a tree must do in spring when the sap begins to rise. Shay pulled the curtains. The rain had stopped and the sky looked fresh and blue outside, waiting to be conquered.

'I take it you didn't ask Mooney for your job back?'

'I'd starve first,' Shay said. 'It's no harm you got the bullet. You could be there till you drop without ever learning more than that E comes after D.'

'It's a big cold world outside.'

'Who the fuck are you telling kid?' he said.

He paused. I think we were both remembering that unreal world, the long table of clerks, the clock put forward, the wage cheque every other Thursday, the snug boredom of permanent people who could never be sacked. He shrugged his shoulders.

'No, "The Winner's Enclosure" is your only man. No hitches this time Hano. We'll even get Carol in a corset posing in the window. Fuck them all, eh.'

We joked on as I finished breakfast and then over cigarettes I told him about my father and what I felt I could about Pascal Plunkett. We had the radio on. There was talk of the government falling again. It seemed as if the electorate trusted nobody anymore, were terrified to give either party power. Suddenly Patrick Plunkett was interviewed. 'No one is more tired of elections than me,' he said, 'after two in the past eighteen months. But if we go to the polls, this time the people will give us the mandate we need. A strong government for a strong people: one party, one voice, one nation.'

He bladdered on with the usual shite like that. Once Shay wouldn't have bothered listening but I noticed his attentiveness as the voice droned on, his face uneasy again, drained of light. I pulled the plug out and stared at him.

'I hate this country,' he said. 'What the fuck did I come home to this kip for.'

He took a roll of clean notes from his jacket pocket, peeled some off and threw them on the bed for rent. Once I would

194

have asked him where he'd got the money from but now I said nothing as he picked the tray up and left. I dressed, standing beside the window. Although the cloudburst had cleared, the tail-end of the wind was still blowing itself out. The bushes behind the tumbledown cottages across the road were twisted double, the huge metal bridge beside them creaking like a ship about to slip its moorings. The radio had said that trees were down all over the country, roads had given away under flooding, the Dodder had burst its banks, everything that wasn't solid had been torn apart. Now as I gazed out at the power of the wind I was suddenly scared. Shay shouted from the kitchen.

'Will you get up for fuck's sake Hano! You'd swear you were looking for compensation after an accident. Come on and I'll roll something I brought home in my jocks to put us in the mood down the Botanics.'

I laughed as I walked out to the kitchen but I was still scared.

Our strolls in the Botanic Gardens had always been an oasis of tranquillity, but to go there that afternoon seemed like lunacy. Over forty trees had blown down in the arboretum overnight, and though the wind was dropping they were still reluctant to allow us in. One tree had crashed through the wall into the oldest part of the cemetery and smashed a dozen faded headstones. Workmen in yellow oilskins were using chain-saws to clear it. The Tolka had also burst its banks and the lower half of the gardens was under water. The conduit where I had followed my father's bier in my mind was a swirling torrent, covering the pathway, crashing down through trees and sweeping the smaller plants away. Even to light the joint in the wind was difficult. I inhaled. It was the first time in months I had tasted hash. It made me feel sick and I handed it back to him.

'You go away,' he said, looking around, 'and somehow you imagine life stops in your absence. You know it's stupid to think that, but deep down you do. Let's get the hell away from here.'

But all day desolation seemed to follow us. Almost every old haunt of Shay's had changed, often just slightly, but

195

enough to make him feel not quite at home. That night as we drank our way through the city streets, now deserted and sullen under the torrent of rain, there was something manic about Shay. Wherever we stopped he picked up old friends until there were ten or twelve of us on the pub crawl, drunkenly crowding in from the wet streets. The crowd was as large as the night he went away, only now Shay got annoyed when people left. The night had to go on at all costs. At closing time he ordered a taxi and brought four of us up to Mick's flat. We knocked for ten minutes before Mick came down.

'Party time,' Shay shouted, thrusting the bottle of whiskey into his hand. The girls in the flat above banged on the ceiling when Shay turned the record player up full blast. He wandered upstairs to try and lure them down. A stream of abuse came through their door and when I went up a few minutes later I found that he had somehow hauled an old wardrobe across the landing to block their door in the morning.

The storm grew again throughout the night. The Royal Canal flooded in the midlands and a wall collapsed in Cork, killing a man sheltering under it. I thought of the youth huddled in his blanket near Christchurch, of all those night-time figures I had seen while driving the Plunkett brothers.

We left Mick's at five in the morning. Cables and phone wires had snapped and hung down at street corners. It was nearly impossible to walk straight in the wind, yet Shay strode ahead of me drenched in jeans with his light jacket open. We reached Rathmines Road as the lights turned green and a taxi began to move off. Shay darted forward with his hand out and then did something that I had never seen before. He hesitated and instinctively reached into his back pocket to check he had money before waving his hand again. He was too late, the cab was gone. We headed towards town, looking for another one. He zipped his jacket up and walked beside me in silence, suddenly preoccupied, wet and unhappy.

Plunkett spent the next afternoon sniping at me. Normally if he was going to remain in the garage he would tell me to wander off and I'd sit over a newspaper in the coffee shop down the village. But when I arrived at lunch-time he shouted from his office for me to wait beside the car. I sat outside waiting for two hours, watching the mechanics find excuses to wander out and enjoy my discomfort. I thought he was just angry but later, from our brief snatches of conversation as I drove between sites, I realized that he was jealous. He tried to maintain the stony silence but finally his curiosity overcame him.

'When did you leave home?' he asked.

'A few days ago.'

He was silent again for a while.

'Who's this flatmate?'

'Just a friend.'

'What sort of friend?'

For the first time I knew that I had him. I shrugged my shoulders quizzically, smiled and didn't reply. He glowered out of the window until I thought he was about to put his fist through the glass. I drove on, suddenly feeling strong, enjoying his discomfort. That night in Mother Plunkett's Cabin he made his offer. The house was too big for him alone. Why not move in with him instead? I could have my own rooms, bring my own friends in if I wished. It would be straight friendship; he would not come near me. I asked him what people would make of it.

'You can ... tell them ... something ... tell them you're my shagging butler.'

When I started laughing he got furious. I could tell them whatever I wanted, he roared. He would take my mother's account off his ledger. I could name my salary, I wouldn't even have to work for him. I could go to university, study anything I wanted, he'd pay my fees. As long as I just gave up that flat and came to live with him.

For four months he had bullied his way into my life with that utter self-assurance. And I had cowered, terrified of his every word. He had been invincible, a man with no weaknesses, no feelings, knowing nothing of pity or mercy. Now, seated across from me at that table, while the strains of Country and Western music filtered in from the lounge, he suddenly looked like the tired sixty-year-old man he was. For the first time I realized how little happiness I had witnessed in his life. I had seen his success every day: the strokes pulled, the by-laws bent, the money which kept accumulating in his Isle of Man bank account. But it had ceased to mean anything to him; most of the time he was like a ship on auto-pilot. To hundreds like my mother, he was a deity who controlled their lives, but to those that mattered he was, at best, his brother's brother. Even Patrick often looked embarrassed when he turned up at official receptions. The State driver once told me that when they called in on their way to certain functions he was instructed to knock on the door and inform the minister instead that he would be late for some routine departmental meeting in case Pascal decided to go in as well.

And I realized how much Pascal craved respect, not among the cowering housewives or the traders he did business with, but in places he would always be excluded from. His own money and his brother's position might allow him to glimpse inside, but he would always remain the awkward figure in the monkey suit, ignored by the crowd discussing the symphony in the concert hall bar. He was still talking, low and earnestly, still making promises. There was nothing I could not be. I could do medicine, law: he would pay for any course I wanted. If I hadn't the points he'd bribe my way in. Partly it was the whiskey talking, but I think he suddenly wanted his youth back, wanted the chance to live his life again through my life; to bury the poverty of his youth, the suitcase and the train ticket in that station in Kerry. His eyes were more manic than the night he had chased through the hallway, but they had bulged with strength then. Now they were jaded and pathetic.

'Been working all my life,' he said. 'But for what? For who? I held you on my knee Francy when you were just a child. Your father had come down to me. I took him on. I was jealous, wanted a son, but without some bitch round my neck, getting in my way. I've been trying to show you . . . my world . . . all you can have.'

He lowered his head, then lifted his eyes again. I could barely make out his voice above the noise his staff made, anxious at his presence, trying to show their worth.

'I know it,' he mumbled. 'I'm frightened by it . . . I'll die alone . . . for what? A jumped-up nephew who won't even cry

... people who'll lose their fear ... forget. I want to be remembered, Francy, just come and live with me. This time we'll have the suits, the respect. No more scraping around like I did, or your father. Don't leave me, do you hear, waking at night by myself.'

I don't know how much of my courage was due to Shay's return, but that moment was like a cloud lifting from a mountainside, giving me my perspective back. I wasn't lost any longer. I rose from the table. He pushed his chair back, as though afraid I was going to strike him. Behind us the barmen were clearing out the last drinkers. Two lounge boys stood near the door clapping irregularly to annoy people, while a tape recording of the fire drill repeated loudly. He shouted words I was unable to hear in the noise. I knew if I didn't do it while I felt this strong I might never have the courage again. He shouted again.

'Anything you want, just don't go. Damn you, don't leave me! I've built all this, for what ... I own ... you can't just leave ... I'll die ... what'll I do when I die?'

I reached in my pocket for the car keys and, throwing them on the table among the empty glasses, turned and walked towards the door. I kept waiting for him to come after me, I could almost feel his hand gripping my shoulder to swing me around. But when I reached the door I could see his reflection through the glass panel, still slumped at the table with the half-empty bottle. For the first time in my life I felt sorry for him as I pushed the door open and walked out into the night air.

It smelt so pure, so fresh. I remembered again my father in that hospital bed, how I had longed to carry him out beneath the stars. I had felt a numbness since his death. Each day walking into that garage I had been shamed by his memory. But that night, as I walked through the sleeping fields towards the outskirts of town, I seemed to sense him, not quite beside me, but somehow near at hand, at ease at last. I had no idea how I would feed my family or keep the flat on, but for now nothing mattered. I was discovering what it was like to feel clean again. Shay was sitting up in the kitchen when I got home. He was still hung-over, slightly ashamed at his madness the previous night. He had rigged up a soft light in the corner that took away the harsh look of the walls. A record was playing. He had a joint rolled which he offered to me. I sat across from him and grinned. He looked closely at me.

'Hey, you don't look shit any more, Hano,' he said.

'I quit working for Plunkett.'

He went to the kitchen press and produced the bottle of champagne. The only glasses we had were two pint ones we had stolen in town one night. He fetched them, worked the cork off the bottle slowly with a cloth so that it made little noise when it popped. The liquid fizzed along the edge of the glasses.

'It doesn't matter how broke you are,' he said. 'That family are dirt. When you touch them you become dirt too, dirty inside and that's not easy to wash off.'

I didn't want to ask him any questions. I picked up the glass Shay handed me. He had not drawn the curtains. The night outside was a rich, deep blue. I could make out the shape of the old Protestant church and, stretching beyond it, the pin-pricks of light burning in a thousand homes. The suburb seemed to enclose me, with its continuous cycle of life. We touched pint glasses, swallowed deeply.

'Welcome home, Shay,' I said.

He put his head to one side, grinned quizzically at my nervous euphoria, then lifted his glass to touch mine lightly again.

'Welcome home yourself, kid,' he replied.


*Your tale doesn't end and mine begin. Your life flashes past intermixed with mine. A profusion of images I can make no sense of. I smell of clay, I dream of earth, I have no name for this place. The last faces I remember are a young couple in the ruins. I open the window to throw cigarettes down and turn, knowing I have finally come home. I never slept so deeply before, only it wasn't like sleep but like falling forever down a tunnel of light, hazy as an after image when you close your eyes.*

*Then my body crumples awake into an unbearable silence. It is all embracing, filling my ears as I try to sense what is* wrong. Is it the silence that wakes me or is it a final shout? I call Hano's name as I wake, no longer even able to hear my own breathing. The room is as it should be, sunlight penetrating the curtains. I cross the floor naked to pull the cord open, gaze at the Triumph Herald back in its old spot. I know no reason to be afraid but my hands tremble as the silence sweeps me again. Everything outside is immobile, slotted neatly in its place — the twin barber poles jutting up from the power station, the unplanned jumble of estates. All that's missing is movement and noise.

I walk to Hano's room, try to be casual as I push the door in. The blankets are thrown off hurriedly but the sheets that I touch feel as cold as death. The flat door is still locked so this has to be a joke. I search every corner for a sign or a note. The television carries a blanket of static, the empty airwaves hiss on the radio bands. I try to phone every number I know, but not even the speaking clock answers.

I know that I must be dreaming but still my eyes are mesmerized by the locked door. Will it open or am I trapped inside? 'Go to the door,' I tell myself, 'just open it and you will laugh at this irrational fear. Something has happened that you have slept through. There are friends outside who will tell you.'

My keys clank loudly as I draw them out. Six steps to the door, through the hiss of static from the television, the unanswered beep of the telephone. I wipe sweat from my palms against my shirt, draw in my breath and twist the key round. With a faint click the handle turns under my hand. I press the timer switch and make my way down.

Everything outside is in its place, that crooked street looking the way I love it after dawn. Becalmed trees search for a breeze in the graveyard. The metal bridge betrays no iron creak; no birds sing on the telegraph poles. Traffic-lights shift colour like a medium trying to summon cars. Nothing seems more desolate than their futile cycle. It must still be dawn I tell myself. Hano has vanished for a joke, the station's gone off the air. Somebody soon is bound to appear: an office cleaner as grey as stone; the obligatory old man on a bone-shaker *bike. Then I turn to look back up and see Hano at the window. His hands are spread against the glass, his shoulders white, his hair still tossed from sleep. And he is looking over my shoulder towards the middle of the street. I gaze up at him in purgatory and know that he is staring through me.*

On the next Monday I joined Shay in the queue under the ornate ceiling of the Victorian labour exchange. I still couldn't think how to tell my mother what had happened. On Tuesday I went home with whatever money I had, dreading the scene I would have to face. She was in the living-room with bills spread in front of her on the table. I closed my eyes and when I opened them she was looking up with the trace of a bemused smile on her lips. I had forgotten what her smile looked like. It made her look younger and suddenly I saw why my father had chosen her thirty years before. She beckoned me over, searching to find the words in her excitement.

'I'd overpaid him. That's what they said. Can you believe it? I don't know Francy, I think your daddy up in heaven must be looking after us. I prayed to him to explain these bills to me and now I can pay them all.'

She had the look of a kitchen girl who had woken to find herself a pantomime princess. I made her go over it all: how she had gone to the garage with the usual weekly payment and had been made to wait on the stairs for a quarter of an hour before Plunkett sent word down that her account was paid in full and she was due a refund of one hundred and fifty pounds. She took the money from her handbag and counted it out again like a child with sweets, and even when I told her I had stopped working I don't think she really took it in. I tried to give her my money but she refused it.

'You've been the best son I could ever ask for, Francy. You keep it for now. Enjoy yourself.'

After the wildness of that first night I had begun to see how Shay had changed after his seven months in Europe. He had grown serious, more inward. Before he would have been out almost every night, but now he was more at ease in the flat with the door locked on the outside world. Some days he was still the same Shay, trailing the flex of the electric kettle out the window at the convent girls and cooking excessively hot chilli. One night he phoned up a man across the street and impersonated his outraged neighbour complaining about his wife's infidelities while he was at work. When the man slammed the phone down Shay immediately phoned the other neighbour and reversed the process. We took our seats behind the lace curtain to watch the two figures storming out into the street to roar abuse at each other. Their wives came out and dragged them in. When I got up Shay was sitting smoking and staring down at the empty road. He leaned his chair back after a while and asked me to describe Pascal Plunkett. I called out details from the kitchen.

'I think he wants you back,' Shay said. 'He's been sitting across the road in a car staring up here for the past ten minutes.'

As soon as I pulled the curtains aside the engine started and I could see only the tail-light moving down to the carriageway. Shay stubbed his cigarette out and went into his room without asking any questions.

There were parts of each other's recent past which we instinctively knew not to ask about. In the first few days I had plied him with questions about Europe and when no answers came I realized he had to tell or not tell me in his own way. The memories he chose were selective: a junkie who tried to knife him off Dam Square; two teenage German girls who wanted to lure him off to bed when he had arrived in Essen after travelling for days and just wanted to sleep; the usual intimidation from the British police at customs; the sun rising over Danish orchards as he climbed a ladder to work. But always the memories came from the early months when everything was a new adventure.

One night we called into Murtagh's for the first time since he returned. The top part was closed off; the long-haired singer finally redundant. We both grew silent when Justin Plunkett came in towards closing time and we refused his offer of a drink. He went to the bar anyway and returned with three large brandies. Ten minutes later I saw Shay discreetly rifle the pockets of my jacket before slipping past Plunkett to the bar. I had only two quid and knew Shay hadn't much more. If he bought a round we would have to walk home. Justin raised his hands in protest when Shay returned with the drinks.

'That was just my present Seamus. There's no need, I know you're not working, man.'

'I'm doing okay,' Shay replied curtly.

I was relieved that Justin didn't mention me. I had no idea if he knew that I had worked for his uncle. I had always just been Shay's sidekick; I wasn't even certain if he was aware of my name. We finished our drinks quickly and left.

We walked across town, up along Capel Street and through the jumble of ruins that had been Ball's Alley and Parnell Street. Watchmen in huts surveyed the last few cars parked on the uneven gravel where houses once stood. A hot smell of grease and vinegar came from the chip shop left standing by itself. A man tried to sleep in what was once a doorway; a deranged woman in slippers wandered happily by herself. We walked past the Black Church and through the park where a canal had once run. The flour mill was deserted now; the wives and children back among the lines of estates; the workers on the dole swapping memories of jail. The long, straight road home was ahead of us now, past the ominous black railings of the cemetery.

'You know something Hano?' Shay said. 'I missed this kip. It's strange isn't it, you don't even need to like a place to miss it. Just look around you – this is a ghost town now, and there I was in the heart of the future, if you like; not actually homesick but hauling around this incomplete feeling. I mean, how can you leave somewhere when it's walking around inside you?'

We reached the V in the road by the wrought-iron gates of the torn-down orphanage. Three youths were climbing over the wall. One hurled an empty flagon back on to the littered grass. For the first time Shay began to speak about those final months. I let him talk on, not daring to interrupt in case he stopped again. He described the things I knew first: the workers' dormitories, the autobahns, the railway stations. Then he paused, remembering. We were passing the petrol station where I used to work, another anonymous figure waiting for dawn among the banks of video screens inside. Shay laughed, an ironic, bitter sound.

'One factory in Germany was so bad,' he said, 'that we had to sleep in communal tents in the grounds. We were the lucky ones, the Irish workers; we had some rights, we were part of Europe – even if they couldn't figure out why they had let us in. If you had seen the way they were treating the Turks you'd understand what I'm talking about. One girl from the local town was seen talking to a young Turk at a night club and nobody in the canteen would sit beside her. I saw young Germans from the office spitting when she passed in the street.

'The harvest had to be canned as it came in, so we were working twelve-, fourteen-, eighteen-hour shifts. It was a bumper crop; people were being forced to work impossible hours. We used to catch frogs and put them in the tins hoping that whoever found them would sue the company. There were eleven of us Irish lads, so needless to say there had to be a strike. We weren't actually looking for much, we were just pissed off with the way we were being treated. There were a load of Brits there, they came out at once and most of the others joined in the next day. The Turks were the last to come out, they were the worst paid and had the most to lose. We made it one of our conditions that they received equal pay with the rest of us before we'd go back. The place was swarming with company officials from Bonn within a day. It would have been over in half the time had they agreed to pay the Turks.

'It was great crack actually. Before then none of us had really mixed much. We knew we had them by the balls; the fruit was starting to rot in the containers outside. Two days after the company gave in the Turks invited some of us over to their tent. It was designed to sleep a hundred people but had a hundred and seventy crammed into it most nights. The drink was flying, some men had wives and kids in Turkey and started passing around photographs. The leader of the Turks must have been nearly sixteen stone. He had a tiny moustache and the saddest face I ever saw. I'd never seen him smile until that night, but he was in great form. He went out into the field for a piss and when he didn't come back after quarter of an hour the Turks started murmuring among themselves. I went out to see what was keeping him.'

Shay paused again. He pulled his jacket closer and stared in at the overgrown tail-end of the cemetery falling down towards the river.

'It must have taken at least six of them to overpower him. He was built like a heavyweight boxer. I heard the moans and had to search with my hands to find him in the wet grass. His arm was twisted awkwardly behind him, obviously broken. I lit a match, Hano, and could hardly distinguish any features on his face. It was smeared with thick blood except for his mouth which kept opening in a small, round O. I was still staring at him when they caught me. The first kick got me in the back and I kept my arms over my face and tried to curl into a ball as the boots came in on all sides. They stopped after a few minutes. I was a European: the police might get involved if they went too far. Here's the bit I can't forget Hano, where it all starts to fall apart on me. I heard them moving off and had half-risen when one turned and, despite somebody calling him in German, ran back. His boot caught me just above the eye and as I keeled over I heard him shout, *You'd give that scum the same pay as us, would you, you Jackeen bastard*. It wasn't the bruised ribs Hano or the blood streaming down my face; it was his accent. Pure, unmistakable bog Irish.'

We had reached the new bridge over the Tolka. Ahead of us the dual carriageway stretched up to the old village. He pointed down towards a pile of rubble where I could still make out the outline of four mud walls near the swirling water.

'My mother used to bring me down here through the woods,' he said, 'before they built the carriageway. Her sister's buried in the cemetery. And always as a bribe we'd go down into that old woman's cottage for a wafer of ice cream. Remember wafers? Was that this century or last I keep asking myself?'

When he mentioned it I suddenly remembered that cottage, the half-door, the shop in the woman's sitting-room. I understood the bewilderment in his voice. It did seem like a distant century: my dead father in his shirt sleeves; my mother pushing a pram as I ran excitedly ahead of them.

I walked up that long curve of carriageway with Shay, remembering the vanished icons buried in my past: an old green pump; a half-buried granite milestone; religious processions to the holy well that was now forgotten and boxed in by houses. As I listed each one I found he remembered them too, that we did share a past. And I realized that it wasn't the bright streets of the city centre that had brought him home, but this invisible, unofficial city which we both inherited.

When we crossed the high metal bridge Shay climbed up on to the railing. For a second I thought he was about to hurl himself into the path of the trucks below. Instead he jumped to his left on to the old graveyard wall. He scrambled over it and jumped down, then grinned and beckoned me to follow. We walked through the broken indecipherable headstones and into the ruins of the old church. It had been roofless for over a century. Through the half-tumbled-down gothic windows, curtained by ivy, we could see the lights of the houses around us. Shay lit two cigarettes, handed me one and lay back on top of an old vault.

'Remember the stories from school?' he asked. 'The secret tunnel from here out to Dunsoughly Castle, the grave robber who died of fright in a vault here when he caught his coat in the lid he had screwed back down. What do you say? I doubt if the kids tell them to each other in school anymore. We caught it Hano, the very tail-end of one place and the start of another. And it's fucked me up till now. But I don't want to drink or smoke or travel or fuck any more. I just want to lie here in my own home place which no longer exists except in my head.'

He sat up and tossed the cigarette away.

'Hey, we'll go home Hano before the Plunkett brothers rezone this and build an amusement arcade here.'

One morning, a fortnight after I had quit working for Plunkett, Shay came into my room and threw a letter in a brown envelope on to the bed. It wasn't a bill we figured, so it might possibly be a rebate cheque. He cautioned against haste in opening it, the longer it remained sealed the more interest might be accumulating inside. I propped myself up with a pillow and we smoked two cigarettes each before deciding it was safe to open it. It was from Dublin Corporation, offering me a temporary position again for six months while they were updating the new register of voters. I had to confirm my availability to Personnel and report to a Mr Mooney on Wednesday. It was the same letter word for word that I had received a year and three months before. I looked at Shay while below us the girl's voice started announcing the day's runners and riders. He emptied his pockets on to the bed, then picked up my trousers from the floor and turned them upside down. A pound note and some silver tumbled on to his few coins lying in solitary opulence on the bedspread. Rent was due on Thursday, the first ESB bill had arrived that morning. He shrugged his shoulders.

'Phone the fuckers,' I said.

It was uncanny to walk back through the door and see the same benches with the same faces bent over the same newspapers. Nothing had changed, or so it seemed at first. Then I noticed Carol was missing and it was Mary who drew the red line and gave out the orders for the day. I took my old seat inside the door; Mick nodded and tossed a role of Sellotape at me. The newspapers were lowered like a fleet of ships surrendering as Mary vanished into Mooney's office.

'Where's Carol?' I asked Mick.

He raised one finger to his head and twisted it.

'Out sick for the past month,' he said. 'There's talk of Mooney retiring and they had some computer engineer in looking over the records to start designing a new system. She still has herself convinced she'd be taking over from the old bollox. She started staying on with wads of work after we went home. I don't know who she was trying to prove her worth to: Mooney wouldn't notice if she was here till midnight; none of us could give a fuck; and I doubt if anyone in Personnel could find this hole on a map. They found her asleep here one morning.'

My life had changed so much since I had last sat in that office and yet, like a schoolboy returning after the summer holidays, by the afternoon it felt like I had never been away. The same petty jokes were in currency; the same rows over whose turn it was to do the shopping for lunch; the same expectations of transfer lists were whispered across tables. It's impossible to describe the sense of unreality about that office, how the real world halted outside its high windows. Even the noise from the court below failed to penetrate the old walls. The world of O'Brien and Flynn, Shay's story of fists and boots in a German field, the slow moving human snakes in the employment exchange, they could have all happened on a distant planet. Once I'd been terrified of Mooney; I had carried hatred home in my heart. Now, after Pascal Plunkett, all I saw was a pathetic old bastard. I watched him coldly when he came out that morning and knew he sensed the change within me as he avoided the table where I sat.

A week later Carol returned. Subdued in herself, she wandered between the two offices like a displaced person. Although he had tormented her, she asked about Shay with genuine concern. I felt sorry for her now. The graduates with their jargon and computers were waiting to bring the office into the twentieth century. Till Mooney went she was useful, keeping the office turning. I knew she would be left, a curious anomaly, spinning out her final working years, unwanted and unneeded, in her pensionable job – left behind as her family had left her; living in two rooms of that crumbling ruin in Deansgrange. She was convinced that in her absence Mary had been plotting to take her job, and now rarely spoke to the younger woman. Each lunch-time she locked herself in the office rechecking the figures done when she was away, desperately searching for the reassurance of mistakes.

Lamenting his sold Triumph Herald, Shay began to wander back towards town in the evenings and arrive home laughing and stoned like in the old days. He'd rush into my room and hurl pillows and shoes at my bed until I'd finally get up and sit with him in the kitchen, smoking joints and swapping jokes for hours. There was an intimacy about those conversations when we were relaxed and jaded. Ideas became tangible in

209

ways I could never recapture in the morning, when I'd curse him as the clock jangled through my sleep and I'd stumble in late for work to be nursed back to health by Mary's ironic tongue and the baby Power in our tea she now sent me across to the pub each morning to buy.

One night of torrential rain, Shay accepted a lift home from Justin Plunkett and I woke in a sudden sweat when I heard his voice, remembering the feel of his uncle closing in behind me. I lay awake reliving it until I heard the door slam, then pulled on a pair of jeans and went out. Shay was sitting at the table, wasted from the bottle of whiskey Justin had purchased. He looked at me and shrugged his shoulders before going unsteadily towards his room.

Whatever money he had on his return was gone, and he was anxious for work of any kind. Over the next month he worked his way through the usual jobs: a late-night kebab shop that lasted four days; washing dishes in a restaurant; helping out a mate on a furniture van. He had been working for two nights as a kitchen porter in a top hotel when he called the chef an animal for spitting into the soup. Half an hour later, as he was scraping pots with his hands buried in boiling water, the assistant manager threw his wages into the sink and gave him two minutes to be off the premises before they set the bouncers from the disco in the basement on to him. The Friday after that I arrived home to find him dressing to go out.

'New job Hano,' he said, pulling a second jumper on. 'Security man up in a factory in Raheny. Black economy like the rest of the shagging city.'

He was given no uniform, no radio and no form of identification, and said his major fear wasn't burglars but trying to convince the police he worked there if they ever stopped. Two Alsatians paced around the boundary fencing. They growled but would not attack him as long as he kept between them and the building. They were trained only to assault anything that moved between them and the fence. He had no key to the factory and nowhere to shelter from the rain except beneath the overhang above the side door. He spent his nights peering in through the wire shutters over the windows and trying to guess what was manufactured there. The security firm's brochure described it as *Twenty-four-hour Personal Protection*. At the end of his ten-hour shift a young student came to relieve him. They had to wait until the dogs were at the far side of the building before switching places. When he came home the first morning I asked him that it was like.

'Ever spent ten hours looking at an Alsatian's anus?' he asked, throwing his jacket on the chair and yawning. 'Look on the bright side. In Amsterdam they'd probably have charged me a hundred guilders for the privilege.'

Over the following weeks I began to see less of Shay. Mostly he would still be in bed when I came home. He'd rise when I had finished eating and we might sit together for an hour before he began his journey to work. The next morning he would stumble in just before I left for the Voters' Register. We'd nod and go our separate ways.

One evening I arrived home to find you, Katie, seated at the table in the kitchen. You stared up at me blankly when I entered, as though I were the intruder. Besides taking an instant dislike to you, there was little more I thought except that Shay's taste had deteriorated. The girls he had always brought back were open and uncomplicated. The flat was an adventure for them; they talked and laughed openly. But you sat in your coat, hunched up as if trying to fit into the smallest space. Your black hair was tightly cropped which gave your face a stern, almost aggressive look, and you refused to say a word back to Shay until I had left.

The next evening you were there again in the same seat, with your coat still on. Shay was rolling a joint on the table, you watched him intently, then lifted your eyes to stare at my face as if daring me to stay. I sat down and took the joint when Shay passed it to me. I looked between the pair of you, trying to understand what was happening.

Remember Katie, how you said you despised me on those nights you called to the flat? I grew to hate you too, to hate your long possessive ring of the bell, your sullen face which stared at me but never spoke till we reached the kitchen. In the next weeks I cursed you as often as you ever cursed me. Some evenings you called when Shay was out, both of us brooding

211

in silence, watching the television with the sound turned off. Every few minutes you'd ask, *Are you sure you don't know where he is?* Your voice full of suspicion as though I were hiding him in the next room.

Those few rooms were my Ark. I had built a life there with Shay, lost it and managed to reclaim it against the odds when he returned. Now you were there each night, intruding on its intimacy like a cold wind breaking up a fire. It was not that I wanted Shay exclusively to myself; I had welcomed a dozen girls through those rooms. But they were different. There had been vast breakfasts cooked in the mornings, Shay teasing them as he turned pancakes expertly. There had never been accusations or tears, more often than not he had let the girl choose him. They were walked to the bus-stop, kissed when the bus came, and rarely seen again. I had come to see them as part of the atmosphere of the new flat, like the mammoth poker sessions back in his old one.

With you, it was as if you brought in all the tension of the streets outside each time you came. But I was fooling myself when I blamed you. The tension was there already, branded deep inside Shay by Europe and as deeply inside me by Pascal Plunkett. Even before you came the flat had ceased to be what it was: the past was the past, and Shay and I had grown into different people.

Once I had always understood him, but now I couldn't fathom his relationship with you. You seemed to be constantly in that kitchen, either sullen, or else laughing in a high-pitched, hysterical voice as if on something. Through his bedroom door I could see the bed neatly made and he never brought you in there in my presence. I used to wonder cruelly if he took you on top of the table because you never seemed to leave it.

Sometimes, just to avoid you, I'd wander up to my mother's house, but I felt uncomfortable there too. If she had asked me straight out about Pascal Plunkett I might have overcome the feeling, but instead she chattered on nervously about my job or my sister's forthcoming confirmation, wondering if I could get a day off to be there instead of her father. The whole period of my life when I worked for Plunkett hung like a sheet of ice between us. She knew he never gave money back and since that day he had avoided having to meet her. He wouldn't visit the undertaker's on the evenings she scrubbed the floors there, and if he did accidentally confront her when she worked late he was nervous and kept his head down. I knew he was terrified about what she might know, that the small world he ruled totally could be sniggering behind his back. I had thought I could escape him but he had even taken away the house where I was born. I couldn't enter it without being reminded of the morning when I had staggered home, my face bruised by his hands.

If my mother was out I'd leave a small pile of notes for her with my brothers and hurry away, lingering in the streets until I knew Shay had left for work and you would be gone from the flat. Then I'd come back, make myself coffee and sit with the lights off, looking down at the children still playing on the street in the darkness, and think of Shay circling that empty factory where dogs ran along the wire fence, their breath turning to vapour in the moonlight.

My lunch-times in work were still spent in the Irish Martyrs Bar, but now I drank more from habit than pleasure. The jokes Mary and Mick cracked were the same ones I had laughed at a year before, but I couldn't fit back into that cosy world. I knew that it was only a matter of months before the same letter was left in the attendance book and I realized I would welcome it this time. Sitting back in that child-like office I knew that I was ready to leave those streets behind me at last. When Shay wanted to move again I would go with him, out into the grown-up world of Europe.

I remember it was late on a Friday afternoon in midsummer. The office windows were pulled down and the noise of the cars below could be clearly heard. A fresh breeze was blowing in, and a giddy feeling of weekend euphoria swamped the room. The clock had been pushed on ten minutes when Carol went into Mooney's office after the break, and work had almost stopped while we kept an eye out for her return. The lads at the bottom table were playing twenty questions, the girls in the centre giggling as they discussed the previous night's party. When I stared across at Mary she caught my eye

213

and held it. Like herself and Shay had spent years doing, we played statues, not moving a muscle, daring the other to laugh first.

A cigarette was burning itself out in a long worm of ash beside her and Mick was muttering blue jokes to distract me, but neither of us moved. Ten minutes had gone by when the noise in the office instinctively ceased and, like Shay used to, I nodded towards the Ladies. Mary stood up, grabbing her cigarettes, but Carol had spotted her and almost trotted to reach the door of the cubicle and shut herself in before Mary had time to leave the table.

We laughed and argued about which of us had moved first. Then Mary took down the attendance book to rule out the pages for the week ahead. I collected a new pile of slips and began collating the information on to the ledger before me. Time passed more quickly when we bothered to work. The court had finished for the weekend below and I thought about wandering down to the solicitor's room for a smoke, but decided it was too much effort. I leaned back to yawn when something puzzled me.

'Mary?' I asked across the pile of books on her table. 'Do you think Carol's trying to outdo you? How long is she in there?'

Mary looked at her watch and then at the altered clock.

'Twenty-five minutes. Maybe she's going to sit in there for spite till five.'

Her voice was doubtful. We both looked over towards the door. Mary rose and tentatively knocked on it.

'Carol, are you all right?'

There was no reply. She knocked harder and put her ear to the wood. The girls at the table noticed and asked each other if they had seen her leave. Mary banged louder and tugged at the handle. It was locked.

'Hano, go into Mooney's and see if she's there,' she told me.

I knocked and entered. He sat in that perpetual twilight, his desk littered with papers. Although he picked one up when I entered, I knew he hadn't been reading anything. He seemed to have just been sitting in some suspended state, without thoughts or emotions, waiting for the outside office to clear before going home to whatever strange woman had married him. He snapped at me that he had no idea where she was. As I closed the door I could see the sheet of paper being lowered, the eyes rising up to remind me of an old frog waiting with infinite patience beside a pond.

Everybody had gathered around the door of the toilet. When I told Mary that Carol wasn't with Mooney she asked me to break the door down at once. Behind us the girls muttered excitedly. They knew Mooney would be furious at not being asked first. There was only a thin bolt holding the door shut. It almost gave at the first kick. I stood back and heard the silence behind me as Mooney's door opened and his footsteps approached. I ran at the door and kicked it again. The wood splintered and there was the jangle of metal falling to the floor as the door swung open with such force that it hit the wall and flew back again. In the second it was open I saw Carol slumped on the toilet seat. Then, slowly, this time as though being opened by an invisible hand, the door swung backwards once more. Her head was resting against the wall of the narrow cubicle, her eyes closed as though asleep, but her face was horribly twisted. A pair of faded red knickers hung between her outstretched legs beneath which a small pool of liquid had gathered. As I kicked the door I had sensed Mooney only a few inches behind me but when I turned he had miraculously drifted to the back of the crowd. I looked at him for a command but he lowered his eyes as Mary rushed in and knelt beside the pathetic figure.

'She's still breathing, Hano. Phone an ambulance quick.'

Mooney stepped back out of my way as I went into his office and dialled the number on his antiquated heavy black phone. When I returned the girls had laid her on the centre table. She was alive, but nobody was sure if she knew where she was or what was happening to her. Mary leaned over her, whispering. It was hard to make out the words but I swore I heard *I'm sorry*. Two of the girls had begun crying, one of them in near hysterics. I asked Mick to take them down into the canteen. Those of us left stood awkwardly around in silence. Mooney remained in the corner near the smashed door. All the blood seemed drained from his face and it looked as if one push would shatter him into thousands of dry, crumbling pieces. Within minutes the ambulance men had appeared, professional, reassuring. They lifted her on to the stretcher and automatically Mary and myself followed them down to the ambulance. The siren started as soon as we began to zigzag our way through the evening traffic. They had placed an oxygen mask over her face and strapped a cord on to her wrist that led to a machine. A blip moved languidly across its screen and then, as we reached the hospital entrance, it ceased with a sudden loud buzzing. The assistant thumped on her chest, but she was gone. Mary had been holding her unshackled hand since leaving the office. Very gently the man separated them and folded Carol's arms across her chest.

'Do you know the name of her next of kin?' he asked.

Mary shook her head.

'Had she any?'

'Sister and two brothers in Dublin. One sister somewhere in America she was always talking of visiting. Since the day I started work she was talking of visiting her, only she was afraid she'd be in the way.'

It was half-six when we left the hospital. From habit I suggested a drink but was glad when Mary declined. I think we both wanted to be alone, not to have to talk. Though we were going in the same direction we parted at the gate and I took the long way through side-streets until I was certain her bus had come. I thought of Mooney, guessed that he would still be in that office above the court-house, sitting with his frog-like stare. Suddenly I felt pity for him and decided to take a taxi back.

The cleaner, on her hands and knees in the hall, looked up in surprise when I entered. I realized he had told her nothing. Without speaking, I went up to the main office. It was eerie in the evening light with the high windows still open so that papers had blown on to the floor. The toiler door was still open, as though nobody had had the courage to touch it. Carol's cardigan was draped over a chair, Mary's spent cigarette still intact in the ashtray. Mooney's door was half-open and I pushed it with my hand to look inside. At first I thought it was empty and was about to turn when a slight movement inside caught my eye.

'Is she . . .?' he asked.

I nodded and stepped into the gloom. He seemed to belong there, at one with the dull mahogany furniture, the wooden presses and rows of dark filing cabinets.

'Thirty years,' he said. 'Thirty . . .'

He looked shrunken in the semi-darkness. If he left that desk and walked on to the street outside he would be a dwarfed insignificant figure sliding around the darkest corners. Then I realized that I had never seen him outside this building, had never even arrived or left at the same time as him. He bowed his head down and his bald forehead looked like a knob of polished wood. Even his fingers, stretched like a keyboard player's on the table's edge, seemed crudely carved.

'Your wife,' I said. 'Shouldn't you phone her?'

'Thirty years . . .' he began again in a low voice and then, as if only hearing my words, stopped and looked coldly up.

'What wife, boy?'

'Your wife might want to know.'

His head rolled back. It was the first time I had heard him laugh, an unearthly bitter sound from deep in his throat.

'Wife, boy? What wife, you fool? I have no wife. No wife, no son, no daughter. I have this desk, boy, this room. Soon I won't even have that.'

His head rolled down again. Without wanting to, I began seeing Pascal Plunkett in that chair. His words filled me with a sense of horror, like an innocent who stumbles into a haunted room. The previous winter the pipes had frozen and a workman was dispatched from the maintenance section to clear the damage. He had left a wrench on top of one of the filing cabinets and it had remained untouched, a subject for countless memos ever since. In the light, filtering in over my shoulder from the main office, its silver steel shone among the dull browns and greys.

'But the photographs on your desk? I've seen them.'

'A godchild in England, boy. I send a present every birthday and she sends a photograph.'

'But the stories, the schools . . .'

He just looked at me and I shut up. How many had known or guessed? I remembered the vague smile that crossed Carol's face whenever a problem occurred in the office and she'd say

*Mrs Mooney will have the dinner burnt tonight.* That's why he never left this place on time. I suddenly imagined him stalking through the main office with the lights out, touching the seats where the girls had sat, reluctant to leave his kingdom and venture out under the huge night sky. He lowered his head again.

'Carol . . . one time it might have . . .'

It was hard to catch what he was saying. My eye was drawn back to the shining wrench. I wanted to be rid of the thought but it persisted. If I approached now as I had so often dreamed of doing a year ago and raised that piece of metal above his head, would he look up, welcoming it, his eyes urging me to bring it down and end the pain locked inside that room? Would what had once been dreamed of as a gesture of revenge become one of compassion? I thought that he was sobbing but when he lifted his eyes they were dry and cold.

'What do you want, boy?' he demanded. 'Work is finished. Go back to your pup friend.'

That familiar, contemptuous voice released me from the spell of the room and any pretence of kinship. I was about to call him a pathetic old bollox. Once fear would have stopped me, but now it was simple indifference that made me walk silently out, past the cleaner who stood in the main office, through that old doorway, and down to the park where a crescent moon hung above the rich clumps of trees.

There were thirty-one of us at the grave side. She was buried after eleven o'clock Mass in Deans Grange. Mooney was in before any of us that morning. Occasionally the buzzer went and Mary disappeared into his office. Apart from that we never saw him. At ten o'clock she came out with a pile of annual leave forms.

'As many of you can go as you like. But take your time coming back, he's taking a half-day's annual leave off yous.'

Mary sat down in Carol's old seat as I put my coat on. I asked her if she was coming.

'He won't allow me, Hano.'

Once she would have cursed his spite but now she only put her head down. I didn't know that Shay was coming, but as the cortège reached the cemetery I saw him slip from the queue at the bus-stop across the road and join the small scraggle of mourners. It was too close in time to my father's death for me to feel comfortable at a grave side. I left when the priest began to intone his prayers. Shay caught up with me and we walked in silence down through the ugly ranks of stones, glancing at the names of the dead, watching the occasional widower set out for his morning's work, carrying flowers and water in a plastic bottle. I knew Shay was wondering where Mary was. I felt I should make some sort of an excuse for her and yet I said nothing. Once we would have gone to the pub and I would have found my way back to work unsteadily at five to two, suffocating the room with the smell of peppermint. But that morning we just parted at the cemetery gates with a few words. I got a bus back to town, and Shay – I'm not sure what he did. There were bits of his life which didn't fit any more.

> *I left him behind, I left the hotel,*
>> *Katie, the streets were buckling around me.*
> *I had no idea of where I was going,*
>> *Just knew that I had to keep travelling.*
> *It was late with few trains running,*
>> *I thrust the note at the bored cashier.*
> *'Anywhere,' I said, 'that it will take me.'*
>> *He picked the night train to Berlin.*

> *The carriage of the train was empty,*
>> *Its lights sped across the flat night,*
> *And stopped along anonymous platforms*
>> *With names that I could not pronounce.*
> *When we reached the customs check-point,*
>> *I no longer knew which country I was in.*
> *Infinte lines of tracks stretched out,*
>> *With containers rusting down sidings.*

> *I felt that I was suffocating,*
>> *And went to pull the window down.*
> *A guard was shining his torch along*
>> *The iron wheels of the train.*

*I clutched my passport like an icon,*
  *Trying to breathe the icy air*
*But his face came back into my mind*
  *And sickened me with nausea.*

*I longed to feel clean again,*
  *Wanted a sense of belonging back,*
*My reflection was staring at me*
  *From a carriage window opposite;*
*So old, so stale with experience.*
  *I can't explain why I panicked,*
*Why I felt if I stayed I'd pass*
  *Through infinite cities into nothingness.*

*I just turned the handle and jumped,*
  *Ignoring the guards shouting after me*
*And dodged past shunting goods wagons*
  *To scale the floodlit iron gates.*
*I found myself racing through woodland,*
  *Towards the lights of trucks on an autobahn.*
*Then veered, and stumbling into the forest,*
  *Came to what looked like a ruined mansion.*

*It was a building where Jews had been shot,*
  *Its shell preserved as a monument.*
*Through the night I smoked cigarettes*
  *Leaning against the bronze plaque,*
*Turning a green passport over in my hands,*
  *Remembering the person I had been once,*
*And all I could think of till dawn*
  *Was 'Hano will be there when I return.'*

Two weeks after Carol's funeral, Shay lost his job as night security man. I am not sure why. Maybe he tired of the provocative wiggle of Alsatians' arses; maybe the long hours spent alone in the darkness were slowly turning him inwards; maybe the firm turned over people before they got too familiar with any job. One morning he just came home and didn't go

220

to bed. It was a Saturday. I heard him come in and sank back
to sleep. When I woke again at eleven, he was sitting by the
kitchen window, staring down at the usual cluster of men
outside the bookies. The ashtray was littered with butts,
smoked down to the tip. He didn't reply to my greeting and I
knew he'd been sitting there since eight o'clock. If I had left
and returned that evening I think I would have found him in
the same position, his hand rising and falling from his lips
even though the cigarettes had long been exhausted.

I remembered how special Saturdays used to be. Three cross
doubles picked over breakfast, the air of relaxation after a
night's drinking. Now an atmosphere of gloom possessed the
flat and I didn't bother even trying to talk. At noon you came,
Katie. I let you in silently, and just as silently you took your
place beside him at the window, lit one of his last cigarettes
and followed his gaze over the row of dilapidated cottages. He
never acknowledged your presence, but that morning you both
seemed almost one person, fitting perfectly together. Now it
was like I was the intruder. I slammed the front door as I left,
cursing you, swearing it was all your fault, that you had
dragged him down to your level of despair.

When I returned you were both gone. Coffee had been
made. I took the cup you'd drunk from and smashed it in the
sink, using a piece of wood to pound it into a thousand
fragments. Every curse I ever knew was hurled at those ragged
splinters of delf. When I was finished I took his cup, raised
it above my head and then, slowly, brought it down under the
jet of warm water, dried it carefully and waited for him.
Dawn had broken before he returned. The noise of the door
woke me in the grained light and I went out. He was climbing
the stairs stiffly, too exhausted to even curse.

'You okay?' I asked.

He dragged himself to a chair, bent down to take his shoes
off. He looked so old in the grey light that it was impossible to
believe he was only twenty-two.

'I was walking home,' he said, 'around a quarter past
twelve. I was after two pints in Murtagh's and had stopped for
a piss at the Black Church when the squad car pulled up. *What
are you up to at this hour, boy?* I told him I was walking home.

*You never heard of taxis, boy?* I said I was broke. *Do you work atall or are you one of them spongers living off the rest of us?* I ignored him, Hano, and started walking on. The squad car crawled along behind me till I reached The Broadstone. Then he flung the back door open. *Ah sure get in, boy, we're all Irishmen together. I'll give you a lift some of the way.* They drove out to Rathfarnham, Hano, the foothills of the fucking mountains. Knocklyon, the last place on God's earth. I was squeezed between two of them in the back. Then they let me out. *Don't go mistaking a church for a piss pot again, boy.* I've been walking Hano, ever since. Walking. Fucking walking!'

Shay couldn't let it rest. What possessed him to complain I don't know. Was he so long in Europe as to forget how things worked? I went down to the station with him, waited outside among the crowds returning from mass while he made his complaint.

'Why the fuck did I bother?' he said when he came out. '*We'll be in touch*, they said.'

'Let's just hope to God they won't, Shay.'

A car had slowed to a halt across the road from the station, the passenger in the back watching Shay talking to me. The BMW had been traded in for a Merc like his brother's official one and it took me a moment to recognize Pascal Plunkett. I pulled Shay on and when we reached the corner I looked back. Pascal had got out and was crossing the station forecourt. An instinct ingrained from childhood made me want to bless myself against evil.

For two days nothing happened. Then on the Wednesday we went into town. It was after midnight when we left Murtagh's. We walked home through the streets, familiar from a hundred other nights. It had rained earlier and now a steel-eyed moon lit rainbows in the oil slicks along the carriageway. Over the weekend a car speeding down from the South had overshot the junction and ploughed through the railings into the gully below by the stream. Broken glass still sparkled on the grass verge. I asked Shay to wait and climbed down past the scrape marks where they had hauled the twisted vehicle up, unzipped my fly and watched the arc of urine splash on to the rocks by the edge of the stream.

I was paralysed like that, unable to stop pissing, unable to run, when I heard the screech of tyres and the faint crackle of the radio as the doors burst open. I turned to look up through the bushes and distorted bars to where I heard Shay's voice bemused at first and then alarmed. There was the thud of wood striking flesh followed by a sudden terrifying silence, and when Shay's voice came again it was crying out above a chorus of boots and curses, punctuated by gasps for breath, pleading for them to stop. The silver-green arc of urine had trickled to a halt. If I wished to I could have turned and raced up among them, but I stood as though still paralysed, my penis in my hand, my shoulders hunched. *He'll call me now*, I thought, *and I'll burst into motion, my fists flailing as I charge into the huddle of gardai to get my share of belts and kicks.*

But Shay never once used my name, never gave my presence away and I never moved until I heard them dragging his body into the back of the squad car. As the door slammed and it was too late, I found myself scrambling up the slope, roaring suddenly with a rock in my fist. The car was pulling out, I could see the back of Shay's head slumped down between the two blue uniforms. If the police heard my shouts they didn't even consider me of sufficient interest to be bothered with.

I knew that Shay would never have hesitated; he would have gone in with fists flying if I had been caught. Nothing I could do now would be important; no action could redeem me in my own eyes. I walked up to the station and hovered nervously outside. Streaks of blood stained the gravel where the squad car was parked. I knew there was only one number I could call to stop what was happening inside. And suddenly I knew that Pascal knew it too, knew that he was waiting beside the phone in his house beyond the final street light, a whiskey in his hand, patience and power on his side.

A car pulled up and a man got out. Even in plain clothes I knew he was a detective. A young guard came to the door, his face ashen white.

'I don't know who they are,' he began in distress. 'They just came in, took over the station . . .'

He saw me in the shadows and stopped. The detective came over. He was in his thirties, already going bald. He looked tired.

'What do you want?'

'My friend. He's inside.'

'Wait here.'

I went to follow him inside and he turned to gesture with his hand. I knew what he was saying: I was safer out there. The lorries were trundling down the road from the north, air brakes squealing as they hit the traffic lights. I watched the drivers in their cabs, the vehicles trembling like frightened calves before shooting down the carriageway. Across the road the stream that gave the village its name ran behind the gardens of a few old houses and vanished into the pipe that bore it beneath the concrete to the far side of the carriageway. The glass door opened behind me and the detective whistled. He was supporting Shay who staggered and put his hand against the wall. His jacket was smeared with blood, his jeans spattered in it. His cheeks were puffed out and discoloured. He tried to grin when he saw me, the lips already grotesque, too large for his face.

'Get him to hell out of here, son. There'll be no charges this time.'

'What do you mean no charges? He did nothing.'

'Drunk and disorderly. Resisting arrest. Assaulting an officer. Can't you see I'm trying to do you a favour? Just take him home and make sure he doesn't come back. Of his own free will or anyone else's.'

We had to stop every few yards for Shay to rest. I remembered the night before he left for Europe. Our crazy fight along the main street where nobody had dared come out. How tough we'd felt then, how cocksure of ourselves. If nobody came out it was for a different reason. We crossed the metal bridge and I sat him down on the pavement while I looked for my keys. He keeled over to one side, supporting himself with his hand.

'You were dead right, Hano,' he mumbled, 'not to come out of the ditch. They would only have beaten the shite out of the pair of us. I would never have got out of there.'

I helped him to stand and got him upstairs. I boiled a kettle and tried to clean up his face. He mumbled again that I had done the right thing. I wasn't sure which of us he was trying to convince.

For three days Shay rested in bed. I fed him chicken soup and bread rolls — he seemed to find everything else hard to swallow. You came over, Katie, to sit with him during the day and every evening I'd find some trace of you left behind. When I returned on the third evening Shay was gone. I waited up for him. Afraid of what he might have done. It was after midnight when he returned. The bruises on his face had yellowed in colour, his lip had gone back closer to its normal size, and he was accompanied by Justin Plunkett.

Even after Justin had left I still couldn't sleep. I couldn't explain the terror I felt in my heart. I went to work, not knowing if I would find Shay there when I returned. The lunch-time sessions in the Irish Martyrs had ended. Once or twice since her promotion Mary went over, but our conversation was stilted. Now at lunch-times she remained in Carol's old chair as I slipped on my coat and walked out, looking back sometimes to catch a wry smile on her face. A new bloke had started and we'd wander off to eat fish and chips by the canal. Talking to him was strange. A woman gives her life to a place and, within weeks, all traces of her have vanished. Carol was just a name he had heard of, Mary a boss to be wary of, Shay . . .? Shay by now was hardly even a name.

The previous week another temporary girl had started. She was blonde, nineteen, diminutive. The other girls took a dislike to her. They bitched in corners, inventing nicknames for her, mimicking her posh accent, her naive ignorance of the world outside her Southside suburb. It was her first job and she could sense the antagonism, which made her nervously retreat deeper into the stereotype they had created for her. Shay would have spent days slowly coaxing her out, deliberately talking to her and showing her things, until people came to accept her and she relaxed. I had done nothing beyond watching her daily crucifixion.

That afternoon she came out of Mooney's office and ran into the cubicle where Carol had died. I was taking files down from the dusty shelves outside when I heard faint sobbing. I stood on the step-ladder for five minutes, not wanting to get involved. I had grown bitter and stagnant over the past month, each day there folding drearily into the next. I felt like a

225

hibernating creature, burrowed right down inside myself, waiting for a spring I felt would never come. Hesitantly, I climbed down from the ladder and tapped on the door. After a moment the bolt was drawn back. Her eyes were red, she stepped back surprised when she saw me. We had never spoken.

'I thought one of the girls wanted to . . .' she stopped, confused as to why I had knocked.

'Take three or four of those old cardboard boxes Jennifer,' I said quietly. 'And just slip out the door. Nobody will say anything.'

She peered anxiously through the rows of shelving at the figures bent over the desks. I nodded towards the door again and she grabbed her coat and was gone. I took the sheaf of files and placed them beside my chair before opening the door on to the landing. She was looking down at the crowds milling around the door of the court room as though she expected them to devour her. I touched her lightly on the shoulder and she followed me, still confused and carrying the boxes awkwardly. I dumped them down outside the front door. We had the back lounge of the Irish Martyrs to ourselves. I ordered coffee. She kept darting her head towards the door, expecting Mooney or Mary or possibly the whole office to suddenly descend on our table with fingers pointing.

'Don't mind the fuckers,' I said. 'Nobody will notice. Just relax.'

It took quarter of an hour for her to unwind and when she did I sat back and listened as she blabbered. Then I began to talk, telling her she was young, that this place was just for a few months before she found her wings and started her real life. I'd be ashamed to repeat the nonsense I said, but if she heard any of it it seemed to work. Then I realized that the girls were not the problem, it was Mooney himself.

He had done nothing major that people would notice, just kept catching her alone, keeping his hand on her shoulder when he explained her work to her, touching her as if by accident on the breasts, brushing against her buttocks, placing his hand over hers as he talked about his daughter who, he told her, was almost the same age as herself. He would never

226

dare be so blatant with the other girls but he was aware of this girl's isolation, knew that in another week or two the pink resignation form would reach his desk. She was crying again and I didn't know what to say to comfort her now. The barman had retreated into the front bar. I could hear racing on the television, the curses of a customer as the crowd roared the horses along the finishing straight.

'Go to Mary,' I told her finally. 'Tell her everything you told me. She'll look after you. She'll understand.'

It was nearly five when we returned. Mooney was in the office. He glared and the girl stopped, frightened. I pushed her softly on and she took her seat at the middle table. Mooney and I stared each other out for a minute, then he turned like a cautious animal, and retreated back into his lair. We had not spoken since the night of Carol's death and I had never told anybody of our conversation. I saw Jennifer remain seated as the girls rose to leave. She glanced at me for reassurance. I nodded and as Mary passed she touched her hand. Mary bent down to listen and then sat beside her. I took my coat and slipped out, down the hill where the girls ran for buses, and across the park towards Shay.

A water main had burst near the old monument across from the shopping centre in the village. The water soared up from the hole in the road and splashed down on to the tarmacadam. Two girls with a ghetto-blaster had climbed into the enclosed green triangle around the mock Celtic cross that had been paid for and unveiled by the Plunkett brothers in honour of their grandfather. Graffiti was smeared across its patriotic inscription. Reggae music blared out as children twisted and jived, running in and out of the high spray. I paused to watch.

They were an autonomous world, a new nation with no connection to the housewives passing or the men coming home from work in the factories. And little even in common with me, though I was only a few years older than them. Because in those few years the place had changed beyond recognition. I could piece together obscure images that to them would seem from another planet, Corpus Christi processions through these streets; Christmas concerts in the old cinema where shoppers now queued at cash desks; dances in

227

the parochial hall that was now a semi-derelict ruin. All I had known, as Shay had said that night in the graveyard, was the tail-end of it, the buggy squeaking as I cried, but enough of it remained that evening for me to feel as though I had lived in some other time, in a distant place where I would always be trapped.

Two workmen, still in overalls and boots, checked the winners on the sheet pinned on the door of the bookies. Their heads were bent, eyes concentrated on the list of names as if it was a map of an uncharted universe. Nothing in their expression betrayed whether their horse had won or lost. Perhaps for the first time ever, as I turned the key I hoped that Shay was out. I was tired and I felt embarrassed now after the scene with the girl in the pub.

The flat was empty, smelling of must after the heat of the day. I opened a window and the lace curtain billowed back into my face. When I turned I knew something was different. Nothing had been moved but the flat stared back at me as if trying to tell me what was wrong. His bedroom door was shut which it never was in the daytime. I was suddenly afraid as I approached the door, not sure of what I expected to find. I pushed it open with my hand. The bed was neatly made. He possessed so little that there was nothing to suggest his presence in the room. A few old T-shirts lay on the chair, an old pair of jeans tossed beside them. Everything seemed the same as when I had last been in there, but I could still sense a change. Furtively, not knowing how I would explain it if he walked in, I opened his drawer. The green passport he always kept there was missing. I checked the other drawers, half their contents were gone too. I knew he had left and for some reason I was glad. Shay was still my hero, my other half who was afraid of nothing. He belonged to the world of night-time streets or out among the autobahns of Europe.

I remembered one Sunday a few weeks before, when I had seen him walking up the laneway towards Dalymount Park. The crowd at the match was so small that you were only aware of them outside when there was a goal. Shay had paused a few feet from the turnstile and then walked quickly onwards. I was about to call him when I realized what he was doing, and that there were a dozen like him there, circling the ground as if going somewhere else, waiting for the officials to open the gates early in the second half so they could slip in and see the remainder of the match free. If Shay was broke he would have accepted drink from you all night, but been insulted at the offer of a loan of the bus fare home. I knew he would be ashamed to be seen there, so I left him walking the red-brick length of Connacht Street, checking over his shoulder that nobody was noticing.

The figure I had seen return to grow defeated and sullen seemed like some impostor – too human, too much like myself to be looked up to. I had needed my image of Shay almost as much as I needed him, like a torch for me to live up to. The first time he had left it had seemed as if my life had ceased; this time I felt his leaving meant in some way that it could begin again. Now I would follow him, not the Shay who had returned, but the Shay who had originally left. I too would take a cheap flight, find work where I could, until eventually, out among those cities and factories, I would meet Shay again, cured of his malaise, as strong and vibrant as the first day we had met.

I sat on Shay's bed like a widow, listening to the shouts of children playing around the burst water main outside like a giant wave of life washing over the crowded streets.


Katie walked ahead of him, straight into the rain, hobbling from the soreness of her feet. They hadn't spoken since the dancehall, afraid that words would break the mood that held them and provoke a quarrel. His feet had ceased to ache: they were numb now, no longer part of him. Would this march ever end he wondered, or would they just vanish into the rain, stooped ghosts walking for eternity?

He remembered how, years before, on the last day he had spent with the old woman it had rained like this. All day he'd rarely ventured from the caravan, gazing across the bleak fields through the window, stroking the wet animals who came and went, talking as he had never been able to talk before. Near midnight it had stopped and he'd borrowed a pair of her wellingtons, slopping his way across the wet earth to the small road, thankful to be out in the air. A cold breeze had blown the clouds towards the east where they hung like crumpled blankets pulled down on one side of a bed. The moon was full, igniting the damp tarmacadam into silver, the village silent.

Flashing her small torch on and off, he took the small road that led down towards the bog, leaving the sanctuary of street lights behind, feeling a marvellous thrill of fear tingle through him each time he passed underneath the trees with their gnarled, mysterious shadows. Lights shone in the few houses set back from the roadway where dogs barked, suspicious of his footsteps. As the road curved downwards towards the bridge he noticed another light ahead of him. Puzzled, he switched off the torch and approached. There were no houses there and he wondered whether there was a poacher on the river, before remembering that since the factory opened outside Sligo all the fish had died.

He reached the old bridge and saw the light clearly now, a phosphorescent column the height of a child hovering on a small bank of reeds, cut off on all sides by the swollen water. He could see through the light yet couldn't tell where it came from. The ground was swamped on each side of the bridge and there was no way of getting any closer to it. Occasionally the light sank down slightly and rose again in a straight column, but otherwise it remained stationary. If it were gas rising from the polluted river surely the wind that was swaying the branches overhead would disperse it. But instead it rested above the reeds like a presence, an echo of something lost.

He ran back to the caravan and brought the old woman down to the bridge. It was still there, brighter now than ever. He was relieved she could see it too, even though she had no explanation to offer. All she said as they walked home beneath the trees was that a child had died from drinking the water near that bridge soon after the factory opened.

'When I came here first,' she'd told him, 'all the village took their water from the river. For three months after my husband's death we were so poor we lived on trout my son caught there each evening. I could never eat fish again and later on meat.

Now the women warn their children to stay clear of it, to let it carry its filth away through the fields.'

Katie had stopped at a crossroads ahead of him where road signs pointed in three directions. It was difficult to decipher the lettering and it took him a moment before, with a thrill of recognition, he made out the name of a village near the old woman's. It was five miles there and then possibly another seven to her village. He knew if they had descended the mountain properly they would have been nearer but, despite this, felt a sense of pride at getting so close, and, suddenly, of fear at knowing their journey would have to end.

The new road was larger than the one they had left, with what little traffic there was heading in towards the village. When they saw headlights they pressed themselves clumsily into the ditch, knowing they could become no wetter. His clothes stuck to him, caked in mud; his feet were raw, frozen inside waterlogged shoes. They had walked for an hour when they heard music blaring across the fields. It grew louder and less muffled but still they couldn't place the tune which sounded eerie in the darkness. Then he heard the familiar words.

> We are the soldiers, we are the party
> We'll march together on the long road.
> We are one nation, we are one people
> With one strong leader to bear our load.

Before they realized what was happening, the convoy was upon them, a police car with its revolving light flashing against the bushes, and the two speeding coaches of the victory party behind it. One man with his shirt sleeves rolled up glanced out into the rain and, seeing their outlines, clenched his fist. Although they couldn't hear it, they saw his mouth opening to let out an animal roar. The drivers were beeping their horns to the tune, drenching them with spray as they passed, well over the speed limit, careering from side to side along the road and leaving them in blinding darkness. Hano had forgotten about the election and, looking after the convoy, realized with a shudder that Plunkett's party had won again. Then he asked himself what difference did it make which of them held power. His generation would still be forming long snakes outside the American and Australian embassies or scraping together the money not for the boat this time but for cheap Apex airline tickets.

'Don't worry about hiding tonight,' Katie said, 'they'll all be too pissed to notice.'

They walked on, raindrops striking his skull like Chinese water torture. His shoes squelched as he walked, the water dripping from his chin and nostrils. His stomach was too sick to want food. After midnight they reached the village. The rain had slackened and then temporarily stopped. Both pubs were open, people milling in and out of their doors. Two policemen smoked as they leaned against the bonnet of their squad car. Hano and Katie watched from the shadows as party officials argued and looked up at the sky. Finally one shouted over to a van and a man climbed down with a microphone. He tapped it with his hand to test it and then called for attention, his voice echoing through the main street. The drinkers began to drift from the pubs and cluster around the doors with their glasses still in their hands. A squat man in a pinstripe suit emerged with men clapping his back as he strode towards the microphone.

Katie wanted to push on but Hano stopped her, mesmerized by the scene. The face was familiar from television. He was a TD famous for arriving early at party conferences, and clinging in boredom to the same seat through all the resolutions and debates, so that when the platform filled up for the leader's speech he would always be positioned two rows up, jutting out like part of the leader's right shoulder on the television screens. The TD began to roar into the microphone as though speaking in a parish hall without amplification. It muffled his words but Hano could still follow them.

'You all know why we are here!' A huge roar went up. 'Today is a historic day for the party and for this constituency. This evening, on the fifteenth count, we have captured a third – a rightful third – seat in this constituency. And our tally men say it was transfers from this village that swung it in the end.'

The screams were wild, inhuman. One man near the front shouted, 'That's enough speeches, Conor. Come back in here and buy another round.'

The politician raised his hand and laughed. 'There'll be time enough, don't worry, and rounds enough! There are no guards here tonight, only Irishmen. There'll be no licences endorsed this night!' The two policemen shifted uncomfortably as the crowd laughed. 'We in the party have always held this village dear. We have always looked after you and you have always looked after us. It is time this village had a new parish hall. It is time this village had a sports complex. Our new TD, our third TD, whose aunt is the postmistress across the road there, is going to say a few words to you now. And by God, let me remind you if this party does not forgive its enemies, it does not forget its friends!'

The main street was a mass of bodies as the new TD, a fresh-faced man in his twenties, was carried shoulder high towards the microphone. Hano turned and caught sight of an evening paper displayed in the window of the closed news-agent. The victory was proclaimed in black headlines and, in a corner underneath, his own picture stared back at him, cut in half below the eyes where the paper had been folded. He knew the picture, taken a few weeks before at his sister's confirmation when Hano had stood beside his mother in a suit, trying to be like a father. The eyes in the window made his plight real at last, filling him with terror. He grabbed Katie's hand before she saw them, and began to walk quickly and then run until they reached the edge of the village and were lost again out in the black night, blundering along the road, away from the country they were exiled from.

The next day in work Mary was more tense than I had ever seen her. When Mooney was out on business she vanished into his office and as I passed the door I could hear her arguing on the phone with a woman from Personnel. The girls were friendlier to Jennifer, she was more relaxed, laughing for the first time in the euphoria that swept the room whenever Mooney was absent. At lunch-time I asked Mary if she wanted to go across the road. Butts were piled in the ashtray at her elbow. She sighed and gave a wry smile.

'I'd love to Hano, you know I would.' She squeezed my

shoulder momentarily and was gone, out among the girls heading for the coffee shop. Mooney only returned for half an hour in the afternoon. At three o'clock he emerged in his hat and coat and left without speaking to anyone. As he retreated down the stairs I felt a sudden surge of joy. Like a dictator in disgrace, heading for the last helicopter as his regime collapsed, he vanished slowly through the hallway. He had never left that early before. The girls at the middle table began to sing, working their way brokenly through the charts. Every person in the room was smiling except Mary, and, when I looked down after Mooney's departure, Jennifer. I gazed at Mary, trying to lure her into a game of statues, to coax a joke from her. She kept her head down, eyes trained on the rows of figures. Once I would have put the clock on five minutes but now it seemed like cheating on a friend.

At five o'clock the girls ran down the steps into the freedom of the weekend. I put my coat on and left the room where Mary and Jennifer remained sitting, divided by two long benches. I meant to walk out and leave them, but on the landing I paused and, ashamed, eavesdropped on their conversation.

When she finally spoke I could hardly recognize Mary's voice. The same Liberties accent was there but the words were delivered in the slower, more precise tones of an older person. Personnel were willing to ignore Jennifer's remarks this time, but she would have to control her imagination. She was no longer a schoolgirl; this was a job for adults and she would have to decide for herself if she was mature enough to take it. The incident was closed but if word of it got out it would be held against her at the highest level. The voice droned on, growing harsher with each sentence. I came to the door. Mary was still sitting at her desk with her back to the girl. She didn't see me but Jennifer did. A look of shame and hatred crossed her face as though I had set her up for my own amusement. She grabbed her coat and ran from the room.

Mary still didn't look up when she heard the footsteps. I crossed over to stand behind her and placed my hand on her neck. She put her own hand up to rest on mine.

'I feel like dirt, Hano . . . feel like dirt.'

234

I should have felt angry, but I wasn't even surprised, just disappointed with myself for being so naive.

'Six months, Hano. They were making him take early retirement anyway. Six months from now there'll be computers, databanks, the whole works in here. The place will be gutted apart. But for now they don't want to know, they don't want any trouble that could complicate their plans. Jesus Hano, did you hear me talking? Good Jesus.'

Her hand gripped mine tightly. Her head was bent down, she may have been crying.

'There isn't a girl here he hasn't touched at some stage. Years ago there was one girl from near his own place in Monaghan he used to follow home. If she looked out her flat window at night she'd see his car parked across the street. I told Carol and when she did nothing I despised her. I never forgave her for it Hano, never mentioned it but never let her forget. Now I just despise myself.'

I waited a moment before taking my hand away. I left her with the dusty light pouring in through the high windows, blinding me when I looked back, so that she seemed no more than a silhouette of some lost person who had always been there and always would be: efficient, servile, discardable.

Heading into town that evening I caught sight of Pascal Plunkett. I was crossing the metal bridge and, looking down the little V of roads that had been amputated like an unapproved border crossing by the carriageway, I saw workmen refitting one of the small row of old shops there. Two men were mounted on ladders erecting a large neon sign with *Plunkett Videos* in curved red lettering across it. A sign writer was outlining opening times in white paint on the plate-glass front, where posters of muscular soldiers and half-clad victims were being displayed. Pascal stood impassively on the footpath watching the men work. Shoppers who passed greeted him respectfully, proud when he condescended to nod back. I wanted to run but stood watching by the railings of the monument, until after a moment I realized that, although he had never turned, he knew I was there. It was the way he deliberately kept himself at full height like a girl sensing she was being watched at a dance.

I felt flushed and guilty as I quickly walked on down the old main street that bore the litany of his name on every second shop front. I thought of the recurring dream I still had of him, where I lay in my old bed while he sat on the chair beside it, father-like, concerned, dressed the way he was when he visited me there, his hurt face wondering why I had abandoned him. In the dream I wanted to order him out and yet his power held me, made me feel ashamed for not trusting him. Then he would lower his face to whisper something, and when I lifted mine to hear, his tongue came out, slipped between my lips and was rooted there. I would feel it, coarse and slippery like an earthworm, making me sick as I found myself too paralysed to shake him off. I'd try to scream, knowing that if I did I'd choke. And then I'd wake and lie in the flat, not sure if I had woken Shay in the next room, and wonder how I could explain it if he came in.

That would be one less worry from now on, I thought, wondering in what country Shay was by then. There was a party for a girl leaving work in town that night. I didn't want to be alone in the flat, so I went. Mick was there as always, same battered hat, same cheerful indifference to everything, same appetite for drink. We drank at the bar while the chit-chat of work went on around us, girls still filing cards in their minds, lads opening ledgers in thin air. At closing time, when feelers were being put out to procure a flat to party in, we left.

People were leaving a fancy-dress night in a pub off Dame Street. Girls dressed as French maids and tarts, youths in giant nappies clutching bottles of whiskey. A decapitated gorilla, sporting a man's head, took a slug from a brown bottle and flung it down a cobbled passageway. The city was coming alive. We made our way to the Home of Billiards. Smoke stung our eyes as we climbed the steps. Men clustered around the top table where the sharks played. An ancient black-and-white television blared above the counter, ignored by all. The bottom table was free. We played till two o'clock in the rich, melancholy silence – figures bending over the baize, the quiet click of balls in the chalky light, the intake of breath at the perfect track. I can't remember who won, it was of no consequence. Afterwards I took a taxi from O'Connell Street to the top of the carriageway and walked up alone to the flat.

The hallway was empty. I was at the top step before I saw the bottle of champagne parked exactly where it had been the night Shay first returned. He was not only marking his home-coming, but serving warning in case I was with a girl. I picked the bottle up, feeling both fear and elation. He was lying on top of his bed, dressed in a business suit, his hair cut and carefully brushed. There was still traces of bruising, but he looked now as if he had received them not in a street fight but a Lansdowne rugby scrum. Without him needing to explain I understood. He flicked a small roll of notes across the room towards me.

'Back rent,' he said.

'We could have managed.'

'Take it.'

I put it in my jeans pocket and turned to go.

'Hey, Hano.' He paused. 'Pleased to see me?'

'I don't know, Shay. I don't know.'

He thought about it for a moment.

'There might be a game of ball in the Fifteen Acres tomor-row. We chance it and take a taxi up?'

I didn't reply. I went to bed and dreamt the dream about Pascal Plunkett again.

Over the next six weeks my brain cried out daily during the hours of work. Some evenings if Shay asked me what had happened that day, I was unable to even recall leaving the building at five o'clock, or couldn't be certain if an incident had occurred that afternoon or the day before. The work was automatic, numbing in its simplicity. Mary stayed out of my way as much as Mooney. I sat in silence at the small table by the door with Mick. We had exhausted our blue jokes, swapped all our experiences, considered the probable contents of every take-away which had ever made us sick, and were now too apathetic to talk. At morning and afternoon break we both went down a quarter of an hour early to lie on the canteen tables while the kettle boiled. If the afternoon was mild we burnt cardboard boxes. Now we only drank on pay-day in the Irish Martyrs; without Mary and Shay it seemed pointless.

Once a week Shay would don the same business suit, leave on a Thursday, return late on Friday night. We never mentioned his departure or arrival, they were just the latest forbidden topics. You called to the flat less often Katie, but when you did it was with greater desperation. You'd sit sullenly in the corner, digging yourself deeper in the chair as the night progressed, as though it were a refuge. You'd want dance music always, complain if we put on Tom Waits or Randy Newman, take the record off so violently it scratched, and sulk when we shouted at you. I could see Shay's irritation but he would never ask you to leave. Before when you'd come the ashtray would be littered with the butt ends of joints, the air heavy with cloying scent. But now Shay never carried and never rolled. I had wondered if you only came for the dope but I was wrong, you still banged on the door, stormed in from the night, only now that we were straight there was even less to say. Or at least Shay and I were straight, often you staggered on the stairs, and from the glazed brightness of your eyes and your edginess I knew you had taken something.

I'd grown used to your presence, Katie. In some ways you belonged to the flat now as much as the laughter of Shay's girls once had. I no longer bothered trying to understand your relationship, I just left the pair of you alone and went back out into that jaded world of parties and bedsits. Coming home in the early mornings, and again on my way out to work, I'd step over your body curled alone on the floor beneath a ruck of blankets, and remember myself, like a distant creature, a year and a half before, longing only to be allowed to lie down and feel that I had found a home.

Justin Plunkett never came near the flat now. I had no idea where the pick-up was, except that it would be far from him. He would sit surrounded by alibis, waiting for any danger to pass. I wondered if he knew that the cuts and bruises to Shay's face had been ordained by his uncle. The bruises had long healed, but it was a different Shay who emerged along with the new skin over the cuts above his eye. A third Shay: not the open figure I first knew nor the indecisive, defeated one who had wandered the city like a ghost after his return, but an empty figure, a man who had stepped out of feeling.

Each Thursday he would dress methodically in the bathroom, comb the hair which was cut that afternoon, don the suit, take the briefcase and with a sort of indifferent nod, as though walking to the shops for cigarettes, step out the door when the taxi appeared beneath the window. Sometimes on the Friday nights I would be asleep when he returned. If I got out of bed I'd find the living-room lit only by the television's flickering rays and Shay staring intently at the figures in the late movie with the sound turned off. The next day we would talk as normal, but in those moments when I watched him from my doorway I had the impression that he would not hear me if I spoke, that some papier mâché creature had returned in his place and sat waiting for flesh and blood to bring it to life.

When he'd been broke I had carried him and now whenever I went to the bookie I found that Shay had paid the rent in full. If I offered him my share, Shay looked at me with a quiet smile that was a thin-blooded descendant of his old one, waved his hand dismissively and turned his gaze back to the window. I gave the extra money to my mother, guilty that I didn't call to her more often. She never crossed that metal bridge dividing the village, except to work in Plunkett Undertaker's. If she wanted anything in the West she sent one of my brothers. Each Saturday morning I called to leave the small envelope and drink tea while my young sisters circled me like a curio, no longer sure what relation I bore to them. She was disturbed by the way Pascal Plunkett treated her. She had grown used to him over quarter of a century, both as the wife of an employee and later an employee herself, and then as one of the hundreds of desperate women driven to him for loans when no one else wished to know them. Always she had received the same burly contempt, but now he crept around her. If she asked for time off she received it. Even the manager was terrified of her as though a single word of complaint from her mouth would see him back hoovering corpses again. She had always known anonymity, sheltering her like a cloak. Now she stood out and was frightened. I was the only person who could explain it, but I knew she would never ask the questions she wanted to, and that even if I told her everything it would still make no sense to her. I could never bear to stay more than a few minutes there.

One Tuesday evening it rained non-stop. We hadn't bothered to put the television or radio on. When the showers stopped at half-seven there was a scurry of feet on the road outside, the noise of men's voices and cars pulling up. Shay went to the window and cursed out loud.

'Not again,' he said, 'not all this shite so soon again.'

I looked down over his shoulder. Party officials were racing between lamp-posts with ladders, jockeying for position, those standing below handing up the same old tired posters. A few feet from our eyes a man in a business suit was fixing a poster of Patrick Plunkett below the street light which formed a halo over his face. It had been a miserable petty day filled with miserable petty events. I could think of none more suitable on which the government could fall for the third time in two years.

'Who will it be this time Shay?' I asked. 'The Soldiers of Density, The Warriors of Cuchulainn or The Progressive Shan Bhean Phochters?'

He laughed at the idea that it might matter. The Sucky-Fucky-Five-Dollars government would replace the Five-Dollars-Johnny government for another few months before the electorate got sick of them. No party won elections any more; people just got sick of seeing the same smug faces in power and switched them round for variety. I remembered as a child my father coming home on an evening like this, a coloured poster in his hand for each front window of the house. He'd harass my mother to get them up quickly, uncertain at what time Pascal Plunkett would make the rounds of his employees. Elections had been rare then, posters printed specially. Now they just put them in storage. Often nobody bothered taking them down. Like leaves in autumn they fell in their own time.

'I need a drink,' Shay said. 'Three weeks of this! Will we go?'

All the way into town it was the same, rival workers fighting for the best positions on lamp-posts. Two derelict shops in Phibsborough were being transformed into advice centres, the first loudspeakers being mounted on to the roofs of cars. In Murtagh's the clientele were quiet, election weary, dreading the hype and noise of the weeks ahead. Justin Plun-

kett came in, more soberly dressed than usual, had a few curt
words with his troupe of ladies in the corner from The Clean
World health studio and hurried off. He nodded to Shay who
shrugged his shoulders. Mick came in and told us he had had
three phone calls already from party workers in Donegal
offering him a lift home to vote on the big day. We caught the
last bus, the conductor frisking each youth who boarded it at
the stop beside the waste ground at the cemetery. When we
reached the flat I remembered the last election.

'Hey,' I said, drunkenly. 'The phone. Let's do them one by
one. Go on, Patrick Plunkett first.'

During the last campaign each candidate had put leaflets
through the door informing us they were available to solve our
problems night or day. At four o'clock one night we'd collected
all the leaflets from the hall, filed them into alphabetical order
and dialled the home numbers. Shay's voice had been iceberg
innocence. He apologized profoundly for disturbing them at
that hour, spoke of his admiration for the great work they did,
said that he was in a serious dilemma about who to vote for
and wanted to know whether they had any objections to gay
people.

'Oh, no. No,' each candidate said. 'We're available at all
times to help *all* our constituents.'

'Oh, I'm so relieved you said that,' Shay would reply while I
fell about the floor. 'My *friend* and I here are stuck together
and we were wondering if you could pop over with a bucket
of cold water.'

He'd slam the phone down and break his shite laughing
while I read out the promises listed on the next card.

But this time Shay shook his head and suddenly I sobered
up and was glad. That flat was still our tiny Ark. The thought
of hearing a Plunkett's voice there filled me with foreboding,
like a cold wind rushing in to destroy whatever warmth we
had managed to retain in our lives.

*Now I've exhausted every memory, there's nothing left
that I've held back. Sometimes when I seem to sleep the
faces are so real I could touch them. Was it a Friday*

*evening centuries ago that I stood at the court-house to*
*watch the girls wheel their bikes from the shed? A new*
*girl with red hair whose name I didn't know mounted her*
*push bike and waved back to the crowd. Her slim*
*ankles bare, the outline of panties through her white*
*jeans. She stood on the pedals to get going, her whole*
*body curved against the sun. On the pavement behind her*
*two old women were approaching, cautiously holding*
*hands in case they might fall. And, behind them, two*
*girls carrying a cheap locker to furnish a bare bedsit*
*down some side lane. They laughed as I passed, like*
*they'd exposed something personal. Nothing seemed*
*to happen, so why has the moment stayed locked,*
*almost the last one left in my mind, routine then,*
*even dull, but now so extraordinarily overwhelming.*
*It seemed all so clear a moment ago, the girl's red*
*hair, the mole on the old woman's lip, all I had to do*
*was reach out to touch them. And what seems*
*inexplicable is that none of us spoke. We shared the*
*same space grudgingly, each passing through that*
*moment in time.*

> *I can bear this loneliness,*
> *    Can lie here through eternity.*
> *If there was fire I'd welcome it,*
> *    To lose myself in its pain.*
> *Just one square of light*
> *    like a window boarded up,*
> *Just a sense that someone*
> *    has waited here in the past.*
> *And just the final torment,*
> *    the pain that can't be endured,*
> *This perpetual sense of waste,*
> *    Of words too late to be uttered.*

The three weeks before last Sunday passed, as always at
election time, with a confetti of cards littering the hallway.
Newspapers discussed the grip of election fever while the
nation shambled apathetically on: housewives with children

trying to dodge candidates outside supermarkets; unemployed men ignoring all knocks on the door and cursing every crooked bastard in power, knowing in their hearts that when the time came they would troop to the polling stations to re-elect them. The tally men, sitting beside the election agents, would number the names as they were crossed off, and later trace them back to the numbered ballot papers. There were ways of finding out who voted for who and there would always be favours needed to survive: the reference for the daughter; the hospital waiting list; the cert. that had to be signed.

Mooney was at the summit of self-importance now. The phone rang all day with party officials seeking clarification of boundaries. The huge map on his wall had been redrawn so often that it resembled the wrinkled face of an old man.

On the morning before the last election, trees had been planted in the green space between the carriageway and the first line of houses. Twelve hours after the polling stations had closed, the Corporation workmen returned to uproot them. Now the workmen were back landscaping the verge. A crude fountain, resembling a garden hose stuck between two rocks, was constructed where the old horse trough had once stood, below the bridge on the main street, until the Plunketts had knocked it down. Bored photographers took photographs of Patrick Plunkett opening it. Before they arrived, party workers took down the crude posters an unemployed candidate had stuck up. We found them dumped over the wall of the ancient graveyard. Shay climbed in to rescue one and stuck it on the kitchen wall. It read: *Hush – five TDs sleeping!*

Last Thursday evening, Katie, there was a knock on the door. Shay was cooking in the kitchen before leaving for the airport and nodded for me to get it. Justin Plunkett pushed his way quickly into the hall, annoyed at being seen by me.

'Is he here?'

I pointed and followed him upstairs. Shay came into the living-room with a pan in his hand.

'I need you, Seamus. Get your coat,' Justin told him.

'What?'

'Listen, I haven't time. I'll have you back in time for your flight. Just get your coat.'

'We agreed you'd never call here.'

Justin glanced angrily over at me.

'I've no time to argue,' he hissed. 'I shouldn't even be here myself this time of all times. I'm a man short. Just get your coat and come on.'

Shay considered for a moment, then lowered the pan, picked up his jacket slowly and went with him. Dinner was half-cooked. I walked into the kitchen, breathing in the smell of flour and eggs. New potatoes were boiling in their jackets, stalks of celery cut up on the table. But the place felt violated, like a home after being ransacked by thieves. I was hungry but I couldn't touch the food there. I turned the cooker off and walked across to the Chinese take-away in the village.

An hour later Shay returned. I heard your screams first, Katie, then the sound of a key turning. You cursed him as he pushed you up the stairs. Your hair was tousled from struggling, your jacket ripped and there was blood on Shay's neck from your fingernails.

'Let me go back, you fucking bastard!'

He shoved you towards the chair by the window and you ran at him blindly, clawing with your hands as he caught you and pushed you back.

'You've no fucking right, I want to go bleeding back.'

I remembered the Gypsy girl carried into the court room beneath the Register's office. You had the same sensual fury, the same glaring eyes. You looked around for something to smash, cursing him and me. Shay blocked the top of the stairs, never speaking or taking his eyes off you.

'What are you so high and mighty for, you bollox,' you shrieked at him. 'It's you that was selling it, you that was ripping us off! They're my friends; I want to go back. Good Jesus, how can I face them again? They'll kill me if the men don't return!'

I took my coat and left. Shay moved to one side without looking at me. His face was white. You had sat down at the table and as I closed the front door I could hear you sobbing. The light was drying up outside. I walked down the tiny laneway by the cross. Two punks sat on the steps of the old graveyard, a half-empty plastic bottle between them. A bus turned up from the village, its lights blazing like a galleon in full sail. Far off, loudspeakers blared out slogans in the estates. I didn't want to go back to the flat, not that night, not any night.

I walked for three hours, remembering how I'd paced those same streets on the nights when I worked for Plunkett, taking different routes but always ending up outside the bookies, gazing up, longing to be back in there. When I returned at eleven o'clock, it was because there seemed nowhere else to go. I let myself in and slowly climbed the stairs. The lamp in the corner was lit. Shay sat by the window in a sweat-shirt. He looked jaded. He gestured towards his closed bedroom door.

'She's asleep at last. Don't talk too loud or you'll wake her.'

I pulled a seat from the table and sat back to front on it.

'You don't like me very much any more, do you, Hano?'

I couldn't answer him. I lowered my head until my forehead was cooled by the wood of the chair.

'Don't like myself either.' He sighed. 'You think you can fool yourself, you can pretend things don't matter. You can say that's the way the world is run, if you don't want to get left behind you've got to be a part of it. You can even be like a guard at a prison camp, justifying yourself by saying you're doing nothing in comparison. But it's all a crock of shite, Hano, you can't fool yourself, even when you try as hard as I did.

'It was supposed to be my way of getting back, on the cops, this country, that joke of myself. Remember him? The laid-back dude arsing around, thinking the world was a cuddly place.'

'I loved him, Shay,' I said, 'I miss him.'

'Never saw it through before, Hano; I made sure I never did. Always kept it impersonal, Boy's Own stuff, feeling big because of the risk, walking past the fuckers in customs. I suppose that's what it's like for the bomber pilots, eh, high above it all, just little clean bursts of flame like flowers exploding below them. Collect the stuff from some hotel bedroom, conceal it, take the risk at the airport, drop it at a new pick-up point, a pub toilet, the rubbish bin in a park. Collect your money for the next drop. Your only contact a phone call on the Wednesday. Never see anybody this side; never see where it goes. Finally know you've made it. You're the cool clean hero you dreamt of as a child.'

I looked up. Shay was staring at me as he spoke, wanting me to look back.

'Remember when Justin was just a joke, eh? Those poker sessions slagging his leather jacket. It was like I'd never known him, Hano. You could smell the fear when he walked in, the power he held. Was hard to see anything at first in the gloom with just the noise of water dripping. Then the shapes started coming closer like hunted animals through the dark. Jesus, Hano, if you'd seen them. Mostly they'd money but some tried to barter goods. He'd two men with him who did the work. He just smoked cigarettes and nodded occasionally, standing back in the shadows, putting a value on some item. Normally one of his cronies oversaw it, you could see he didn't trust the two men. I was the look-out, keeping watch at the doorway out over the car-park.

'I mean, it wasn't real Hano, it was some fucking nightmare. One girl had a camera she'd stolen. She kept saying *It's worth enough! It's worth enough!* But Plunkett shook his head. She tried to grab a bag from one man's hand but the other yanked her back by the hair, pushed her over to one side. She stood there, unable to leave but afraid to go back, holding up the camera for Plunkett to see, pleading to him with her eyes. Then I saw Katie, waiting in the queue. There was a puddle on the concrete floor. She stepped into it when the line shifted and stood, waiting patiently for it to move again. Her eyes were down, Hano, her hand clutching a bundle of crumpled notes. And she never looked up, just shuffled forward in turn.

'I remember a film I saw one night on the box above some bar counter in Holland. It was in Dutch so I couldn't understand a word of it, but I recognized the black-and-white newsreels. We've all seen them: train stations; people with stars pinned to their coats waiting to be loaded on to a truck. They had the same lifeless look, you know, that numbed indifference, that she had in her eyes when she reached the two men and held the money out.

'I grabbed her shoulder, Hano. She screamed, looking at me in terror like an apparition from another world. *Let me go*, she kept saying, *Let me shagging go!* The men were confused, they looked back at Plunkett. *Quit messing Seamus*, he said. *Don't handle the merchandise. You want to fuck her it's your own business, but not on my time.* I began to pull her screaming towards the doorway. I could see her mates huddled together, whispering among themselves. *Let her alone, Mister, or I'll split you*, one of them called. *Cheap meat Seamus*, Plunkett said. *Back to work and I'll fix you up with any of them later.*

'Katie was trying to bite my hand and I wrapped her in a headlock. The men were advancing, spreading out to cover both sides. I knew one was armed with a gun and kept trying to keep my body between him and Katie. They were almost at me when Plunkett spoke. *I don't like it. Take the gear, let's go.* They turned, just like that, picked up the suitcase at their feet and suddenly everybody had forgotten about me. Katie's friends clustered around the men, frantically holding up money, radios, credit cards. I dragged Katie through the doorway, past the driver smoking on the bonnet, as Plunkett slipped out ahead of the horde. Seconds later the engine started. I looked back, half-way across the car-park, and saw the two men climb in as the car gathered speed. Girls were running behind it, screaming, trying to climb on to the bonnet. The lights came straight at me, swerved at the last moment and headed for town.'

Shay took out another cigarette. The ashtray beside him was overflowing with butts.

'Were the men called O'Brien and Flynn?' I asked.

He nodded, surprised as he struck a match.

'I don't like myself much either,' I said. 'When I was a kid my daddy would shake his head and say, *Be anything you want, but no son of mine will ever work for a Plunkett.* I don't know how much he knew about what went on, Shay. He'd never hear a word said against them. He had a wife, five children, all the commitments of the world, but he'd look at me and say, *No son of mine.*'

Outside there was a shout and then footsteps. A siren in the distance startled my nerves. I crossed to the window and closed the blinds as if I could keep the world out. Shay looked at the bedroom door.

'It took me hours to soothe her ... like I'd torn her from her mother, or something. I thought it was just the drugs, but it was more than that, it was like she was terrified of being different, of standing out by herself. You don't like her much, do you Hano?'

'I don't really know her.'

Shay looked down and shrugged his shoulders, trying to decide whether to tell me something or maybe just to understand it in his own mind.

'Never told you much about Europe, did I?' he asked.

I shook my head and Shay paused, remembering.

'First few months were great, all the freedom I ever dreamed of. Even after I got the shit kicked out of me in the field I was still together. I knew I'd built up enough money to survive a month or two, but I was concussed after it, shaken, like. Few nights later I fell out of that hostel bunk and everything was taken. But I still thought I'd get fixed up; I even got taken on at another factory. I was only there a morning before the manager came down. You'd be surprised how quickly word gets round a city about a trouble-maker.

'Amsterdam seemed the place to go, but it was the end of winter, few tourists there, shag all casual work. I'd trudged through the streets for days, sleeping down behind Central Station, waiting for my luck to change. I'd met a Turk there when I was passing through in the summer. His family were in prison in Kabul; he'd been given political refugee status on condition he said or wrote nothing in Holland. I remember his talk fascinating me. He was a bizarre mixture ... twentieth-century Marxist and nineteenth-century peasant, completely unlike the fey Dutch around us. One summer evening we went drinking and the most beautiful Dutch girl I'd ever seen asked him for a light. She was no more than seventeen, white-skinned, in a loose T-shirt and skin-tight jeans. Back at her table she kept glancing at him, letting him know she wanted him to fuck her. I could see how tempted he was but he stayed

248

talking with me even though I was egging him on. And suddenly I realized that what he was most lonely for, amid those glossy streets, was somebody to talk to from his own world, somebody who could grasp what the fuck he was on about. And from what he'd heard of Ireland, he presumed I was a refugee too.

'That winter I spent eight days searching for a familiar face and in the end it was he who found me. I was huddled outside the Aithain Bookshop watching an organ grinder across the road, the metal figures jerking in and out of the freezing air, when this voice said, *Hello Irish.*

'Spent three weeks, kipping on his floor, Hano, looking for work each day, putting off my return until it was too wet or cold to stay out any longer. His flat overlooked the back entrance of one of Holland's most select brothels. Each evening I watched the red sign across the road switching on and off, silhouetting him where he sat in the window with his memories and thwarted plans, motionless except for the glow of his cigarette burning down. I think I could have spent years there and he wouldn't have complained, but I could feel myself sinking into it – waiting endlessly, like him, like a real refugee, for something to happen.

'All that I had left was that Irish pound you'd given me the night before I left. I'd kept it as some sort of good-luck charm, and the two times I tried to change it the men in the booths looked at me as though I was insulting their intelligence. And one address in Amsterdam that Justin Plunkett had given me. Don't even know why I'd kept it, I never meant to go there.'

Shay's cigarette had gone out. He lit it again, pulled on it, blew the smoke out. He smiled to himself.

'When you're that broke you just can't lift yourself. I hitched to the Irish embassy in The Hague ... don't know why, to feel I belonged somewhere, I suppose, that I was still part of something. That ninth secretary was some spring chicken, hair dyed blond, those rimless glasses, and a voice like the speaking clock. I didn't want repatriation, I didn't want to go home thinking I'd failed in my own mind. I was looking for the fare down to France where I figured I'd get work or a loan of a hundred guilders, just something to get myself back on my feet. I never even saw her hand touch the bell, before I found myself in the street outside. The two porters were Dutch. They grinned at me and one tossed out a cigarette as if to a beggar.

'I walked for hours till after it was dark. I tried dustbins, watched to see if people left food on the counters of the open-air cafés, drove myself crazy staring in the windows of restaurants. You should see it some day, Hano; a city of embassies and government. The streets smell of it – money and privilege, centuries of uninterrupted wealth. Even the red-light district is discreet.

'Near it there was a street of gay bars. Young men stood on the pavement outside them, hair groomed, tight jeans, sweatshirts. You know how they say you're getting old when the policemen look young? Well, the youngest cop I ever saw was riding on horseback down the centre – fair skin, blue eyes, hair so blonde you'd swear it was dyed – the perfect Aryan specimen. An old queen stumbled into his path and the cop shouted impatiently for him to stand aside. The queen looked back and blew a kiss in the air as he reached out to rub the leather boot in the stirrup. It was gas. The gays drifted out of the bars till they surrounded the cop, smiling seductively up at him, rolling their eyes and winking as he started to blush. I could see his face swamped in red before he lashed the horse and broke through the jeering men, and as they drifted away I saw a face I knew cruising down the far side on the street.'

Before Shay said his name some instinct told me. I didn't want him to continue. It brought back too many memories of things I would never have the courage to tell him.

'Must have been some meeting of Junior Ministers on. Patrick Plunkett may be famous over here but most people in Europe were amazed we even had our own passports. I was used to seeing him on the box, or watching the chauffeur open the door for him outside his advice clinics on Saturday mornings when I was small. Always surrounded by people and shaking hands. He looked so odd there, just another face in the crowd. I felt like crying, Hano. Weeks searching for a familiar face and who did I get? I'd only met him once, years ago in Justin's apartment. I remember Justin stubbing out his cigarette like a guilty schoolboy when he saw the Merc outside, even though that night in Murtagh's he'd laid two white lines down for us on the counter inches from the barman's pumps. The da couldn't resist the political handshake when I went. *Well shake the hand that shook the hand of three American presidents*, he'd said. *Shake the hand that's after scratching me arse*, I'd replied. Okay, I was pissed, but I never forgot the look he gave me. It was like, *I own you, son. It doesn't matter what you say, you'll need me one day and I'll make you bleed.*'

'I don't want to hear this, Shay,' I said. Just hearing that family's name mentioned in the room made me feel dirty again. Shay's voice was low, insistent.

'Listen to me Hano, sit down and fucking listen. I want this out, I want to tell you. I'm sick of carrying it around inside of me. So I followed him, right. I don't know why – maybe I couldn't think of anything else to do. There was nothing for me to do. I knew I wasn't going back to the Turk, knew I couldn't stay there, and I just couldn't face another hike up to Denmark again or down to France. Not without food or money, some dignity. I was starving and filthy and the old bastard had been right. I was just like those housewives I'd seen standing outside his clinic in the rain. Finally I did need his help.

'He must have known someone was behind him. Most of the streets we passed through were deserted, our two sets of footsteps conspicuous. He turned a corner and, when I reached it, the avenue before me was deserted. I'd walked a few steps when a hand grabbed my shoulder from a doorway. He swung me round to face him.

'"What are you at, boy? Why are you following me?" His eyes were suspicious, without any recognition in them. Seeing him face to face, I realized I'd been crazy even to bother. There was no kudos to be got from the party for helping emigrants, except by encouraging them to leave. He'd probably get a dressing down if he'd helped me to return. I had been going to mention knowing Justin but suddenly I didn't want to be beholden to that family in any way. I mumbled something about mistaking him for somebody else. His hands still gripped my jacket, his face inches from mine. When he asked how long I'd been following him I said since the street with the policeman on the horse. Saw him frowning, Hano.

'"I saw no policeman on a horse! Didn't say that I did. Do you hear? You're thinking of somebody else. Now get away. Off with you before I do call the police."

'I backed away but had gone only a few yards when he called me. He had recovered himself, his voice as polished again as the government handlers had shaped it.

'"Wait," he said. "You just took me by surprise. Where are you from?"

'I thought for a moment. I've not much of a Dublin accent and didn't want him to know I recognized him.

'"Essen," I said, thickening my voice, "in the Ruhr. And you?"

'"Manchester," he said, pronouncing each word distinctly. "Denis Law? Georgie Best? Remember them? No, you'd be too young. I'm in engineering. We have important clients over here. Your English is good."

'"Ya," I said. "Sehr gut."

'I could see him trying to size me up, Hano, but I was bored. I wanted to get away, yet didn't know of anywhere to go. He asked if I often went down the street with the horse and, when I shook my head, he said I was wise, that it was a dangerous place. "You get all kinds of people down there, all kinds," he said. He shut up and eyed me speculatively. I knew I was getting ensnared in something I wanted no part of. I turned to go.

'"Hey Essen, when did you last eat? Don't try and kid me. I can see the hunger in your face."

'I told him I had to meet some friends. He laughed, fully in control now. I knew he'd had this conversation a dozen times before.

'"You don't fool me Essen," he said. "You've nowhere to go. Look in a mirror – you haven't seen food or a bed for days. Oh, I know what you're thinking but you're wrong. I'm no queer, I'm just alone. I'll not lay a finger on you. Sure, I've a lad your age back in Manchester. If he was stranded I hope someone would do him a turn. Come with me for a meal, keep me company. European to European eh, we're all one big

252

community now. Look, I'm not even paying for it. Company expense card." '

Shay stopped speaking. A sound came from his bedroom. He listened. You, Katie, were moaning something in your sleep. The untouched cigarette beside him had burnt down into a worm of ash. He touched it with his finger and it broke apart. I rested my elbows on the chair and cradled my forehead between my palms. Shay went on.

'I refused, of course, but he knew all the tricks to work on my hunger. Finally I told myself that I was younger and stronger and could handle him. He had good taste in restaurants. The manager took one look at me and ushered us into a dark corner. When the waiter brought the menu, Plunkett. ordered two large beers for me and a glass of wine for himself. I began to ask him wide-eyed questions about engineering and England. Jesus, his knowledge of Manchester didn't extend beyond United's first team twenty years ago. Kept contradicting himself with that mixture of arrogance and stupidity. He reminded me of this book I read once about South America. There was a quote in it from the mother of a Bolivian general: *If I had known my son was going to become president of the Republic I would have taught him to read*. When he asked me to name things in German I cursed him to his face in Connemara Irish without him recognizing one word of it. He was trying to get me drunk but I knew my limits, or at least I thought I did. I was weak from hunger and unused to alcohol after that past month. It was taking its effect sooner than I expected. I rose, a bit unsteadily, to use the toilet.

' "Sit down!" he snapped and, when I looked at him, he repeated it more quietly. "This is my evening, Essen. I'm asking nothing, so just do what you're told. If you leave this table I'll be gone before you return and you can explain half the bill to these oriental gentlemen." I sat down and we stared at each other in hostile silence.

' "Drink up," he said. "The food is coming."

'I realized how drunk I was becoming on my empty stomach and left my glass untouched, but he ordered two more beers for me when the food came. It was an Indonesian rice table with eighteen dishes. When I saw it I forgot everything,

253

Patrick Plunkett could be handled later, I thought, for now my body just wanted food. He smiled at my appetite and asked were we friends again. Even his pretence of an English accent was gone. I laughed at the ridiculousness of it all, thinking how I'd slag Justin whenever I got home.

'Neither of us spoke after that. I ate and ate and when he ordered more beer I was grateful for it. Beneath the table I fingered the buckle of my belt. The moment he laid one finger on me I'd let him have that. My bladder and bowels were aching, but somehow I controlled them until I'd finished everything on the table and had downed seven large beers. I was in severe pain now. He'd paid the bill and we were outside. I knew I had to get away from him but I could hardly move. My eyes kept closing Hano, my head spinning.

' "The toilet," I said to him. "I've got to use the fucking toilet."

'He took my hand. I was too weak to shake him off. At any moment my bladder would burst all over the pavement. His voice came from close to my ear.

' "My hotel is just on the corner. You can use the toilet there and go on. You'll need to sober up. I'll help you."

'I remember nothing about entering the hotel or reaching his room. Perhaps I blacked out. When he helped me on to the bed I struggled up, determined not to black out again. I was shouting out for the toilet. There were two doors at the end of the room. Through a blur, I watched him lock one and enter the other.

' "It's in here," he cried. "The toilet's here."

'I staggered in the direction of his voice. When I went in there was just a bath in the room. I knew instinctively that the toilet was behind the door he'd just locked. He lay naked in the gleaming white bath, Hano, a bloated carcass with a thin coating of hair on his chest standing out against his child-like white skin. I felt sick looking at him. The same face I'd seen on a thousand posters stared up, pleading, old looking and wrinkled without the coating of make-up.

' "Do it on me," he begged. "Please, I don't want anything else. On my face, on my chest, please, that's all I ask."

'I swayed in the doorway. Just being in his presence made me feel I'd never be clean again. I felt guilty, felt I'd sold myself for food and drink, felt the sick power of his voice I'd been hearing since childhood. If I delayed any longer I'd soil my clothes. I went through the motions, Hano, in a state of shock, like I was in somebody else's body – seeing his cock harden as I turned to sit over the rim of the tub and listening to him squirm to get his face directly below me.

'I cried out in relief as my bowels and bladder opened in a rush. And I never looked down, just covered my face with my hands as I heard the slap of shit hitting his face and the hiss of piss splashing over his body, knowing how his hand was pumping away. He never made a sound through it all and though my eyes were closed I could see his face in my mind, the mouth open, eager to swallow the torrent of piss, the brown streaks of shit smearing his forehead and hair, the white necklace of his sperm sprinkling over his chest. If he had even reached one finger out to touch me, Hano, it would have broken the spell, but he made no contact at all with my body. And even after I had finished I was unable to move, I perched there with my buttocks exposed to his eyes, numbness replacing the feeling of degradation. Then he spoke with the pleading gone, in the voice I remembered from those television programmes, in the assured tones of a man of state addressing an underling:

' "I shall lie here a while longer, Essen. You will find a one hundred guilder note on the bedside table. Should you try to take anything else I shall have you arrested before you reach the lobby. Now get out."

'There was no paper to clean myself, and when I thought about it it seemed a futile thing to do. I fixed my clothes and left the bathroom without looking back. A small lamp was switched on beside the bed, the crisp Dutch banknote shining in its circle of light. I thought about it before bending down to pick the money up. I had sold myself. I took his money, folded it neatly in my wallet and left your crumpled Irish pound in its place. Across it I wrote, *Fuck you too, Mr Plunkett, TD, Junior Minister*. I walked till I found a train station and blew the money on a ticket anywhere.'

Shay went silent. Though he was gazing straight at me I wasn't sure if he was still aware I was there.

'And then?' I asked.

'It gets complex then, can't understand it myself. Anyway I

left the train, eventually made it back to Amsterdam and phoned the number his son had given me. That phone call was a once-off Hano – or that's what I thought. Twenty-four hours later I was sleeping on the stairs here, waiting for you to come back from that simple world I once belonged to. I've never felt clean again, Hano, never fully after that. It's funny, I used to enjoy having you around because you were so innocent you amused me. Now I'd envy you.'

Shay stopped speaking. It was my turn to come clean, to tell someone, to share the burden inside me. I wanted to but I couldn't. I didn't know the words. Some of it he guessed because he smiled.

'But you're not innocent no more Hano, are you? They get you, always get you some way or other. I gave in Hano, never confessed, could never tell you even. In the end I just became a part of it. Surrendered myself in slow stages. Screw the world because the world is screwing me. Keep your head down as you build your nest egg and say you'll stop some day. Make yourself forget things. Do you believe in sin, Hano?'

'Do you mean like in school, that shite?'

'No . . . never had time for the organized stuff. Used to watch the converts coming out of the Mormon church by the cemetery, middle-aged men in suits having orgies of ice cream. Perpetual bleeding adolescence, perpetual abdication of re-sponsibility. Don't think, just follow the rules and get an Apex ticket to heaven. I don't mean other people's versions of sin. I mean your own, your own judgement, your own penance.

'I left that hotel Hano and it was like I would never feel again. There was a shop for leather goods on the corner. As I passed the window I looked in. My face Hano, it scared the fuck out of me. I never saw such desperation before, it was a face that would gladly welcome death. I came home to forget that face, but I couldn't. I only found it here again.

'You were at work one day when I saw her first. It was nothing major, just the challenge of another girl on a wall. Remember them here, the little schoolgirls thinking they'd entered the big dangerous world? She was watching the trucks. She turned when I spoke to her, and I was back Hano, back in that street in The Hague. It was the eyes, the same fucking despair beneath the mock toughness, the same desperation that would risk anything. She thought I was bent when I brought her back, thought there was something wrong with her. But I couldn't touch her. I was powerless; I was dazzled. I wanted a second chance, I wanted . . . I don't know, it doesn't make fucking sense . . . wanted somehow to save her, to save myself, to atone in my own mind. I didn't know how Hano. For once in my life I didn't know what to do.'

I had never heard Shay talk for so long before, for months I had hardly heard him speak at all. Now it was like a wound opening and the pus pouring out. He had stopped and was looking over my shoulder. His bedroom door was open and you were standing there, wearing one of his shirts. Your legs were bare, thinner than I thought they were. I'd no idea how much you had heard. You closed the door again with a soft click. It was half-three in the morning. Shay borrowed a pillow and a blanket from my room. I slept for a few hours, then stumbled into work.

*I smell of clay, I dream of earth,*
*Remembering until there's nothing to forget.*
*Where is this place?*
*One high square of fading light,*
*Old bits of glass and stone,*
*Dry leaves that have blown in.*
*Somebody was here before me,*
*I'm waiting for someone to come.*

*My leather belt feels like flesh*
*That has begun to rot.*
*How long have I been lying here?*
*My memory is choked*
*With flashes from the past*
*Hurtling by like cars*
*Towards a city I can't reach.*
*Now I've no past left*
*That hasn't been burnt out*
*And I lie in this oblivion*
*Without even knowing my name.*

*God, if you were ever there*
*what more is left to recall?*
*It's all got jumbled up.*
*A girl somewhere with cropped hair*
*Someone waiting for me once.*
*Every memory's been sucked*
*Till my mind's a shrivelled ghost.*

*I want to pass on!*
*I want . . . Oh Jesus wait:*
*There is a last memory I can't escape.*
*A roadway, morning from a window,*
*Birds that never sang,*
*Down streets that were abandoned,*
*I must have had some destination.*
*Then it's night, suddenly like that;*
*Beneath Dalymount's lights*
*the pitch greener than green.*

*But there's nobody inside,*
*The stadium gates left open wide.*
*The city strewn with abandoned cars,*
*Bronze statues gazing down*
*As I stared, willing them to speak.*
*Why was there no one around?*
*Two voices I couldn't hear were calling*
*like night birds in distant buildings,*
*Holding me back with their cries.*
*The night turned black,*
*The moon dim as a tunnel's mouth.*
*I drifted towards that host of light*
*But their voices weighed me down.*
*When I woke I was trapped*
*In this black void.*

*I smell of clay, I dream of earth,*
*Remembering until there's nothing to forget.*
*Where is this place?*
*One fading square of light high up,*
*Eternally out of reach.*

*Faces that I cannot name*
*Run like a film through my skull.*
*God, when will the reel snap*
*The spool spin wildly by itself*
*And let me escape?*

*I smell of clay, I dream of earth,*
*Remembering until there's nothing to forget*
*Somebody was here before me,*
*I'm waiting for someone to come.*

Everything seemed unreal at work the next day. The clerks' voices buzzed around me from another world with their clichés about interviews and transfers. At break I stood on the stairs, gazing down at the mill of faces crushed against the court door. I was trying to remember two youths with cardboard boxes laughing as they sneaked away. You were gone when I got home, Katie. I didn't ask Shay where. He was edgy. I knew he was waiting for Justin Plunkett to call.

All that evening canvassers were knocking on doors, lists of voters in their hands, immune to whatever abuse they received. Others skulked along, careful not to touch the bell as they dropped little cards with messages, printed to resemble a handwritten note from the candidate: *Sorry you were out when I called. Please remember I am always at your service.* A mobile advice clinic for Patrick Plunkett tore down the street blaring martial music, the young woman driver ignoring the men who put their hands out for a joke as a recording of Plunkett's voice announced his availability within. Every time I heard footsteps on the pavement I moved to the curtain. Shay sat impassively at the table. I knew my movements were beginning to irritate him but I was unable to remain still. When the doorbell rang Shay placed his hand on my shoulder and nodded towards the bedroom.

'This is between him and me, Hano. Don't get involved.'

I watched him go down to open the door. It was two elderly women campaigning. Once Shay would have played along, gently sending them up before moving in for the kill. Now he just shook his head and closed the door. He was turning to go back up when someone put his finger to the doorbell and held it there. We both knew who it was. He looked up at me and, after a moment, I obeyed, walking over to the unlit bedroom and lying down to listen. They climbed up together, Justin Plunkett's voice as brash as ever, mocking the canvassers who were trudging door-to-door for his father – and whose children, in a few years' time, would walk those streets for him. But it was no longer the words of a friend, more the small talk of a boss about to come to business. Shay said nothing. When they reached the top of the stairs I heard Plunkett shout, his tone suddenly as raw as his uncle's.

'Don't do that to me again. Ever! You hear Seamus? Are you fucking crazy or what? Over some fucking chick. And then you don't make your flight. You don't like getting your hands dirty is it? You're a part of it, man; you bring the stuff in. What do you think I do with it? Pour it down the toilet?'

'I want out Justin. Full stop.'

Shay's voice was calm but I knew he was fighting to control his temper. Justin Plunkett backed off.

'Right, Seamus. Listen, I'm sorry. I shouldn't have called on you last night. I was a man short, I even had to go out myself, this week of all weeks. Look, it won't happen again. I promise. You're a good courier. Let's leave it at that. You've missed this week's run but I'll give you a cut anyway. We'll set it up again for next week. Will you do it?'

'You heard me, Justin. I'm through.'

'You going chicken on me Seamus?'

There was no reply. I could imagine Shay staring at him.

'Only joking Seamus. We were friends long before this and we'll be friends long after. I've never asked you to do anything you didn't want, but just do this last run for me. You're pulling out without notice, leaving me badly exposed. Just one more run Seamus and we're through.'

Again the only reply was silence. Plunkett was growing impatient.

'Listen Seamus, just because of some tart you want to . . .'

I heard the scrape of a chair being pulled back and a thud against the wall beside me. The sentence wasn't finished.

When Shay spoke he was just a few feet from my head. I heard Plunkett's breath as he was pinned against the wall.

'Don't fucking annoy me Justin. I'm out, do you understand? You needn't worry about me going to the police or anyone else, but you go near that girl again with your shit and I'll come fucking looking for you. In person. Right?'

This must be life to a blind person I thought, only having the words, sensing the fear, having no other clues to what was happening. But instinctively I felt the grip on Plunkett's jacket being relaxed, his weight easing from the wall. Justin laughed nervously.

'Take it easy, Seamus. It's cool. My mistake. It's bad to do business with friends. You want out?'

Shay still didn't reply. I knew he hadn't released the jacket fully.

'You've got out. Come on. No hard feelings. Hey listen, you want your wheels back. I mean, no offence but they're a crock of shite. I only took them off your hands as a favour. They're no use to me. Come over later this evening, we'll have a beer and you can take them away. A parting gift right? We'll have a laugh about this in Murtagh's some night. Come on. Friends?'

In the silence a loudspeaker outside began to hail the virtues of Justin's father. I could imagine Justin holding his hand out with his father's same professional smile. Shay must have finally taken it.

'You'll be over?'

Justin's voice moved further away, heading for the stairs.

'I might.'

'I'll expect you so.'

When I heard the front door close I waited for a moment before coming out. Shay was coming up from the hallway.

'Will you take it?'

He smiled wryly.

'You can step on my blue suede shoes, but leave my Triumph Herald alone. I'll buy it back.'

He counted a slim roll of notes in his bedroom.

'Have you twenty spots?' he asked.

I gave it to him and he put it with his own money in an envelope with Justin Plunkett's name on it.

'No more obligations to nobody from now on. It was good here once Hano, wasn't it?'

'It was the best, Shay. It still could be. Remember, the massage parlour? "The Winner's Enclosure". It's never too late. I'd be bouncer. We could install Katie as a madam now that Carol's gone. A bit young but it would certainly keep her off the streets.'

Shay grinned at me. I'd forgotten what his grin looked like. We joked about the future until you knocked on the door, Katie. You were shocked by my smile when I answered. It was the first time you ever asked could you come in. You seemed embarrassed by the previous night and felt the need to offer some excuse for coming back.

'It's just that . . . I've nowhere to go,' you said. 'I've nowhere else where I really belong any more.'

'Don't worry,' Shay said, 'none of us have.'

We left you behind us when we went to Clontarf for the car. I waited for Shay outside the apartment block. The car was parked fifty yards down the road. Through a line of trees I watched Justin come to the door. He smiled and said something but Shay shook his head. Justin handed him the keys and closed the door and Shay waited a moment before pushing the envelope through one of the letter boxes. The car had a full tank of petrol. We parked in town and went searching for Shay's old snooker hall. The old man was gone, the dusty crates of orange bottles carted away. A girl in a bow-tie kept watch beside the computer screen. A monitor above her head showed the tables upstairs.

'There's a five pound deposit,' she said. 'You'll be a half-hour waiting.'

'What happened to Joe?' Shay shouted above the disco music. She looked at him, baffled.

'The old lad who used to own this gaff?'

She shrugged her shoulders.

'I don't know. He died I suppose. Cancer I think it was.'

We found another place along the quays and played four or five frames. Two friends of Shay's came in, a gay couple who hadn't even known that he had got back from Europe. They slagged him and he laughed, tossing his head back. It was like the Shay I first knew, woken from suspended animation, like the stories of Oisin I once learned. We wandered back to their flat in the markets and Shay found a deck of cards. He cleared everything from the table and rubbed his hands.

'Straight poker,' he said. 'Jacks or higher to open. No butter vouchers in the pot.'

In the narrow cobbled street below, refrigerated lorries hummed in the night. Watching the lads, relaxed and open as they leaned against each other on the sofa and laughed with Shay, it seemed impossible that men such as the Plunkett brothers had ever existed. I leaned back in the chair in exhausted exhilaration and let their warmth banish the pain of the last six months.

It was three o'clock when we left, our pockets rich with silver. I expected to find you still there, Katie, but you had gone home. There was a young couple across the road, squatting down beside a fire in the roofless cottages. Not cider drinkers or vandals, just a broke boy and girl putting off the moment of returning to their separate houses. Shay made a noise at the window and threw down a packet of twenty cigarettes. The girl ran to get it as though it were a hundred-pound note. Shay turned and his face was radiant. I don't have the words to describe it. Not physically beautiful or just happy, but suddenly young. We didn't talk much, we were both too tired. He touched my shoulder for a moment on his way to his bedroom.

'Hey Hano,' he grinned, "The Winner's Enclosure." We're skint but we've made it here at last.'

After the drunken turmoil of the village the road seemed even blacker. The rain began again, heavy sodden drops thudding against his wet flesh. Hano no longer bothered to brush them from his eyes, so that he stumbled along as though underwater, with the dark shapes around him unfocused and unreal.

Was it only two nights since he had walked the roads of North Dublin with her footsteps following his into the darkness? Now he could no longer distinguish them, but through the rain felt he could hear a faint humming as if a song without words was coming from deep within her throat. He knew she could sense it too, that they were going home in a way that they had never gone before. Even though nobody waited there for them, when they reached the wood there would be no place left to return to. Home was not the place where you were born but the place you created for yourself, where you did not need to explain, where you finally became what you were. The cars had stopped. Even the dogs, sheltering in the outhouses of the farms they passed, no longer ventured into the teeming rain to bark at their presence. They would never be more alone.

'I loved him Francis,' Katie said. 'Big and gruff. Packy, they'd called him in Leitrim; Uncle Pat in Dublin. Part of me never believed they were dead. When others said, your parents are with God, I knew they were lying, but when he said it, I just felt sorry for him. If I could have said goodbye to them Francis, it would have meant ... would have been a moment when one life stopped and a new one began. But there wasn't ... I'm sorry Francis ... had to go back to find they were gone, find there was nothing to go back to. I ... do you pray?'

If she couldn't see, she sensed him shaking his head in the blackness.

'I did. I wish I could still. But not to their God, not since the day they left. But to my mother. And not really pray but talk; you know, tell her things in my mind. Never had nobody to tell things to again ... could never shake the feeling she was there, somewhere, aware of things.'

The surface of the road was uneven with pools of water lurking beneath their feet. Lights of houses shone across the flat expanse of poor land. In a hollow the empty windows of a ruined mill kept watch. Two hours after they left the village the road curved down towards a small stone bridge. Hano recognized it as the bridge with the light. He grasped Katie's hand and began to pull her on, excitement replacing his exhaustion. The road veered right beneath a clump of trees, then twisted left again, allowing him a glimpse of the street lights of the woman's village. There was a Spanish feel to that old row of sleeping buildings: the four pubs, two with petrol pumps outside, one an undertaker's, the shop unchanged for half a century. They walked up by the side of the old national school. The main road through the village had been widened.

A lorry sped past at high speed towards Donegal, splashing water over the loose gravel outside the shops. A cat crept from a doorway, paused to watch them and then moved on, leaving stillness in its wake.

It must have been half-two in the morning. Half a decade had passed since he'd stood there, yet never had he felt such a sense of coming home. Every memory was vivid now; he'd only to cross over and slip up the side-road past the single street light at the crest of the hill to reach the site of the caravan. He didn't dare imagine that the caravan might be there itself. How old had the woman been? She would be over eighty now if alive, living on a tiny pension, buffeted by storms in winter, searching for dry wood to keep the stove burning. Like Katie with Tomas, he hoped she was dead rather than in a hospital ward. She belonged out here, away from drips and charts.

Lately there had been raids on old people throughout the West. Men in vans arriving at four in the morning, breaking down doorways, beating pensioners up, searching for the discoloured hoards of banknotes hidden beneath beds and carpets. It was an act of faith to imagine she could have somehow survived. Katie was waiting, staring towards the lights of an oncoming car which lit up a row of new bungalows. Automatically they stepped back till it had passed, then he took her hand and led her up the side-road, by a field of sleeping geese which stirred at their footsteps, towards the street light shining on the white walls of the farmhouse, and beyond into the darkness by the graveyard. There was an overgrown turn to the left, a row of bushes hiding the field from view. He walked slowly towards them and saw his ark, his old caravan with the windows broken and the door open in the rain. Katie's hand touched his shoulder as he lifted his head, welcoming the coolness of the rain that ran down his cheeks. Then, in the silence, a dog barked.

The noise was indistinct, like a ghost calling, but it came again as Katie pushed him forward. They'd gone past the bushes now, the field open before them with a long dark shape in the corner beyond the abandoned caravan. Suddenly a door was thrown open and, framed in the square of light, they saw

265

the tiny figure in boots and a yellow oilskin gazing out. By her feet, an old dog was barking and swaying back and forth. Hano remembered the cries of the injured cat on his first night. He climbed over the gate, pausing for Katie, and began to run. The dog was growing more excited, the old woman still staring out into the dark. Her face had a quizzical look, child-like in its delicate bone structure. When he reached the corridor of light thrown across the grass he stopped and walked nervously forward. The woman stepped forward uncertainly and then smiled.

'Francis,' she cried. 'Francis, come in quickly, you're drenched.'

She stepped backwards, beckoning them into her new mobile home. In the narrow space he kissed her lightly but she brushed him off, concerned only to give them warmth and shelter. It was all still there: the crowded bookcase, the cast-iron stove, the faded paintings and the row of photographs from the old caravan.

'Look, he remembers you,' she said as the dog came over, brown eyes looking inquisitively up into his. Katie remained in the doorway, uncertain of herself. The old woman didn't bother with introductions. She pushed the girl towards the seat and, opening the iron stove, began to pile twigs and small pieces of wood inside. The dog whined and licked his hand. He stared at Katie over the woman's bent back, trying to reassure her. She straightened up and turned to them.

'Now we'll have warmth. First a cup of coffee, then we can talk.'

She handed Hano the kettle to fill and, smiling at Katie, led her into the bedroom at the end of the mobile home. Hano could hear their voices as he ran the tap. The dog lay down again on the rush mats. A white cat stretched luxuriously and eyed him from a cushion in the window. He ran his fingers down the spines of the old books, staring again at the rack of photographs above the window. The light filtered through a slender red shade above the small table. When he stood beside the jet of flame at the cooker he was in shadow. A black cat climbed in the small open window, balanced on the frame and sprang on to the table. She shook herself, spraying drops over the piles of paper, yawned and then padded her way into the corner. He bent beside the dog who turned on his stomach, raising his legs to be rubbed. The old eyes stared at him with extraordinary sadness. As Francis rubbed him the eyes turned to look towards the woman's door, low sounds coming from the animal's throat. The kettle began to boil. He found the cups and filled them, the scent of coffee filling his nostrils, making him dizzy. But he waited, wanting to share the first taste with her.

The door opened and Katie emerged in an old jumper and jeans belonging to the woman. The dog rose and went towards the woman, pressing his paw against her leg and staring up as if to tell her he had not been unfaithful.

'He knew,' she said. 'He woke me an hour ago. He was whining. I knew something was wrong.'

'I had nowhere else to go,' Francis said. 'I wasn't even sure if you'd still be here, if you'd be . . .'

'You can say the word. I'm not afraid of it. I only hope the animals die before me.'

'Deep down I never thought of you as dead,' he said. 'Somehow . . . I think I would have known; you would have given me a sign. That doesn't make sense, but . . . You don't know what I've done. If they find me here you'll be in trouble. I shouldn't have come to you, but . . . I don't just need shelter, I need to tell someone. I don't know anybody else it would make sense to. I'll go then.'

'Sleep now,' the woman said. 'Eat some food and then sleep. Whatever you've done nobody will find you tonight. Tomorrow we can talk.'

The dog, looking carefully back at the woman, came to lick his hand. Cait sat beside the open stove, her bare feet held up close to the flames. Hano knew there was no need to explain anything. Nobody in that caravan would be his judge or jury.

# CHAPTER FIVE

# *Wednesday*

It was the oldest dream, the dream Pascal Plunkett had displaced. Hano dreamt it again as fresh as if it had never occurred before. Walking in slow motion beneath the trees towards the low branches which framed the ruined house. The curious stillness as though life had stopped. He knew it was a dream this time before he stooped beneath those branches, knew that the figure would emerge through the wild foliage that covered the slope leading down to the basement. And he knew too that he had dreamt it often before, that at this point in the dream he had always begun to struggle. But this time he didn't fight against the dream. *I'm no longer scared*, he thought, *I'm no longer running; whoever you are that has haunted my sleep for years I know you are a friend.*

A man's head and shoulders began to emerge from the cellar, the features indistinct, a hand raised in greeting. And Hano felt himself lifting from the ground, letting himself float, allowing the heat to penetrate his limbs. His body turned like a plane in a spin, buckling in the intense warmth, seeing the forest below him, the tops of the trees, the roof's broken slates flashing into view. The heat was drenching through him in waves and he knew that he was not alone. There was a presence floating close to him. Momentarily they soared together before the figure rose and Hano fell away. He was alone now, drifting awake, still soaked in the surging heat, gradually recognizing the outline of the dark caravan, the eyes of the cat in the corner.

He would never know the dream again: it was fulfilled. He felt no sense of loss. He heard the slurp of a dog's tongue at the water bowl, felt Katie's limbs like toast against his. He said his own name, Francis, understanding for the first time that he was just himself alone. The caravan rocked in the tide of the wind. He turned over on the narrow bunk, carefully so as not to wake her. Still bathed in sweat, he slept.

I keep wondering, was it a first ring or the silence which woke me? It was so rich, completely swamping the world. I lay a moment breathing it in, imagining the street outside: the chrome of cars glistening in the Saturday morning light; the blue tar of the carriageway sloping down towards the city. It was too early for punters to loiter outside the bookies, too soon for the women to push plastic bags of washing to the launderette in old prams.

I lay for a moment savouring the euphoria of the night before. The faint aftertaste of whiskey burnt my throat; my limbs were suffused with sleepy warmth. The weekend lay before us, like the ones of a year before. Three cross doubles decided over breakfast; the click of snooker balls where sunlight shafted through the skylight of some dusty hall; prowling the Fifteen Acres in search of a football match. Each memory came back as though it could be reclaimed.

I had turned to drift back to sleep when the doorbell rang. I ignored it and had curled into the warmth of the sheet when it rang again. Curiosity overcame me. I thought it must be you. I reached for my jeans and stumbled into the living-room to open the window and look down.

Nobody stood at the door. The road was bereft of traffic. Old papers blew along the pavement past a brown stain below the window where somebody had pissed coming home the previous night. I had taken my head in when a noise from across the street made me look back. A skinhead was bent over Shay's car, trying to force the door handle. I shouted at him and he looked up briefly but continued working the iron bar. As I roared again Shay came into the room.

'It's the middle of the shagging night, Hano,' he said. 'What are you at?'

'Your car,' I said. 'Shay, there's some bastard at your car.'

One moment he was behind me, leaning over my shoulder, so close I could feel the warmth of his skin, the next moment he was gone. I turned as I heard his boots on the stairs and was about to follow when I saw the skinhead raise his right hand, look towards the corner and let it drop swiftly. The front door opened, and Shay was already on the roadway, wearing only his jeans and that old pair of battered black boots, when I heard the car engine rev up. It must have happened in seconds but watching from that height it all seemed to occur in lengthy individual stages.

First Shay was running towards the Triumph Herald, a solitary figure in the still morning. Then his head turned as he heard the engine approaching from the right, and his body shifted till he was facing the oncoming car. His hand reached out to point towards the driver: his face changing from surprise, through a momentary grin of recognition, into sudden realization. And then he was somersaulting like a ballet dancer, shoulders first, on to the bonnet of the car, legs rising behind and turning in a full circle to land on the concrete behind the car. His head hit the ground last of all, at an odd angle to his neck, bounced once and lay there, twisted and still.

I knew the car before it had even appeared. Not only knew the engine's roar but instinct told me it was the BMW which Justin Plunkett had bought from his uncle. I knew every inch of it, could feel the leather grip of its steering wheel. Before looking across I knew that the skinhead would be gone. I heard another car start on the carriageway. Then I was staring down at Shay and at Plunkett, none of us moving and it seemed we could have stayed that way for hours, only the three of us left in the world, locked in those postures. Suddenly a woman screamed from a doorway down the street and, like a flock of startled crows taking off, every doorway came to life.

I closed my eyes and Shay's body somersaulted again through the air, his head hitting the ground at that angle, the half-smile of recognition still on his face. When I opened them Justin Plunkett had left the car and was racing back to kneel beside Shay, lifting him up in his arms and crying. I was still detached from the scene below, in shock, still believing somehow that I had only to reach my hand back to touch Shay's skin, warm as it leaned against my shoulder. Then I saw

Plunkett's fingers slipping something into the pocket of Shay's jeans just before the crowd reached them. People were still running, still shouting. The noise stopped and a silent circle formed around the couple on the ground. Though nobody could have called one in that time, a squad car turned off the carriageway and glided to a halt before the crowd who parted to let the policemen through.

I found myself running down those stairs and out into the brightness of the morning, scrambling my way through the people until I reached the centre of the crowd. Justin Plunkett was talking to the officers, his face ashen white.

'Just at that corner. From nowhere he came. He looked half-crazed like he was coming down from drugs or something. Good Jesus, what could I do? I tried to swerve but it was too late, he just ran straight out.'

I know it was the worst thing to do but I wasn't thinking anymore. My first punch caught him on the side of the head and as he went down I kicked him in the face before I was lifted from behind and thrown against the side of the squad car.

'Murderer!' I screamed as he knelt on the ground holding both hands to his head. 'You murdered him, Plunkett. Murdered him because you couldn't control him, because you're afraid of him. Afraid he'd tell the world you're a pimp and a pusher! But I know! And I'll tell it, every fucking bit of it! You bastard! Bastard!'

Then I was in the back of the squad car that was driving off at high speed, one policeman holding me down and punching me on the head whenever I tried to speak, and the other radioing for a second car and an ambulance to go to the scene. At the station the officer held me by the hair until we were inside and I was pushed into an empty room. It had no windows, just a table and two plastic chairs. I sat and buried my head in both hands, started to cry with loud choking sobs that seemed almost to convulse me. I didn't hear the door open and don't know how long the detective was standing over me until he touched my shoulder.

'Your friend?'

I didn't look up.

'You know he's dead, don't you?'

I nodded, searching my pockets for a handkerchief and when I couldn't find one, using my palms to dry my eyes. I was in my bare feet and wearing only a pair of jeans.

'Murdered,' I said.

'So you claim. It's a big word, murder. Do you know what it means? It doesn't just mean to kill but to kill with intent. A traffic accident is not murder.'

I recognized the detective who sat down on the other chair. He was the one who had brought Shay to me that night two months ago. His hairline was receding and, in the glare of the light, he looked even older, well into his forties, but policemen who've seen too much always look older than their years. There was a vague taste of blood in my mouth and when I put my hand up I realized that I was bleeding from a cut over the eye. He handed me a packet of paper tissues.

'We'll have that seen to in a moment,' he said. 'You were pretty hysterical, you know, had to calm you down. I'm going to take a statement from you, but if you're claiming murder I want you to understand what you are saying.'

His eyes looked as tired as my father's had those last evenings when he had struggled home from Plunkett Motors. I decided to trust him and made a statement, leaving nothing out. On the gravel I could hear the motor cycles coming and going. A single bird began singing somewhere nearby. It could have been no more than half-nine but in that room without light there was no time. Once or twice he interrupted to clarify a point, but otherwise he just wrote down what I said carefully and clearly. He read it back to me in full and passed it across the table to be signed. When I did so he read through it, sighed and shook his head.

'I'll get coffee,' he said, and returned with two paper cups, having left the statement with somebody outside.

'Justin Plunkett is in the next room,' he said. 'His statement says he was simply driving home from his uncle's house where he had been staying overnight. This skinhead, you're saying he just vanished into thin air. Two of your neighbours claim to have heard the crash and been at their doors in seconds. Both of them say the street was totally deserted.'

'They were too busy gawking at the body.'

He smiled for the first time.

'You have a point.'

He began to question me again about the dates of flights to Amsterdam, arrangements I knew about for payment, the details of Shay's final conversation with Justin Plunkett. There was something unreal about the interview. Shay was dead and yet life was going on as usual. Already I was discussing him in the past tense with a man taking careful, professional notes.

'Why do you hold the biro like that?' I asked.

'The tendons are severed,' he answered matter of factly, gazing down at the scar on the back of his hand. 'It was a drunk on a pub roof one night. He kept saying he was going to jump. I'd talked to him for an hour till he seemed to have calmed down. I took my eyes away for a moment and he tried to bring a slate down on my skull. I just got my hand in the way on time. Tell me about the Health Studio beside Murtagh's.'

Somebody rapped on the door. I didn't turn round when he opened it, only heard the whispered voices and the noise of the door closing. The voices rose in argument in the corridor. Where was Shay's body now I wondered? Had his family been told? Shay had invented bizarre stories about his parents – that his mother was into leather bondage and his father wore a mouse outfit around the house. The only time I had ever called on them they were timid and normal, mystified by the eldest son they worshipped who rarely came to see them. I could imagine the ban garda calling, declining the obligatory offer of tea, and the silence which would never leave that house when she had left. The detective returned. This time he didn't sit down but leaned against the door. I turned around in the chair.

'Will I go on about The Clean World Studio?' I asked.

He didn't reply for a moment, just stared at me until I lowered my eyes and turned back to face the table.

'We're not discussing The Clean World Health Studio,' he said. 'Let's get this clear for your own sake, Hanrahan, we're discussing a traffic accident. I suggest you make another statement, this time restricting yourself to the facts about the accident and nothing else.'

'I'm happy with the statement I made,' I said.

He stepped forward. Instinctively I ducked, expecting a blow. When I looked up he was resting both hands on the table in front of me. His fingers were brown from nicotine. I had presumed he was just beginning duty. Now, looking at his eyes again, I realized he had worked all night.

'Hanrahan,' he said in a low voice. 'I've got your word against that of the son of the Junior Minister for Justice and two independent witnesses. You say Shay was on nothing. What's this they found in his pocket?'

The small plastic bag he placed on the table was filled with white powder.

'Plunkett planted it. I told you I saw his hand in Shay's pocket in the statement.'

'I don't have your statement. It's away being typed.'

'It will be in it when it comes back.'

Even as I said the words doubt entered my voice. The sentence that began as a statement had become a question he didn't answer.

'You'll find nothing in his blood stream. You'll see . . . the coroner's report at the inquest . . .'

'The inquest won't happen for weeks,' he said. 'The newspapers come out in a few hours. Listen, I have your word Francis, and nothing else. Pascal Plunkett claims his nephew was in his house at a campaign meeting from six o'clock yesterday evening until he left this morning. Two election workers claim he was with them all evening Thursday. All you have is words. Give me a witness, give me anything.'

'It's all there. Raid the Health Studio. Raid his apartment. Round up the girls who were in the factory on Thursday night. Shay said there must have been thirty of them.'

He sat down. For the first time he looked uneasy in himself. He spoke in little more than a whisper.

'We're dealing in the possible here. There is a general election in two days' time. What judge is going to sign a warrant for that raid? You seem a nice lad. I'm sure your friend was too if he could only have learnt to stay out of trouble. In a week's time it could be a very different situation. A new government always likes public inquiries, show trials, so to speak, dirt on their predecessors to keep the heat off themselves. I'm not forgetting what you told me and I'm not discounting it, but you could be in a lot of trouble if you start making wild allegations in the next two days, and not even I could save you then. There'll be an inquest soon. You will have your chance then. For the next few days it might be wiser not to be around.'

'Fuck you,' I said, 'I've made a statement and I'm sticking to it.'

'You lived with this lad, didn't you?'

'We shared a flat, yes.'

'A search warrant has been issued. But it's one for your flat. We found this on him and God knows what else they might find if they go through the place.'

'That flat is clean as a whistle.'

'So you tell me. But it wouldn't look too good for Shay – or for you – if we found speed there or mescalin or morphine sulphate or maybe even a few gay magazines, vaseline, K-Y jelly, two beds made up as one. Shay's parents seem a nice couple. It would be a nasty shock for them. Even your own mother . . .'

He let the sentence hang. I should have felt angry. Instead I felt foolish like the day I had sent Jennifer to Mary. When something is dying it rots all over. The detective was more uncomfortable than I was.

'How much do they pay you for this job?' I asked.

He held his hands open with what could have been the shadow of a smile or a frown.

'The art of the possible.'

'What's happened to my statement?'

'I don't recall a statement. Would you like to make one?'

'I'd like to go now.'

'You left the door of your flat open,' he said. 'One of the cars picked up some clothes. I'm not sure if they're yours or your friend's.'

The shoes were mine, the shirt and jumper had belonged to Shay. He walked with me through the hallway and out on to the gravel. I could see the mechanics across the road in Plunkett Motors, Eddie under a car with only his head sticking

275

out, Sean and Matt smoking in their overalls. Inside the corrugated iron doors of the garage somebody was respraying the bonnet of the BMW.

'A week,' he said, as if to himself, 'is a long time.'

Then he was gone and I was by myself. Two hours before I had lain in bed, luxuriating in the thought of the weekend. It could have been weeks ago. Wearing a dead man's clothes, I walked slowly through the village, if village it could still be called. Plunkett Motors, Plunkett Undertakers, Plunkett House, the ugly façade replacing the Georgian mansion that once stood there. I surveyed the twisted wreckage of the main street which had been bought and sold by the Plunkett brothers: a mishmash of shapes and plastic signs; the ugliest fountain in the world which would be switched off after the election; the grotesque metal bridge over the carriageway. Home.

I had known every corner of it. Home. The small post office that closed for *The Kennedy's of Castleross*; the old man in the wooden bicycle repair hut; the cobbler with the tiny glasses in the old cottage; the stooped gardener behind the high walls of the last big house they had demolished; the mystery of the picture house; the haunted cabin by the stream where the old man was said to live and where a long-dead dog barked if you approached; the last green pump; the vanished woodlands in autumn. Home, before the Plunketts came. Home, before the family shops were bought or intimidated out; before the planning laws were twisted in the heady sixties; before the youngest TD in the Dail and his brother bought the lands that were rezoned. Home, where my mother would kneel that evening in the funeral parlour which would receive Shay, thanking the man who paid her the wages of a slave. Home, where a detective spoke without looking at you; where crowds pushed themselves flat against the sides of buses; where queues were already forming both inside and outside the prefabricated community centre for Patrick Plunkett's clinic – respectful, worried faces, hoping for a reference there, a claim here, a word with the guards or health inspectors: the subtle everyday corruption upon which a dynasty was built.

And walking through it last Saturday morning I realized I loved that home more than any place in the world for no reason that I could explain, except that I was a part of it and so was Shay. Now suddenly, with his death, part of it seemed to have died too. That morning all the defiant strength seemed to have ebbed from the village, the ordinary courage with which people survived in the face of indifference. There was just the anxiety left, the worried shoppers pulling home their trolleys, the parents waiting for the State car, desperate for favours.

I didn't want to go back to the flat. I didn't want to meet anybody. Perhaps I felt that if I walked far enough the sick empty feeling would be gone, perhaps I would stop seeing Shay tumbling through the air; I could pretend for a little longer that I had not fallen for it all, I had not sent Shay racing down those stairs to his death. But I couldn't. There was no corner of that suburb where I didn't see Shay, no group of youths in which I didn't hear his laugh. I had to turn back, to face my own conscience. Back by the graveyard he had loved, by the tiny lane with the last of the old cottages, back to the crowds outside the bookies, to the women with the prams of washing. Back to you Cait, waiting at the locked door. Waiting for whom? Your hands were jammed down in your jeans' pockets and your eyes said it all – why Shay and not me? I let you in without speaking and made tea because it seemed the thing to do. We both sat in that living-room letting the cups go cold. After a while, maybe half an hour – time that day seemed to have no meaning – I told you about it, the doorbell, the death, the detective, all in a flat even voice. Just the facts, with no attempt to say how I felt myself. There was silence after I finished, then you looked up.

'And you let them,' you said. 'You just stood here, above it all and let them! You were his friend and you let them. You let them! Let them!'

I had to push the chair back or you would have scratched my eyes out. I covered them with my hands and let you pull at my hair as you screamed. In the end I used my fist to send you staggering back across the room. You fell against the wall and sneered.

'Friend? A friend would have been down the stairs with him, a friend would have called a warning, done something.

277

You think you're great 'cause you went to the police. You can keep your fucking police and your fucking inquests, but I'll murder that bastard.'

You didn't need to accuse me. All that morning I had been accusing myself, remembering the beating Shay got by the carriageway, my own cowardice. I got up and walked into my bedroom. I never heard you leave.


They took the small lane that led away from the village, crossed over the main road and were gone down a tunnel of trees. The edges of the road were scarred by the tyre tracks of trucks that had passed up and down to the chemical dump. It was too late in the evening for them now. There was no traffic as they walked towards the entrance of the wood. The ruins of a tiny gate lodge stood like a skull in the undergrowth, thick brambles covering the walls, trees and moss reclaiming the stone. There was a smell of wild garlic as they entered the forest path.

The gate to the wood was covered with rust, the bottom bar had broken in two. They climbed over the stile and began to walk up the curving avenue. It was like that evening over a half decade ago when he had first walked here, watching the light like a living object through the leaves. The grass was overgrown, still damp after the previous night's rain.

'Last winter,' the woman said, 'it snowed heavily. I did not come here for a month. A sheep-dog found its way in and gave birth to five pups in a badger hole. She was so weak she was unable to run away when I found her. She lay trying to cover the five starved pups. Further up in the trees I found a donkey. Some farmer had decided it was not worth keeping and let it loose in here. It was as bloated as the dogs were thin. All it could find to eat was moss. There is no water here. It was dehydrated. I came each day, carried up what I could. The dogs survived but the donkey was too far gone. When it died a farmer in the village approached me.

' "I'll take it off your hands, mam, if I can bring the lorry up the avenue."

' "What do you do with the meat?" I asked him. He

278

hummed and hawed for a long time. "Dog food," he said; and then, "corned beef for the third world". He could see how upset I was and kept explaining how the cooking of it killed any germs.

' "Would you eat it?" I asked him, and he looked insulted.

' "Do you want the carcass moved or not, mam?"

' "Would you eat it?" I asked him again, and he looked around even though the street was deserted.

' "I wouldn't even eat my own beef, mam."

'I left the donkey alone. Each time I came back a little more of him would be gone. I think even the dogs had some. But it was better that way, more natural, part of the real cycle. When only the skull was left I buried it.'

There was a stone wall built against the bank. It was covered in moss. Katie ran her hand against it as sensually as if it were skin. She was carrying the parcel with the food inside it. She rarely spoke but he knew she was not unhappy. They walked in silence till they came to the old tree with its broad canopy of branches. Beyond it he could make out the corner of the house. This was the moment in dreams when he had always flown, had woken bathed in that wave of warmth. Hano knew this time there would be no flight, no figure would appear from the corner of the house. They moved on in the evening light until the whole house came into view. The wood was slowly reclaiming it. The shutters had fallen through on the great window to the right of the hallway, and he could see the rafters hanging down from the ceiling. He walked closer and peered through the hole in the floor at the cellar beneath. He shivered involuntarily and turned away. Katie was behind him. She stared silently down at the jumble of stones and wood in the two cell-like rooms exposed below.

'If we walk around the back there is a way in,' the woman called. They followed her down what had once been the lawn, through overgrown bushes by the side of the house. The window of the cellar gaped in the wall as they passed the remains of what had been outhouses. There was a sort of courtyard at the back with an exposed doorway. They walked down a bare passageway. Below them was a crumbling stone staircase. He knew the others could feel it too, the sense of overwhelming pain that emanated from down there.

'It's strange,' the woman said. 'It feels like fifty years ago; like something has come back.'

Katie stared into the darkness below and then bent down to search among the piles of old papers and brass pots on the floor. When she stood up, Hano saw that she had a few pages from a torn bible in her hand. The edges were brown as if the rest of it had been burnt. He put a hand out to stop her as she began to walk. She ignored it and descended into the dark. He could barely hear the words as she read from the page. It was the psalms, that much only he could recognize. She had reached the bottom and turned to look back up at him. Her eyes were scared. He knew she was feeling stupid and exposed. Her voice faltered and then she began to read again, only it was so dark that he knew she was reciting from memory now. There was a noise in the darkness below, faint enough to be an echo, a sound like the wingbeat of a tiny bird. She continued reading as Hano heard the beating slowly ascend the stair, drawing closer until it seemed to merge with his own heartbeat. There was a sensation of lightness, of flight, though his feet were firmly on the ground, and then it was gone past him, up the corridor, dissipating into the evening air. Katie had stopped reading. She let the pages fall and cleared a circle on the floor around her with her foot. She smiled up at him.

'It's time you came home, Francis.'

The woman handed him the bag she had been carrying. He turned to thank her but she had waved and was gone. Katie called again, kneeling to open her own bag and produce a blue candle. She struck a match, lit it and stood up, cupping the flame with her hand as he walked cautiously down.


That night I began to tour the bars where we used to drink, early in the evening, before they were cluttered with noise – the time Shay liked them best. I followed the route we had taken the first night after work a year and a half before. Two had changed their names, new interiors replacing the scarred wooden counters, strings of soft-focused lights pock-marking the ceilings, snatches of Beatles' songs that lasted a few seconds, the barmen suspicious of a solitary drinker. Murtagh's was empty downstairs, the front door open at that early hour. I sat at the long table, noticing for the first time how faded and cracked the paintwork was. In what countries were they now, those twenty friends who rolled joints at that table with him on nights when music was a presence in the blood?

I abandoned his haunts before anyone who might know Shay came in, and walked home half-drunk down streets I had followed on the nights when he was gone. Beyond Phibsborough and the canal. Remembering the loneliness I had felt then, each landmark like a station of the cross I'd pause at on my way back to the empty flat. The scent of bread near Cross Guns Bridge; the rusting barges where grey swans nestled among the scum of cider bottles and floating debris; the crumbling silos of the deserted flour mill. But all those nights I had had at least the hope of his return. Now there was just the memory of that car, the thud as a body was flung through the air, the empty sickness that refused to leave my stomach.

I went home and stood at the darkened flat window to stare down for hours at the spot where he'd died. Blood still stained the road. It was too dark to see it but I was convinced I could. Do you know what I wanted Cait? I wanted him. Not alive; I knew there was no hope of that. No, I kept saying: Shay, I'll not be frightened if you're here. If you can come back, even just for a second, do so. Give me a sign, anything to tell me you're not just rotting flesh in a box supplied wholesale by Pascal Plunkett.

When I was a young boy I had loved a girl. I wrote her a note and hid it beneath my pillow, convinced that if I wished hard enough in my mind it would vanish and appear beneath hers. Now I was like that child once more, standing at the dark window, praying for a sign which never came. There was nothing except my own tiredness, the sickening aftertaste of drink and a numb, futile anger.

There should be no removals on a Sunday but I knew the party could not resist the photo opportunity. All day I sat alone in the flat, watching the photographers begin to gather outside the undertaker's next to the Protestant church. The crowd was still small when the hearse arrived: less than half that which had gathered for my father's removal. Then I had stood down there in a black suit and tie, taking over the duties of a diligent man. Now I remained at the window. There was nothing more I could do for him. They had him neatly in their power at last. One brother was in the office joking with the bored chauffeur; the other mourning professionally, gathering votes with a handshake.

I watched Patrick Plunkett posing with the bewildered parents and could see the morning's headlines already: *A Tragedy For Two Families, parents unite in grief*. They were talking as the lens zoomed in on them. From his face, I knew Shay's father had found himself apologizing for his son's death. The professional smile was reassuring him. I could almost read the lips. 'Poor Justin, he's been on sedatives ever since.'

Tomorrow the first preferences of all there would flood again into the Plunkett stronghold. I only realized I was banging on the glass with my palms when the crowd began to look up.

While the cortège was crawling its way out on to the carriageway and along the awkward route to the far side of the street, I walked over the metal bridge to be there before them. I didn't think I would be able to go in, but when the service began I ventured hesitantly up the steps. I knew the chauffeur well, an oldish, quiet widower who lived with four children in the West. I remembered my father organizing a collection for him in the garage when his wife died years before from cancer.

'Drugs, wasn't it?' he asked when I paused outside. 'An awful thing that, everything to live for and yet they still take them. Wandering around like zombies in the daylight. Patrick Plunkett's talking of launching a personal crusade against them in the new Dail. You should have seen poor Justin's car. I drove it myself up to Pascal's house after the respraying.'

I went in past him. I had not been there since my father's funeral and not for six years before that. But Shay and I must have shared this place often without knowing it. The long snakes of schoolchildren brought over class by class to hymns and confession. How many hundreds of times had I passed him in that whirling school yard, the seagulls swooping down for bread as the teacher drilled us behind a 1798 pike? How far we had come and now here we both were again.

At the end of the service mourners filed up the main aisle to console the family before slipping back into the shadows at the side. I wanted to go up, I knew it was an insult not to, but I felt excluded from the circle of people. He was murdered, I had watched him die, and yet if I had screamed it at the top of my voice not one person there would have believed me.

In the porch, more mourners were shaking Patrick Plunkett's hand than were clustering around Shay's parents. I stared at him, wanting him to know that I knew, wanting to damn him to hell, to tear at him with my fists. He looked up and when he saw my angry gaze he replied with a slow, steady smile for ten or fifteen seconds above the heads of the crowd. It was the smile of one who knew that knowledge was a cheap and not very valuable commodity. The smile of somebody confident that everyone had their price. And instead of being cowed by my stare his smile reminded me that my turn could be next.

In the end it was I who dropped my eyes, and when I raised them again he had already climbed into the back seat of the State Mercedes, which the other drivers were waving into second place in the procession behind the black car carrying Shay's family. The photographers were gone, the crowd starting to disperse. At the turn on to the carriageway I watched the State car indicate left and swerve into the fast lane, away from that place.

Why did I go back to Pascal's house? I told myself that I wanted revenge, I wanted the head of Justin Plunkett. If the chauffeur was right then that was where I would find him. But I was also terrified and intensely alone. In the midst of my anger I was scared. I remembered Patrick's smile which seemed to say you have not been forgotten. I walked back out through those half-built fields along the North Road into the countryside to Kilshane Cross, the plastic bags of litter burst open in the ditches, the slip-streams of big trucks blowing through my hair. I tried not to think of you Cait, as I walked, but your voice haunted me, shrill as you screamed. I wanted to be away from those memories, to escape those thoughts, just to walk forever out through the cold dusk: a numb creature moving through the dark, a man longing to turn to stone.

Justin's BMW was parked in the driveway of Pascal's house. A new Alsatian on a chain began to bark furiously when I approached and then stopped suddenly to whine from hunger. I pushed the button and heard the tape recording of a bell booming deep within the house. After a few moments Pascal Plunkett opened the door a few inches on the chain. He stared at me before undoing the chain and stepping back.

'My old friend.' His voice was half a sneer. 'A social call I hope.'

I looked around, scared, wondering in what room I would find the man I wanted and not knowing what I would do if I found him.

'Well come on into the library. Never let it be said a Plunkett didn't show a guest country hospitality.'

I followed Pascal down the hallway carpeted in red with the family crest embroidered on it and into the library, and stared at the rows of red and black leather-bound books that had been bought by the box and never touched. The door closed and I found myself thrust against it. His hands were at my throat.

'If you've come here thinking of blackmail, don't, little boy. Do you hear me, wee Francy? I've been good to you. I've let you off the hook. No paper in this country will print a word about a Plunkett and don't you forget it.'

Behind his words I could sense fear.

'I'm not,' I choked. 'Pascal, let go of me. Do you want somebody to come in?'

'Somebody?' he said, slackening his grip. 'There's nobody here except you and me.'

'Justin?'

'Oh the car? He's gone abroad. The party thought it better. Let any publicity die down. It was a genuine accident, Francy. You know that, don't you?'

I said nothing, but for the first time since leaving the police station I began to cry, leaning against the doorway with my head down. As I did Pascal changed. His arms came up again but not in anger this time. I was too weak to prevent him embracing me.

'I lost a friend too once,' he said. 'A very special one. Your age he was and your colour hair. He was all I lived for when I had nothing, down in Kerry with that old bastard of a grand-father collecting rates. My friend went to England for work. I was to follow him. He fell four storeys – a loose scaffold. Francy, the heart recovers. You have me again now and I have you. I'll look after you, Francy – properly this time. No more flats and poverty. Like a son Francy. I always said you would come back.'

He tried to kiss me but I moved my face away. I could feel his breath against my cheek, feel his trembling excitement as he half-shoved me towards the stairs and up back into his nightmare world. And I just clung to him now, unwilling or unable to resist. He undressed me in the bedroom with the light out. I lay on the cool sheet and just wanted to feel nothing, to be anywhere or nowhere, to be dead like Shay, away from all this. And in that room, that bed, I was as dead as I could ever be while breath still came from my body.

When I raised my hand I could feel the sweat of Pascal Plunkett's back. It seemed to break profusely through the man's skin like clammy discoloured blood from a thousand invisible wounds. Although the room was dark as a coffin, I seemed to see the grotesque whiteness of his blubbery flesh. It did not feel human or warm in the dark; it was some monstrous thing consuming me, drawing off my youth, my life force, some spider living off my blood.

And I kept seeing Shay where he was lying in the church, the skin as white and surely no colder than this icy touch, his arms folded and that old bewildered smile facing the nailed-down board. That dark church, where both of us had made our communions and confirmations, to which my father – who had lain in that same alcove – had once carried me three days after my birth in a frozen February to be baptized. How long was it since Shay had been there? And now they possessed him again. Tomorrow morning the two long aisles, still segre-gated when we had first knelt as children, would be half-filled with neighbours and friends, talking of him already as a distant, legendary figure. Shay with the wounds from the Bath Wars, a general leading his army of short-trousered soldiers with stones and clipped hair; Shay the scholar off to secondary school; Shay the rebel expelled; Shay the wild boy; Shay the lover; Shay the European emigrant.

Pascal grunted as he ran his tongue and teeth down my chest, a hog wallowing at home in mud. 'I knew you'd come back, I knew,' he mumbled. 'I'm your man, I'm the man for you.'

*Shay*, I whispered in my mind, *remember the bottle of whiskey we finished in the basement in Rathmines. The time there were no glasses at the party. One slug of neat whiskey followed by a slug of mixer. So outrageously drunk as we fell home, phoning Patrick Plunkett at four in the morning and asking him to raise a Dail question about why our stuffed hamsters wouldn't breed. Falling about outside the phone box as the voice cursed us down the receiver. That night we got talking of death for some reason, staggering down Rathmines Road, past the kebab shops and the beggars. 'Anything but a coffin,' you said. 'Fuck me into the Tolka in a plastic bag, but don't put me into a hole in the ground.' I promised if you died first to scatter your ashes over the North Road some night. You know, that last rise before the countryside where the trucks come swooping in.*

I lay in Pascal's bed and spoke to Shay in my mind, apologizing over and over. *Tomorrow they'll take you Shay in the polished box that broke your parents' savings and wheel you on a trolley to the hearse. I won't be there Shay when the clay falls like a thousand blows on your skull. I don't know where I'll be, but I'll not be there. Oh Jesus, Shay, what could I have done? It was me who called you to the window. I saw it all Shay and could do nothing. I need to know Shay: do you forgive me? Do you forgive?*

Plunkett shifted his body down lower, fingering my penis that was limp and tiny. 'What's wrong with you, Francy?' he said. 'I'm giving you a good time, boy. Respond. Respond.'

I was crying. *Shay*, I thought, *I'm crying for you and I'm crying for me, back in this trap, looking for something I lost, needing to go back before I can move on. Once it had been so good, Shay, before we touched this family, and every time we've touched them since we've fallen more and more away.*

286

The feel of Plunkett was like the feel of death. He was kneeling above me in the bed, trying to puzzle out my face in the darkness. He was out of his depth, no longer in control of the situation. He looked pathetic. I knew he longed to explode in anger and yet he was afraid. He had lost me once, he would wait till I was back in his web before making demands.

'What do you want, Francy? I'll do it for you. Just tell me. I've been taking care of you, son. Have you spoken to your mother? I've let her off those loans. The pair of us, we'll make a great fist of it together. Are you thinking of your friend still? Tragic, tragic. But it brought us back together again. Lie back, Francy. I'll make it good for you this time, I will.'

He ran his fingers up to the wetness of my face and I flinched when I felt his touch. He moved his face closer towards mine. It felt like suffocation, but at least it felt. I was moving from the numb shock I had been in. I had to do something, I still didn't know what, but if his lips touched mine I knew I was lost. My strength and courage were draining fast. *Oh, Shay, Shay*, I prayed, *what the fuck do I do?*

Then the door burst open like a sword of light exploding. Both of us blinked and turned our heads away from its brilliance before peering back again at the form revealed in the doorway. I think we both thought that you were the ghost of Shay; certainly at that moment, Katie, you did not look like a human thing. And then your hand reached up for the light switch to let reality in. Plunkett moved like an animal. He had left the bed and was running towards you while the pair of us were still staring across the room at each other. You had a knife clenched in your right hand, the blade so large against your tiny wrist that it looked comical.

'Where's Justin? I want that bastard!' was all you had time to scream before Pascal's first blow sent the knife flying one way and you the other. He bent to pick up the knife, and as he did you climbed on his shoulders, scratching at his face with your nails. He spun round in circles, one hand defending his face, and the other gripping your hair, trying to dislodge you from his back.

'Don't just lie there!' he screamed. 'The knife, get the knife, boy. Come on, move boy, move!'

I had pulled the blanket up over my naked shoulders and was hunched in the bed crying. I hardly heard his words. You were screaming as he tore at your hair and banged you against the wall, and then he roared and sank to his knees as your fingers penetrated deep into both his eyes. I could see blood running out through his fingers as he fell and you jumped from his back to go for the knife. I got there a second before you and sent you crashing back against the wall with my elbow. As I clenched my fingers round the knife, you lay panting, looking from me to the door and back to Plunkett. He had risen to his feet again. The blood was smeared down his hands on to his chest and the ugly bag of a stomach. He put one hand out groping for me.

'Hold her, Francy. Hold her!'

I lifted my left hand to link with his outstretched fingers. I could see him try to smile through the blood. For the first time in his life he needed somebody. He moved closer and closer towards me, walking towards the blade. I don't believe I would have had the courage to have used it otherwise. He stopped when he felt the tip against his breast.

'Francy?' There was a note of alarm in his voice and the jerk he made as he moved back released a fury within me. All three of us were screaming but it didn't sound like my own voice I was hearing as I stabbed and stabbed. He fell to his knees clutching me with both arms, and kept repeating my name in a choked voice between screams as I moved the knife in and out. I have no idea how long I kept stabbing away. Long after he was dead, I think. Eventually my hand went slack by my side and when I stepped back his body keeled over at my feet. I was covered in his blood, as was the wall behind him. But I felt nothing, there was nothing left I could feel. I turned, having forgotten you were there, and maybe even who you were, and began to walk naked towards the bed.

How can I describe that look in your eyes when I finally looked down? There was silence, and when you spoke it was in an almost dream-like voice, as though part of you was pleading with me.

'Am I next? Are you going to kill me next?'

288

If I had moved with the knife towards you would you have welcomed me? Did Shay mean that much to you as well, that there was nothing left after his death? I felt a stutter return from childhood and had to force the words out.

'Get out! Leave me alone. Go!'

Did you want to leave and found your legs too weak to move; or had the world ceased to exist for you too outside that blood-splattered room? I became aware of my nakedness and reached for a sheet to cover myself. Plunkett's blood seeped through it as soon as it touched my skin. I shouted at you to go again but you were no longer looking at me. Your eyes were mesmerized by the corpse on the floor, the red eye sockets staring back at you.

'What did it feel like, Hano?' you said in that dream-like voice. 'What did it feel like to kill?'

During the struggle the mirrored doors of his wardrobe had slid open. A row of suits hung inside like echoes of him, reminding me, bringing back the shame of it. Everything in his house made me feel unclean except the blood that was caking into my flesh. I started pulling out the suits and the neatly folded shirts and jumpers. I was filled with a fury as I ripped them, as though his possessions were mocking me. The more of them I destroyed the wilder I became. The sheet had become a hindrance and I lost it as I ran from room to room, searching for traces of Patrick and of Justin. I wanted them both, wanted to kill every one of them, to destroy that family who corrupted everything they touched. When I overturned the bed in the spare bedroom a stack of bondage magazines fell out. Justin's leather jacket hung from the back of the door. There was a cigar butt in an ashtray on the bedside table and a box of matches had dropped on to the floor beside it. I lit one, watched it catch in the tangle of bedclothes and begin to lick the mattress above it. I had forgotten about you until you were suddenly beside me with a wet towel and my clothes in your arms.

'Put these on, Hano,' you said. 'You have to get out of here before somebody comes.'

'Leave me alone,' I screamed. 'Did you not hear? Get out or I'll cut you fucking open. Do you hear me?'

The room was starting to blaze, thick suffocating smoke filling my nostrils. You looked at the knife but this time differently. You raised your hand slowly to take it from me.

'What good will it do you to die here, Hano? Put these clothes on, we're leaving now.'

The heat was becoming unbearable. I lowered my head.

'Just go on, Katie. Are you blind or what? What do you want with me after what you've seen?'

'I don't give a fuck what you are or what he's tried to make you. We're just getting out of here.'

You took my hand and began to lead me down the staircase. I was bewildered and ashamed and crying again by the time we reached the bottom. I sat on the step while you dressed me like a child, coaxing me to lift this arm or leg, wiping the blood from my face and hands, cajoling me until we were out in the night air and crossing the manicured lawn where the alsatian was straining on his chain, barking in terror at the fire. At the far end of the lane we saw the rolling white and blue light of a police car. It was that flashing light which brought me back to my senses. I knelt quickly to tie my shoes and, grabbing your hand again, began to race for the cover of the hedgerow, to plunge into that blackness overcome with a new strength and a savage joy like a convict breaking free. We plunged onwards through the briars and hedges while the sirens of the police, and then the fire trucks, filled the countryside around us and when we hit the tarmacadam we ran joyously onwards, breast to breast without speaking, no longer having to think, just careering outwards into the darkness till the lights of the first car sent us cascading down into the sanctuary of the ditch.

I built a small fire from the dry timbers on the floor. You used a broken rafter to clear a space for us. Two birds outside gave their final cries and settled down to sleep. We had a sleeping bag and a single blanket. I hung the torch from an old nail near the ceiling. It cast a dim arc of light downwards and left the rest of the cellar in shadow. Why I asked I don't know; maybe it was just to finish something in my own head.

'Would you sooner be here with Shay?'

You looked up at me as you unpacked the food.

'I preferred Shay as Shay. I prefer you as you.'

We ate in silence and then undressed. I removed your blouse, you unzipped my jeans. I took each nipple under my tongue. To taste them was a shock of freshness. Your head was thrown back. I licked the expanse of your neck. You lay on the blanket and I fumbled in my jacket for the condom. Your hand reached out to halt mine.

'It's too late, Francis, for being safe now. It's time to take chances. Let's see what comes of it.'

I entered you. The feel for the first time of flesh upon flesh, the incredible tightness, the almost painful sensation of my foreskin stretching back. When I came you pressed your hands tightly against my buttocks. I lay inside you drifting towards sleep. How long has passed since I woke? I do not want to sleep. Each moment is so important now when it could be our last.

I hear the pad of animal paws outside, twigs snapping, dry leaves crinkling underfoot. Fox or badger, it means us no harm. Tonight at least you can sleep and I can watch and listen.

I think I'm understanding, Cait, why this place remained so important for me, why I kept it secretly in my head all these years when I was in exile from myself. I used to think of here as the past, a fossilized rural world I had to fight to be rid of. I got the conflict wrong of course, though she had always understood it. When we walked this evening along the avenue of old trees up to here, she was not leading us back into the past, she was bringing us onwards into the future.

Those rows of new bungalows clinging in deference to the main road, how brightly painted they looked, like a bulwark against what will come. How solid they seemed, like the terraces of houses where I was born. But this crumbling house in the woods is the future, is our destination, is nowhere. I never understood it until now; soon it will be all that's left for the likes of you and I to belong to. City or country, it will make little difference, ruins, empty lots, wherever they cannot move us from.

For a while longer the lorries will keep coming, widening the roadways with their tyres, dumping the plastic sacks into the quarry until the holiday homes grow so close that the continentals will object. Our role is to offer tranquillity, not rivers awash with the eyes of dead fish. Some day soon a law in Brussels will silence the convoy, will close down the factory. Like the women I saw outside the flour mill in Dublin the workers will camp in for a while, jostling against the lorries as the machines are shipped out to the Third World.

I wonder, will Patrick Plunkett have made it by then: Euro MP, commissioner? I can hear his speech now to the half-empty chamber – the French, the Germans outside waiting for the important business. The few Irish rooted to their seats like puppets, joining in the voting as if they somehow counted.

In time, some workers will die from contamination, the rest subsist on the dole or merge into the exodus, stand in the foreign production lines where Shay once stood. The paint will peel on the bungalows, the multinationals will buy out the building societies and foreclose. The hire-purchase cars withdrawn, like toys from children at bedtime. All that once seemed permanent, what people had imagined they possessed. A foreign accent will supervise the bulldozers burying the last of the waste; an Italian expert shaking his head before the television cameras. No more fires will begin accidentally here, no more trees in the wind path will wither up. The last corner of Europe, the green jewel free from the paths of acid rain. A land preserved intact for the community. German tongues clicking in amusement at how it was run in those last years.

I can see it, Cait, though another century will have long opened before I'm released back into a city ringed by golf courses. Exclusive restaurants between the green canals, sporadic insurrections still in the shanty towns. The crowd of youths not dispersed by the water cannon but by the bored cameraman finally screwing the cover over the lens. Out here electric fences will hum in the evenings, crackling when a stray dog stumbles against them. In the white pillar beside the solid wooden gates an intercom will wait for messages. Motorists gliding silently through the woodlands, the drone of Dutch and French over the car telephones.

And the chosen million Irish left: red-haired girls in peasant aprons bringing menus to diners in the converted castles, at one end of the scale; at the other, middle-ranking civil servants who will close their eyes at night, knowing that once we could have stood up as equals, not been bought out like children by the quick lure of grants. Irish officials, knowing they began too late to reach the top posts, will swap electronic gadgets with their neighbours, wondering some evenings about the times of their youth, never speaking of them in front of their children, like parents a century and a half before ashamed of their Gaelic tongue.

Maybe Pascal died well; maybe I did him one final favour. A bull-like man, living on instinct and animal strength. He died as he had lived before a thousand officials cut him into pieces with triplicate forms. He was too much himself to ever adapt to their world: too burly, too steeped in his past. His brother will purr like a lap-dog but they will soon tire of that. And Justin? The chosen one. In a bar full of emigrants about to depart, I once thought of him as the angel of death. His childish games are over now. Farmers up for the markets in the frozen dawn will knock in vain on the door of The Clean World Health Studio, students will no longer reach Holland with phone numbers in their pockets. When you are a child you play with childish things; you play with grown-ups when you inherit the earth.

From this night we will have a son. I feel it as surely as I know they will catch me. When his turn comes, will he join the queues at the airports, or will you teach him to run like his father tried to? Woods like this have sheltered us for centuries. After each plantation this is where we came, watched the invader renaming our lands, made raids in the night on what had once been our home. Ribbonmen, Michael Dwyer's men, Croppies, Irregulars. Each century gave its own name to those young men. What will they call us in the future, the tramps, the Gypsies, the enemies of the community who stay put?

I do not expect you to wait for me, Cait. Just don't leave, stand your ground. Tell him about me sometime; teach him the first lesson early on: there is no home, nowhere certain any more. And tell him of Shay, like our parents told us the legends of old; tell him of the one who tried to return to what can never be reclaimed. Describe his face Cait, the raven black hair, that smile before the car bore down and our new enslavement began.

I can hear that animal creeping closer, paws barely touching the grass, nose alert for danger. Sleep on, my love. Tomorrow or the next day they will come. I will keep running till they kill or catch me. Then it will be your turn and the child inside of you. Out there, across the cities and villages, the celebrations must still be going on, the newspapers full of statistics, shifts and voting patterns, commentators discussing the reaction of the nation. It doesn't matter to internal exiles like us. No, we're not exiles, because you are the only nation I give allegiance to now, sleeping with some strands of your hair caught in the torch light. When you hold me, Cait, I have reached home.

# FOR THE BEST IN PAPERBACKS, LOOK FOR THE 🐧

In every corner of the world, on every subject under the sun, Penguin represents quality and variety – the very best in publishing today.

For complete information about books available from Penguin – including Puffins, Penguin Classics and Arkana – and how to order them, write to us at the appropriate address below. Please note that for copyright reasons the selection of books varies from country to country.

**In the United Kingdom:** Please write to *Dept E.P., Penguin Books Ltd, Harmondsworth, Middlesex, UB7 0DA.*

If you have any difficulty in obtaining a title, please send your order with the correct money, plus ten per cent for postage and packaging, to *PO Box No 11, West Drayton, Middlesex*

**In the United States:** Please write to *Dept BA, Penguin, 299 Murray Hill Parkway, East Rutherford, New Jersey 07073*

**In Canada:** Please write to *Penguin Books Canada Ltd, 2801 John Street, Markham, Ontario L3R 1B4*

**In Australia:** Please write to the *Marketing Department, Penguin Books Australia Ltd, P.O. Box 257, Ringwood, Victoria 3134*

**In New Zealand:** Please write to the *Marketing Department, Penguin Books (NZ) Ltd, Private Bag, Takapuna, Auckland 9*

**In India:** Please write to *Penguin Overseas Ltd, 706 Eros Apartments, 56 Nehru Place, New Delhi, 110019*

**In the Netherlands:** Please write to *Penguin Books Netherlands B.V., Postbus 195, NL–1380AD Weesp*

**In West Germany:** Please write to *Penguin Books Ltd, Friedrichstrasse 10–12, D–6000 Frankfurt/Main 1*

**In Spain:** Please write to *Longman Penguin España, Calle San Nicolas 15, E–28013 Madrid*

**In Italy:** Please write to *Penguin Italia s.r.l., Via Como 4, I-20096 Pioltello (Milano)*

**In France:** Please write to *Penguin Books Ltd, 39 Rue de Montmorency, F-75003 Paris*

**In Japan:** Please write to *Longman Penguin Japan Co Ltd, Yamaguchi Building, 2–12–9 Kanda Jimbocho, Chiyoda-Ku, Tokyo 101*